D0953750

STREET MUSIC

Books by Timothy Hallinan

The Poke Rafferty Series
A Nail Through the Heart
The Fourth Watcher
Breathing Water
The Queen of Patpong
The Fear Artist
For the Dead
The Hot Countries
Fools' River
Street Music

The Junior Bender Series
Crashed
Little Elvises
The Fame Thief
Herbie's Game
King Maybe
Fields Where They Lay
Nighttown

The Simeon Grist Series
The Four Last Things
Everything but the Squeal
Skin Deep
Incinerator
The Man with No Time
The Bone Polisher
Pulped

STREET MUSIC

Timothy Hallinan

Published by
Soho Press, Inc.
227 W 17th Street
New York, NY 10011

Hallinan, Timothy, author.
Series: The poke rafferty thrillers; 9

ISBN 978-1-64129-123-1
eISBN 978-1-64129-124-8

Subjects: 1. Suspense fiction.
LCC PS3558.A3923 S77 2020 | DDC 813/.54—dc23

Printed in the United States of America

10 9 8 7 6 5 4 3 2 1

Once again,
for Munyin Choy

STREET MUSIC

Part One
IT'S A BOY

1

Look Like Who?

"O H-*ho*," S A Y S T H E woman at the cash register, looking at the baby formula and the stacks of disposable diapers. "How old?"

The woman is in her middle forties and contentedly plump, hair dyed the color of a lit jack-o'-lantern. He can see the hair glowing at him from anywhere in the store. He'd spotted it, as always, the moment he entered the supermarket—ice-cold after the steam bath of Bangkok's late afternoon—and immediately he'd thought, feeling like a dog wagging its tail, *Here's someone I haven't told yet*. The city's number of uninformed people is dwindling, if he doesn't count total strangers, but the impulse to share the news remains irresistible.

"Almost two week," he says, in Thai. The language isn't rich in plurals.

The cashier, whose badge reads NIT in both Thai and English, has worked at the local branch of Foodland for two years, and for two years Rafferty has been speaking to her in his fractured but serviceable Thai and she's been speaking to him in the cheerful, optimistic string of approximations that many Thais believe to be English. If pressed, Rafferty would have to admit that her English is a lot more like English than his Thai is like Thai.

Postponing the transaction in favor of a chat, she leans over the counter toward him, looking concerned. "Wife okay?"

"Wonderful. Better than I deserve."

"This no good, you know," she says, making a face as she opens a palm above the formula. There's a recent and widely hailed law in Thailand to prevent the merchandising of baby formula, some of which is cheaply made, smuggled in like dope, criminally short on nourishment, and occasionally toxic. As with a great many Thai laws, this one was designed to create the *impression* that something is being done without actually doing anything that might cut into the fat boys' fifteen-percent slice of the trade. "Merchandising," whatever that is, is strictly prohibited. Selling it, on the other hand, is no problem.

The cashier, who had picked up two packets of formula, drops them as though they're dirty. She reaches up and mimics squeezing her right breast twice, as quickly and efficiently as a clown squeezing the bulb of his horn, and holds up an instructional finger. "Better."

He says in Thai, feeling almost medical, "Her nipples hurt."

"Ha!" she says, triumphantly. "Suck strong. *Boy.* Very good."

"I don't know. I wanted a girl." He's had almost eight years of experience raising a girl. The only boy he's ever known really well is himself, and he's no recommendation.

"Boy better," she says, with the kind of total confidence Rafferty can remember experiencing perhaps twice in his life. To the woman in line behind him, who has been fidgeting throughout the conversation, the cashier says "Just a minute" in Thai. Then, to him, in English, she says, "Boy better. Girl, worry, worry, worry."

"I'm sorry, but I'm in a hurry," the woman behind Rafferty says in English. She's Thai, runway-model thin, well-dressed, and worried-looking, and he suddenly recognizes her as a teller in the bank he and Rose use most often. He's about to step aside when the cashier says to her—in English, for his benefit—"Him have baby."

"Really?" The woman's face lights up. "Boy or girl?"

Rafferty says, "Boy."

"Wife him," the cashier tells her, "very beautiful. Thai lady, beautiful too much."

"That's wonderful," the woman behind him says. "Girls are just one problem after another. How old now?"

"Him almost two week," the cashier announces before Rafferty even opens his mouth. She points at the formula. "You think good, no good?"

"I think that kind is, mmmm, okay." The bank teller scratches her head, a Thai gesture that means, *I'm thinking*. Rafferty sometimes wonders whether they picked it up from bad American movies. "Just stay away from Baby-Lac. That's the one I keep reading about."

Rafferty says, "I use your bank all the—"

"Oh," she says, hand flat over her heart, "Mr. *Rafferty*." Her smile is broad enough to suggest that this is the first good news she's had in years. "So this is for—how *wonderful*, and yes, your wife *is* so beautiful. How old now?"

"I tell you already," the cashier says, reclaiming her territory. "Almost two week."

"Right, right, sorry," the bank teller says. "Well, we'll send you some flowers."

"Thank you," Rafferty says, trying to remember whether any American bank ever sent him flowers.

"Baby look like who?" the cashier demands.

"Like, like—well, I'm no baby expert," he says, holding up a modest hand, "but he sort of looks like both of us."

The cashier, who has begun to ring up his purchases, says, "Too bad."

* * *

"How old now?" After an unprecedented absence of almost a month, Bob Campeau has reclaimed his immemorial stool at Leon and Toot's Bar. It's been *Bob's stool* for so long that the bartender and owner, Toots, who is responsible for the wayward apostrophe on the bar's sign, occasionally dusts him. But that doesn't mean he's universally loved, and without him on hand, the place has felt lighter, at times almost cheerful. Still, the first time Rafferty came in and found Campeau's stool empty, he felt a disorienting pang of loss, as though he were looking at an aerial photo of Washington, DC, with the Potomac River missing.

Rafferty has detoured to Leon and Toot's to dodge the heat and to see whether there's anyone there whom he hasn't told about the baby. Much to his surprise, it's Campeau, and he's actually evincing interest. Putting the supermarket bag on the bar, Rafferty says, "Almost two weeks."

"Why the hell aren't you home?"

"Buying for the baby." He props up the sack, which seems to be contemplating falling over sideways.

"Look like Rose?"

"Like both of us, I think." Toots sets down a glass of carbonated water with a discolored lemon slice floating in it. She'd given him a disapproving twist of the mouth when he asked for a Singha. Rafferty says to her, "I'm not the one who's nursing."

"Too much to hope for," Campeau says with a regretful shake of the head. "That kind of beauty, I mean. It's like lightning. Not gonna strike twice in the same place." Campeau, whose reign over this room began more than fifty years ago, when it was still called the Expat Bar, was Rose's occasional patron back when she was working on Patpong. He remembers her fondly, a favor she does not return. For years he's held a grudge against Poke for, as he put it, *taking her off the market.*

Rafferty says, "It's a *boy*, Bob."

Campeau shrugs off the detail. "Still."

"I'm not such a terrible-looking guy." Toots is squinting at him and sucking on a tooth. "Am I?"

"You want we take a vote?" Toots says, pronouncing it *wote.*

"You're okay," Campeau says. "Right number of arms and legs. Kid'll probably walk upright."

Rafferty says, "So where were you?"

"Land of cotton. Alabama. Brother died."

"Sorry to hear it."

"Aaaahhh," Campeau says. "He was a horse's ass."

"Why'd you go, then?" The bubble water tastes like water with bubbles in it.

"My mother," Campeau says. "Hadn't seen her in forty-two years. Figured it was now or never."

The notion of Campeau having a mother slows Rafferty down for a moment. He says, "Alabama, huh?"

"Asshole capital of the world," Campeau says.

The front door opens and Pinky Holland comes in, wiping his bald head with what looks like a woman's T-shirt in a shade of pink that would make a shrimp squint. "Jesus, it's hot," he says. "Hey, Bob, back in the Land of Smiles, huh?"

"And not a minute too soon," Campeau says. "I'da killed the next person who said *y'all* in my presence."

"Poke had a kid," Pinky announces.

"Not unassisted," Poke says.

"Yeah, yeah, we were just talking about it," Campeau says. He scratches a cheekbone. "So, bar fines go up again?"

Pinky takes the glass of Something Toots has put down in front of him. "You've only been gone, what? A week?"

"Almost a month."

"Well," Pinky says, "time flies when you're enjoying yourself. Still, it's only a *month* and you're worrying?"

"Month is plenty long," Campeau says. "Bar fine's the only thing in the world that goes up faster'n the price of oil."

"Far as I know, not here in Patpong," Pinky says. "Over at Soi Cowboy, maybe."

Rafferty says, "The first week after the kid—"

"Soi Cowboy," Campeau says. "For fucking Rockefellers. Who cares about Soi—"

"You'd probably be surprised to hear this," Rafferty says, "but the thing about a kid this age—"

"Lookit that," Pinky Holland says. He's mopping his neck with the pink thing and squinting past Rafferty toward the street. "It's that horrible old woman again." Rafferty turns to look through the bar's small, ambitiously unwashed front window and sees a dark-skinned, battered-looking woman, gray hair in an exploding bird's nest, nostrils wider than her downturned mouth, peering in. The moment she realizes she's being looked at, she disappears.

Campeau says, "An admirer."

Poke says to Pinky, "What do you mean, *again?*"

"Third time I've seen her. When I came in just now, she was sitting on the curb across the street, looking at the door. Like Buddha was gonna come through it."

"You're a chick magnet," Campeau says.

The bell over the door rings and the man Rafferty privately thinks of as the guy with the hair comes in, raking his fingers through his carefully sculpted waves to peel them back from a glistening forehead. With the conversational panache that makes him welcome everywhere, he says, "Hot out."

Campeau says, "You're *kidding.*"

"No, look at me. I'm all wet."

A moment of silence glides by to acknowledge a straight line the entire company is allowing to pass. Toots says to him, "Usual?"

"Ummmm," the guy with the hair says, slowing to give it some serious thought. He chews his lower lip as Campeau crosses his eyes. "Sure," the guy with the hair finally says. "Why not?" To Campeau, he says, "You're back."

Looking down at himself, Campeau says, "Jesus, I *am*. You gotta break stuff like that gently." To Rafferty, he says, "So. Mother-in-law there?"

"First four days, until she certified the child as likely to survive. Now she's back up north and I've got an apartment full of former bar girls."

Campeau's ears practically prick up. "Names?"

"Lek," Rafferty says, feeling an unanticipated bloom of irritation heat his face. "They're all named Lek."

Campeau's anger, never far offstage, makes an entrance. "Don't be a jerk. What do you think, I'm going to fucking come over and *bar-fine* them?"

"What I *think* is that they're in a different phase of their lives and happy to be there."

"Sheesh," Campeau says, shaking his hand as though he'd burned his fingers. "*What I think*," he says in a high, feminine voice. "Nothing more self-righteous than a recovered sinner. What'd you do, cut it off and donate it to the dick of the month club?"

"You know, Bob." Rafferty gets up and drops some money on the bar. "I'd tell you to grow up, but if you did there wouldn't be anything left."

"Just 'cause you snagged the hot one—" Campeau begins.

"Arrested development," Rafferty says, raising his voice. "With a life sentence. And fucking *can* it, Bob.".

The guy with the hair says, "You guys having an argument?"

Campeau says, "Ooohhh, he's *cranky*. Not getting any since the *baby?*"

Rafferty is very, very tired. For twelve days he's been banished from the big bed—which Rose is sharing with the baby—sleeping on a lumpy couch in two-hour stretches, in between fits of squalling from what used to be his bedroom. His adopted daughter, Miaow, has an unattractive case of the just-displaced-only-child sulks. He's feeling guilty that he doesn't seem to love the baby the way he's supposed to. He's dully aware of all this—and on a quest for a reasonable perspective he factors all of it into his response—and he *still* picks up his remaining half glass of bubble water, takes four irretrievable steps, and pours the cold drink onto the crotch of Campeau's jeans.

Campeau leaps up, knocking his stool over with a bang, making everyone straighten up, and the guy with the hair, who has just hoisted his Usual, drops it onto the bar, and everyone jumps *again* at the noise. Toots shakes her head in a way that expresses a long, profound weariness at the limitations of men and picks up a damp and malodorous bar towel to mop up the Usual. Rafferty steps back, more than half hoping Campeau will take a swing at him. Only Pinky Holland is having a good time, sitting, chin on hand, bright-eyed with expectation.

Rafferty says, "Come *on*, Bob. Let me give you a real Arkansas welcome."

Campeau says, "You hypocritical fucker," and steps toward Rafferty, who sidesteps, swipes the filthy towel out of Toot's hand and pushes it, wadded-up and stinking, into Campeau's face. He keeps pushing it until Campeau steps backward, tangling his feet in the legs of his overturned stool, and goes down, hard, on his butt.

"*Any time*," Rafferty says to him, seeing him through a haze of red as if someone had atomized blood into the air.

A *bang* from the right gets his attention. Toots has grabbed the

billy club that hangs near the cash register and slammed the bar
with it. Everyone is frozen, wide-eyed, their ears ringing.

"Him old man," she says, pointing at Campeau. "You. *Poke*."
She gives him the unambiguous thumb jerk over the shoulder that
means the same thing all over the world. "You eighty-sick."

Rafferty does the only smart thing he's done in the past minute:
he doesn't correct her pronunciation. But he does say, "If you can't
wash old Arkansas down there out of that rag, I'll buy you a new
one."

From the floor, Campeau says, "Alabama, you asshole."

"Who cares?"

"*Out*," Toots says.

Rafferty says, "When can I come back?

"Not today." She picks up the supermarket bag and extends it
over the counter. "Here. Give Rose kiss for me."

"It'll be a pleasure."

From the floor, Campeau says, "This isn't over."

"Yeah? You going to burn a cross in my yard? You gonna poison
me, slip some of your nine million tabs of fake Viagra into my
drink?"

"Out, out." Toots is making little *scram* gestures, flopping the
backs of her hands toward the door. As it swings closed behind
him, Rafferty hears Campeau growl at Toots, "Whaddya mean, *old
man?*"

2

The Adoration

"You go long time," Fon says, shaking her head in disapproval. It had taken her years on Patpong to polish her immaculate, note-perfect bar-girl English and to flash-freeze its development before it started to threaten her customers' insecurities, and she's proud of it; it supported her family for decades. She sees no reason to abandon it just because Rafferty wants to exercise his Thai. "You go to bar?" She'd opened the door for him because the deadbolt was fastened from inside, and behind her he could see that she, or someone, had remade the couch he'd slept on, folding more neatly than he had the blankets that, in theory, soften the lumps.

"A *bar?*" he says, helpless against the infallibility of bar-worker radar. "No. No, why would you say that?" It's not a *real* lie, he thinks; at least, he hadn't had anything to drink. Now that his anger has receded, he's feeling wayward pangs of regret about having essentially decked Campeau in front of virtually everyone the man knows. Fon, who loathes Campeau, would get a kick out of the story, but he can't tell it now that he's lied to her. What a tangled web, etc. He says, "I need some sleep."

"So sleep," she says, pronouncing it *saleep*. She extends her arms for the bag. "Give me."

"I can't just sleep in the middle of the day."

She takes the bag and heads for the kitchen and he follows,

feeling like the extra puppy, the one people step on occasionally. "Can sleep any time," she says.

He knows that's literally true for many Thais. He's seen them out cold, head resting against the driver's back on a motorcycle taxi that's weaving wildly through traffic, inches from death by glass and steel. He says, "Is Rose asleep?"

"Maybe. Baby, him cry maybe one hour. Now quiet." She pulls out the formula packets and regards them critically, her nose wrinkled and her mouth pulled to one side. "This good, no good?"

"It's not, uhhh, Baby-Lac. That's the one you're supposed to avoid."

The glance she gives him has doubt dangling from it like Spanish moss. "Who say?"

"A woman who works in our bank," Rafferty says.

"Woman work in bank?"

"That's what I—"

"Okay," Fon says with a decisive nod. She pulls the other packets out and then the diapers.

"Wait a minute," Rafferty says. "Why would you believe a woman who works in a bank when you're not sure you believe—"

"Her *woman*," Fon says, as though speaking to a four-year-old. "Her work in *bank*. Have school too much."

"*I* went to school."

"Yes? You are woman? You work in bank?"

"No. Forget it."

Fon is Rose's oldest friend, the veteran bar worker who took her in hand and into her heart when Rose, a bewildered, unworldly seventeen-year-old from a tiny dirt-road village deep in the rice country of the Northeast, was towed down to Bangkok by a bar worker who had skipped over the specifics of *being nice to customers*. After the bewildering and painful evening in which Rose lost her virginity to the first man to take her out of the bar—an influential cop who went back and complained about her performance—Fon moved Rose into her apartment, opened Bangkok for her, and taught her what Rose came to think of as *the dog tricks*: sitting up, rolling over, panting, wagging your tail, and so forth, to shore up the customers' ids and keep them asking for her. Fon also eased Rose into the rockier aspects of her new life, both emotionally and spiritually, by reminding her over and over that she was following an essential Buddhist precept by helping her mother and father, and that the money she was sending home would keep her younger sisters in school, sparing them their own trips to Bangkok. There were times, during that first year especially, when that was almost all she had to hang on to.

And the night the baby came, after Rafferty bundled Rose into the back of a cab to get her to the hospital, trying to remember the name of the hospital and where it was, trying to look like he wasn't paralyzed with terror as he fidgeted beside her in the backseat, Rose had said, "Call Fon," and Fon had arrived before they did, no small feat in Bangkok traffic.

Fon had seen the baby at the same moment Rafferty did. She had held it *before* he did.

Standing there, looking at her, Rafferty can't believe how he's been taking her for granted. She's small for someone with so much good in her, dark-skinned and blunt-featured, a little rounder than she used to be and almost morbidly conscious of it, and solid gold. He says, "How are you, Fon?"

She looks a little startled. "How I am? No problem. Why?"

"Just, you know, you've been such a good friend. All these years—"

"Never mind," Fon says, shutting down the conversation.

"But I *need* to say this."

"Say what?" Rose says.

Rafferty says, "Oh."

"Something I shouldn't hear?" Rose says in Thai. She's wearing white shorts and a blinding white T-shirt, looking as chaste as a saint's pipe dream. She must have just put them on, because he's heard her complain about how quickly she stains her clothes since the baby was born and she started nursing. He has, and immediately abandons, a brief hope that she put them on for him. "Has my nightmare come true? Are you running away together?"

Fon puts her hand under the hair hanging down her back and flips it dismissively in Poke's direction. "I only like handsome man."

Hand splayed over her heart, Rose says, "What a relief."

Rafferty, feeling like it's the only line anyone ever writes for him, says, "The baby asleep?"

The doorbell rings.

"Maybe not now," Rose says. She turns to get it, and for the millionth time Rafferty loses himself in the black shimmer of hair cascading down her back.

Fon, though, is all business. "You sit," she commands Rose. "I get."

"Yes, Mommy," Rose says, and goes to sit on the couch.

"*I'll* get it," Rafferty says, feeling that a little male domination is long overdue.

Fon turns back to the bag, mumbling "*I'll get it*" in a surprising baritone. But she allows him to get it.

When he pulls the door open, three women crowd through, stepping around him as though he were a pair of shoes. They all wear the street uniform of jeans and T-shirts, two of the shirts decorated with bright smiling animals and the third with a full-color print of a thousand-baht bill. They kick off their flip-flops as they enter. He knows all of them: Noi, Ning, and Cartoon.

Rose gets up with a high squeal of happiness and the girls rush to her for a group huddle-hug as the bedroom door opens and two more women, Dao and Fanta, come into the room. Dao's T-shirt is of a Korean boy band, all tiny waists and blinding teeth, and Fanta's says BUT DIFFERENT, meaning she's got it on backward, since the front is supposed to say SAME SAME. At the moment Rafferty makes that deduction, the baby, perhaps waking up to a momentary loss of attention, begins to cry. All seven women fall silent so abruptly that the soundtrack might have cut out, and a couple of the new arrivals cover their mouths and chortle with anticipatory glee as Rose leads them through the bedroom door, an unwieldy herd jostling for position. Rafferty, smelling chewing gum and shampoo and a faint citrus perfume, follows along. He stops just inside the doorway, and Fon muscles past him.

The baby is waving his arms and squalling, red as a radish, but the moment Rose picks him up he falls silent and rolls his head around, his surprisingly blue eyes wide to take in his new fans. An unidentifiable vowel goes up from the women and then chatter breaks out, sharp-edged as dishes hitting the floor, and they gather so closely around Rose they might be competing for the baby's autograph. One of them, Cartoon, says in Thai, "So handsome," and Rose, her eyes finding Rafferty's over the heads of the women, says, "Looks like Poke."

Two of the women glance back at him for a second and catch him in full blush, but it's no contest: the baby wins in a walk. He stands there, taking in the adoration of new life, and male life, at that, by women who have been victimized by men at so many turns in their own lives, and he finds he's getting a little teary. Fon would make merciless fun of him if he sniffled, so he leaves the crowded room and turns aimlessly toward the bathroom. From behind Miaow's closed door he hears voices, low but not whispering—energized, in fact, even urgent—and he pauses, considering for a moment, indulges himself in a sniffle Fon won't hear, and then knocks.

The back-and-forth dialogue on the other side of the door continues as though there's been no interruption, so he knocks again, waits, and pushes it open to see Miaow sitting at the head of her bed with her back to the wall and her legs stretched in front of her. She has a paperback book open and balanced like a little personal roof on her head, and her ridiculously handsome school friend and not-so-secret love, Edward, stands at the foot of the bed with a matching book. Miaow's gaze darts to Rafferty and then back to Edward, and she says, "*You're* no gentleman, you're not, to talk of such things. I'm a good girl, I am; and I know what the likes of you are, I do."

Her Cockney accent is much improved—amazingly so, considering that she first heard it less than two months ago in a 1930s movie adaptation of the play on YouTube.

In a ridiculously deepened voice, Edward says, "We want none of your Lisson Grove prudery here, young woman. You've got to learn to behave like a duchess. Take her away, Mrs. Pearce. If she gives you any trouble wallop her."

"No," Miaow says, grabbing the book off her head and jumping up. "No! I'll—I'll—" She opens the book and glares over it at Rafferty. "I'll call the police, I will." She stops, the image of someone whose train of thought has been derailed, perhaps for life, inhales deeply, and blows it out in his direction. He's struck yet again at the spurt in height of the past six months or so: a short, slightly boxy little girl of fourteen or fifteen is turning into a slender, angular young woman. She avoids mirrors as though they were sources of contagion, and he wonders for the hundredth time whether she's even noticed the transformation.

"Sorry," he says. No one reassures him that it's no problem, so he adds, "Accent sounds great."

"I've been working on it," Miaow says. "In fact, I'm working on it *right now.*"

"Sorry. Hi, Edward."

"Hello, Mr. Rafferty," Edward says. Miaow has said she thinks Edward is too polite, although that seems to be the only fault she's perceived thus far.

"Edward is *helping* me," Miaow says. She blinks at him meaningfully.

"Well, then. I'll just . . ." He steps back and quietly closes the door. Instantly, he hears a stream of irritated Cockney, picking up Eliza's speech a few lines back to give Edward his cue. When Miaow learned—in Leon and Toot's bar, of all places—that the upcoming school play, *Pygmalion*, was not some old, dull Greek classic, as she had thought, but rather the story of a street girl who is transformed into a lady, she had instantly locked on the part of Eliza, which, to Poke's total lack of surprise, she won. Edward had wanted to play the male lead, the unfeeling dialect wizard Henry Higgins, but had settled instead for Eliza's vapid upper-class suitor, Freddy. Rafferty likes Edward, and he's secretly happy, as the father of a girl who seems to be in love with the boy, that Edward is in some important ways more like Freddy than he is Higgins. Not that Edward is vapid; it's just that, despite having a dreadful, compulsively womanizing father and an unloving mother, Edward lacks Higgins's icy, unemotional core, which has greatly eased Rafferty's mind. Someone as handsome as Edward could be a disaster for Miaow if he didn't have a good heart.

When Miaow announced she was going to master all of Eliza's dialects and win the role, Rafferty had been, to put it mildly, apprehensive. The barriers seemed forbiddingly high in such a short period of time. She had spoken only rudimentary, present-tense English eight years earlier when he first met her as a smudged, lice-ridden child selling chewing gum to tourists in the "entertainment district" around Patpong. The first task she had set for herself after he and Rose adopted her—after Miaow realized they were going to keep her and that all those new shoes and nice clothes actually *belonged* to her—was to master Poke's language, which she went after like a lion tamer, with a figurative whip and chair. And now here she is, speaking English like a native Californian and devouring all these new variants: Eliza's native Cockney; the upper-class diction Eliza masters under Higgins's domineering tutelage; and several transitional phases between the two.

So it's an understatement to say that Rafferty admires his daughter. He's often dazzled by her. Until the baby's arrival remapped Rafferty's emotional landscape, his two strongest feelings in life had been a kind of helpless, infinitely deep love for Rose and an uncertain mixture of pride in, and anxiety about, Miaow. He was proud of how strong and even how fierce she was, and anxious about the fragility of the self-esteem beneath the thin shell of bravado she showed the world. She'd had periods of despair during her first year at the international school where Rafferty had enrolled her. Comparing herself to her worldly, upper-class schoolmates, she'd felt like an impostor, a household pet that had been briefly allowed to sit at the dinner table because it was mildly amusing, and all the time dreading the moment when the joke would become stale and she'd be banished back to the floor.

It almost breaks his heart to look at her now and see how she's grown; the little beggar girl he and Rose used to worry about all the time has become someone almost completely new. And, he thinks more and more often these days, someone who will soon be gone.

Approaching the couch, he stops in his tracks. As though the thought of Miaow's departure has had some kind of magical effect, the living room, empty for the moment, seems suddenly immense, as big as he sometimes imagines it will feel when he and Rose are rattling around the apartment alone. It takes him a moment to remember why the place seems so spacious: the giant flat-screen TV he bought Rose the night he learned she was pregnant has been pushed back against the room's longest wall, opening up the space and clearing the view to the precarious balcony for the first time in nine months. He's settling into the couch when he hears a unison *awwwww* from the bedroom, followed by a ripple of laughter.

My son. He still doesn't actually know how he feels about that.

Looks like Poke, Rose had said, and he feels himself blush all over again. But he has to do something about the baby's name.

The name, the result of a generous but misguided impulse on Rose's part, is Frank, in honor of Poke's extremely dodgy father, with whom he has never been close. Still, he thinks, it can probably be changed, and even if Rose defends it, the child also has a Thai name that delights him—Arthit, in recognition of Rafferty's police-colonel friend, with whom he's gone through a lot. The name Frank, although it grates on him, is just a minor blemish on the new and somewhat daunting panorama of parenthood. He can tell people it's just an English synonym for *honest*.

He leans back and lets out a long breath, thinking this is supposed to be the happiest he's ever been. And he isn't. Not by a considerable margin.

"What," he says at a conversational volume, "is wrong with me?" And instantly recognizes that he's generated at least one of his problems all by himself; he can't blame anyone else. With a deep sigh he looks across the room and through the glass doors that open onto the balcony. The sky is the royal purple that announces bat-time and the oncoming edge of full-scale darkness. Down at ground level, certain parts of Bangkok are disguising their drab and slapdash buildings behind lurid fantasies of neon. It's a time of day he most happily spends indoors.

But. Whatever's wrong with him—here's *one* thing he can do something about.

He sighs and gets up, grabs his keys, and slips into his shoes. A moment later, the front door closes behind him.

3

Chocolate Moose

ON PATPONG, RAFFERTY thinks, every night is Friday night. A really *cheesy* Friday night.

Patpong Road is actually two stubby, parallel, charm-free streets, imaginatively called Patpong One and Two, that connect two busy boulevards, Thanon Surawong and Silom Road. During the day they're a dreary automotive shortcut, but around five in the afternoon the night market starts to open up, the neon stutters into life, the bar workers stream in, and an area that's an unassuming urban Dr. Jekyll in the daytime turns, with a vengeance, into Mr. Hyde. Wearing heavy mascara.

Despite the hundreds of millions of dollars that have changed hands here over the decades, Patpong is even shabbier now than it was when Rafferty arrived in Bangkok to write his book. It had been dusty and makeshift then, as though it were slapped together at dusk every evening and taken down at dawn like a stage set. But today, Patpong One is bisected by the enormous, garish night market that metastasized from the modest row of street vendors he remembers from his early days. The bars, however—other than the occasional name change—have remained much the same. Whatever furtive appeal the place held for him when he arrived has been replaced by a kind of rancid glimmer, the greenish sheen on meat that's going bad.

Dragging his feet on Silom, in no hurry to get to Patpong, he realizes he hasn't eaten anything since breakfast, so he climbs the three steps to the Baskin-Robbins store just a few yards away from the corner. *Being an adult means I can have ice cream for dinner. When my wife isn't watching.*

As he shoves his way through the swinging door into the freezing shop, the thought clobbers him for the hundredth time: *I have a son.*

Well, he thinks, pushing aside the more complicated reactions as he eyes the list of flavors, *I'm going to make sure the kid eats right.*

"Three scoops in a cup," he says to the boy behind the counter, who looks all of fourteen and has a little fake diamond stud sparkling unconvincingly just below his lower lip. "Chocolate almond, chocolate chip, chocolate."

"Have also chocolate ripple, chocolate mint, chocolate mouse," the kid says, counting off on his fingers, beginning with his pinky.

Rafferty says, "*Mousse.*"

"*Moooozz?*" the kid says experimentally.

"*Mouse* is same as Mickey Mouse. Chocolate Mickey Mouse."

"No *good,*" the kid is laughing, waving away the image like smoke. "Chocolate mooooze. Give you, okay?"

"No. I've got to exert *some* self-control."

"Give you free. You teach word, I give you."

"What the hell," Rafferty says. "Go for it."

"Go . . . for . . . it," the kid repeats under his breath several times as he digs into the tubs of ice cream, substantially exceeding the capacity of the scoop with each dredge. He stuffs all four scoops into the cup and counts, out loud: "One. Two. Three."

Rafferty pays and says, "Keep the change," and the kid says, "Too much," but drops it into the jar anyway, and Rafferty retreats to the back of the store and sits, downing chocolate like he had when he was twelve, and watching, without much interest, the traffic on the sidewalk.

He's seen this particular show so *many* times. It seems to him that people who say that some things never change are rarely referring to things that cheer them up. The stream of foot traffic into Patpong is no exception. This early in the evening, the pilgrims are mainly solo men. It's safe to assume that most of the patrons are either freshly showered or newly drunk, or both, for their plunge into the long string of largely interchangeable bars that have begun to pump passé music into the street. Bangkok is one of the few cities in the world in which "Hotel California" is still played without irony, and he's wondered for years what kind of karma it would take to sentence a young woman or man to dance to it literally a thousand times a year.

Patpong One and Two were once Desire Central in Bangkok, a gaudy heart of darkness, but now they're adrift, outdated, and out-glittered by the once dusty Soi Cowboy and the three-story emporium of squeeze called Nana Plaza, both over on Sukhumvit. And then there are the specialty locations such as Soi Kathoey a few blocks away, offering boys and ladyboys, and the rich vein of trans clubs scattered in and around Soi Nana. Not to mention, of course, the monotonous metropolis of skin down on the Gulf, Pattaya, which to Rafferty is ultimate proof of the notion that too much of anything can become not only boring but repulsive and even allergenic.

Still, Patpong trudges on, relying mainly on a peculiar mix of relatively young, wide-eyed, first-time visitors and the geriatric lifers in whose memories the place still shines bright: old soldiers like Bob Campeau and a few dozen others who patronize ancient holes in the wall such as Leon and Toot's and the Madrid Bar. These are the guys who remember when everyone was an amateur, when nobody went for short time, and when a bar girl and a patron—sometimes on leave from Vietnam—had no way of knowing when commerce might be shouldered aside by love.

At the thought of Campeau, he scoops up the last of the chocolate almond, which he's saved for the finale. In a world in which pleasure is justifiably regarded as fleeting, chocolate almond has staying power.

As he gets up, his attention is snagged by someone battling the tide on the sidewalk, heading away from Patpong rather than toward it. At first glimpse it seems to be a pile of discarded garments that has somehow become mobile, but by the time it passes the window it has resolved into an old woman, battered as a wrecked car, her spine curved into a painful-looking C and her shoulders hunched almost level with her ears. It's the wild scrabble of gray hair that rings the bell, though; this is the street woman he'd seen earlier, peering through the dirty window of the bar. Slung from her shoulder is a jumbo plastic tote bag, ragged and dog-eared, that says LOUIE VUITTON on it, either a misspelling or someone's notion of how to duck a lawsuit. He makes a mental note to give her a few baht if he spots her on his way home. The plainclothes cops who keep Patpong running don't tolerate beggars. No profit in them.

The boy behind the counter bids him a cheerful goodbye and says "Moooooze" as Rafferty pushes his way back into the heat and falls in with the herd. He's already back to thinking about Campeau, a man whose emotional compass seems to be frozen halfway between misery and resentment. And really, Rafferty asks himself, what is there in Campeau's life that would inspire a broader spectrum of reactions? This is what he's got: a barstool, a meager pension that dwindles as prices go up, an almost operatic comb-over, an empty apartment, a spotty disposition, dying friends, and—in his late seventies—the Big One, the final station on the line. Sooner or later, when it's finished messing around with his friends, it'll be staring him in the face.

If he were in Campeau's shoes, Rafferty thinks, he'd probably be even more miserable than Campeau seems to be.

In the nine years he's known the man, he's only made one lighthearted remark about the life he was dealt: When some dick-head, bucktoothed kid, obviously in the wrong bar, called him a *fucking duffer*, Campeau had said, "The whole *world* is duffers, jerkface: duffers-*in-waiting*, like you; *duffers*, like me; and *former* duffers, every single one of whom would give his soul to get back across the line and be a duffer again. *And*," he'd said to the kid, whose top incisors jutted out at such an acute angle he could have used them as a shelf for tiny toiletries, "why don't you give us all a break and get your fucking teeth fixed?"

Campeau may not be the man he once was, Rafferty thinks, but he's still got a formidable edge. And he's owed an apology.

4

Pieces of It Fall Away

IT'S A NARROW road and relatively dark, and she's not sure how she got there. If she could remember *that*, the path she'd taken, she'd know where she is.

She took a fall not too long ago, recently enough that she still hurts, recently enough that she's still trailing the pink ghost of pain and her palms still sting. She tripped over a paver—it must have been a paver—and went down. She's heavy now, so she went down hard. Her tote bag slipped off her shoulder. The fall made her lose track of herself the way something sudden and painful will: it shakes the day and cracks it so that pieces fall away and all that's left is whatever hurts and a vivid impression of the moment everything went wrong, glaring at her like a spotlight, beyond which she can see only the broken bits of what happened before. She looks at her skinned and filthy palms and is surprised to see a ballpoint pen in her left hand. It says something, some kind of bank, on the side. KRUNGTHAI BANK, that's what it says.

She thinks, *I don't keep any of my money in Krungthai Bank*, and then she laughs. She had a bank account a long time ago, but it's too many days or weeks back. Maybe years, *certainly* years. And hard to find in her memory: the days or years in her deep past that haven't broken into pieces around something impossible to forget are folded away now. Hard to locate. She used to read comic books, and her days now sometimes seem like the pages in

a comic book: when she's turned a few of them, the old ones disappear. They're hiding back there somewhere, she knows. She
could look for them, but she can't always expect to find them.
And even if she does find them, they might be in the wrong order.

But when you turn a page to something blindingly *bright*, like
pain or a thief or a too-strong dose, or a bad cop, that brightness
can make everything that went before it go dark and kind of
loose, for a while, anyway, hard to figure whether it was then or
now, here or there, or rattling around somehow *between* here and
there.

The cop. There had been a cop. He'd kicked her. Sideways.
She'd been sitting on a sidewalk and he came up beside her and
kicked her over onto her right side, his foot on her shoulder.
Then there was some pain and some shouting and his hands all
over her, in her bag and in her clothes, and then she was walking
away.

On Silom. Walking away from . . . She'd been waiting for . . .
Wait.

The *cop* . . .

She slaps at her pockets, dropping the pen. It's *gone*. The fifty
baht that was left of the two hundred the Sour Man had given her
that morning. Breathing heavily, she stands still and closes her eyes,
seeing the moment again, putting its pieces together: the cop, the
push, the shouting, the hands. The money. Panic crackles deep
inside her. The *money's* gone, but what about . . .

She opens her eyes and very, very slowly looks up and down the
street to see whether anyone is watching her. There are people
across the way, but they're not paying any attention to her. Still,
she waits until their backs are turned, and then she slowly,
slowly—quick movements draw attention—reaches inside her big
loose outer dress and pats the pocket of her T-shirt. Feels the tablets, the bright orange tablets, still in their aluminum foil. There

should be three of them. Three warm visits to the place where everything is fine, where she's not frightened and tired and hurting. Where the street music is.

One. Two. *Three.*

The sigh she releases is so deep and so long that she imagines herself turning inside out and laughs at the notion. Old lady, inside out, on the sidewalk. Who would they call? The inside-out squad? *Bet they sit by the phone a lot,* she thinks, and she laughs again, laughing herself all the way down into a sitting position, knees up in front of her. That puts the scrape on her knee at eye level, and she studies it for a moment, thinking *look, I'm meat,* until it stops interesting her.

Still, the cop got her money. That's one of the things the *bag* is for, to carry her extra plastic sheet and her blanket and to get snatched by thieves. It's so big they just grab it. She doesn't know how many times it's been taken, but it's been more than she can count on one hand: the yank, her fall, the thief running around a corner, and then the bag thrown to the pavement. But this time, the cop hadn't even looked at the bag, he'd gone straight for one of her pockets.

She stops, reliving it. He'd found the money in the first pocket he invaded. That was why she still had the pills. He'd hit the money and then he'd stopped.

So *where* was she when the cop . . .

Patpong. She's supposed to be on Patpong *now.* Or maybe it's too late. Maybe everything's all gone dark already. The Sour Man will be angry. She needs to do what the Sour Man says. The Sour Man has the money.

The Sour Man terrifies her.

She puts her hands down to push herself up and something rolls beneath her right palm. The pen. She sits again, picks it up, reads again the name of the bank, and has a brief flashbulb of memory, of seeing the pen, practically under her nose on the pavement, when she tripped on the sidewalk.

She clicks it a few times, click *click*, click *click*, and she's a girl again, sitting in a hot wooden classroom up in rice country, some of the students asleep with their heads on the desks, and in her hand is a gleaming pen, the first new one she's ever seen. And she does now what she did then: she uses the pen to write on her left palm, a bigger, much dirtier left palm than the one that little girl had. What she writes is her name: *Hom*, meaning sweet-smelling.

She had been sweet-smelling once.

She closes her eyes and rocks back and forth for a minute or two, thinking about the orange tablets. Thinking about taking one and going into Lumphini Park, which can't be far from here, and reclaiming her bush. Maybe the extra pill she buried will still be there: she'd patted the soil down carefully. It had been almost dark when she finally left the park, and it would be hard to see the little mound. She's got three with her, but four is better than three. At one pill each night or even two, four is better than three.

But then, in her mind's eye, she sees the Sour Man, and the image puts strength into her legs. Slowly and stiffly, she gets her feet beneath her and stands up. Little red fireworks pop in the air just in front of her eyes, and she waits until they're gone. There's a big street to her left, she knows that much. If she can find a big street she can find Patpong. She knows now what it is that she needs to do in Patpong. She looks at the name on her palm again, the name of that long-ago little girl, and starts to walk.

But it might be too late.

She *hates* the way she smells. *That little girl with her new pen*, she thinks, and then there's only the walking and the pain.

5

The Only One

THE BELL RINGING over the door brings every head in the place around, reminding Rafferty of a herd of antelope that's just scented a predator, a unanimous shift of interest that makes it clear that nothing really hypnotically interesting is going on. Toots is glaring at him with her fists planted on her hips, a stance that usually signals fireworks. Pinky is grinning at him with a kind of gleeful expectation. The guy with the hair seems to be checking for split ends. The Growing Younger Man sips something so green it might be the essence of a million Aprils and studies a chessboard with an unfinished game on it; he plays by mail and cheats at every opportunity. A couple of leathery, self-styled *old Bangkok hands* whose barstools have been drawn up to Campeau's, probably to commiserate or plot some Byzantine revenge that they'll never get around to, are staring at him wide-eyed and open-mouthed; and Campeau has sprung off his stool with the intensity of someone who's been stung by a wasp. Instantly Rafferty realizes, *Bob's enjoying this.*

As the door closes behind him, Rafferty gives Campeau a high, respectful *wai*. He says, "I'm sorry, Bob, I'm sorry. Toots, I'm sorry to you, too. Can I ring the bell?"

After a punitive moment, Toots nods, reestablishes her authority by saying, "*I* do," and yanks at the rope dangling above the bar. A rusting bell makes a noise somewhere between a chime and a quack, and everyone in the bar starts to chug whatever he's drinking to clear the way for the free one coming up. Toots says to Rafferty, who's still in the doorway, "Come in, come *in*, air-con all go outside."

Rafferty says, "Okay with you, Bob?"

Campeau says, "Shit, yes. I can't say I've missed you, but if you're buying, what the hell."

A LITTLE LESS than an hour later, Campeau says, "You're the only one."

They're in Pinky Holland's plastic-upholstered booth. Poke had offered Pinky an additional free drink to vacate it when it became evident that the members of Campeau's posse were unwilling to let him and Poke talk without listening in.

Since Campeau is at the stage in his evening when he doesn't necessarily identify the topic under discussion and he seems disinclined to elaborate, Poke can't be sure why he's just been called *the only one*. So he says, "Really."

"Well, *yeah*," Campeau says, going instantly to his default tone, irritation. "I don't mean the *only* only one, but *one* of the only ones. I know thirty, maybe thirty-five *farang* guys who married locals. And look at 'em. There's you and Rose, there's Jerry and Lamyai, there's Leon and Toots and, shit, Leon's dead so he doesn't really count. And a couple others, maybe. But you're the only one I know who married a working girl and wound up with a whole skin."

"I don't think of Rose's time in Patpong as a formative experience," Rafferty says, hearing the stiffness in his tone. "It's not like she grew up dreaming day and night about coming down to Bangkok to screw strangers in crappy hotels. If her father hadn't been about to sell her to—"

"Ahhhh," Campeau says. "*You* know what I mean. Mine,

Malee—you ever meet Malee?" He focuses on Rafferty, squinting a little bit as though to hold Poke still. He's had quite a few during Rafferty's absence.

Rafferty says, "Not that I remember."

"Nah." He shakes his head. "You wouldn't. She was gone long before you got here. Damn, she was beautiful."

Poke waits, sipping his bubble water. Toots is absolutely not going to let him drink alcohol. "Didn't work out?"

"Worked out for *her*." He picks up his bottle and puts it down several times, making a pattern of wet rings on the tabletop. "Oldest fucking trick in the book. Needed a house, right? I mean, she was gonna be married, gonna have a baby, needed a house."

"A baby."

"Don't even ask," he says. "Goddamn rainbow baby. No matter how close you got, it was still the same distance away. But I *believed* it. I believed everything. She *loved* me, right? So I buy her a house, and since this is fucking Thailand it has to be in her name 'cause foreigners can't own, *et cetera*. Up in some village in Nakhorn Nowhere, I go up there one time before I sign the papers and people sort of nod at me, not a big welcome, but they seemed to realize I was there. House is a crappy little dump, a few regular rooms in back and a couple open rooms in front, you know, no wall, so the whole fucking village and its chickens can come in and say hi, but I figure, hey, it's what she wants, so I buy it, just buzzing with goodwill, and then I fly back to the States to arrange things. I'm gonna live here, right? So I gotta get banking stuff set up, sell some property. Takes me about a month, and she's not answering the phone but I figure she's up in Dirtville putting up curtains or some fucking thing, and there's like three phones in the whole place. I get back here, and the first surprise is that my apartment is for rent."

"Oh, no," Rafferty says.

"*Yeah*, oh, no. So I get all heavy with my landlady and she says my wife told her I wasn't coming back. She took everything that wasn't cemented down, bed and all, even some of my clothes, so I make a sort of panic run to the bank, and the joint account's been cleaned out. About nine thousand US. And I re-rent the apartment, buy a bed, get a motorbike, and break the world speed record from Bangkok to Nakhorn Nowhere, and there's nobody in the house and the people in the village tell me they have no idea in the world who my wife was. She'd never lived there in her life."

He swipes his mouth with the back of his hand as though he's wiping away suds and says, "Later I find out half a dozen guys have bought that house and not one of them ever lived in it." He takes a pull from his bottle. "Woulda been a good investment."

"I'm sorry."

"Yeah, well, I've had a lot of time to get used to it. And it could have been worse. I know a guy, it was a condo down in Phuket, right on the beach, cost him most of what he had in the world. Sold out from under him while he was on a four-day visa run to Singapore. At least mine chose a dump."

"But it's not just the money," Rafferty says.

"No," Campeau says, studying the pattern of rings on the table as though they were a code of some kind. "It's not."

Rafferty is adrift in the conversation. He'd wanted to apologize, but he hadn't been looking for sad tales, especially not one that makes him feel even more fortunate than he had when he came in. He says, for lack of anything interesting, "Sorry to hear all that."

"We've *all* got *stories*," Campeau says with sudden force. "I know to someone like you, who comes here late, when things are pretty much shot to shit, we probably look like useless old fuckups, guys hanging around a mirage hoping for a glass of water, but you know, we all got to where we are one fucking day at a time. This place was magic once. The girls came down from the villages, *nice* girls, girls you could fall in love with, you know? Clean, modest, honest. Sweet. They worked a year or two, sent money home, and then packed it in and went back, and more new ones came in. They were *nice* to us, *interested* in us. Wasn't all just boom-boom. Nobody even knew what a short time was, not like now. Back then you'd take a girl out and she'd stay with you for a week. Now the girl's clock starts running the minute you leave the bar with her, just tick tick tick. In the old days, people fell in love all the time. Hell, *I* fell in love."

"So did I."

"Yeah, and you got *the last good one*, you asshole. Most beautiful girl ever. Now they got tattoos, they smoke like chimneys, they got half a dozen fucking poultry writing them love letters on the Internet, sending them money every week so they can *go to school* while they're popping in and out of the bar, getting fined out for a short time three, four times a night. Getting a degree in the old horizontal mambo. You get them in the room, you hide your valuables, 'cause they'll swipe them any chance they get. Making more money than we are, making as much money as a fucking *banker*, and they'll still kipe your stuff."

Rafferty chokes back the suggestion he was about to make, that what really pisses Campeau off is the transfer of power from the customer to the bar worker, but he knows that's only part of it. As atypical and remote from the normal American moral code as Campeau's life on Patpong was, it had been his *youth*, and almost everyone mourns the loss of his or her youth. And for certain kinds of men, of which Campeau was a prime representative, this shoddy, banged-up old street was once Eden, an improved Eden with multiple Eves, whole *teams* of Eves, and no pissed-off God polishing his thunderbolts just around the corner. Guilt-free wish fulfillment forever and ever, amen. Until it wasn't.

But, of course, Rafferty has had eight years to get Rose's perspective, the view from the other team, a look at the things they endured: the ever-needier family at home, the drunks, the rough guys, the occasional woman-hater like the one who had tried to murder her, the ones with *special tastes*, the incremental degradation of being displayed and sold night after night like varieties of hard candy, the corrupt cops who could be depended on to take the customer's side and the woman's money, no matter what the problem was. And then there were the women who couldn't handle it, the friends damaged beyond recognition, the cutting, the booze, the *yaa baa* and all the other dope, the despair of waiting for life to change. The ones so ruined they could never go home, might never have a home again.

"God damn, she was beautiful," Campeau says, his face almost soft at the memory.

"I'm sure," Rafferty says.

"I'm talking about *yours*, you idiot. Rose."

"She is. I'd never argue that."

Campeau nods a couple of times. After the second nod he keeps his chin lowered, staring at the center of the table. Just as Rafferty is about to push back and go home, Campeau says, without looking up, "So you got all the bar girls keeping watch over the kid."

"You know, if she was home in the village every female relative within fifty miles would be there, but since she's down here—"

"Since she's down here, they're her sisters," Campeau says, surprising Rafferty. "That's one of the things about women, isn't it? They can slip into families like that. Woman needs a sister, she's got one. Probably more of them than she wants. Men don't do that."

"No," Rafferty says. "We'll punch somebody for each other, but it's not like we brother up. It might get embarrassing. Might need to hug or something."

"That fucking *guy-hug*," Campeau says, "with two pats on the back so it looks *manly*." He sighs, and when he looks up at Poke he seems surprised to see him there, but then he nods. "Yup," he says, although Rafferty isn't sure what he's agreeing with. "Yup, two different tribes. We got the good end, though."

"How do you figure?"

"We get to look at them and they gotta look at us. And they do all the work when the kid comes. It's hard enough for me to clear my throat, can't imagine pushing out a kid."

"Hadn't thought of it that way."

"What's the kid's name?" Campeau raises a hand with two fingers extended, toward Toots. "Two, on me," he calls. "And give my friend a fucking beer, wouldja?"

"Thanks. The name is a problem. Rose honored my father by calling the baby Frank."

"Not a bad name. Kind of 1940s, I guess."

"Well, the actual name isn't the issue. The issue is my father."

"Don't get along, huh?"

"You remember Top Forty?" Rafferty says. "When I was a kid, there were radio stations that played records—"

"'Course, I remember Top Forty. They played *real* music. What about it?"

"If my family were the Top Forty, my father would be about number fifty-seven."

For a moment Rafferty thinks Campeau will laugh, but he

gets it under control. "My old man was a pile of shit. Drank himself to death the hard way a year after I went to Nam. Got so drunk he fell into a threshing machine. My mother said it was the best thing that ever happened to her although it was hard to clean up." Toots puts two beers on the table with unnecessary force and wheels away.

"So," Campeau says, and tilts the bottle. He gets about a third of it down, celebrates with a seismic belch, and says, "So how *is* the kid?"

"Seems to be fine," Rafferty says. "Sleeps and eats and everything. Fills his diaper. Cries. Pretty much the full complement of skills, far as I know."

"Not *that* kid. Probably shouldn't say this, not now, anyways, but I'm not a baby guy. I'm talking about your daughter. Even the times when I don't like you, I have to remember the job you've done with that little girl."

"Not so little now, but I don't think I've done anything. Miaow is like Rose. She's who she was when I met her. I've probably learned more from them than they have from—"

"Oh, bullshit. You know, you don't gotta do the *who, me?* thing every time someone says something halfway nice. Rose, sure, she was born complete, everything in place, like a fucking butterfly, minus the worm stage. But that little kid, she's *different* now than she—"

"That's not to my credit—"

Campeau puts down his bottle and softly backhands Rafferty on the shoulder. "Stick it up your ass. She was *a street kid*, dirty as Pittsburgh, didn't trust anybody, thought she was ugly. Spoke beggar's English. Now she's acting in Shakespeare."

Rafferty feels a little electric sizzle he identifies as pride. "She did that, Shakespeare, I mean, couple of years back. Now it's George Bernard Shaw."

"Yeah, yeah. *My Fair Lady*, I remember how she lit up, like a fucking billboard, when Louis told—"

"It's not actually *My Fair*—" Rafferty says, and then he replays the second part of Campeau's sentence. "Who? *Louis?* Who's—"

"*Him*, for Chrissakes," Campeau says, lifting his chin in the direction of the Growing Younger Man, who now is supervising the preparation of his next drink, a concoction that involves a great many stalks of celery. He brings in bags full of vegetables daily for Toots to pulverize in a special blender he purchased and installed, a deafening whopper that could probably puree a pound of nails. "Bet he poops green," Campeau says. "Like a parrot."

"I'll take the bet," Rafferty says, "but you'll have to take the picture."

"You don't *remember* when he said that about the play, when Louis did? Swear to God, I never seen anyone light up like she did. It was all that—that stuff about a street girl, learning to be a princess."

"I remember the conversation. It's his name I forgot. Him and the guy with the hair. I can never remember the—"

"*Ron*, you fucking snob," Campeau says. "You know what she looked like? She looked like someone who'd just had Christmas explained to her."

"Yeah, well, the whole idea of, of turning into somebody else . . . I mean, I'm probably to blame. I put her in this snotty school, and she felt like everyone looked down at her. And then, she's dark-skinned, which doesn't help. But listen, you should *hear* her work on this accent, it's—"

"Exactly what I'm saying," Campeau says. "She wanted to be somebody else, and you—"

"She was *always* somebody else. She just didn't know it."

"Probably easier to shoot you than to pay you a compliment. You changed that kid's life, and just shut up about it."

"Well," Rafferty says, "thanks."

Campeau rests his head on his hand and burps. "But I know what you mean, I really do. There was always a high-class kid hiding in there somewhere."

"You've got to be careful, Bob," Rafferty says. "You're going to make me like you."

"Don't worry," Campeau says. "I'll never go that far."

6

A Slum Girl's Idea of an Interesting Man

AN OUTBURST OF laughter finds its way in from the bedroom, followed by a little spattering of applause, like the first moment of rain.

"Wonder what that's about," Edward says, wiping his forehead with his sleeve. He and Miaow are on the living room couch, books face down and out of easy reach on the glass coffee table. He's volunteered to work overtime to drill Miaow on her lines although he's the one who really needs the memory work, and she's compensated him by giving him an impromptu dinner, sharing some leftover *som tam*, the spicy green papaya salad that most Thais can eat for breakfast, lunch, dinner, and, probably, in the casket. Edward, who hasn't yet developed the internal asbestos required by much Thai cuisine, is in full sweat mode from the chili.

"The baby probably drooled," Miaow says. "Blinked both eyes at the same time." She looks down at Edward's socks, visible through the glass top on the table. "How come your feet never smell?"

"I change my socks?" He pushes his plate away. "He's just a *baby*, you know. He can't help it if women get all gooey around him. It's not like he's playing to the crowd. And you shouldn't call him *it*."

"*I* change my socks," Miaow says, "but my feet still smell. *It, it, it*. It's *my* brother and I'll call it what I want." She pulls Edward's plate toward her. "You're not going to finish this, are you?"

"I'm already on fire," he says. "How can you eat anything that hot?"

"You'll get used to it." She had hoped the thing about his feet not smelling was a compliment, but he'd shrugged it off, so she tries a new tack. "You're getting really good as Freddy."

He shrugs. "I *am* Freddy. I'm ornamental and dull."

She sits up, pushing the plate away. "You're not dull."

"I wanted to play Higgins."

Miaow looks down at the food. After a moment, she says, "You're not right for Higgins."

He lifts his chin a little and looks down at her over his large, but to her perfect, Western nose. "Really. Well, thanks."

"No. *Dieter* is right for Higgins. He's dry and kind of old-papery and he doesn't seem to have anything except a head. I mean, he doesn't feel anything except getting pissed off, far as I can tell."

"And he's smart," Edward says.

"So what? *You're* smart. But you're a *good* kind of smart, you don't use it all the time to make other people feel dumb. Dieter's always keeping score. He's perfect for Higgins."

"I still wanted it."

"You have a *heart*. It shows. That's why you were so good as George in *Small Town*."

"George," Edward says gloomily. "Another hole in the air." He picks up his book. "You're perfect as Eliza."

"I was born," Miaow says, "to play Eliza."

Edward says, "Oh, for Christ's sake."

"Well, *look* at me. I mean, I'm sitting right here with you, short and stubby and as dark-skinned as a farmer, and you can't see me on a sidewalk somewhere? Selling flowers? Or maybe gum?"

"Miaow," he says. He puts the book back on the table and slides it side to side with his fingertips. "I already know about that, remember?"

"You know the—the *fact* of it. You have no idea what it felt like."

"It makes me admire you."

"I don't want admiration. Well, I do, but that's not what I really want. What I *really* want is never to have been that girl." She closes her eyes and says in a careful British accent, "My aunt died of influenza: so they said." Lapsing into Cockney, she adds, "It's my belief they done the old woman in."

"*But* it's my belief," Edward says, picking up his book.

Miaow snatches up her own copy. "No way." She's flicking through the pages.

Edward says, "You know what your problem is?"

"Poop," Miaow says, looking at the book. "*But*"—she makes a *tsssss* sound, like something landing in a hot pan. "*But* it's my belief they done the old woman in." She marks the place with her forefinger. "I don't have a problem."

"Oh, *well*," Edward says. "Fine. You don't have a problem." In a falsetto intended to suggest a woman's voice, he reads, "Done her in?"

With her eyes closed, Miaow says, "Yes, Lord love you, why should she die of influenza? She come through diphtheria right enough the year before. They all thought she was dead; but my father he kept ladling gin down her throat till she came to so sudden that she bit the bowl off the spoon."

Edward is laughing, but he says, "You missed a couple of—"

"No. We cut them to get to the laugh sooner."

He stops laughing. "You *cut* them."

"Sure. They were just slowing things—"

"*I'm* in this scene, Miaow. Why don't I know about that? Are there any other cuts I might want to hear about? Any of my lines, for example?"

"No. And so what? We made my speech shorter, not longer."

"Who's we?"

"Me and Mrs. Shin. She cut *Small Town*, too, you must remember that. And you weren't in *The Tempest*, but she cut that—"

"Fine. Are there other cuts? Are the two of you planning to share them with the rest of us any—or, wait a minute, was it the *three* of you? Was Dieter in on the, the script conference, too?"

"I don't know why you're—"

"Maybe we should go through them *now* and I could, you know, write them down? Might be good if we all had the same script."

"You were being so nice a minute ago."

Edward leans back on the couch and closes his eyes, and Miaow briefly envies him his lashes. Why couldn't *she* have lashes like—

"I'm sorry," he says. "We'll do some more tomorrow."

"What's wrong? I mean *really* wrong?"

"I just—I just—" He raps his knuckles, hard, on the glass tabletop. "I just can't stand this part. Freddy. I feel like that, that thing in a, in a department-store window that they use to show off stupid clothes."

"A mannequin."

"*Thank* you for that. Yes, as you remind me in your second language, a mannequin. They could put me on a dolly and wheel me around the stage. That way I could keep the crease in my pants."

"You hate the part that much?"

"I do. He hasn't got an idea in his head. He's—he's a slum girl's idea of an interesting man."

Miaow nods and busies herself straightening up the table.

Watching her, he dabs the tip of his index finger into the *som tam* and touches it to his tongue, then wipes his tongue on the back of his hand. "Is it really always this hot?"

"Fon likes it that way." She looks at the plate he's just touched and says, "Are you finished with that?"

"I might take it home and sneak some of it onto my dad's plate. Then maybe lock the door to the toilet."

"I'll wrap it up for him," Miaow says, and picks up the dish.

He says, "You are *not* a slum girl."

"But I *was*. It doesn't just wash off." She starts to get up but he puts his hand on her arm. She pulls away and says, "So what's my problem, then?"

"What do you mean, what's your—"

"A minute ago. You said, *You know what your problem is?*"

"Yeah," he says. "That sounds like me."

Miaow sits forward, as though to get to her feet, but instead looks over at him. "Well, what is it? You must have had *something* in mind."

He looks down at his lap for a moment. "Do you really believe you can—anyone can—turn into someone else?"

"That's a trick question. If it wasn't, you wouldn't ask me. You know too much about me to ask that unless you've got some stupid argument in—"

"Do you think you'd be who you are now if you'd never lived on the street? It you'd been some, some brainless, useless rich girl who thinks God dealt her a royal flush for no reason, who spends her time counting her dresses and getting her hair done and practicing makeup tips from YouTube, do you think you'd be who you are? If the worst thing you ever worried about was that your dimples weren't the same size or you were wearing last year's shoes, do you think you'd be who you are? Do you even *know* who you are?"

"I know exactly who I am."

"Excuse me, but you haven't got the faintest fucking idea who you are. At least, you don't have any idea who you are to me, or to the people who—who care about you."

It takes her a moment to work her way up to it. Then she says, "Who I am to you?"

"*Miaow*," he says. "I only took this awful, stupid part so I could be with you."

She's looking directly at him as he begins the sentence, but the moment he says *be with you* her eyes slide past him to the wall. She's still holding the dish.

He says, "Are you just going to make me sit here?"

"Well." She very carefully puts the dish down and sits back. "What am I supposed to do?"

"I don't know." There's a chorus of *ooohhhs* from the bedroom. "Maybe we could hug each other?"

It seems to take her forever to slide down the couch to him, and the moment he puts his arms around her, they hear Rafferty's key in the lock. In less than a second, they're pressed against opposite ends of the couch like a pair of mutually repellent sub-atomic particles, staring at each other, and then Miaow begins to laugh. By the time Rafferty has kicked off his shoes and come into sight, they're both laughing.

7

Like Struck Matches

ONE BAR AT a time, the street is blinking out, going dark from one end to the other.

The evening exit has crowded the road with pedestrians, driving her up onto the sidewalk, which is set one tall step up to allow people to walk, rather than wade, during the rainy season. From her perch above them, with her back pressed to a wall—which always makes her feel safer—she can see over people's heads. As she settles back, she feels a sudden twinge of fear, like a low string plucked somewhere inside her. She'd been sitting on the sidewalk only a meter or two away when the cop appeared. He is probably still here; he probably doesn't leave until the street has emptied out. She scans up and down the block for him and then looks again at her scraped palms, at the pen clutched in her right hand, at her name written on the left.

She hates Patpong. She has a long list of hates, which, fortunately for her, is usually tightly folded and tucked out of sight, but Patpong is different. After all these years she still feels a hot rush of shame at what she did here, up those stairs, what she was forced to do here, what was done *to* her here. If she had her way, a two-story wall of filthy water would churn through it, smashing the bars as though they were cardboard, sweeping up the customers and the touts and the police and floating their corpses all the way to the Chao Phraya, where they would be carried out to the broad emptiness of the Gulf. No cremation, no funeral, no rites, no priests, no sad farewells, just howling *phi tai hong*, ghost-souls severed abruptly from their bodies, raging and weeping eternally as they ride the winds that scour the cold surface of the sea.

But not the girls. The girls don't deserve that.

In a life that seems to have taken her from one island of unhappiness to another, Patpong stands out, a broad smear of black ash that defaces—but does not, unfortunately, obscure—a period of several months, months she tried for years to forget.

She has avoided this street for years.

And now she's been ordered back here with the threat of harm and the promise of money. She's not sure how many nights ago the Sour Man first put her here, but it seems now as though she never left; she's seen this end-of-the-night transformation often enough for the sequence to be familiar, even predictable. First, the clash of music that comes from all directions begins to shut down and the vendors in the night market start to pack up their wares. Then the crowd in the street thickens as customers leave the bars, some of them with women beside them. After that, the bars— beginning with the few that never seem to be full—switch off the colored lights that shine on the women who dance there, and turn on the cold overhead tubes, light the color of sour milk that makes everything look smaller and dirtier and colder. People sweep, mop tables, count money.

So much money.

And soon, she knows, the last doors will begin to close.

It's beginning even now: doors slamming, people flooding the street. Everyone moving in one of two directions, depending which cross street they're headed for, Silom or Surawong. It's not like when the bars are open, with everyone looking everywhere, wandering from one side to the other. At this hour she can stand up here, still as a window, watching the river of people without feeling their eyes on her, without them staring at her like she's some kind of animal and stepping aside to pass her at a distance, as though there are things living on her that might jump onto them.

She can smell beer and wine on the breath of the men pushing their way down the street, she can see it in the glaze over their eyes. She regards them without interest or curiosity, looking at them mainly just because they're moving; but she's not really seeing them, simply smelling as she breathes them in and watches the flow. The man she is supposed to be waiting for will come out of a bar at the other end of the street. She should go down into the slow current and let it carry her down there.

Except that he's probably gone by now. That low fear-string is plucked again and she feels a twisting in her gut. She's probably too late. The Sour Man will be angry.

Her heart crumples like paper at the notion of his anger. He's already hit her twice, once hard enough to knock her down. Now he may withhold the money he's been giving her each day. And she's sure that he knows—the thought arrives on a cold wave of dread—that she's already turned away from two chances to do what he wants, trying to keep the baht coming. She's gotten used to the man's money. People don't give her money the way they once did, when she was still pretty or looked like she had once been pretty. It takes no effort to remember (even if they're not in order) whole successions of days when no one gave her a baht, when she either starved or ate a handful of cold food some other beggar gave her. *Begging from beggars,* she thinks, *this is my life now.*

Without knowing she's doing it, she transfers the pen to her other hand, reaches inside the filthy outer dress, and presses her fingertips against the pocket that contains the paper with the pills in it. Three of them, and the one she buried makes four. She's pretty sure she's never before possessed four of them at the same time.

She's never *taken* more than two at a time. A kind of vista, beautiful and terrifying, opens before her.

Go somewhere. Back to the park. Take one. Swallow it whole or crush it and smoke it in an aluminum foil pipe she can make with her eyes closed. Then another.

No. He'll find her. He probably knows where she sleeps.

He could be here *now*. Here in Patpong.

She *hates* . . .

She shakes her head to bring herself present and takes a tentative step, realizing that her scraped knee has stiffened. Still walking, she looks down at it, half-expecting to be able to *see* the stiffness surrounding it, like the ghost of the cast she wore years ago when she broke her foot and she still lived in a world that had doctors in it. At that moment someone throws open a swinging door directly in front of her, and she walks into it, banging the top of her head in a starry burst of pain. She freezes for a moment, waiting to see whether she's going to fall down, and by the time she realizes that she won't, she's lost her purpose. Idly, with one hand pressed to her head, she lets her gaze sweep over the slow tide of people in the street until her vision is snagged by a glimpse of white.

A smile.

Smiles, she sees, are going off here and there in the crowd, like struck matches. She's watched this procession often enough by now to know that the smiles belong to the women from the bars. As they're towed along they gaze at nothing, or at the people coming in their direction, until the man they're with looks down at them, and then they smile. She feels *herself* smile, the same absolutely meaningless smile the tall, slender woman is giving the short, tubby man who's hauling her toward the waiting taxis. The smile is the one called *yim mai ork*, forced and without any spark of happiness or pleasure behind it. The young woman knows, and so does Hom, that the *farang* won't see through it; to a *farang*, a smile is a smile. A little farther away, a younger girl, probably new to the bars, offers her suddenly attentive customer a *yim sao*, the smile that masks sadness. That's the smile Hom is most familiar with; she can feel its muscle memory in her own face. Her destination forgotten for the moment, she searches for her favorite of the smiles, the one that makes her feel kinship with all these sad, beautiful girls: the *yim yae-yae*, the smile someone assumes when she's facing something hopeless and is determined to make the best of it, no matter what. *There* it is, on the face of a woman who's trying to match her steps to a drunken man's stagger.

She can feel her own smile broaden as she watches the man stumble and go down on one knee and then put both hands down to grope for his glasses. By the time he looks up again his companion for the evening has melted into the crowd.

Hom is searching for the fleeing girl when her ear catches fire and then is yanked—hard enough, it feels, to tear it off. Her world solidifies sharply and comes to a tiny, buzzing point with the hot flame of pain at its center, and she finds herself looking up at the face of the Sour Man.

"*Idiot*." He pulls at the ear again, and this time she follows it, stumbling toward him to avoid more pain. His nails are long and yellowish, filed to points, and they've definitely pierced her skin; she can feel a warm trickle of blood down the side of her neck. She's still trying to regain her balance when her right foot catches on one of his and suddenly she's down again, landing heavily on the bloody and stiffening knee, and she hears a high sound, like something from an injured cat, escape her.

She's put down a scraped palm to break her stumble, and that produces another sudden pink explosion of pain. He's bent down to follow her fall, not relinquishing her ear, and he steps on the back of the hand on the pavement and puts his weight on it. He's leaning directly over her now, her ear still impaled by the sharp nails, and he tugs on it to pull her face up until she's looking straight at him, diverted momentarily by the hair in his nostrils, which she's never seen before, but then he's talking and she knows she's *supposed to listen.*

"One more time," he says to her. It's as soft as a whisper and as hard as a slap. "Are you hearing me?"

"Yes." People in the street are slowing, turning to look, and he extends his free hand and more or less drags her to her feet, and it occurs to her, as it has before, that he's stronger than he looks. He's thin and starved-looking, someone who probably never got enough to eat as a child, and not much taller than she is. But it's all bone, sinew, hatred, and nails.

"*Well,*" he says, resting his right hand on her shoulder as though they're having a chat. The left, with its nails still piercing her ear, is between her and the wall, where no one in the street can see it. "I'm not sure you *are* hearing me. I'm not sure you ever *have.* Do you understand what I just said? One more time? Do you even *remember* it?"

"I—I think you . . ." She trails off and swallows what feels like a stone.

"It means *one more night.*" He tugs on the ear with each syllable, turning her entire body into an escalator of pain, darting from her ear all the way down to her toes, and her knees loosen, but that just makes it worse and she forces them to lock. She's trembling all over, and she hates it. His breath reeks of cigarettes, making her want one. "After that, it's finished. And if you don't succeed by tomorrow night *you* will be finished." He squeezes his fingers together, digging his nails deeper into the tissue, and her knees buckle, but he's slipped the other hand beneath her arm to hold her up. "After tomorrow night, if you haven't done what you're supposed to do you'll be fed to a cage full of *soi* dogs, very *hungry* *soi* dogs. Do you understand?"

"Yes."

"Do you know what you're supposed to do?"

For a moment, she has an instinctive surge of hope: over his shoulder, she sees a police uniform. She hates the cops, but they routinely break up any conflict that's visible to tourists, that might sully their memory of the Land of Smiles. But then, as fast as her hope had risen, it evaporates. It's the fat-bellied cop who kicked her. He slows for a second and peers at her face, and then he registers who she's talking to, touches a fingertip to the brim of his hat, and moves on. She says, "Yes."

The Sour Man smiles as though she's pleased him. He's filed one of his eye teeth, too, the left. The foot traffic in the street continues to flow: just two people talking, nothing to see. "Tell me what it is."

"Find him in, in—that bar . . ."

"Which direction?"

"Down there." She nods toward the Silom end of the street, but she's forgotten about his grasp on her ear, and she lets out a little yip of pain.

He says, "Quiet. And."

"Follow him."

"And."

"When I get to where he lives," she says, and then she steps back, bumping up against the still-open door behind her, and yanks her head away, sharply enough to make him lose his grip on her ear. She feels more blood on her neck, but she doesn't reach up to stanch it.

Something flares in his eyes, and he takes a quick step toward her, closing the gap she's just opened. The nails find her ear again. "And then."

"I—I call you."

"Let me see the phone."

She has a moment of profound gratitude for not having sold the battered phone he gave her. Only terror has prevented her from doing it. She digs it out of the pocket in the men's walking shorts she wears beneath the dress, and shows it to him.

He checks the battery and then the screen of recent calls, which has nothing on it. Who would she call? "And then."

"Then I—I listen to you."

"And if I have to meet you?"

"Oh," she says. "Wait, wait a minute."

"*Now.*"

"Around the corner." She can hear her voice scale up. "Some kind of store."

"A store that sells what?"

She says, "Ummmm."

She feels his fingers move on her ear and she lets out a yelp. But he surprises her by pulling his hand back and making a *T*— no, a cross—with his index fingers. His eyebrows go up: a question.

"Medicine," she says. "Drugstore."

"*Good*, good." He reaches out once more and she flinches, but all he does is pat her cheek, a little harder than is necessary to demonstrate affection. "Follow, call, wait outside the store if you have to. Right?"

"Right." She takes a breath. "Why don't *you* follow—"

"*Sssssssss.*" Suddenly his face is almost touching hers. "*Because I have you.*" It's a hiss. He pulls back and continues as though she hadn't spoken. "And how many more chances do you have?"

"One." Someone in the street bursts into laughter.

"Two, of course, counting tonight. Guess you'd better get to work."

"It's . . . it's late."

He leans toward her again, and she holds her breath. He says, sounding amused, "Two chances, one of them tonight? For five thousand baht? And you're going to waste tonight?"

"No," she says, and then she says again, "no, no."

"Well, then." He steps back and turns away from her while she fights to keep her knees from buckling. Over his shoulder as he steps down off the curb, he says, "You'd better get down there, hadn't you?"

She says, "Yes," but he's already at the edge of the crowd's current, and she watches as it carries him away, and she's surprised yet again—seeing him among the others in the crowd—at how small he is.

SHE'S PINCHING HER ear between her fingers to stop the bleeding. It hurts, but she can't be seen with blood all over her. Some cop is sure to notice and use it as an excuse to shake her down, accuse her of having done something violent, search her for money, maybe take her pills to sell, and have her hauled off to the monkey house.

She's not giving up her pills and she is *not* going back to the monkey house.

So she hobbles down the sidewalk on her stiff knee, one hand raised to her ear like someone talking on an imaginary phone. The Sour Man is gone now, but he has people up and down this street at all hours, and someone is probably watching her. She's nearing the end of the street, now; she sees the usual tangle of taxis and tuk-tuks, and, across the street . . .

Her heart sinks.

The lights on the little sign above the bar she was supposed to be watching have been turned off. From where she stands, her back to a club that plays very loud live music when it's open, she makes out a rectangle of pale, chilly-looking light and identifies it as the window she's peered through several times. Just to be sure that the man whose picture the Sour Man has showed her so many times isn't in there—and to look like she's being thorough in case she's being watched—she zigzags through the thinning trickle of people, fingers still pressed to her ear, threads between two night-market booths, and steps up onto the sidewalk on the other side of the street. She looks right and left to avoid colliding with anyone, and then presses her face to the dirty window, cupping her hands around her eyes to block the light from the street.

Behind the bar, the stocky, gray-haired woman who is always there is lining up glasses on a shelf, pulling them dripping out of the sink behind the bar, giving them a quick swab inside and out with one end of a towel that hangs over her shoulder, and placing them upside down in perfectly straight rows, with a casual, inattentive precision that says she's done it a thousand times. The woman, Hom thinks, must be ten or fifteen years older than she is, but not battered by bad karma and exposure to too much sun and too much of the kind of dirt that won't wash off. Most people, she is certain, would guess that she, Hom, is the older of the two. Watching the bartender dry a glass, Hom has an instant, full-color memory of a warm, dirt-floored house, its rooms smelling of food, of herself washing dishes in a big yellow plastic tub, of someone laughing in another room, and then the memory shrinks to nothing and fades like the black ghost of a camera flash, and she's looking at the bartender again.

There's only one other person in the room. She saw him here earlier today, when the man she wanted was in there, too, before the cop attacked her: a lanky, too-thin old man with a beaky nose and long, straight, gray-streaked hair parted just above the ear on one side and then pasted across his skull with some kind of grease, right to left, as though he hopes people will think it grew that way.

His mouth pulls down on both sides, so sharply it looks like the corners are weighted somehow. A bottle of beer, obviously cold from the way it sweats, stands on the bar in front of him. But he's not drinking, not talking, not even holding the bottle, just sitting there with his elbows on the bar and his fingertips at his temples, leaning forward and studying the bar's wooden surface; it almost looks like he's staring down into water or something transparent, reading a message that's been written there. The woman moves repetitively—pull a glass from the water, shake it, wipe it dry, turn it upside down, line it up on the shelf, turn back to the sink, pull another glass from the water. She doesn't seem to be thinking about what she's doing, and she never glances at the man. The two of them could be on opposite sides of Bangkok, she thinks, for all the attention they pay to each other. Either they're strangers or they know each other so well that everything has been said too many times; they've used each other up. The lights set high on the walls are off; there's just the glow from a couple of the milky tubes on the ceiling above the bar, making them both look as pale and shadowless as ghosts.

Hom gets a little sprinkling of fear-bumps on her arms, a prickle at the back of her neck. They both, especially the thin old man, really *do* look like—

Breaking the rhythm of her routine, the woman places one more glass on the shelf and then stretches her arms wide, fists closed like someone who's just waking up. She reaches deep into the sink and comes up with her hand empty, her arm glistening wet. She's obviously pulled the plug. She wipes her arms briskly with the other end of the towel and drops it into something behind the bar, and then she leans over and raps her knuckles several times on the bar, just inches from the thin man's beer. The man sits up, blinking like someone who's received an unexpected slap. Then he blows out a lot of air, his cheeks belled out, and takes a survey of the room as though he's surprised to find it empty. Hom ducks aside as his eyes near the window, and when she dares to look in again he's up off his stool, the beer bottle upended in his mouth. The gray-haired woman watches without any apparent interest, just following his movements. When he puts the bottle on the bar, sharply enough that Hom can hear it through the glass, the gray-haired woman turns around, bends down, and comes up with another bottle, which she pops open beneath the edge of the bar. She hands it to him, grabs his empty bottle, and drops it into something that's out of sight. Then she reaches under the bar again, and the overhead lights go off.

And Hom is backing up as fast as she can, turning and stepping down from the curb and scurrying across the street, not so full of people now, until she's once again in front of the bar that plays the loud music. She sits, huddled tightly, arms wrapped around her knees to make herself smaller, and finds that the men who are taking down the night market have removed a section that would have blocked her view of the door to the bar. In a moment, the door across the way opens and the woman sticks her head out, looking up and down the street as though she expects someone to run up with a gun to rob the place. When she finally comes through the doorway she's followed by the old man, who still has the bottle in his hand, hanging loosely, as though forgotten. The woman uses three keys to secure the door as the old man stands there, looking at something invisible hanging in the air at chest-level, and then the woman turns to him and pats his cheek, as though to get his attention. He starts, obviously surprised, and his eyes come up to her. She says something, eyebrows raised in a question, and he nods a yes. She returns his nod briskly, like someone who has settled something, and they separate, the bartender going to Hom's left, toward Silom, and the thin old man trudging slowly, even aimlessly, in the other direction. In a moment or two, though, he turns around to see the bartender go right, up Silom and out of sight, and then he comes back, walking carefully with his eyes on the sidewalk as though he's making sure there's nothing that might trip him, until he's in front of the bar again. He leans back against the window and slowly slides down into a sitting position, bottle in hand and knees upraised and folded, as angular as a grasshopper's. He passes his hand over his hair, smoothing it right to left, lowers his head so he's looking down at himself, and leaves it there. His eyes could be closed, or he could be studying something on the pavement.

Not wanting him to see her watching him, she puts the bag over her shoulder and begins to rise as he sits, but he's obviously lost in his thoughts or stranded in an empty moment, so she stays where she is and studies him. His head is tilted downward at such a steep angle that she can see a patch of bare scalp at the crown of his head, behind the long plastered strands of hair. *He probably doesn't know he has it*, she thinks, and without being conscious of it she reaches up and runs exploring fingers over her own head, still reassuringly covered in stiff, graying hair. For a moment, it seems that there's a kind of thread running from him to her, but then a man and a young woman walk between them and the thread is broken. The notion vanishes. There they are, just the two of them, each of them old and alone, sitting on opposite sides of a road that could be a million miles wide. Nothing connects them. He doesn't know she exists.

Still, she stays put. He seems as abandoned as a collapsing house. She knows what it is to lose everyone she ever loved. He should be a grandfather or even a great-grandfather with his children's children around him, giving him a sort of immortality, a resemblance or a tone of voice passed from one person to another, the way, back in the village, she had seen fathers' eyes in their sons'. A footprint in time that would last longer than the old man would. Instead, here they are, the two of them: dead ends.

For a moment, that warm house with the dirt floor surrounds her again, but a blink chases it away. So she rises with a grunt and a wince against the pain in her leg and the stiffness that's patiently accumulated in her knees, and she heads up Patpong One, away from Silom, toward the cross street that leads to Patpong Two, heading for Surawong and then the Rama IV Road to the park. Turning toward Patpong Two will take her in the wrong direction—to her right, although the park is to her left—but she does it anyway: it's become a habit now, whenever she feels someone might be watching her. Try not to leave a trail. Take routes that allow you to double back without seeming to look behind you. At this point in her life she has no walls, no door she can lock behind her.

When she reaches the corner she glances back. The thin old man is still sitting, his knees jackknifed up and his arms crossed over them. He looks like he might sit there until the bar opens in the morning. The bottle dangles from one finger jammed into its neck. His eyes seem to be closed, but then he leans his head back and brings the empty hand up to scour his face, and she sees that he's wide-eyed and looking at nothing. It's the attitude of someone who is very, very tired, someone who is no longer waiting for anything, someone who probably feels—as she does—surrounded by nothing. For an instant she has an impulse to go back and talk to him, ask how he is, but then she remembers what she looks like now, who she is now, and without thinking about it she reaches inside the big dress to pat the paper-wrapped tablets in her pocket.

One. Two. Three. Smoke or swallow? One or two? She can almost feel it already. Her joy at the sheer fact of possessing them drives the old man from her mind and she lumbers off down the

street to make her dogleg toward the park, her heart pounding in
anticipation of the moment, not too long after she's taken the first
one, when the terrifying whisperers, the demons who always visit
her first, give way at last to the street music.

Interlude
NOCTURNES

8

Green Screen

LATER IN HIS life, whenever Rafferty looks back on the events that followed his fight with Campeau, they seem like part of a long, dim night sequence filmed in "green screen," the magical technique that allows actors to put down their donuts or their crossword puzzles or their organic kale smoothies, walk eight or ten steps, and dodge nonexistent meteorites or fight invisible dinosaurs without messing up their hair. In his memory, all the things he saw too late or failed to anticipate had been looming right behind him on that screen—not *always* something terrifying, but something important that he'd missed, something invisible to him, something that might have changed the course of events, and he could see it only in hindsight, when the special effects were all in place.

And, in fact, when he forces himself to think about that time, he realizes that much of what happened then—both to him and to others—had happened at night.

ROSE WAKES UP in almost total darkness. Automatically, in a new habit that already seems lifelong, she holds her breath until she hears the baby exhale, and then she slowly extends her arm to let her fingers brush the little fence of couch cushions that Fon built to surround him so Rose can't accidentally roll over on him and because he seems happier when he's enclosed by softness. He's

content to be in the crib when he's awake and has some attention, but he won't sleep there. She curls her fingers into a soft
fist to get her nails, clipped shorter than they've ever been, out
of the way, and moves her hand, a fraction of an inch at a time,
until she touches the warm, soft skin of his cheek and the fine-
spun flaxen hair he was born with, absolutely straight, standing
at vertical attention atop his head as though his toe were in a
socket. Poke had laughed the first time he saw the baby and then
stopped abruptly, afraid he'd committed some un-fatherlike sin
until she started to laugh, too. She feels, a little sadly, that it was
one of the closest moments they'd shared since she and the baby
came home.

The moment the palm of her hand senses the child's warmth,
even before her fingers find the skin and the erect, startlingly soft
bristle of hair, she has an overwhelming sense of *reconnection*, as
though she's found a bit of herself. But then she's all business
again, verifying that her child is sleeping on his back, as all the
women say he should.

No, not a bit of herself, not anymore, but someone new, complicated, and demanding, right there beside her as though she had
dreamed him into being. And now it—*he*—is actually present,
warm and solid and within reach, breathing into the darkness and
seeing—what? The faces of the women who have surrounded him
almost since he was born? The bright pool of daylight that edges
its way through the room's sole window, partly blocked by the air
conditioner Rafferty put there? Or the warm darkness from the
time *before* all that, time marked and divided by her breathing and
the beating of her heart, the darkness in which the child had
floated until he emerged, squalling angrily at the interruption of
his long meditation, into this noisy, stop-and-start world?

Maybe, she thinks, maybe at this age, when he's still so *new*, he
dreams about some past life. There must be a week or two before

past lives disappear completely, shouldered aside by the details of the new world into which he's been born.

It would have been a blameless life, she hopes, a life that sent him into this one with a comfortable stockpile of good karma. Although, to be candid with herself, she's never been able to visualize a truly blameless life except, perhaps, for the Buddha, a very few priests, and children who died in infancy. She energetically leaps past *that* thought and settles for a life that was good *on balance*, a life in which others, at least at times, had meant more than oneself, hard as that is to imagine. *She* certainly hasn't lived that way.

Running through the list of people she knows, she can only think of one who fits the description, and that's Fon. And even for Fon, this is a new phase; back in the old days in the bars she'd been nicknamed *thǐ peid khwad*, "the bottle opener," because of her skill at prying customers away from their regular girls, most frequently during the regular's turn on the stage. Late one night, not long before Rose met Rafferty, a woman had looked across the room from the stage to see Fon waltzing toward the exit with her arm around one of the dancer's repeat customers. In the time it took to blink, the dancer had taken a flying leap into the middle of the customers, zigzagged to the bar, and gone after Fon with the first thing she could grab—a cocktail fork—which she sank into Fon's shoulder before the larger brawl broke out between the cliques of women who coexisted so uneasily in the bar. When it was over, the wayward man was clucking maternally and using a wad of paper napkins to apply pressure to Fon's shoulder as they left together, and the woman who'd stabbed her was in the dark, malodorous bathroom holding an ice cube to a split lower lip.

I lived that way, she thinks, feeling the warmth of her child's breath on her hand. *I stole customers from girls I didn't like. I lied to the men. What karma have I accumulated?*

She adjusts the little valley of cushions, just to be doing some-thing, and suddenly remembers where the cushions came from.

Poor Poke. The couch was lumpy even *with* cushions.

It must be late. No women are chatting in the other room, keeping Poke awake. (*Poor Poke.*) No muted back-and-forth in strange accents seeps in from Miaow's room. She's never seen Miaow work this hard. The girl had been almost obsessed when she played Ariel in *The Tempest*, fixated on understanding every word the character said and every thought behind it so that she could speak the lines as though she'd thought of them at just that moment, while all the other actors seemed to be reciting some-thing that had been chiseled into an ancient tablet half a mile away. Julie, the girl she'd played in *Small Town*, had been easier: Julie hadn't seen one-fiftieth as much of life as Miaow had, but she'd only been a little older and she had a soft heart, like the one Miaow tries so hard to hide. Also, the English that Julie spoke was a lot like the English Miaow had learned from Poke.

And, of course, Julie fell in love during the play, which was something that had been happening to Miaow at the time. With, naturally, Edward, who played Julie's naive and somewhat dull boyfriend, Ned. Poke is worried that Edward might turn out to be like his awful, womanizing father, but Rose, who learned the hard way how to judge males, knows better: Edward is like Ned, sweet all the way through and a little bit dull, and she's pretty sure he's falling, or has fallen, in love with Miaow.

The baby makes a whispering sound like wet paper tearing, which she knows is his way of snoring. *If he's snoring*, she thinks, *he's probably out for at least a few minutes*. Moving in slow motion, she slides to the edge of the bed and brings herself to a sitting position with her feet on the floor. Then she holds herself very still and listens for a count of ten. Nothing, and she thinks the baby might have floated up toward consciousness, but then she hears it again, that tearing of soft paper. Feeling like she's moving underwater, she gets to her feet.

The apartment is so quiet she can hear her heartbeat, but there's a faint ribbon of light beneath the door. Not from the living room; that would be much brighter. It must be from the lights over the kitchen counter, at the room's far end. After one more glance at the bed—dark as the room is, she can see the baby's shape as though it emits its own pale light—she goes to the door and quietly, just in case Rafferty is actually asleep, she turns the knob.

THE WORLD: BLINDINGLY bright and so hot she can feel the air hum. The sky is an unmarked, clean-swept blue, but there are no shadows. It's as though the sun has dissolved into the sky and turned the whole blue ceiling into a burning source of light. Light from all sides, heat from above and below, radiating from the city's walls and the paving on the sidewalk.

And yes, there's a sidewalk. There is *always* a sidewalk. And this one is just another sidewalk that might be passing through the center of a nothing, a nothing that's hot and bright, and she's sweating, she's dirty, she's itchy with fleas and bedbugs, and there's a hole in her shoe. She can smell herself. She *reeks*, and she's out of breath. The world is the sidewalk, and the sidewalk is still and empty except for the girl far, far in front of her, the girl she's trying to catch up with. Miaow is running, and the other girl is walking as though she has all the time in the world. Wherever she's going, it will wait for her, and no matter how fast Miaow runs she'll never catch up.

The girl wears white clothes: a brilliantly white long-sleeve shirt, untucked above loose-fitting, beautifully creased white trousers and spotless white shoes, clothes that have never been soaked with perspiration, that have never brushed up against dirt, clothes that make Miaow think about boats, although she's never been on a boat. Her clothes are so white Miaow has to squint when she looks at them. So white they hurt her eyes.

Miaow is already running, hard enough to be short of breath, but she's not catching up. The girl in white doesn't seem to be hurrying; she walks at a pace idle enough, casual enough, to suggest that she owns the world she's passing through.

The sole of Miaow's right shoe, the one with the hole in it, detaches itself where it supports her toes and begins to flap. It makes a sound like someone clapping, one, two, three, a kind of sarcastic applause. The heat that's been baked into the pavement burns her bare toes, and she has to suppress the desire to hop on the other foot. If she doesn't run, she'll *never* catch the . . .

Far ahead, the girl slows and turns her head. Looking for something.

Miaow grabs a breath that feels like the air is on fire, forces it down, and shouts something that's supposed to be *wait,* but the only sound she can produce is a kind of strangled gargle. When she inhales to call out again, she sees the other girl, whose profile Miaow has glimpsed for only a second, turn away and begin to move again. Miaow tries once more to run, but now she seems to be in waist-deep water, churning heavily and slowly through nothing that she can see, but every step forward is more difficult than the last. Still, she has *begun to close the gap*—she's close enough now to see the sheen of the other girl's immaculate, blunt-cut black hair, the hair Miaow has always wanted, swaying with every step the girl takes, brushing the white cloth of her shirt at precisely the right length—and then the girl turns a corner Miaow hadn't seen, one that seems to have opened up out of nothing. Somehow the corner is farther away than the girl had been when she disappeared into it, and even though Miaow pushes herself to the limit, by the time she rounds it, the girl is gone. When she *does* round it, she sees it's not really a corner at all, it's a blind alley, a setback of three or four meters that ends abruptly in a high, gray building, the first thing she's seen that doesn't seem too bright. It's the restful hue of pigeon feathers, smooth as polished stone and windowless, and there are columns on either side of the huge, triple-wide door, which is slowly swinging closed. Through the narrowing gap she sees a drift of color, a pink as pale as a blush, the swish of soft fabric, and then the door is closed. She hears laughter.

And *that's it*, that's the tip that she's dreaming. She's heard that laugh dozens of times, always on the other side of a closing door, and she knows that the dream is about to turn too sad to bear and that there's only one way to end it. So she does it: she runs at full strength toward the hard, smooth gray wall, leaning toward it, leaping at it head-first so that her face, with all its nerve endings and delicacy, will take the full, shattering force of the collision, and she flies through the air toward it, anticipating the shock and the pain, and then she hits the wall; and when the pain doesn't come, the surprise wakes her up.

. . . COMPLICATED, H E writes, and then he leans forward, his elbows on the counter, and rubs his eyes with his free hand. He lets the pencil drop: at this point, he needs a two-handed rub.

Complicated? And he's supposed to be a writer? Using a word like that to describe *this* state of mind is like performing heart surgery with a can opener: it's just not up to the job. He leans back and makes the yoga lion face, eyes wide, tongue out, mouth so far open he could bob for apples. Then he relaxes, blinks away the tears from the yawn that had seized him by surprise, and looks down at the page again.

Words. He might as well have picked them at random. They could have escaped from a thesaurus in a poorly coordinated jailbreak, emerging into the light as absolute strangers, blinking at each other in total incomprehension.

This is his *life* he's trying to write about. And perhaps the word he's searching for is *schizophrenic*.

On the one hand, there's the baby as an abstract, as a new life, a blessing, the creation of the love between him and Rose: in short, the way he feels when he's wandering around Bangkok, looking for someone he hasn't yet told about it. It's an *event*, the kind of event that he recognizes as absolutely architectural; he feels like most of his life he's been slippery as an eel, slithering through the world without changing anything, not even himself. Here and there, getting snagged on something of consequence: writing his first book, moving to Thailand, meeting Rose and Miaow, the kinds of things that, if he were to look at his life as a house he's creating, might be painting the walls or washing the windows. But this, the arrival of—oh, just say it, of *Frank*—this is a whole new wing, a major change to the floor plan, the addition of new rooms as yet unexplored, uncounted, and even unmapped. On the theoretical plane he can accept it in its full magnitude, with the uneasy and unfamiliar sensation of having been present at the miracle. A miracle he prattles to strangers about.

But. The thing was . . .

. . . the thing was the other level, the day-to-day *living* level, that he'd had *all this time* to prepare himself for, during the past eight and a half months, the months they were all trapped in the seemingly endless white-knuckle thrill ride of Rose's pregnancy, with its tight curves and sudden drops, the endless terror of miscarriage, that yet another child would be turned away, just inches from the door to the world. And then, a week and a half early, the terrified cab ride to the hospital to find Fon waiting for them, the coolly amused nurses guiding him to a chair as impersonally as someone moving furniture, the squeaking wheel of the gurney carrying his wife and—still unseen—their child into the room Rose refused to let him enter.

He'd protested, but not very energetically. He'd been fairly certain he would pass out when the big moment came. His own parents had treated biology as a kind of unseen force, something like cosmic radiation; it might be important, but it was better to not look at it too closely. His mother, when he had pressed her for details at the age of eleven or twelve, had described it as *undignified*.

But all that was over now. Undignified or not, it had played itself out, with a positive—he mentally erases the word and replaces it with *happy*—outcome. He is a father, a *biological* father. He has a son to complement his adopted daughter. Of course, part of the problem is that his only experience as a father had been with a child who could already communicate when she joined them, who could make her wants known and wasn't shy about doing it, who could take better care of herself than he could. She'd been dirty, unhappy, self-loathing, and morbidly sensitive, but she'd been a *person*.

Unbidden, the words of a British king come to mind: presented with his swaddled, screaming heir, the king had nodded approval at the number of fingers and toes and said, "Bring him back when he can talk."

He could *relate* to a person.

But living with this tiny-fisted, squalling, diaper-filling, bristle-haired whirlpool of need—this is something completely new to him. This is miles off his map. Looking at the baby, he supposes he is in there *somewhere*, represented obliquely, like one of the smaller states on an election-night tally, but he hasn't spotted himself yet. He is feeling unnatural, he is feeling superfluous, he is feeling *left out*.

And she'd called it—oh, shit, *him*—Frank. Honoring his own

wretched father. To go back to politics for a moment, doesn't he get a *vote?*

He lets out a sigh that ruffles the pages, picks up the pencil, and writes, *I feel like I've bought something with no guarantee and no return policy. I feel like the three bears must have felt when they found that someone had been eating their porridge and sleeping in their beds, and it turned out to be someone they'd never heard of. What I feel like is an absolute shit.*

And he remembers that two nights ago he had turned off the living room lights and then cracked open the bedroom door, as he had every night since the baby came home. As he was trying to negotiate with the lumps in the sofa, he'd heard Rose laugh. He'd gotten up and tiptoed into the bedroom, and she was on her back, eyes closed, sound asleep, and then she did it again: she laughed in her sleep.

He leans forward and underlines the words *absolute shit.*

HOLDING HER BREATH without being aware of it, Rose slowly pulls the door open.

And there he is, all the way across the room, hunched over at the kitchen counter, writing something with a yellow pencil in a hardcover notebook. She can hear the skritch of the lead on the paper. He's resting his forehead on the fingers of his left hand as the right hand loops its way across the page. Even at this distance, he looks tired, and she knows he'll wipe all that away, replace it with some semblance of energy, some slightly forced sunburst of pleasure, the moment he knows she's there.

So for a long, secret moment she just luxuriates in the feeling of being invisible, and she drinks it all in while it lasts: in the bedroom to her left, her new son, breathing almost inaudibly; to her right and down the hall, behind the door she closes each night, her adopted daughter, probably fighting her way through some uncertain dream of the street. And there—across the long room in front of her, silhouetted against the rain-jeweled glass of the balcony door—hunched over and looking weary, the one for whom she had risked everything, the odd foreigner who'd persuaded her to quit the job she loathed but which supported her family up north, who'd assured her over and over, in the wake of all the men to whom she had lied and who had lied to her, that his love wasn't *bar love* but something real that would endure and even deepen and grow, and that her mother, father, and sisters would be cared for. *And he's done it*, she thinks, on the strength of a trickle of book royalties, some magazine and newspaper articles, and even—in several tight pinches—a surprising amount of money earned writing catalog copy for some company that sold, he told her, "adventure clothes for people who avoid adventures."

She steps all the way into the living room and glances at the couch, minus its cushions, beneath the thin, wadded-up blanket he'd obviously thrown off. It looks seriously uncomfortable. She tries to fight the smile, but she can't deny that it amuses her. *Poor Poke.*

His head snaps around, eyes wide and startled, and she realizes she's said it out loud.

"On the contrary," he says, closing the notebook and resting his arm on it, "I feel pretty rich."

"This bed is *awful*," she says, indicating the couch.

"There are *so many* things you're going to have to make up for later. Once that kid can walk and sing bass, I'll be in paradise."

"You make a list?" she says in English, tilting her chin toward the notebook as she crosses the room. "Do I get to see?"

"You do not." He pushes the book away as though that will lessen her interest. "I'm making notes for my autobiography. I need to remember *all* of this, every grim, lumpy detail. In the part I've written so far, I have to confess that I come off a lot better than you do." She comes up behind him and puts her arms around him, bending down so she can rest her chin on top of his head, and he luxuriates in the warm, soft fall of hair over his neck and shoulders.

"You have . . . surprise me so many time," she says. Thai lacks a past tense and doesn't pluralize the way English does, and she's never felt a need for either when talking to him.

"All I've ever asked for," he says, "was a chance to have to put up with something really *unreasonable* so that you'd owe me. Not necessarily something as big as sleeping on that couch, but, you know, something I can take advantage of later on. Emotional money in the bank. Maybe buy a pardon if I lose the remote again."

She blows into his hair and says, "You not lose, you hide. I like the room better with teewee over there."

"I'd like it better out on the balcony." The stool squeals as he swivels to face her.

She warns him: "I haven't brush my teeth."

"One *more* gold star on my report card. You'll pay for it later." He wraps his arms around her waist, and she bends to kiss him. It lasts a little longer than he'd thought it would, but he still feels cheated when she pulls back. He says, "I think Miaow and Edward are finally noodling around a little. When I came in this evening, they were sitting as far apart as the couch allows, laughing like lunatics."

"Noodling?"

"Ummm. Messing around. Romantically. What my mother said *her* mother called *canoodling*. Moofky foofky." He laughs at the expression on her face. "*You* know what I mean. I'm certain I interrupted something. Edward was as red as Rudolph's nose."

"Rudolph—oh, Rudolph. He give the light to Santa Claus." She runs her index finger down what she calls his *big foreigner nose*. "Moofky *what?*"

"Foofky. Never mind, very obscure."

She says, "Is time, I think."

"*Time?*" He looks startled.

"She not a baby, Poke. Big girl now."

"Like *hell*," he says. "A little canoodling, no problem. But within limits."

"You have limit? When you are her age?"

"At her age, I was terrible."

She leans up against him. "*Ooohhh*. Tell me."

"Yes," Miaow says from the hallway, "*tell* us."

"Wow," Rafferty says, stretching like someone who's wanted for hours to go to sleep. "*Look* at the time."

"You don't have a watch," Miaow says.

"It's two-twenty," he says. "Give or take. I always know. And you should be asleep."

"Two-twenty-four," Rose says, flipping her wrist over. She's worn her watch with the face on the inside of her wrist for as long as Poke has known her.

Miaow comes the rest of the way into the room and stakes a claim to her end of it by sitting on the white leather hassock. She's wearing a faded T-shirt that's got a sprinkling of pale little abstract ghosts ornamenting its front, courtesy of some over-enthusiasm with a bottle of bleach, and a pair of athletic shorts with Chuck Jones's Road Runner on the leg. It's her third pair. She once told Poke she wore them so she could outrun her nightmares. Her hair is standing straight up on one side, looking like it's been crocheted. "So," she says, settling in. "When you were my age, what?"

"When I was your age," Rafferty says, "I was a boy."

"Wow," Miaow says, "that's *so* grandpa. So you were a boy, what does that mean?"

"When I was your age," he says, "I knew it was impolite to ask adults questions they didn't know how to answer. Why are you up at this hour?"

"The baby wasn't crying. Woke me up."

"*Miaow*," Rose says, and Miaow sits back as though someone had swung at her. Rose's tone has real disappointment in it.

"Umm," she says. "I'm sorry?"

"You have barely come to see him," Rose says in Thai.

Miaow says, "I don't think he misses me."

"He can hardly see you at all. He's still nearsighted. Anyway, you're practically a stranger to him."

"Well, then, he doesn't miss me."

Rose says, "I love *both* of you, Miaow. It would *make me happy* if you came in sometimes."

Miaow pulls the neck of her T-shirt up over her nose, like an outlaw in a western. Through it, she says, "I will." Rafferty can barely hear her.

"Why are you awake?" he says.

"The play." She grabs some of the little volcano of hair and tugs at it. "I don't know if I can do it."

"It keeps you awake at night?"

"No." She scrubs at her eyes with the heels of her hands. "I go to sleep okay, and then I wake up after some stupid dream, and I feel like something's wrong. Like something horrible followed me out of the dream and it's in the room with me. Sitting on my chest. And then I realize what it is. It's me."

"The middle of the night," Rafferty says. "It's the most defenseless time."

"When I first came to Bangkok," Rose says in Thai, twirling Rafferty's stool so she can sit in his lap, "I could get through the day and the nights in the bar, and even the time I spent with customers. But when I woke up in the dark, I was at the bottom of a deep, deep hole. I didn't want to live."

Miaow has pulled the neck of her shirt down to reveal that her lower lip is caught between her teeth. Lately, Rose almost never talks about that time in her life. Miaow says, "What did you do?"

"I lived," she says. She grasps the counter's edge in one hand and swivels the stool back and forth by a few inches. It squeaks. "What was the other choice? It would have been selfish to die. My family needed me." She ruffles Poke's hair, something she knows reduces him to putty.

Clearing his throat, Rafferty says, "You're *nothing* when you wake up in the middle of the night." He pats Rose's hips a couple of times to get her attention, says, "*Up* we go," and crosses the room to the bookshelves he put up in the corner where his desk stands. "All your defenses are gone. You're a naked, helpless glob of protein without anywhere to hide."

"What did you just say?" Rose asks, reclaiming the stool.

"You tell her," Rafferty says to Miaow, pulling out a big book and thumbing through it.

Miaow does the best she can to translate, and Rose starts to laugh.

"Here," Rafferty says, "just to let you know that everyone goes through this."

He crosses the room and gives her the book, and she looks at it and breaks into laughter. "It's not *this* bad." She holds it up for Rose to see: a woman on her back in bed, one hand thrown up helplessly, with a demon squatting on her chest and a bone-white, ghostlike horse, its nostrils flaring, staring through a gap in the heavy curtains beside the bed.

"Almost two hundred and fifty years ago," Rafferty says, "a guy named Fuseli painted it. And he made a lot of them. This thing has been duplicated a million times because everybody instinctively recognizes it. It's a nightmare, but it shows you why you're so helpless when fear gets hold of you in the middle of the night.

Who's there to defend you? How sure are you, really, whether you're awake or asleep? And you, in that room, you don't even have a window. You're in the darkest room in the house." His face lights up. "I know—you can sleep *here*, on the couch, and I'll go into—"

"You *would*, too," Miaow says. "You'd put me on this collection of lumps and grab my bed—"

"It's not much of a bed," he says.

"*Now* you admit it. I've been saying it for—"

She breaks off because Rose has risen quickly, and then they all hear the baby crying.

"I'll be right back," she says, hurrying to the door. "Maybe." She stops next to Miaow and puts a hand on her shoulder. In Thai, she says, "You can play that part, you silly girl," and she hurries into the bedroom.

"You can, you know," Rafferty says, drifting toward the fatal couch. "You've already played it, haven't you? It's your story."

Miaow ignores the comment and smooths her hand over the open book. "Do *you* get like this at night?"

"How do you think I found the picture so fast?" The bedroom door closes behind Rose, and he sits on the couch and sees that Miaow is still waiting for an answer. "Not as much as I used to, but yeah, sometimes."

"When it happens to you, what are you afraid of?"

"Losing what I love. You, your mom, the baby. Our lives, just the way they are. I used to believe in evil spirits that would sense when you were too happy, same way a moth finds a light, and swoop down and eat the happiness, leave an empty hole."

"Not very cheerful."

"I'm Irish," he says. "We're always mentally running out of potatoes. And since most Irish are also Catholic, there's always a new baby to feed."

As if it had heard its cue, the baby stops crying. "She must be breast-feeding him," he says. "She couldn't have gotten the bottle ready that fast."

Miaow says, "You always call the baby *him* or *it* or *the baby*, never his name."

"Well, don't tell your mother, but I'm not crazy about the name. I think I'm going to call him Buster."

"I'd like to be called Buster."

"Too late. Why don't you leave your door open when you go to sleep? That way, we'd be, I don't know, closer. Sort of."

"I never had a door before I came here." She closes the book and puts it on the table, beside her paperback of *Pygmalion*, which is still open and facedown. "Well, I had *doors*, but there were a lot of people behind them with me. I didn't get to decide whether they'd be open or shut. This is my first very own door." She reaches out and uses her index finger to push the paperback a few inches farther away. "So I close it. I suppose I do it because I can."

"Well," he says, "I'll be right out here all night for the next eight or ten years, and you can always wander on out and talk to me. I won't be asleep."

She grins at him, and the sudden smile almost breaks his heart. "You *won't be asleep*. You're as much of a phony as I am. I get up to go to the bathroom every single night, and you're snoring in here like the buzzer on my alarm clock."

"I do that on purpose, just for you," he says. "Just letting you know that it's safe to sleep. And that the couch is actually really—"

"It's *not* always safe," she says, and she gets up and goes around the table, where she flabbergasts him by kissing, very quickly, the top of his head. "You're right, Edward and I were—what did you call it?"

"Well, my mother called it canoodling."

"And we *were*," she says, heading for the hallway. "So you know my secret. I'm a canoodler. Thanks for the talk."

"Any time," he says as she disappears into the hall, but a moment later she peers around the corner at him, just half of her face in sight.

"I know you mean that," she says. "When you say *any time?* I know you mean it. And I know why you mean it, too." And then she's gone again, and he sits there feeling a warmth so definite, so unmistakable, that he thinks it might be what he'd feel in the first few moments of getting microwaved.

9

The Face Trees

A TOE-POPPER EXPLODES beneath his boot.

It was the thing he'd most dreaded, death from below—a cheap Russian land mine, a fucking snake, a punji pit, whatever: you can get smoked *and* catch it in the gonads, all at the same time. His eyes snap wide, wide open.

No jungle, no steaming air. A dark street, a hard sidewalk, the grainy smell of beer. A cop stands over him, thick-necked in his tight brown shirt, with a gelatinous-looking belly that spills over his pants. "Cannot," he says.

"Yeah, yeah, yeah. Cannot do fuck-all. Go away."

The cop raises his foot to kick the sole of Campeau's shoe again, and Campeau pulls his leg back, obviously surprising the cop, who takes a little stutter-step back to regain his balance, and Campeau thinks, *He's drunk.* Drunk cops are dangerous, and Campeau immediately parks the notion of getting up; he isn't very tall, but he's taller than the cop. He takes a more submissive tone. "Sorry," he says in Thai. "I was waiting for someone."

"*Waiting*," the cop says scornfully. "You *sleep*." He stretches his foot out again, and this time he tips over the bottle of Singha, which topples to the sidewalk with a musical sound, rolls at a dignified rate to the edge of the curb, and disappears. There's a sound of breaking glass and a little geyser of beer.

"See?" Campeau says, reverting to English "I didn't even drink it."

In English, the cop says, "What hotel, you? You stay where?"

"No hotel. I—"

"You sleep in street? You no money?" During the last decade, both here and in Cambodia, homeless Westerners have become a problem, men who came looking for their notion of paradise and couldn't handle it when they found it. Filthy, often toothless, and frequently scrambled by drugs, they're an international embarrassment, begging in the street and swiping leftovers off people's dishes in food courts. Some of them, like the man who walks an invisible tightrope between fast-moving vehicles on Sukhumvit and screams about Jesus to the startled drivers, are clearly psychotic.

"No, no," Campeau says. "I have an apartment. I just—I was just waiting for somebody. Look, I'll get up and—" He tries to get his feet under him, but the cop leans forward and puts a hand on top of Campeau's head, and Campeau sits back down.

The cop, his face only a few feet from Campeau's, exhales a cloud of fumes—the distinctive, oddly rumlike smell of Mekong whiskey—and demands, slowly and with quite a bit of emphasis, "You no *money?*"

"Ahhhh, right. *Sure. Money.* Given the cheap shit you've been drinking, it's a reasonable question. Hang on a minute." He slides his right hand into his pants pocket, difficult to do in his semi-collapsed seated position, and tries to work a single bill free; it's not good policy to show too much money to a cop, who is likely to regard it as being his by the simple, unarguable Code of the Uniform. Campeau keeps his money strictly organized, folded once into a single wad with bigger bills on the outside, a holdover from his first days in Thailand, when the money all looked the same to him and he occasionally overpaid substantially, mistaking the surprised smile for Thai good manners until he realized, usually quite a bit later, that he'd forked over something like ten times what had been required. It takes him a moment to slip aside the four bills on the outside of the wad, which, he's sure, are purplish five-hundred-baht notes, and then to tug out the one below them. It's not until he sees it between his fingers that he realizes it's an American twenty and remembers that he's still got a wad of American money on him.

"See?" Campeau says, internally kicking himself as the bill seems to launch itself out of his hand and into the cop's. The twenty is worth about five bucks more than the purple note he'd been trying to avoid. "Make friends with it," he says. "Say hi. Fold it, sniff it. Sing it a song. Practice your English on it. What the hell, take a bite out of it. Show it to your grandkids, if you live long enough to have any."

The cop says, "Quiet." He folds the bill and tucks it into his shirt pocket. "I come back, maybe twenty minute. You not here, okay?"

It's not actually a question, and Campeau lets it pass until the cop kicks his foot again. "Okay, *okay*," he says. "You meet crappy people on this street anyway."

"Twenty minute," the cop says. "You here, I look your pocket." He tugs his trousers up over the bottom of his belly-bulge, but they immediately roll back down. And then he's off, heading up toward Surawong.

"Land of Smiles," Campeau says in the W. C. Fields voice that always got laughs in Nam. Nobody even knows who W. C. Fields is, these days. No wonder the world is so fucked up. He waits until the cop has turned the corner, and then he scoots on his palms and his butt until he's at the edge of the curb, looking down. Sure enough, the bottle is broken. He sits there, just inhaling the beer, and suddenly he's thinking about Malee, about the sad brown eyes, the softness of her voice, and the sudden laugh that seemed to come out of nowhere as though a much happier person occasionally peeked out from behind the woman he thought he knew. About how often she literally laughed until there were tears in her eyes, and, for the ten thousandth time, about the night he'd been beaten up by a three-pack of Marines—he'd picked a lot of stupid fights in the bad old days, unable to let go of the war he'd lost—and how she'd furiously run a warm bath for him and washed the places where he'd been cut or scraped, swearing at him in Thai and English as she pressed a cold compress, with super-human delicacy, against his broken nose, and gradually turned the water colder to reduce his swelling. How she'd put lemongrass and spearmint leaves into the water, just for the fragrance. How he'd drifted in the tub, the pain waning, breathing in the fragrance, and watching the grace of her slender fingers as she ministered to him. How, when she was finished and she'd bandaged the open cuts and put salve on the scratches, she erupted in anger, berating him for being so stupid, for fighting like that and frightening her so badly. "You not young man," she had said. (He'd thought he was.) How, the next morning, she'd looked at his swollen face and broken into laughter that had her gasping and gripping her sides. How he'd made monster faces at her, feeling the pain as he con-torted his features, until she ran for the bathroom. When she laughed too hard, she sometimes needed to run for the bathroom.

How he'd known her so well that he knew even that.

How she'd swindled him on the house and emptied their bank account and fled Bangkok for almost a year. She never came back to Patpong; instead, she worked the other "entertainment areas."

Several people have told him recently that she's working in one of the outdoor bars at Nana Plaza, playing mother hen to the younger waitresses. She must be in her late sixties, maybe even her early seventies, by now. He's thought dozens of times of walking by, free as a bird in the open air, just to see if it's true. He's thought of confronting her and demanding his money, even though it's been long spent, dropped into the bottomless hole of *mama-papa*, and she's obviously been reduced to cadging a small percentage of the waitresses' tips. He's also thought about going in and telling her he loves her.

Fucking Patpong.

How many weeks, how many months, how many *years*, has he spent on this stubby little shithole of a street? He half-closes his eyes, trying to remember it as he'd first seen it on R&R from Nam. It had been cleaner, more respectable-looking, dotted with little businesses: airline offices, shops of various kinds, a few relatively decorous bars, Mizu's Kitchen at the far end, where it has been, probably, since Columbus bumped into America. On the same side of the street, Madrid, and the Expat Bar—now Leon and Toot's—the only original joints that are still here. A small number of bars with girls in them, farm girls just down from the country, and a barbershop with an infamous massage parlor on the second floor, where paradise came cheap. Then, after ten days in a dream, it was back to the meat grinder.

By the time he returned, a year later, there were more bars and fewer offices, and now the women in the bars were *dancing*, although they were all clothed, if somewhat scantily: the "upstairs" bars, ratholes that had nothing to recommend them but nudity, hadn't opened until later. One night, in one of the downstairs bars, he'd broken out of the Nam funk he was in and looked up to see a young woman who didn't seem to belong there. She had something reserved about her; she looked embarrassed about being on the stage and she gazed at the floor or at the air above the customers' heads while she danced. The other dancers gave her space; she got none of the joking, roughhousing camaraderie they shared with each other. When she wasn't dancing she sat at the bench closest to the stage, hands folded in her lap, as far from the customers as possible, making no effort to cadge the drinks that would earn her a small commission. While she was sitting there, she kept her eyes on the floor. She might as well have been alone in the room.

He'd called one of the other dancers over and told her he wanted to buy a drink for the girl by the stage, but he didn't want her to know who'd sent it. One wall of the bar was mirrored, and he'd sat with his back to the girl, watching her reflection as the cola was delivered, seeing the indifference of the woman who took it to her—no smile, no joking congratulations, she just put the glass down and retreated, offering a shrug when the girl asked who'd bought it. He'd focused on his glass of beer as the girl searched the room, trying to spot her benefactor, and out of those bits and pieces he'd constructed a small-scale tragedy: a young, inexperienced woman who didn't want to work there, who was ashamed of her new station in life as a prostitute, who was alone in Bangkok, dancing isolated on a stage with no friends on it, too shy to approach the men whose patronage she needed if she was going to send home the money she'd left her village to earn.

Looking back at it all later, when some of the pain had faded, he realized it had all been true, virtually every detail. He'd been right about all of it, and he'd seen it because he was so weary of war and loss and killing and the stink of blood that there was a part of him that simply demanded tenderness, and here was someone to whom he could offer it. And, even though it *was* true, even if he'd gotten her story largely right the first time he saw her, he'd simplified her, painted her in two dimensions. He'd taken a complicated, conflicted, unhappy, humiliated young woman and turned her into a doll like the ones his little sister loved, the ones whose clothes she could change, whose hair she could style, to whom she could give multiple names: Marilyn with her hair *this* way, Tammy with it *that* way, Anita when she was wearing the blue dress, but always the same doll underneath it all, the doll that had come out of the box. The changes were an illusion. With people, he learned, it didn't work that way. People were moving targets.

Eventually he sat beside her, chatted awkwardly with her, got her to smile, paid her bar fine, and took her to the little hotel on Patpong Two. After the second time he made her his only Bangkok girlfriend. Each time he came back to Bangkok over the next year and a half of the war, he went straight to her, arriving just a few minutes after the bar opened. And he continued to see her as the same person she'd been when he left her, although she'd obviously changed: she was less lost, more certain, more instinctive about what would please him. Her English improved in his absence, and that made him uneasy. She had, of course, learned it from customers. But to him, she was still the doll out of the box: the details—the externals—might be different, but she was still Malee, the girl who got so furious at him when he was hurt.

He'd seen other guys fall in love with bar workers, talk about them as they would about some presumably virginal "good girl," some pillar of virtue, some small-town banker's daughter back in Iowa, and he'd had those same bar workers hit on him when their boyfriends were back in the field. He'd felt sorry for those guys.

What a fucking idiot.

He gets up, surprised, as always lately, at the stiffness in his joints and the heaviness of his legs, and he looks up the street, seeing its cold, drab ugliness. For the thousandth time, he asks himself what he's doing here. It's not the women anymore; they've become more trouble than they're worth. And they've changed, as he's complained to Rafferty and anyone else who will listen: they've gotten harder and older and brassier and, well, more independent. Decades ago, he'd felt like a few of them were delighted when he walked into a bar he hadn't been in for a while. Whereas now, if he's honest, he has to admit that they don't remember his name. And if he's *really* honest, he has to admit that he's changed even more than they have. The handsome young kid they had smiled at, all that time ago, had been wrapped inside this aging, increasingly creaky husk for years.

Malee, he thinks.

He takes a couple of aimless steps and then turns so he's facing the right way. Go home. Take a sleeping pill.

Take two.

HOM SHOULDN'T HAVE smoked two. Big mistake.

The night had begun well, which should have warned her. Things stopped beginning well for her a long time ago. Good beginnings just raised her spirits so they'd have further to fall when the truth finally grinned at her to reveal the sharp, irregular gleam of its teeth.

But it *had* begun well. Halfway to the park, she'd stopped, shaken her head, and turned around to go back to Silom, steered helplessly by her stomach, which had turned into a fist-like knot to remind her that she hadn't eaten all day long. As late as it was she knew of only one place where she might find something. *If* he remembered her. *If* it hadn't all been taken already, as it so often had been.

When she had first come down to Bangkok, her husband—the man she had *thought* of as her husband—had taken her to a restaurant on a little *soi* just off Silom, not far from the park. The restaurant was called Isaan and was run by a man from an Isaan village not far from Hom's home, a man whose life was a success story, told over and over to young people who were brave enough, or foolish enough, to think about leaving the rice paddies behind and striking out toward a new life in the capital. The famous man's nickname was Jit. He had started, everyone said, with a small sidewalk food cart and in five years he owned a restaurant that served the food Hom had grown up with, the food her mother had made. Jit was talked about in the villages as a man who was willing to help those who followed him down to Bangkok or had been driven down by hunger and hopelessness. He was still Isaan in his heart, people said. The city was full of sharks, they said, but Jit would help you. She'd envisioned him as a beaming, benevolent man, fat on his own food, who would welcome them, comfort them, reassure them.

So she'd been unprepared for the dark, knife-thin man who had glared at them when she, her husband, and the baby had come through the door. Not happy to see them at all; in a hurry, in fact, to get rid of them. But he'd told them, his eyes going to the door every time the bell rang, of a place where they could probably stay, a rundown tumble of shanties where a few baht would buy them a night or two on someone's floor. Those people could teach them the tricks of life in the city. They could mention his name, he said. As he'd shooed them out, she'd been surprised for a second time when a woman bustled out of the kitchen with two small boxes of hot food. Hom's husband had grabbed the cartons and Hom had said *thank you*, the courtesy winning her a new glare from Jit, but she'd smiled at him, and his glare became a brief crinkling around his eyes, although the smile didn't quite reach his mouth.

She hadn't gone back until much later, years later, after all the losses, after the pills and the alcohol, after the lost jobs, after the last time she saw her husband, after Patpong—long after the bottom fell out of everything and her husband made the final demand, the ultimate sacrifice and even *that* went wrong, and she deserted him and learned for the first time in her life that she had no resources left, none whatsoever. Several weeks after she'd been forced to realize that *everything* was gone and that none of it would ever return, she'd gone back to Jit's restaurant, hungry this time.

Jit had recognized her at once, and had grabbed her arm and hurried her through the dining area into the kitchen, away from the big windows in front. Her husband, he said, had come in twice, and when they'd thrown him out he'd waited across the way, watching the restaurant. About an hour before she'd arrived, Jit had paid a cop five dollars US to chase him off. "But he'll be back," Jit said. "He's too stupid to stay away."

Then he showed her his secret.

He took her out through the back door of the kitchen and into a short alley that reeked of dog shit and the sharp-edged urine of rats. Screwed into the wall beside the door, just low enough for her to reach them on tiptoe, were five metal hooks, each sticking out two or three inches. Hanging from two of them were white plastic bags, weighed down by something inside, something with corners.

"This is food that was sent back to the kitchen," he said, "usually by some *farang* who wants to prove that he can eat food that's *phet maak maak*, as hot as the Thais order it. Usually it's a man who wants to show some bar girl how strong he is. We throw away the little bit he tasted before he began gulping all the water in sight, so what's in here is clean. You can take one of these, but *only one*. They won't always be here. It's best to get here late at night. One, but only one. Take the box out but leave the bag, or we'll run out of bags. Do you understand?"

"Yes. Can I take one now?"

"Of course. And you have to make me a promise. Don't talk about this. And don't come in through the front door unless you have a very big problem. It's not good for business."

She said, "Thank you," but he had already opened the door to the kitchen and was going inside. It was the last time they spoke.

AT THE ENTRANCE to the alley she looks left and right and then steps into the darkness, thinking about the sad, thin, drunk man she'd seen on Patpong. She should have said something. So what if he shooed her away? She's used to that. She's brought back to herself by the scratchy sound of a skittering rat somewhere in front of her, and she stops where she is until she can find her plastic cigarette lighter and flick it on. The rat has disappeared, but midway down the alley, on the right side, she sees the gleam of a white plastic bag, hanging almost out of reach. She thinks they must have put it out just before they closed, around midnight, or it would be gone by now. Not many people are supposed to know about this, but two times out of three the hooks are bare when she comes looking.

On tiptoe, she eases the bag off the hook and pulls out the little cardboard box, no longer warm but satisfyingly heavy, and rehangs the empty bag on its hook. Then she uses her free hand to rifle through the pockets of her dress and her blouse, and then the T-shirt and the man's running shorts beneath the dress until, in the shorts' hip pocket, her fingers slide over a folded plastic bag, about the size of the one she'd put back on the hook. The box slips easily into the bag and the loops at the top of the bag hook with no trouble over one of the buttons inside her dress. She adjusts the bag a little and buttons her outer dress to hide it. There. Out of sight. It bulges a bit but then, she thinks, so does she.

She had dropped the little lighter into a pocket so she could deal with the bag, and now she pulls it out again and flicks it open for a moment, just to orient herself, but she gets lost in the flame, lost in the way the pale blue at its base flowers into the hot yellow at the tip. She gazes at it until the lighter begins to heat up, and she takes her thumb off it and watches the flame's dark ghost, now imprinted deep in her eyes, dance across the alley as she looks around. *There*, go to the left, that's the street. The street will lead her to the park. Blinking around the flame's ghost, she fumbles her way out of the alley and makes the right that will take her to the park, to the bush she has been sleeping under. And, once there, she sees the evening's second good beginning: first the food, now the hole under the fence. She knows five ways, some more difficult than others, to get over or under the fence that surrounds the park and the gates they lock at ten each evening. This is her favorite, a simple hole, roughly dug beneath the chain link, and it seems to her that someone has deepened it a little since the last time she used it. She can shove her bag through it and then follow on her stomach and elbows.

A short time later, with the bag of food bumping reassuringly against her chest, she weaves her way into the park, which is thick with trees, crisscrossed here and there with concrete pedestrian paths, and slopes down to a small lake. The lake contains large monitor lizards, many of them as long as she is tall, fork-tongued beasts that lumber across the grass and terrified her until she'd been assured by the scattering of street people who also slept in the park that they'd never bitten a human. But a year or so ago, some city workers had come in and pulled many of them out, taking them wherever anyone could take a bunch of giant lizards, and she saw them less often now. Still, she walks with her head down, horrified of the prospect of stepping on one.

She pauses, takes a few deep breaths, and then begins, without thinking about it, the long series of loops and double-backs that will take her across the park in the general direction of the lake: the kind of route that might be taken by someone who either has no destination in mind or has forgotten her way. It allows her to make sure no one is following her. She'd been grabbed from behind twice by small groups of boys who had knocked her down and pinned her on her back, rifling her clothes and her bag and taking everything she had in her pockets. They'd also done things to her that she didn't want to think about now, although one time—the one she remembers most clearly—she'd grabbed the one who was standing over her, wrapped her fingers around his testicles, and yanked, pulling herself upward, her weight literally dangling from his scrotum, squeezing as he screamed. The other boys were already backing away from the noise, turning and taking flight as some of the park's other residents appeared beneath the trees, but she held on to the kid's balls as other park-dwellers kicked him and spat on him and hit him in the face. When she finally let go, the bleeding boy had whimpered all the way out of the park. Ever since then—when she remembers—she takes this random-seeming path that lets her verify that she has no followers, before she makes the turn that will take her to her bush.

Nobody. She stops and counts ten heartbeats, but she's alone. She can move on.

But the thought of boys reminds her of the new boy, the thin, furious-eyed fourteen- or fifteen-year-old who appeared in the park a few weeks ago, and whom she has caught looking at her several times. If she still has any soft spots, she reserves them for kids about the boy's age. Now, feeling the weight of the food carton pulling at the front of her dress as she walks, she finds herself looking for him, thinking that there's enough food in the box to share with him. She's never seen him eating, although, of course, he must eat sometimes, but he looks like someone who is burning himself away and not taking in anything to replace it.

His face; what was it about—his *face*, last time she saw it, had long scratches running down it, the wrong kind of red. Swollen, hot-looking, probably infected. She has cotton somewhere, she has a little bottle of alcohol somewhere. She can't afford to get infected.

So she's thinking about the boy as she hooks right, following the edge of the lake while staying several yards from the water, taking a detour to see whether one of the bathrooms has been left open, as they sometimes are. To her surprise, the first door she tries yields to her, and once it's closed behind her and she's relieving herself she sends up a prayer of thanks: she's been able to pee inside, she's got her blanket and her plastic sheet in the bag everyone tells her says *Louie* on it, and she's learned that Louie was a dead French man who made bags and clothes. And she knows where her bush is, and she's got her pills in her pocket and another one buried under the bush, and maybe she'll be able to give some of her food to the boy with the terrible eyes. Maybe she can make him smile. He doesn't look like he's ever smiled.

Her ear itches, and when she reaches up to scratch it, her fingers find stickiness and set off a little pinwheel of pain. The Sour Man. She hasn't thought about him since—when? Since just before she saw the old man sitting outside the bar, as slack and empty-looking as a paper bag waiting for the wind to take it somewhere.

I should have talked to him, she thinks, wetting a paper towel to scrub the dried blood off her ear and the side of her neck. *So what if he didn't want to talk to me? Maybe I could have cheered him up.*

When she's cleaned as much as she can without further damaging her ear, she packs everything up and goes back out into the night, heading for the bush beneath which she sleeps. The boy isn't where he usually is under the tree to her right, although it's hard to be certain because it's so dark. Maybe he'll come later and she'll still be able to offer him some of her food. She would like, she thinks, to do something for someone. She hadn't spoken to the empty man sitting outside the bar.

At the bush, she kneels unsteadily to check the spot where she buried the other pill, wrapped in a bit of tinfoil. It's undisturbed, so she buries it again and pats it flat. She opens the plastic sheet and spreads it over the damp ground before she sits all the way down. Then she folds the blanket over her crossed legs and undoes the buttons of her dress to get at the carton of food. Without being aware of it, she looks again at the tree, but the boy's still not there.

The moon hasn't showed up. It seems to her that she saw it the previous night.

With every bite she takes, she thinks about how skinny the boy is. As her physical hunger wanes, the tablets in her pocket seem to get warmer, bigger, and heavier. She closes the carton and puts it aside, carefully standing it upright so nothing will leak out and she can leave it beside his tree as soon as . . . well, as soon as she's finished the task at hand. She pulls a flat square of tinfoil from her Louie bag and begins to mold it into a pipe. She's not thinking about it, barely looking at her hands. Three minutes later, it's ready, with a bowl at one end and a mouthpiece at the other.

The pills are damp with her perspiration, making them easier to crush. She puts a piece of paper on the grass and uses two flat stones a little less than three centimeters in diameter that she keeps under the bush to grind them into a clotted powder. Then, very carefully, she folds the paper down the middle, and after one last look around, she tilts the creased page into the bowl of the pipe and taps it very lightly until the paper is clean and all the orange powder is at the bottom of the pipe.

The pipe suddenly feels charged with energy, warmer than the night, warmer than her hand. Turning to face the bush, she leans down, shields the lighter with her left hand, and hits the pipe. Waits. Exhales. Hits it again. The fingers holding the pipe feel like they're on fire but the pain doesn't matter because at the same time a phantom hand squeezes her heart, which is instantly beating triple-time, fast and hard enough to bring her to her feet. A hot wall of energy hits her like a wave, pushing at her and *through* her, turning her into a hot wire, *electrifying* her; and her heart, impossibly, speeds up. She needs to move, *has* to move: she has to distract herself by moving, looking at things outside herself;

she can't let it take her inside, not until she's used to being here, in the world of the pills.

And then she remembers her two good beginnings, the food and the enlarged hole under the fence, and knows this is how she's going to pay for it; she will skip the usual warm flood of well-being and instead will spend the rest of the night lost in the wreckage of her life, the life from which every single thing she ever loved has been weeded out, abandoned, destroyed. By *her*, she's the one who . . . *stop that, stop that right now*. Fat, useless, stinking old cow, not a mother, not a wife, not a friend, and she *needs to cut this off*. She's shifting from foot to foot: Where to go, what to do? She has to move, she has to keep busy, she has to focus outward, on the world, or she knows what will happen: she'll wash up on the cold, empty, stony, loveless island of her life.

And she can't handle that, not yet, so she's walking toward the water. Seen from a safe distance the water is dependable much of the time, there are the reflections of the city lights and the moon, except there isn't a moon, and she feels a surge of fury at the fact that there's no moon. She *needs* the moon. Looking at the moon would hold her in place until she's built her walls against the hot, scouring wind that's blowing through her, stripping her skin off to leave her, grotesque and red and seeping blood, for all to see.

How long has it been? She's been at this stage often enough to know that, even in a journey that begins this way, paradise will arrive eventually. She needs to wait it out, to crawl over the spikes. Ripples, color on the water, color that blows straight through her, a breeze off the lake that cools her, and she can feel the long plunge into the bad unknown slowing, like the elevators that so terrified her when she first arrived in Bangkok, when she still had . . .

Look at the color, colors that seem like they were just invented and no one but her will ever see them. Look how they waver and ripple at the edges, like smoke, and maybe she should go back and crush another tablet and go for three. She's never done three.

Or she could just cut her head off.

The boy, the food. She should take the rest of the food to the tree where the boy . . . maybe she could get him to clean up those scratches on his face . . .

The breeze off the lake smells like the city, but it's cool. Take the boy some food.

Sometime later, she's on the other side of the lake, looking back toward her bush and the boy's tree and feeling like she could walk straight across the surface of the lake to get to them, lizards or no lizards. This is it, this is where she wants to be. There are no problems she can't solve. She can organize her life, get back to who she was. She can clean out her bag, straighten things under her tree, wash her clothes in the lake, get a toothbrush. She can make everything *fine*.

The elation takes her all the way around the park several times—she has no idea how many, but at various times she paused to do chores: she detours to leave the food carton under the boy's tree and she refolds everything in her Louie bag three or four or five times, getting it perfect, and she decides to create a mental map of the park, speaking each turn aloud to herself and drawing it on the air. She's in charge. She's home.

But then the whisperers begin. One or two at first, and then too many to count, and from all sides. Two tablets had been a mistake. The whisperers descend on her like mosquitoes, and they know everything and everyone she ever lost or betrayed, bringing back the dead, terrifying her with the night's *new* horrors—transparent ghosts with enormous jaws and fingers longer than her legs; shadows that detach themselves from their trees and slide hissing across the grass behind her; a baby crying somewhere that gets farther away when she tries to follow the sound, and that she suddenly realizes is a demon that will sink its teeth into her breast and never let go; a gathering weight in the moonless sky that seems to get lower and lower, making her feel like she should lean down as she walks. By the time the whisperers are gone the final joke is revealed: the morning sky is actually going pale as the first light starts to rub away at the layers of darkness, and the day pushes its way in, staking its claim. So, no street music.

She only hears the music in the dark, when she can see the colors the melodies wrap themselves around. The music makes the colors seep through the darkness and dance across its hard black surface, and then, somehow, the colors make the music; and that is when it is best, when the colors pull the music out of the night. But with the weary, flat, everyday glow of dawn shouldering its way into the sky, dragging more light behind it, the colors don't stand a chance. Not even with her eyes closed.

By the time she gives up, she is at one of the park's borders, looking through the fence in despair at the same ugly city she left behind, it seems, only an hour or two ago, although it must be more like five or six. As she stands there, her heart hammering, eyes closed as she fights the beginning of a headache, she's startled to feel the ballpoint pen still clutched in her left hand, or there again. For a moment it absorbs all her attention, and she transfers it to her right and uses it to ink her name again and again on her palm, over the faded letters she had written there—when?— whenever she found the pen. When her name is thick and dark blue, she wraps her left hand around the pen again, and that brings back the stumble, the scraped knee, the pen rolling out from under the palm she'd put down to break her fall.

Yesterday, then. It had been yesterday. So today . . . *what* is it about today?

Right. Today is her last chance to find the man and follow him home. If she fails . . .

She stinks, she itches, she hurts, there's still a fringe of the night's terrors ruffling the frilly ends of her nerves. The guilt and the fear of angering the Sour Man wrap themselves around her and squeeze. Why does she stay alive?

Habit, she thinks.

WITH ALL THE bed's pillows jammed behind her back, Rose sits, looking through the part of the window that's not blocked by Rafferty's air conditioner and watching the dawn declare its intentions. The baby is in the crook of her left arm but no longer at her breast. He had fallen asleep while nursing, gradually letting go of the nipple, but not until he had been making his little wet-paper snore for a few moments; he had nursed his way into a dream. She can smell her milk on his lips, and she raises her right arm, slowly and carefully, just enough to blot her breast with the bedsheet. Fon will change the linens today, as she does every day, acting on one of her three commandments of motherhood: *keep the baby warm, keep the baby clean, give the baby love.*

She's gotten used to being awakened at this time, so easy to identify by the paling of the sky. And she begins, as she has for the past five or six nights, to start a mental countdown of the time stretching between now and 10 A.M.—the time Fon will come through the door, taking charge of the world and towing other women in her wake. Some of the visitors, like Fon, haven't danced in years but (unlike Fon) they preserve the bar worker's internal clock, plugged in until dawn and then rubbery with sleep until the rest of the world is finishing lunch. A few of them are still working nights, mostly in the relative respectability of the cocktail lounges where, as Fon says, "No one will fire you if you gain half a kilo." These women arrive late enough to be rested and leave just early enough to avoid being fined for not punching in on time.

By now Rose has internalized these rhythms, the tide that brings new women in each day and sweeps others away. She has learned the sequence and she clings to it more than she can admit to herself, because the presence of the changing cast of women, with their energy, their bawdy humor, their open-mouthed adoration of Frank, keeps her from focusing on the people who aren't in the room anywhere near as often as she'd thought they would be: her husband and her daughter. As full as the apartment is most of the day, it still feels empty to her much of the time.

She had never thought it would feel empty.

10

The Last Puritan

RAFFERTY WAKES UP late, somewhat surprised to realize that he'd gotten to sleep at all. The first thing he sees is Fon, followed by another woman, tiptoeing across the living room toward the kitchen. The room is very bright, and through the glass doors of the balcony he sees that the western sides of the buildings aren't catching the full weight of the sun, so it must be high in the sky: it could be as late as ten-thirty or eleven. It's a Wednesday, so either Miaow has overslept for school, which she never does, or he's somehow snored through the entire morning mob scene: doors opening and closing, the shower running, the toilet flushing, the smell of the coffee Miaow's taken to drinking after years of deriding it as *bean drink*. (Edward, he suddenly realizes, likes coffee). He's slept through the clatter of plates landing on the counter and the arrival of at least part of the day's squadron of former bar girls. He might have even slept through the baby crying, which would be a first.

In his morning *basso profundo* he croaks, "Time is it?" and is rewarded by seeing the unflappable Fon propel herself four or five inches straight into the air. The other woman laughs at her.

In the second or so it takes her to come back down and turn to face him, Fon has almost, but not quite, reassembled her composure. "Wery late," she says, still slightly rattled; like Rose, Fon conquered the V sound years ago. "Now make lunch."

"Jesus," Rafferty says. He sleeps in his underpants, so he wraps his sheet around him as he gets up, and Fon gets even for "wery" by saying, "You no hide. I see before."

"Not this one, you haven't," he says. "It's had a limited circulation." The woman he doesn't know, cheerful looking and plump as a muffin, covers her mouth and chortles. With the sheet half draped around him making him look, he thinks, like a Roman senator on welfare, he heads for the bedroom.

Behind him, Fon says, "All same-same. Only man think is different." He's trying not to laugh when she calls after him, "You wan' coffee?"

"Does the sun rise in the east?" he says, and he opens the door.

Rose sits on the end of the bed, her white blouse pulled down on one side and the baby at her right breast. The smile she gives him when she turns to face him makes his eyes water.

He has to say something manly. "What about the formula?"

"He like me better," she says.

"But you hurt."

"No problem. Sometime this one, sometime other one."

"Lucky kid. Hi, Brush-head," he says to the baby as he sits, very carefully, beside them. He drapes the sheet over his shoulders and leans over to kiss her cheek. She says, "Mmmm."

He says, "While he's still so small we could use him as a bottle brush."

"I rent him to Toots at the bar," she says. "Make more money than me."

"He'll have to join the baby union. When they're unhappy with working conditions they carry little picket signs and cry." He reaches across her and passes his fingers over the straight shock of hair. "You know," he says, "the earlier they get hair, the earlier they get bald."

"They get hair early," she says serenely, "they have big brain. No room for hair."

The doorbell rings.

"The crew assembles," he says, leaning forward to get up.

"No, no, no," she says. "You stay here. Please? Fon and Claudia open door."

"Claudia?"

Rose shrugs. "She like the name." The baby has pulled away from the nipple, its wide blue eyes fixed on something on the ceiling. Rose follows the baby's gaze. "Him see spirit." A bright morning babble of voices erupts in the living room. They all sound very happy.

"Me too," Rafferty says, studying her.

"Sweet talk. Now I am just fat lady." She turns, catches him in mid-stare, and just barely overrules a smile. "I like when you come in."

He gets up. "I'll come in more often," he says. "I promise." He bends to kiss the top of her head, and Fon announces, behind him, "Coffee."

THE WOMEN—FON, YIM, Nui, Waan, and the one he doesn't recognize, who must be Claudia—crowd into the bedroom. Waan and Yim give him a *wai*, hands pressed together as though in prayer, their fingertips meeting near the space between their eyebrows. This is higher than the ones they usually give him, and he thinks the promotion must reflect his fatherhood. He returns the greeting as well as he can with a sheet hanging from his shoulders and a cup of very hot, very weak coffee in his hand and gets the kind of laugh he usually hears only in sitcoms. Fon could make a pound of coffee last until the baby is shaving. The first time she'd made his coffee, five or six days earlier, she'd let the water drip over whole beans.

So, he thinks as he comes into the living room, re-draping his sheet, *on with the day*. Real coffee, black enough to write with. Eggs and bacon. Fon's favorite dishes are heavy on fish, and he's not someone who can easily contemplate the notion of fish for breakfast. He's passing the counter, planning his meal, and heading for the coffee grinder, when his heart misses a beat.

His notebook. He hadn't put his notebook away, and now it's not where . . .

He literally pops a sweat. He stands there, one hand on the counter to steady himself, and then he sees it. It's closed, at least, but it's all the way down at the far end of the counter, right in front of the sliding glass door.

Where Miaow eats.

This is what comes of not having secrets, he says to himself. *You get out of practice.*

For a moment, he worries about Fon. If *anyone* would tell Rose about his second, third, and fourth thoughts, it would be the fiercely protective Fon. But then he dismisses the notion. Most Thais who have learned English on the fly, as opposed to in school learn it orally. Their reading is usually limited to some relatively simple print, but few of them can find their way through cursive script, especially a cursive script as sloppy as his.

Miaow, on the other hand . . .

Jesus.

It's not just what he wrote *last night*, which had included a few of his misgivings about fatherhood and an addendum about canoodling. He'd been writing down his issues with fatherhood practically since the kid came home. He'd done, for example, a paragraph on his horrified first sight of a full diaper, which had been just a couple of days ago, so what kind of a father *was* he? He'd described it as *the world's worst peanut butter*. He'd written that *the kid could drink his weight in milk every day*. He'd written about feeling left out, pushed to the margin by the crowds of women, about feeling displaced in Rose's feelings, among many, many other things. He'd viewed these reactions, as he wrote them, as bits of a candid and completely private journal of new fatherhood, with emphasis on the areas he couldn't discuss with Rose and also those that made him feel he wasn't up to the job, either practically or emotionally. Or, in the case of diapers and milk throw-up, even aesthetically.

And, he remembers, he'd written about Miaow's play, mostly worries over the size of the challenge she'd taken on. Now, flipping back through those pages, he relaxes a little. His admiration of her courage and his belief in her talent are there, too. She'd be okay with it because the doubts he'd expressed would at least tell her that he was being candid.

Although the paragraph about canoodling . . .

How old am *I, anyway?* he thinks. *When did I become the Last Puritan, the Holder of the Scales of Justice?*

Coffee. If he's going to navigate this minefield, he needs coffee. *Real* coffee.

Still, the first thing he does is take the notebook and put it into the file drawer in his desk with the spine down and the edges of the pages up. That makes it almost indistinguishable from the printouts of his articles and the catalog copy and the hundred or so pages of his new and, if he's being honest, abandoned book. He'd learned the hard way that it was one thing to write a book about a place when he was an outsider who could focus on the impressions, mostly on the surface, that a traveler would experience over the course of a few days, and a completely different challenge when he'd essentially married the country, seen the indifference of the rich toward the poor, seen the enormous engines of exploitation, the endless layers of corruption, the complicated reality and the omnipresent tragedy behind so many of the smiles. Look at his own family, assembled literally from the wreckage: a child abandoned to the streets with no official infrastructure to take her in, and a daughter of the impoverished Northeast—where rice-farming families, including her own, have been methodically cheated for decades—who became a Bangkok prostitute for the sake of her younger brothers and sisters. The story has been told so often that it's woven into the country's urban legends.

So, no, it's not so easy to write about Thailand now. Not, given the Kingdom's current level of censorship, if he wants the book to be sold here.

He closes the drawer. Miaow will still find it if she wants to, but it'll be a little more difficult.

He's grinding the beans when he decides what to do. He texts her: **Found your diary, we need to talk**. She's at school, but she'll get back to him between classes.

Within thirty seconds, his phone rings. "Impossible," she says, without waiting for him even to say hello. "Totally impossible. First, you couldn't find it because it's with me, and second, you wouldn't . . ."

He waits, and by the time he's counted to four she says, "Oh." He lets her stew in it, and then she says, "It was right *there*."

"Was it addressed to you?"

"Of course not."

"Well, that was the *easy* question. Was it open?"

She says, "Um."

He dumps the ground coffee into the filter, slides the unit into place, and goes to the sink to run some water into the carafe. "It was not," he says. "It was closed and as far away from where you sit as it was possible for it to be and still be on the counter. So that means you had to get up and look at it, pick it up, carry it all the way back to your seat, decide to open it, and *then* decide—"

"I *already* feel bad."

"Good. You're supposed to." He smells the first *hello* between the water and the coffee almost immediately. It raises his spirits a little, but he pushes that aside. "And then decide to *read* it, even after you saw what it—"

"I *didn't* know what it was. At first. I thought maybe it was, you know, notes for a new book. About Thailand. Thought maybe I could help you get it right this time."

"Tick. Tick."

"Well." She's raised her voice, something she does only when she knows she's wrong. "What do you want me to—"

"I want to know why you thought it was okay to—"

"Because until I looked at it, I didn't know you feel the same way I do. About the baby. Because I've been feeling really, *really* guilty about it, and there it was all of a sudden. You're as bad as I am."

"I'm not sure I'm as bad as—"

"Maybe badder," she says, and then she's laughing. "*The worst peanut butter in the—*"

"Okay, okay." He pops open the cabinet and takes down the cup Rose gave him, the one with the sleepy eyes that open wide when the cup is tilted. He kicks the underside of the counter to speed up the brewing process, and says, "Hello?"

"I *needed* to read that," she says, "so I'd know I wasn't the worst person who ever lived."

"There were the Borgias," he says. "There was Hitler."

"There's *you*," she says. She pauses, and then says, "Do you know what?"

"Do I *want* to know what?"

"You're the only person I've ever been able to laugh at."

"That's sort of a mixed bless—"

"Because I know you love me. Because you know, umm, that I love you."

He goes absolutely blank for a moment, and then he says, "Okay. But you can't read my diary."

"It's not really your diary," she says, "it's your bitch book. You just needed someplace to bitch about not being a perfect father."

"Well, as long as we're being so honest, you leave a lot to be desired in the Big Sister Sweepstakes, too."

"We're awful," Miaow says.

"So no reading my bitch book. And you'll go in and spend some time with your mom and your brother."

"Or what?"

"Or I'll take Edward away from you."

"You're not his type."

"Wow," he says. "One-upped by my own daughter."

"*Again*," Miaow says. "So, the baby. I mean, what do I *say* to him?"

"How the hell do I know? What do you think, he's going to correct your grammar?" Still holding the phone, he pulls out the pot and slides the cup under the stream until it's full, and then does the switch in reverse, not spilling much; he's gotten good at this. "She—your mother—just needs to know you love him."

Suddenly Fon is at the sink beside him, giving him a hip-bump to move him aside. "Strong too much," she says, glancing at the coffee. She's got Rose's cup and she's running water into it.

"I'm a strong man," Rafferty says.

Miaow says, "That's pathetic."

"Oh, are you still there? Aren't you supposed to be in class? Learning something?"

"It's lunchtime," she says. "*Boy*, were you snoring this morning."

"Takes a lot of sleep to be a strong man. Think about what I said. More time with you-know-who."

"I promise. Sorry about, you know."

"Hell, I'm glad you read it. We would never have had this talk."

"I actually could have done without the talk," she says.

"Good to be appreciated," he says. "Love you."

She hangs up. Fon is looking at him accusingly.

"*Miaow*," he says, and Fon starts to laugh. Vaguely stung, he says, "It *might* have been somebody else."

"No, no," Fon says, and she makes a maternal clucking noise as she reaches up to pat his cheek. "You *good* boy."

FOR THE NEXT four hours or so, he's an exemplary father, the kind that might get a four-column picture in a *New York Times* piece on the shape of the modern family. He learns how to mix, decant, and heat the formula, even though the baby snubs it when he's done. In front of the assembled women, he's given a purely theoretical diaper-folding class, with diapers just out of the washing machine, still warm and clean enough to squeak. Awkward as he felt, the women didn't laugh much at all until Fon said something in Thai that was too fast for him to catch, at which point they all pretty well fell apart. He spends almost an hour and a half beside Rose, watching her as she handles the baby, one hand almost always beneath the bushy head. He even holds Frank, or, as he sometimes thinks of the child, *Arthit*, for fifteen long, uneasy minutes until the baby squalls and waves his arms, a semaphore of distress, and Rose takes over. He can't help seeing the contrast between her and himself: when he's got the child, it absorbs every atom of his attention, while Rose seems almost frighteningly nonchalant. Worrying uselessly about the kid as Rose bounces him up and down in her arms, Rafferty realizes that the baby's warm, milky smell makes him go a little soft in the knees.

That startles him a bit, but what most startles him is Rose's glow. If it were any brighter, and if he had tears in his eyes, which, he's proud to say, he doesn't, it might look like a halo. He dismisses the thought as hopelessly banal but when she catches him looking at her, he says, "You're glowing."

Rose says, "I'm happy."

He says, "Me too," and Fon leads the women in a round of applause that almost makes him jump out of his skin. He'd forgotten they were in the room.

A little after 4 p.m., his phone rings. *Leon*, it reads, and for the hundredth time since his friend died he resolves to change the caller ID to the name of the bar.

"IS TOOTS," SHE says, as she always does.

"Hi, Toots."

"Bob problem."

"You're telling me?"

"You come here. Bob problem. Maybe big problem."

"What kind of—"

"You come here."

"I'm busy right now," he says, and the front door opens. Miaow comes through, followed by Edward. In lockstep, they go straight to the kitchen, and Rafferty can absolutely *not* avoid glancing at the drawer with his journal in it. "Wait, Toots. What kind of problem? And why me?"

"Why *you*?" She sounds incredulous. "You his friend."

"He has . . ." he hesitates, but finishes the sentence anyway, "a lot of friends."

"You friend number one. You come. You come now." She disconnects.

From the kitchen, Miaow calls, "Something wrong?"

"No, nothing, somebody else's problem." He drops the phone into his shirt pocket and stands there, irresolute, thinking, *friend number one?*

"Anything serious?" Miaow is standing in the entryway to the kitchen.

"No. I mean, I don't know, but I know it's not our problem. Don't eat the *som tam.*"

"Why not?"

"Fon thinks it might be a little old. Just leave it alone."

"Will you be back for dinner?"

"I have no idea. Just don't eat the—"

"Yeah, got it. What are you looking for?"

"My phone."

"It's in your shirt pocket." She comes all the way into the room. "Are you *sure* it's nothing serious? You usually know where you put something, especially if it's like ten seconds ago."

"My father's forgetting things, too," Edward calls cheerily from the kitchen. "We look for his keys almost every day."

"I'm not *forgetting* things. It's just . . . you guys going to run lines?"

"When we're not canoodling," Miaow says.

"Well, don't get too involved with the canoodling. There's a quintet of bar workers here. They'll rate your technique, laugh you all the way to Cambodia." He slaps his pockets for his keys, finds them, and says, "And some information *remains within the family,* right?"

"Sure. Will you be home for dinner?"

Edward says, "What information?"

"I have no idea about dinner," Rafferty says. "Didn't I already say that? Listen, I wouldn't eat the—right, right, I told you. Go say hello to your mother. Tell her I'll be back later, okay?"

Miaow is saying, "But Mom will want to know if—" when he pulls the door closed behind him.

11

Queen's Mansion

THE TRAFFIC IS building to its early-evening delirium as he does his much-practiced broken-field running across Silom. He earns a couple of honks, but they're purely ceremonial: the cars are barely inching forward. Only once does his heart rate increase, and that's when he steps between two cars and in front of a motorcycle that's doing about forty kilometers per hour, zigzagging between vehicles that are eighteen inches apart. It streaks past him, a girl with wet, shiny hair clinging one-handed to the backseat. The bike's blaring horn leaves him with his fingers in his ears.

Patpong is glum, dull, ugly, and relatively empty. The colored lights haven't been flicked on yet and women are ambling toward the bars dressed in T-shirts and jeans, many of them with hair as wet from their afternoon showers as the girl on the motorcycle's had been. They look younger and less sophisticated out here; they haven't put on their work faces yet. Making up is a communal ritual performed in tribes in front of the mirrored wall that's a feature of so many bars, the women catching up on the events of the day, each tribe dodging the members of the others.

Once, he thinks, as he often does, *this was Rose's life.* And now she's at home with what's-his-name, *Frank*, his son is named Frank.

The rusty bell announces him to the thin scrum of afternoon drinkers: the guy with the hair, the two Bob Campeau wannabes he'd had to bribe to leave him and Bob alone the previous night, a couple of newbies—tourists, looking disappointed with what might be their first Patpong adventure—and, perched expertly on a barstool, whispering fiercely to Toots, an attractive woman in her early fifties whose hair is the kind of flat matte black that proclaims *dye job* even from across the street. She might, Rafferty conjectures, be having second thoughts about the dye since she's doing nothing to hide the inch of steel gray that bisects her head, straight as the track of a bullet, on either side of the center part. Toots spots him and lifts her chin at him as he comes in, and the other woman turns to glance at him, then looks back to Toots and shakes her head, *disappointment* in any language. Despite the low-budget implications of the dye job, she's wearing a loose, light blouse that's silk even from this distance and a pair of shoes by a guy Rose has intermittently obsessed over, Christian Louboutin, their provenance announced by the blood-red soles, effortlessly displayed by the neatly crossed ankles she's propped on the rung of her stool. There are a lot of fake Louboutin shoes in Bangkok, and he'd bet that these aren't among them. She also has the perfect ankles for the shoes, which is to say flawless. Rafferty is a highly qualified arbiter of ankles.

He waves at the members of the Campeau fan club, nods at the guy with the hair, and ignores the tourists, who return the favor. As he pulls up a stool at the bar, leaving one empty between himself and the woman with the two-tone hair and the expensive shoes, Toots says, in Thai, "Here he is."

"Here I am," he agrees in Thai. He lowers his voice and glances, meaningfully, he hopes, at Campeau's carbon copies, and puts a finger to his lips. "What's the problem?"

The woman with the two-tone hair purses her mouth: he's being too direct. He says to Toots, "Would you please introduce us?"

"*Khun* Ratana," Toots says. "This is *Khun* Poke."

Ratana says, "Poke?" She looks startled.

"Philip," Rafferty says. "My real name is Philip. My father called me Poke." It doesn't look like that response cleared up much of anything, but he's not in the mood to replay the whole thing about how he'd poked his nose into things when he was a kid, so he just says, "American nickname. What's going on with Bob?"

Khun Ratana exchanges a look with Toots, and Toots says, in Thai, "He's stronger than he looks. And smarter."

Ratana glances at Rafferty again, and when she catches him looking directly at her, her skepticism dissolves instantly into a radiantly meaningless smile. "I'm sure he is," she says to Toots in English, "if you say so." She gazes past Toots, studying the bar. "Do you have Dr. Pepper?"

"No. Have cola, have Fanta."

"Which flavors?"

Toots shrugs. "All terrible. Have beer."

"Well," the woman—Ratana—says, "if you say so."

The glance Toots gives Rafferty is so fast he almost misses it, but Ratana slaps the back of Toots' hand in reproach and Toots yanks it back, and they both laugh.

"*Dr. Pepper*," Toots says scornfully. "I know you one hundred year, you never drink Dr. Pepper." She leans down to open the refrigerator.

"It sounds so *healthy*," Ratana says. She turns to Rafferty and says, "I don't know you." Her English is excellent.

"That makes us even. I don't know you, either."

"Although Bob did say you were a friend."

"Ah," Rafferty says, not sure how to react to his promotion; he'd never really thought of Campeau as a friend. "You're another one of Bob's, um . . ." he glances away, but the clones are talking to each other. "His friends?"

"I'm his landlady. I own the apartment house he lives in. Long time now, fourteen years, I think."

"I see." He watches Toots pop the cap from a Singha and decides against asking for one. She probably wouldn't give it to him, anyway. "What seems to be the problem?" He holds up a *wait a minute* finger and says to Toots, "How old is the coffee?"

She closes one eye in concentration. "Two day. Maybe three."

"Well, then. A very small cup, if you can chip it out of the pot."

Pouring into a mug, Toots says, "Joking. Not old."

Ratana says, "I got a call this morning from the person in the apartment next to your friend's. She said she heard things breaking and slamming against the wall, and at some point someone screamed."

"*Screamed?*"

"Well, shouted. I'm just telling you what she said."

"Male or female?"

"I didn't ask."

"What time? I mean, was she calling while it was going on, or—"

"No, later. She said it woke her up about four in the morning and she wanted me to know, but she didn't want to bother me at that—"

"Okay, late last night, early this morning. And so—let me just think this through—Bob's neighbor hears all that ruckus, maybe violence, in the middle of the night—"

"Ruckus?"

"Noise—you know, things banging around."

"*Ruckus,*" she says with the air of someone memorizing a word.

"And she waits until this morning to call you, and you call Toots, and Toots says to call me."

"No, I—"

"And nobody thinks to call, you know, the cops."

Ratana says, "Bob hates the cops."

Toots says, "Everybody hate—" but Ratana says, over her, "He told me to call you if anything went wrong. I didn't know how to get in touch with you."

"He told you to call *me?*"

"If there's a problem. Yes."

"But Toots didn't just give you my phone number."

"Want to *know*," Toots says, as though it were the most obvious thing in the world. "Want to know what happen."

"Well," Rafferty says, "what *did* happen?"

"*I* don't know," Ratana says with the air of someone being asked a stupid question. "He said to call—"

"Okay, okay, I've got that part. So what you seem to be saying is that no one has been in the apartment since all the ruckus."

"I don't think so."

"For example, you. *You* haven't been to—"

"No, no, no." She's wiping the words out of the air as she speaks.

"And you want me to look."

"Yes."

Rafferty says, "He could be dead in there."

"Oh, no," Ratana says, picking up her beer. "He's too mean to die."

FOR THE PAST five or six years it's been evident to Rafferty that Bangkok is under energetic and perpetual attack by developers. Individual buildings, groups of adjoining buildings, even entire streets have fallen prey to the bulldozers, creating new neighborhoods for people to get lost in, vainly seeking their familiar landmarks. Here and there, while navigating a "renovated" area, Rafferty has grown used to seeing the odd building or two that miraculously escaped improvement, as though their bit of the street had somehow been folded out of sight when the heavy machinery showed up, leaving them as they were: low, dumpy, sooty concrete buildings, glum but familiar among the shiny strangers, the only bad teeth in the block's gleaming new smile.

Khun Ratana is a fast walker, and she has the advantage of knowing where she's going. Rafferty scrambles to keep up, one eye on the red soles, as she leads him over a zigzag path through patchwork neighborhoods, carrying on a conversation in which she largely replies to him over her shoulder. Bob, she says again, has been living in the apartment for fourteen years, which tells him it wasn't the one Malee stole everything of value out of, when she broke Bob's heart.

"I bought the building just before he moved in," she says in Thai. The silver hair on either side of her part gleams in the late-afternoon sun. "Most of the apartments were occupied when I bought it, so he was my first new tenant, the first one I really had to talk to. One of the first *Americans* I ever talked to, in fact." She tilts her head to one side. "We'll go left up here."

"So," he prompts, "one of the first Americans you—"

"Yes. I got to know him because I'd spent every baht I had to buy the building, and I was living in it to save money when he moved in, and I was worried about things breaking, maintenance problems, because I couldn't afford the repairs. So, naturally, things broke, and *Khun* Bob fixed them."

Rafferty says, "Really" because it's the only thing that comes to him.

"He wouldn't let me pay him, either. It was embarrassing. I'd knock on his door to tell him what was wrong and promise to pay him as soon as I could, and he always just shook his head. 'What else am I doing?' he'd say. He was my first American, and I remember thinking that Americans were very generous and very sad."

"Sad?"

"I don't think I've ever known anyone sadder than he is. I've met lots of Americans since then so I know they're not all like that. He's still the saddest."

"Really."

She slows and looks back at him. "Don't *you* think he's sad?"

Rafferty opens his mouth and closes it. Then he says, "Yes, I guess I do. I met him later than you did, only about eight years ago. I thought he was mostly angry."

"Broken heart," she said, as if it were self-evident. "Men don't know how to live through having their hearts broken. It changes them."

"It doesn't change women?"

"Women *expect* to have their hearts broken. It's part of being a woman. We live through it the best we can. For men, it's a surprise. They always think they'll get their way in the world, and then they don't."

"You're not worried about him?"

She stops until he catches up with her. "Of course I am."

IT'S A FOUR-STORY building, squat and stubby-looking in contrast with the newer, more ambitious structures on the street, and it encapsulates most of the cheap Bangkok building conventions of the 1950s: colorless concrete; aluminum-frame windows; tiny balconies, no more than a couple of feet deep and five or six feet long. Many of the balconies are decked out with things hung up to dry: clothes, towels, sheets, washrags. In front of the building, to the left of the double glass doors, is a highly conspicuous wooden structure about the size and shape of the prow of a large sailboat. The wood has been stained a golden brown, and incised into it are the words QUEEN'S MANSION.

"Mansion," she says, opening the door with a key card. "Everything in Bangkok is a mansion."

"I've noticed. Is there any way for you to keep track of those key cards?"

"No." She shoulders the door aside and holds it for him. "First floor, stairs on the right. Oh, sorry, for you Americans, second floor. At first I tried to make everyone turn the keys in when they moved, but by then there were people who said they lost theirs or they'd accidentally packed them, and how could I know whether that was true?"

Rafferty pulls open a metal fire door in the right wall of the small lobby, undecorated but for a large color photo of the former king and his queen—Sirikit, now the Queen Mother—in an ornate gilt frame. He holds it open for Ratana, who has slowed to *wai* the royalty, and then he follows her up.

"A gentleman," she says. "So one year I changed the code and gave everyone new cards, and for the next six weeks my life was hell. Everybody got locked out. No one threw away the old cards and they'd try to use them instead, so I was getting calls day and night from people who were stuck at the door. The next year I changed the *color* of the cards and asked for the old ones back, but some people had more than one of the old ones and were apparently color blind, too, so I still got calls. So I gave up." She stops at the switchback and looks down at him. "You think maybe someone broke in and hurt him?"

"For all I know, he knocked over his ironing board and he's still asleep."

"Toots says . . ." She turns away from him and opens the door, but he stops her by saying, "Toots says? Toots says what?"

"That he was very sad last night. Sadder than usual."

"What does that mean?"

"He wouldn't go home. She says in all the time she's been there, thirty years or however long it's been, he never insisted on staying after closing time. But last night he sat there, without saying anything, just drinking until she had turned on the lights, swept, washed the glasses, everything. She finally had to give him a beer to take with him and lock him out, and she said, the way he walked up Patpong, he didn't look like he knew where he was."

Rafferty says, "*Shit*," and comes up another two steps. "But wait, he was alone? All the noise your tenant heard. I mean, do you think he had a fight or something?"

"I don't know. That's why you're with me. And do I think he killed himself or somebody else did? I don't know that, either."

"Well, let's go."

The hallway is narrow and dim and damp-smelling, lighted in the daytime only by a floor-to-ceiling window at each end. The corridor runs east-west, and Rafferty finds himself peering directly into the last moments of the sun, glaring at him with an almost personal ferocity between two newer and higher buildings. By the time he looks away from the brightness he already has the sun imprinted on his retinas, and the hallway seems impenetrably dark. He looks down at the floor, blinking hard, and what he sees, cheap linoleum, does not reassure him: Bob should be living better than this. He's trying to push down a rising tide of uneasiness when fluorescent lights stutter on overhead, probably on a timer, and Ratana says, "Right here."

But Rafferty stays where he is, looking down and hearing his heart pound in his ears. The fluorescents have brought the floor into sharper focus, and now he sees the rust-brown drops of what could only be blood. He rubs his eyes, hoping the image will go away. When it doesn't, he follows the drops visually, eight to ten feet to the spot where Ratana stands, a conventional metal key in her hand, in front of a door numbered *124*.

"One-two-four," she says. "Adds up to Bob's lucky number, he told me. Seven. He said he'd take the apartment even before I put the key in the lock."

Rafferty says, "Speaking of that, I mean, putting the key in—"

"I know, I know." She's shaking her head. "I just don't want to—here." She extends the hand holding the old-fashioned key. "You do it."

He says, "Look at the floor."

"I know," she says, "it's terrible, so ugly. I've been meaning to replace it for—" She stops, staring downward, arm still outstretched, and he watches her eyes track the path of the droplets until she steps quickly away from the door, which is inescapably where they either begin or end. She says, "Hurry," and extends the key again.

Thinking of the baby, thinking of everything that's happening at home, Rafferty says, "Maybe the cops would be a better—"

"Who's going to pay the cops?" she says. "There's no money in this for them. He's an old *farang* in a cheap—I mean, budget— apartment. All they'll do is try to shake us down, say maybe we were the ones who . . ." She puts her hand, the one with the key in it, over her mouth.

"I have a friend who's a cop," Rafferty says. "It might be better to . . ." He runs out of steam. "We don't even know whether these drops are coming or going." Hearing what he's just said, he reaches out for the key and says, "Right. He might be hurt in there."

As little as he wants to go in, the key turns as though the lock has been oiled. Midway through pushing the door open he senses *something* and takes a couple of involuntary steps back. The apartment is dark, and he can't see anything but vague shapes, so when the door begins to swing closed again, he has to jump forward to stop it, which means that he's standing dead center in the doorway as his eyes become accustomed to the dimness. He says, "Oh, no."

"No *what*? No—is he . . . ?"

"No, no, no. I mean, I don't know yet. Not really, not yet." He reaches around the edge of the doorway to his right, locates the wall switch, and snaps it up with his knuckles. Another flickering yields to a cold fluorescent light that brings everything into indifferent, merciless relief.

From where Rafferty stands, the apartment seems to be what the Thais call a studio, essentially one room broken into three areas: the sleeping area, which is right in front of him with its stained, unmade bed and its night table, a fat book sitting on it, and a sort of sitting area along the wall to his right, marked by a sagging couch, a rough wooden coffee table, and a couple of folding chairs that probably originally stood at the near side of the table. The wall behind the couch has a doorway that almost certainly leads to the third area, a shallow space that gives the resident access to the bathroom and, probably, the balcony. The first thing he'd glimpsed had been the bedsheets, the top one ripped most of the way off the mattress and stained in the same rust brown he'd seen in the hallway. Now, with the light on, he registers other details to his right: the cushions torn off the couch and standing upright, leaning drunkenly against the wall and one another at the couch's far end. One of the folding chairs, lightweight aluminum with the seat and back made from that woven plastic that Rafferty has always ranked as the ugliest fabric ever created, is on its side on the table, half-collapsed, all acute aluminum elbows and sagging bright orange plastic. Above the couch is a big framed something that had been covered in glass until, he guesses, the partially collapsed chair hit it and broke it, showering the couch with shards of glass and tearing the picture, whatever it is, jaggedly down the right side. There's a long arc of blood droplets on the wall between the edge of the front door and the couch, as though the source of the blood had somehow been swung through the air.

"Bathroom at the back?" Rafferty calls. He's gone only a step or two past the doorway, but he can already smell the blood.

"Yes," Ratana says, staying where she is. "What is it? What's in there? Is Bob—"

"I don't know yet, but there's blood. Stay out there for now, okay?"

"No problem. Be careful."

"Yeah." He draws three deep breaths and steps all the way into the room.

The top sheet is relatively clean except for a spattered fringe along the right edge, but the bottom sheet caught a lot more blood, two now-dry pools of it, six to eight inches across, over which some flies are circling. Rafferty hates flies, and there's nothing he hates more about them than the way they buzz over blood. He keeps his eyes on the floor, seeing the trail of blood droplets that followed the bleeding person either into or out of the apartment.

A closer look at the bed tells him nothing new except that the bottom sheet has been cut with something sharp that went straight through the fabric and put a short, ragged, deep-looking incision in the mattress. Averting his eyes from the surprising violence of the sheets, he sees the book again and, since there is virtually no circumstance under which Rafferty won't take a look at a book, he does so now, but without picking it up. It's *Once Upon a Distant War*, by William Prochnau, a deadly serious non-fiction comic-opera about a bunch of inexperienced kid reporters in Vietnam, describing to their editors back home a war that had nothing in common with the one American politicians were selling to their constituents. The Halls of Power put the question directly to the *New York Times* and several other national outlets: "Who you gonna believe? You gonna go with the secretary of defense and the president hisself, or are you gonna go with some rookie, wet-behind-the-ears reporter barely out of high school?" The *Times* and the others went with the reporters. Rafferty wonders what Campeau thought—*thinks*—about Prochnau's book. Like a lot of the Vietnam vets Rafferty knows, Campeau seems to hate equally the government that had sent him there and the people who had challenged the government—and by extension, the war. It was *their* war, the soldiers' war, many of them seemed to say: If you weren't there, who cares what you think? Just keep your fucking mouth shut. The cloud of flies over the bed has thickened and Rafferty realizes that he's avoiding going into the bathroom. He turns his back on the buzzing and takes the six or eight steps that put him beside the long, cigarette-scarred wooden coffee table, also speckled here and there with blood. The couch once pretended to be leather but age and wear have revealed its vinyl heart, and Rafferty once again feels a pang at how Campeau was—is—living. His own apartment in college was better than this.

The torn picture is a photograph, head and shoulders, of a Thai woman in her early twenties, fine-boned and slight of build, with huge, luminous eyes. She's wearing a T-shirt and a big, almost comically clunky necklace, most likely big plastic beads trying to pass themselves off as amber, and she's looking straight into the camera and laughing. An out-of-focus jumble of buildings carve up the space behind her, not modern urban structures but the softer lines of low-hanging canvas awnings that obscure the buildings behind them, which were probably modest one- and two-story wooden structures, each set up a step or two from the unpaved street to thwart the annual floods. When the picture was taken, though, the street was dry and dusty and swarming with motorcycles. A village, then, a lot like Rose's village, maybe a little more prosperous if the sheer number of motorbikes clogging the street was any indication.

This must be Malee. Or maybe not: Bob's tone when he talked about her hadn't suggested that he had her picture hanging where he'd see it first thing every morning. But if this *is* Malee, this is probably the village with the ghost house in it. She could look directly and fondly at Bob, Rafferty thinks, and laugh like that when she was in the process of swindling him out of everything he had in Thailand. And Campeau has her picture on the wall? Or maybe it's not—

"You are all right?"

Her voice startles him; he'd forgotten about Ratana for a moment. And he has to face the fact that the bathroom is waiting for him.

"I'm fine," he says. "Checking the rest of the place now."

He turns to his left and walks the few yards to the space at the rear of the apartment, which is broken by a couple of small curtained windows and a flimsy-looking door. There's a waist-high refrigerator against the short wall to his right. It has a small bouquet of sagging flowers on it, jammed into a water glass too long ago; the water is yellowish and malodorous, and petals litter the floor. He pulls open the door in the back wall and finds himself looking at a balcony that's all of seven feet long and three deep. A clothesline has been strung there, and from it, secured with old wooden clothespins bleached white by the sun, dangle two pairs of jeans and three of the drab T-shirts, mostly dark gray and brown and olive, that Campeau rotates all year long. Rafferty regards them for a moment; he's seen these garments on Bob so often it's almost spooky to see them hanging there empty, as though Bob had evaporated while wearing them. He pushes the notion away and opens the door wide to let in the little remaining light; there's no ceiling fluorescent here. Reluctantly, he looks to his left. The door to the bathroom is open a few inches. He sees nothing behind it but darkness.

But the blood spatters beneath his feet are bigger here, suggesting a faster flow in this area. So just do it.

He feels a strong aversion to the notion of touching the bath-room door. Instead, he positions himself, lifts a leg, and pushes the door with the sole of his shoe, gently because he also finds that he dreads either banging it against the wall or hitting something soft when it's partway there. It opens most of the way, unimpeded, and he hears more flies. He takes a very deep breath and holds it, and then puts his arm through the doorway and pats the wall to find the switch.

Brightest room in the place, by far. And, since tile doesn't absorb liquid, some of the blood in here is still a deep heart-wringing red. There's a pool of it on the floor and more, but not much more, in the sink. It doesn't look as though any effort had been made to clean it up. At the far end of the tiny bathroom an opaque plastic shower curtain hangs all the way to the floor. Once again, Rafferty comes up against a deep reluctance to touch any-thing, so he uses his foot to slide the curtain aside. Empty and clean. No one is dead in the shower, and no one bled in there, either. And he finds that it doesn't really make any difference. He feels, all the way to the soles of his shoes, that he needs to get out of that apartment.

"I DON'T KNOW," he says. They've claimed a booth in a small, mostly empty restaurant around the corner from the Queen's Mansion. The place smells of burned fat. "He wasn't in there and there was only one blood trail in the hall, so my guess is that whatever happened, it happened in the apartment and he was still bleeding when he left. Tell me, as exactly as you can, what his neighbor said."

"I told you. Shouting—"

"Shouting? One voice or two? Male or female? Things banging around?"

"She didn't say anything about the voice or voices she heard.

Things banging around, yes. But she'll be back tonight. I'll have her call you."

"She speaks English?"

She smiles. "Sort of. Do you speak Australian?"

"No one can speak it except Australians. But I can understand it, most of the time."

"She's very young," Ratana says. "Maybe twenty-two or twenty-three. She's having an *adventure*, she says. She's teaching English in a high school."

A waitress puts a foam-topped glass of beer in front of Ratana and yet another cup of coffee just to Rafferty's right.

"You don't drink?" Ratana says. When they got to the booth, he'd slid in first and she'd started to sit beside him, but he'd stopped her by saying he was right-handed and didn't want to elbow her. She'd given him a short, moderately amused look and then taken the seat opposite.

"Not much. And Toots stopped serving me beer after the baby was born, almost two weeks ago. I think it was a hint that my character needs improving."

"You have a new baby? Boy or girl?"

"Boy."

"Girls are more fun."

"You seem to be alone in that opinion. Everyone else in this city votes for boys."

"I only met you an hour or so ago, but it doesn't seem to me that your character is in urgent need of improvement."

"Toots has had years to form a judgment. You're just getting started." He sits back and lets his eyes wander over the little restaurant. The waitress, now back behind the counter, is laughing at something the cook has just said over the pass-through. He feels a sigh coming on but bottles it up. He knows the smart thing to do would be to make his excuses and leave, but the time for that would have been before he raised her hopes by following her all the way over here, and before he saw that bloodstained, fly-infested apartment. And though he's never thought of Campeau as a friend, the two of them have been exchanging nods, grunts, and even words for eight years, and the things he'd said about Miaow the previous evening had come from the heart. So he draws a deep breath and dives in. "You seem to know, personally, the woman who lives next to Bob. How many tenants do you have? Do you know them all?"

"Oh, no. I only know her because she took the place next to Bob, and I wanted to be sure she wouldn't bother him too much. There are hundreds of tenants at this point. I own five buildings now and I'm working on my sixth. My husband says I sneeze gold, although 'sneeze' isn't the word he uses."

"Lucky him. Does he sneeze gold, too?"

"No. But he appreciates that I do. Actually, that should be *appreciated*. We're no longer together." She gives him a moment to reply and then lifts her glass. "So I'll have her call you. Then what will you do?"

"Depends on what she says. I'll either phone my friend on the police force or start talking to people who know Bob. I might do that anyway, no matter what the neighbor tells me."

"What do you think happened?"

"I have no idea. Toots said he was drinking a lot last night. Maybe he came home and threw a fit, looked at his life, and tossed some stuff around. Then maybe he went into the bathroom and slipped, hit his head on the edge of the sink, hard enough to open it up. Cuts to some parts of the head bleed like fountains. Maybe yelled some more and went to a hospital."

Regarding him, resting her chin in one hand, Ratana says, "Or?"

"Or maybe he was so drunk he picked up the wrong person.

Bob's got a mean side, but he's not very big. Maybe they argued over money or maybe she never meant to do anything but steal from him in the first place and they had a fight, maybe she cut him—someone seems to have stuck a knife into the bed—and she got out of the room. Maybe he followed her. The one thing we can be pretty sure of is that he left the room, because there's all that blood in the bathroom and on the bed, but only one trail of drops outside the apartment. So he wasn't bleeding when he went in."

She puts her other elbow on the table, both hands supporting her chin and her fingers framing her face. It's a good look. "Toots said you were a writer."

"I am."

"You don't think like a writer."

Rafferty lifts his coffee cup and tilts it to her in a toast. "I'll take that as a compliment."

12

Joot

BY THE TIME he gets back to Patpong, a few of the less gaudy bars are open, the night-market vendors have turned on their million-watt lights, and the street looks—briefly, at least—like a family destination, if for rather odd families. And sure enough, Rafferty spots a scattering of adults leading jet-lagged looking children from stand to stand, Mom spouting a bright stream of chatter to interest the kids in the merchandise while Pop and, perhaps, an older boy or two keep at least half an eye on the open doorways filled with lightly dressed, suspiciously friendly-looking women.

Toots glances up at him, eyebrows raised expectantly, as he comes through the door. He takes a seat at the bar, as far as possible from the Campeau contingent (now numbering three), leans toward her, knowing it's an aggressive attitude, and says, "I want a beer, and it's your fault that I want one, so don't give me any bubble water or I'll pour it on the bar." She regards him, her mouth pulled down at the corners, and then shakes her head and gets him a bottle of Singha. He knows Singha is probably not on the beer snobs' list of the world's great brews, but it's been the taste of Bangkok for him ever since he came here to write his third book, *Looking for Trouble in Thailand*, the one that, until recently, had paid his family's bills.

"What happen?" she says as she puts the beer on a paper

coaster. It's in front of him, but he'll have to reach all the way across the bar to get it, and he has a distinct feeling she'll slap his hand. So he ignores the beer and says, "Well, we went into the apartment, and . . ." and then he stops talking and glances around the bar. "You know what you need? A jukebox or an mp3 dock or whatever it's called now. Liven the place up. What do you think?"

"Inside the apartment, what?"

He looks at the bottle.

She narrows her eyes, moves it an inch or two in his direction, and crosses her arms.

"Yup," he says, nodding in agreement with himself. "A jukebox. Lots of, I don't know, ABBA and Kanye, Maroon 5, see who runs screaming into the street first. You could rename the place, call it the Endurance Test, ban earplugs, go after the masochist market, give the fetish bars a run for their money." He shakes his head. "Boy," he says, "that apartment."

She pushes the beer halfway to him, her mouth as tight as a knot.

"Blood," he says, sitting back on his stool. "Everywhere."

She says, her eyes enormous, "Bob blood?"

"That would be my guess," he says. "It was Bob's apartment." The two of them regard each other for a moment, and then she centers the beer directly in front of him.

"Why *thank* you," he says. "It's like old times, isn't it? I don't know what happened there, and Bob wasn't inside when we got there, but there *was* blood." He picks up the Singha and knocks back about a third of it, and a little coil of unease loosens around his heart.

"Not dead."

"Well, not dead *there*. Tell me about last night."

"Last night," she says, as though the phrase is new to her.

"You know, the night before the sun came up this morning?

You got me into this, Toots, and the least you can do is tell me what I might need to know to get out of it."

"Him stay. Drink one beer long time, look at nothing. Not talking."

"Did you try to get him to talk?"

"No. I think, him want to talk, him talk."

"Was he drunk?"

Toots focuses on something above his head for a moment. "Same every night. Drink many beer before close-up. But last night, after close-up, maybe one, maybe two." She studies the bar for a moment and says, "I give him one when we go outside. This morning, bottle all broke out there, I sweep up."

"Did the whole bottle seem to be there?"

"*I* don't know. I not try to put back together. *Oh*, you mean—"

"No, no, nothing. I doubt he toted a piece of broken glass home. Just a dumb . . . um, was there any blood out there?"

"Not that I see."

"Okay. Last night when he was sitting here alone. He didn't talk at all, he didn't give you any sense of what he was thinking about?"

"Nothing, I think maybe, I don't know, maybe because brother die? Maybe him just . . . tired. You know, tired everything. Maybe him lonely. Not have lady long time."

"How do you know that?"

A laugh explodes in the midst of the Campeau contingent, and Toots leans toward him. "*Poke*. Him here every night. Drink beer too much. Bar close, him go home late. Him old man, not same before. Not strong."

"Okay, okay."

"And have broken heart."

"You mean, from before. Long time ago."

"Girl no good," Toots says.

"You knew her?"

A shake of the head, pure disapproval. "She work Safari bar, over there." She tilts her chin in the direction of the bar across the street.

"How well did you know her?"

"Not know, just see, say hello. We only open short time then. I waitress then, say hello, serve beer, not marry Leon yet. Bob bring her here sometime, like she Queen of Thailand. Her drink water, her drink joot—"

"Joot?"

"Orange joot, apple joot."

"Ah," he says, "*joot.*"

She says, "I *say* joot." She looks down at the bar chewing on her lower lip, the picture of someone who's on the verge of saying something she shouldn't. "Leon," she says, lowering her voice, "Leon and me, we not talk about customer. Customer ask about other customer, we say we not know. Not talk about lady. People fighting sometime, but they not fighting *us.*"

"I understand."

"But Bob, him go back Vietnam, that lady come here with other man, other man, other man, drink *everything.* Drink whiskey, drink wodka, drink everything. One time, take money. Man have money too much, stick out of pant, her take. Leon see. Not tell man, but when man go toilet, him tell her, not come here again. One week, two week more her come back, Leon say *no.* Man very angry, want boxing Leon, but Leon say no. Him go away, her go away."

"What about Bob? Did he ever bring—"

"Yes. She come with Bob, we say okay."

"You know, Toots, not to take her side, but these girls are poor, and they—"

"No, no, no, no, no." She makes a side-to-side gesture with an open hand like someone erasing a chalkboard. "Not same Rose, not same Fon, not same *me*. Not same many lady. Some lady no good. I poor girl, too, Poke. Then I lucky too much, marry Leon, but before, when I have no money, I not *take*. Not good for karma. You know, you are poor and you good, you win. You are poor and you bad, *poor* win."

He sits for a moment as she responds to a rap on the bar: Pinky Holland trying for his first of the evening. After his short dry spell, the bottle feels familiar and comfortable in Rafferty's hand, and he indulges himself in the sheer tactile pleasure of it for a moment. Then he gets up, nods at Pinky, and goes around the bend in the bar to the stools claimed by the members of the Campeau Club. They cut off their chat as he approaches, so abruptly they might have been discussing classified information. One of them, the one to his far right, says, "You buying again?"

"Sure. Toots?" Toots, who is talking with Pinky, holds up a finger, but he says, "One more round here, on me." To the acolytes, he says, "I need to talk about Bob."

"So talk to Bob," growls the one who'd spoken before, who might be the oldest. He has a freeze-dried look, as though something had abruptly brought the aging process to a halt and his skin had responded by thickening instead of wrinkling. Up close, it looks like the faux leather on Campeau's couch.

Rafferty says, "As you might have noticed, Bob's not here. There's been some sort of tussle at his apartment, a little blood here and there. I'm trying to track him down."

The one in the middle, who is emulating Bob's comb-over, says, "A little blood?"

"Yeah. Just enough to worry about. I'm going to have someone check the nearest emergency hospitals, but I'm wondering where else he goes." They look at him with the unfocused attention of hibernating bears who have been shaken awake a couple of months early. "Besides here, I mean."

"You talking about Bob?" rumbles the one on the left, whose voice is almost low enough to make the floor vibrate, and Rafferty notices for the first time that he's wearing a hearing aid. He's the only African American in the group.

"Some kind of problem," says the one with the vinyl face. "Nothing for you to worry about."

Rafferty says, "How do you know that?"

"Bob?" Vinyl-face says. "Bob can take care of himself."

"It was a lot of blood," Rafferty says, suddenly and surprisingly furious. "He didn't fucking cut himself shaving." He regards the three of them and sees, right to left, scorn, uncertainty, and, on the face of the one with the hearing aid, bewilderment. He chooses the one who looks uncertain. "I think he's in trouble. I know he's a tough guy but he's also a borderline alcoholic in his middle seventies, and to some people he's going to look like bait. All alone, half-drunk, old guy—"

"Not so old," says Vinyl-face.

"Not talking to you, Jack. Talking to Mr. Reasonable here."

Mr. Reasonable says, "Huh?"

Vinyl-face says, "Drink or no drink, ain't nobody here wants to talk to you."

"People who think they speak for everyone," Rafferty says, "are almost always wrong."

"Wait a minute, *wait* a minute," says the one on the left, fiddling with the thing in his ear. "He's not speaking for me. Something happened to Bob? I want to know about it."

"Why don't you go get the beer?" Rafferty says to Vinyl-face. "Do something useful."

Slowly and meaningfully, Vinyl-face gets off his stool, which actually makes him shorter without, somehow, making him seem any less dangerous. "You watch it, bub."

Rafferty says, "We seem to have gotten off on the wrong foot.

My fault. Tell you what, you have a couple of beers on me and, umm, your friend here—"

"Lanny," says the one with the hearing aid.

"Lanny and I will go chat for a bit, and then the evening can resume its long slow slide into whatever it is."

"Sleep," Lanny says. "People just waitin' to go to sleep."

"I can sympathize," Rafferty says. "I haven't slept more than three hours at a time for thirteen days." To Toots, he says, "Give these guys two each on my tab, and then bring Lanny and me two more."

"You already have," Toots says.

"They're both for Lanny," Rafferty says. He puts his index finger to his lower lip and tilts his head, Shirley Temple–style. "I'm being good."

Once they're settled, Rafferty gives him a three-minute version: Campeau staying at the bar past closing, the noise in the apartment, what he and the landlady saw there.

"Who else he *hung* with?" Lanny shakes his head. "You wouldn't know this yet, but, Jesus, guys our age, our circles get smaller, not bigger. It's not like high school, where you knew a thousand people. We know—or maybe I should say, we'll put up with—ten or eleven. And that's pushing it. People fall away. People die. And then, you know, when you've been through something like we went through, it's not easy to hang with people who haven't." He takes a pull off the beer, and Rafferty can tell from the way he handles the bottle that he probably won't drink the second.

He waits until Lanny has swallowed a moderate mouthful. "What about women?"

"You kidding? At our age, unless we're married, like old Leon was—" He raises his bottle to toast Leon's old stool, which still has a ribbon running from arm to arm to prevent anyone from sitting on it. "It's pay for it or go without, you know? 'Course, it gets easier to go without, as ol' Henry develops a will of his own, no longer automatically stands for the ladies. Not even in Bob's case. But, you know, used to be, back in the day, you couldn't stop him. The girls called him *old triple-pop*—you okay?"

Midswallow, Rafferty has spurted half a dollar's worth of beer through his nose and segued instantly into a coughing fit, tears streaming from his eyes. "Sorry, sorry, just, uh, just caught me off guard." He coughs again and sniffs deeply, drawing a censorious look from Toots, all her worst fears confirmed. He tries for a jaunty toast, lifting the bottle toward her, but has to wipe his eyes and sniff again. "Sorry. Old, um, triple—"

"Triple-pop. Because, you know, back in the day he was Mr. All Night Long, he could go so many—"

"Yeah, yeah, I know." Rafferty wipes his eyes. "I mean, so they say." He had thought this was Fon's private nickname for Campeau, for whom she possesses a truly concentrated dislike, and Rose had told him it had spread over the years among the women who were unlucky enough to win Patpong's nightly Campeau Lotto. It's a whole new perspective to think that Campeau was aware of it.

Lanny centers his beer on the coaster, making him unique among the bar's customers. "So *who* says?"

"Oh. The, um, the women in the bars."

Lanny nods. "That's right, you're married to one."

"I am."

"Beautiful girl," Lanny says. "You're a lucky man."

"I won't argue with you. So about Bob. No women now?"

"The spirit is willing," Lanny says. "In fact, the spirit is insistent, but the flesh has its own ideas."

"Well, okay. Just trying to cross off—"

"There's one woman he talks about sometimes, though."

"Which bar?"

"No, a massage parlor. It's, ummmm . . . it's got some stupid English name. Not far from here, over toward Soi Kathoey."

"With *women?*"

Lanny puts his thumb into the neck of the bottle and pulls it free with a damp little popping sound. "Things aren't *that* bad. Bob may be past it, but he hasn't turned the corner."

"No, no, I just meant that over there it's mostly boys or lady-boys and—"

"Massage place, it was there first, before the neighborhood changed." He shakes his head. "This is the only place in the world where *before the neighborhood changed* could mean that you got boys in the bars instead of girls. Name of . . . name of—" He snaps his fingers. "Rub a Dub Dub, if you can believe that. Boy, I still got it when I need it. You know the setup, bathtub, all that shit? Maybe you don't do that stuff anymore."

"I know the setup, and no, I don't—"

"Didn't think so. Man got a prize garden at home, he doesn't go pawing through the greens in the market."

Toots knocks on the bar, and Rafferty looks up. "They want two more."

"Tell them to show you their money. But Lanny here—"

"Naw, thanks, I'm good. Most nights I'm the designated sane person."

"Do you know her name?"

"Girl at Rub a Dub Dub? Yeah, yeah, lemme think a minute. Trix, he calls her Trix. With an X at the end."

"Like the old breakfast cereal?"

"Yeah," Lanny says, turning his hearing aid back down. "But he says she's really dessert."

"He probably would," Rafferty says. "Being Bob and all."

13

Abattoir

SHE'D SEEN HIM the moment he turned into the street from the Silom end, heading for the little bar he always goes to, and she'd ducked between two night-market booths to get out of the light. No point in drawing his eye. The guy who runs the stand she's partly blocking glares at her, and she takes a couple of steps back. She realizes she's hungry, and that reminds her that when she woke up that afternoon, the bag she'd put under what she thinks of as *the boy's tree* was on the ground beside her. It was empty and clean and it had been carefully folded. That had touched her; there were always uses for a perfectly good plastic bag, but he'd brought it back and even cleaned it out. This is the fourth time he's done it.

So, that's good, it means that he'd eaten something. On the other hand, it means that she hasn't. And it's getting late. Her stomach growls so loudly she can hear it, and she shifts from foot to foot as the street vendor, who has customers approaching, gives her the smile that means *get out of here*. For a moment she decides to drift over to the Isaan restaurant just to see whether there's a plastic bag hanging beside the back door, but as she backs away from the vendor's stand she sees again the man she's supposed to follow stepping up onto the sidewalk and pushing open the door to the little bar. And she remembers: *this is the last night*. She's almost certain the Sour Man hadn't meant what he said about the cage of hungry *soi* dogs, but her ear is still hot and swollen where he pierced it with his fingernails—when? Last night, it had been just last night, and tonight is the night she has to . . .

Anyway, *there*, he's gone in. She'll have to wait and eat later, after the Sour Man pays her.

But she has to follow him home first. The little girl in her stamps her foot and says a word that had once prompted her mother to take a switch to her calves, one of only three times she can remember being hit. Hurting a child, she thinks, is an unforgivable thing to—

The thought had slipped up on her from behind or she would have sidestepped it, the same way she had tried to sidestep her mother's switch. There are certain things she can't think about because she has no defenses against them: they sweep her sideways, pick her up and spin her around, and when they're through with her and they drop her at last, she usually has no idea where they've taken her. They wipe her memory clean in the same way a fall does: they shine with such a terrible brightness that everything else fades and recedes. She usually has to find something familiar to orient herself.

She can't afford that now. She has to stay where she is. She can't drift; she knows that she drifts. She pats the pocket of her inner shirt, the two tablets reassuring in their predictable solidity, the familiarity of their shape. Out loud, she says, "*Soi* dogs."

Groups of people are separating to pass on both sides of her, some of them turning sideways to squeeze by, unwilling to brush up against her in the thickening throng. She hears music now. From all directions the bright, cold lights of Patpong blink at her, signaling terrible things, glinting off shards of memory she has tried to crush beneath her heel for years and years and years. She doesn't know how long it's been when the door to the small bar opens again and closes behind the man she's supposed to follow.

* * *

COMING OUT OF the bar, back into the heat and the smells and the noise and the neon, he's startled at the intensity of the worry he feels about Campeau.

Unlike most of the Vietnam vets in the bar, who have good days and bad days, it's seemed to Rafferty for years that Campeau has bad days and worse days. For many of the men who were dropped into that meat grinder, and perhaps especially to those who *volunteered*, it had been devastating to realize that the entire enterprise was misconceived, mismanaged, and shrouded in lies, *with everyone from the president down*, as the old song said, *trying to keep it from you*. Vietnam was a clusterfuck on the grandest possible scale. It was an absolutely personal betrayal of the Americans who died there, of the Vietnamese who were killed and maimed there, of the millions of acres of fertile land that were bombed and poisoned into sterility, their only crop the birth defects that scarred the babies of the young women who were exposed to the best that American chemical firms had to offer.

And the vets: the knowledge of what was done to them and what they had done to others had left them with a kind of emotional scar tissue that many of still them carried. It was probably less marked in those who had remained gung ho behind the mission, those who had continued to buy the government's myth of righteous warfare for a humane cause, those for whom the young reporters in Campeau's book were traitors while the rich men in their unwrinkled suits back in Washington were patriots. The gung ho, Rafferty supposed, persuaded themselves that they had fought in, and their friends had been wounded and died in, the pursuit of an objective that was consistent with the shining city on a hill the men in suits were always talking about. For the others, the ones who decided never to go home again, who no longer knew where home was, the war was a brutal, pointless abat-toir, a misguided spasm in the ancient and discredited global shell game of empire. It was a blunt-force con that had destroyed their lives in ways that went as deep inside them as those American poisons had into those once-green fields.

Bob was no fool. He knew that his life and all the other lives sacrificed on both sides of the battlefield had been dropped and stepped on like cigarette butts by men who never gave them a second thought.

And then he'd had his heart, or whatever remained of his heart, broken.

Rafferty made a right and headed toward Soi Kathoey.

He never looked behind him.

14

If I Had a Favorite Aunt

TRIX IS NOT at all what Rafferty had expected. For one thing, in a profession that burns youth as its primary fuel, she's in her mid-forties and seems comfortable with it; she's wearing virtually no makeup beyond heavy, smoky-looking eyeliner that reminds Rafferty of the woman who long served as the White House press secretary, although Trix looks more cheerful than that woman, less likely to whip out an automatic weapon at the first syllable of dissent. She's toting fifteen or twenty contented-looking pounds that seem to have found a place where they can feel secure. In fact, she seems contented with everything: contented and somehow familiar, like a family member you only see at widely spaced intervals but who usually brings a present.

Neither of Rafferty's parents had kept in touch with their brothers and sisters, but the thought that comes to Rafferty as he returns Trix's smile is *she could be my favorite aunt, if I had a favorite aunt.* The homey impression is dented somewhat by the lopsided, vastly complicated sculpture of vaguely country-western hair that's been sprayed into asymmetrical submission on her head. It's been dyed a black so deep that the highlights are blue.

"Bob," Trix says. She gives him an assessing gaze, tilting her head to one side—the side with the majority of the hair on it—and for an instant Rafferty sees it as the beginning of a sight gag in which she topples all the way over, dragged by the sheer weight of the coiffure. Instead, she puts a manicured hand down on the bathtub's porcelain edge, which is where she's sitting, and leans on it. Her nails are a bright corn yellow. The room—small, windowless, and lavender-scented by some ersatz flower that came in a can—contains the tub, a blow-up mattress on the floor, a narrow, rock-hard massage table, and a single metal chair, currently folded flat and leaning against one wall. Trix wears a soft-looking pale yellow terrycloth robe, parted over a crossed leg to display most of a memorable knee. Rafferty is sitting on the massage table.

"You want talk about Bob." Her English pronunciation is excellent.

"I'm going to pay you," he says, reaching for his wallet. "In fact—"

"Talk about customer, not for sale," she says. "Especially some customer."

"I'm a friend of his." Rafferty suddenly finds himself unable to produce any aspect of his relationship with Campeau that might persuade this woman that he and Bob actually like each other. "I know his brother just died—"

Trix says, "He very sad."

"Well, sure—I mean, no." He flips a mental coin and it comes up *candor*. "He thought his brother was a horse's ass."

She gazes at him for a count of three or four and then she laughs. "That just what he say. Zactly. Why you ask about him?"

He runs through a summary of the events of the afternoon, not dramatizing it but not playing it down, either. "So," he concludes, "noise, blood, and he's missing. Looks like some kind of trouble."

"Maybe him fighting himself," Trix says. "Bob not like Bob."

"That was my first thought, too. I might still believe it. But I've known him eight or nine years, and if something has happened, I feel like I should try to figure out where he is."

"Because you are friend."

"He, umm, he named me to some people as the person to call if anything happened to him. So they called me."

She cocks her head again. "He respect you. Maybe not friend, like drinking, laughing, but he respect you."

"I guess." His eyes drift to the bare knee, and he looks away. "I guess that's a kind of friend. But whatever our relationship is, I want to find him, make sure everything is all right."

"And if not all right?"

The very question he's avoided asking himself. "Try to find a way to make it right."

"Yes," Trix says. "Friend."

He sits there, feeling like a pool ball that's just been dropped into the least likely pocket. "I, uhh, I guess what I need to know is who he talks about, if you know anyone he might have gone to if he was in trouble, if he ever mentioned anyone who might help him when he needs help."

"He never think he need help." She uses the yellow nails to drum a little rhythmic figure on the edge of the tub, a noise like hail on a windscreen. Then she reaches over to the head of the tub and turns on the water, full force. He sees for the first time that the showerhead and the faucets are gold colored, perhaps even gold plated. For a minute or so she adjusts the hot and cold controls until she has to yank her hand out of the steaming stream. The room grows warmer and damper. He waits as she continues to play with the faucet, twisting it slowly toward the red. Rafferty feels himself begin to sweat.

"He like it like this," she says, pulling her hand back. "He say he never knew how much he like wet weather, hot weather, until he go to Vietnam and Thailand. He say it slow people down, make them think before they do something, because it too hot here to do something two time. So people not so stupid: do right thing first. He say women here so beautiful because skin never dry out, they not look old same way women in dry country do. How old you think I am?"

This is always a treacherous question. "Thirty-seven, thirty-eight?"

"Sweet mouth," Trix says, and it's not a compliment. She turns the water off and seems quite interested in watching it drain. "I forty-eight, next month I be forty-nine." Delicately, she uses the edge of her left index finger to wipe moisture off the bridge of her nose, first the right side, then the left. "I have three baby. The oldest one is boy. Now him thirty-two, no good. Fight, steal, drink too much. Take my money. Bob boxing him, old man not look strong, my son laughing at him, but Bob win, break my son nose. Tell him he take my money again, Bob kill him."

"Did he ever steal from you again?"

"No, but I give him money. Not tell Bob. I pay for him to fix nose, too, not tell Bob. Money not important. Important is, Bob care about me. Have one daughter, in school for being a nurse. Bob, him help. Help her learn English, help her buy book. She need many, many book. Now she working hospital, still go school but work hospital too."

Rafferty says, "Which hospital?"

She names the one where Rose gave birth.

"Where was your son last night?"

She shrugs. "Him gone from my house now, but I think he never fight with Bob again. Shoot with gun, maybe, but not fight. Anyway, him not Bangkok now. Go Pattaya."

"You said you have three kids."

She passes the edge of the same index finger across her forehead. It's the most elegant reaction to perspiration he's ever seen. "One die. Long time before I come to Bangkok. When I still in village. Die five week old."

Rafferty says, "Oh," but it's actually a response to something that feels like a punch to the gut; he has immediately imagined Rose's devastation if something were to go wrong with the baby—with *Frank*—and the only words he can find are, "I'm so sorry. Boy or girl?"

"Girl. Now, no problem. She come in my dream many time, she say everything okay. Her spirit happy."

"Good." He waits a moment to slow his breathing, and then he says, "My wife's grandmother comes into her dreams. She was the one who said our baby would be a boy."

Trix smiles and nods. Rose's dead grandmother dropping in from time to time is nice, but nothing special. Dream spirits are all over the place.

"I see Bob mainly at a little bar on Patpong One," Rafferty says. "Do you know anywhere else he goes?"

"Sometime him talk about bar in Sukhumvit. Have music, sometime he like."

"I think I know it. Anything else?"

"Expat something."

"Yeah, on Patpong. That's where I see him." He gets up. "Are you sure I can't pay you for your time?"

"Bob my friend."

"Well, thank you. If you hear from him, please tell him I'm looking for him, and let me know that you talked to him." He takes one of his business cards out of his wallet. It's been in there so long the ink sticks to the leather and he has to pry it loose. "My phone number," he says, giving it to her.

"Him have girlfriend one time," Trix says, slipping the card into a pocket of her robe. "Before. Him have broken heart."

"I know."

"Some Thai lady," Trix says, shaking her head. "Some Thai lady no good."

* * *

DOWN IN THE street, he walks for a bit in the general direction of home, considering and then rejecting going to Sukhumvit to check out the new Swizzle Stick, probably the club where Bob had listened to music; the original venue got evicted to make room for God knows what, and he hasn't been to the new location. Unlike Miaow, he can't just order his phone to find it and then lead him, like a docile four-year-old, to his destination. The thought of Miaow brings with it a guilty little prompt: he hasn't called home in a few hours. He stops and pulls out his phone.

"*What?*" she says, sounding like his call has delayed the granting of a lifelong wish.

"Am I interrupting something?"

"Edward and I are on YouTube, watching the old movie of *Pygmalion*. I'm trying to show him Freddy's not just a snooze."

"Good idea, I guess, although I've always thought he was a human Xanax."

"Just the perspective we're looking for." To Edward, she says, "Tell you later."

"Have the troops left?"

"Yeah, and here's a surprise. Mom went with them."

"You're kidding. She took the baby out of the house?"

"No," Miaow says. "She taught the baby how to work the remote, and it's watching a Korean soap opera. It picks better shows than you do."

"*He.* Whatever happened to respect for your elders?"

"Wow," she says. "Maybe we're all old enough to know better? Anyway, Fon said it was time for the kid to see the big city and that if Rose didn't start walking, her legs would fall off."

"I didn't think she was supposed to be—"

"They're *two blocks away.*" There's a voice in the background, Edward's. Miaow says, "Hang on."

Rafferty says, "Hang on, *please*," but he's talking to himself.

"Good idea," Miaow says, but not into the phone. Then she says, "Can you pick up something for us to eat?"

"You're a terrible negotiator. See, when you want something, the thing is to be nice. Maybe even *respectful*."

"Oh, *please*? I'll do anything. I'll listen to your awful music. No, I can't. I've never been that hungry. So here's what I'll do. I'll tell everybody you like the Bee Gees."

In the background, Edward says, "He likes the *Bee Gees*?"

"I have *never* said I liked the—"

"And Linkin Park, and—"

"How do you even *know* about Linkin Park?"

"—and ABBA. And Maroon 5."

Rafferty says, "I was just talking about Maroon—you wouldn't dare."

"*Som tam*," Miaow says. "Edward is going to learn to like *som tam* if it kills him."

"You know, you and Edward have legs, same as me. There are restaurants all over—"

"Yeah, but we're *working*. We can't watch the movie in a restaurant."

"Sure, you can."

"It's too embarrassing," she says. "People would hear how loudly I breathe when Leslie Howard comes on. And we'd have to pay."

"Well, hell. Wait a minute. I need to see where I am. *Som tam*, right?" He makes a slow turn, realizing he's already passed the sidewalk food cart that makes the best in the neighborhood and, in a tardy spurt of resolve, decides not to go back. At the edge of his vision, he sees someone in white step aside and into a doorway, but there's the usual early evening sidewalk glut, and he doesn't think about it. There's a restaurant coming up that's aggressively second-rate but on the way to the apartment. Miaow might make a face, but Edward won't know the difference; he doesn't like *som tam* anyway. Rose avoids the restaurant, but she's not home, so he decides that Miaow is outvoted and slips the phone back into his pocket; second-rate *som tam* is better than none. He has to cross the street to get to the restaurant, so he looks in both directions, catching another glimpse of the person in white, and then he mentally crosses himself and dives into the traffic.

15

I Know Where You Are

HER HEAD IS ringing, high, tinny, electrical sounds, like the music made by a child's cheap toy. It comes from all directions, and it's all she can hear. It's there even when she covers her ears. The world beneath her feet seems to be rising and falling in waves so pronounced and so steep that she has to wrap a hand around the railing beside the driveway and force her eyes wide, wide open to keep from throwing up.

She's already thrown up once, because of what the Sour Man had said after she called to report that she'd followed the man home to his apartment with its doorman, and now she's fighting to keep from vomiting again. She *already* stinks, she's *already* filthy, and now she's come up against the only thing in the world that has the force to wake her up at night, gasping for breath, even after the pipe and the dope have wrung her out, exhausted her.

All she wants to do is turn and run, not to the park or any where she's ever been before, not anywhere where anyone knows her or will even see her, not anywhere that reminds her of who she is. Of what she is. Someplace empty and quiet, just her and the sky and a soft place where she can lie down and die. As she should have done years ago.

But.

But she can't.

But.

He's *there*, somewhere where he can see her. He'd proved it when she called him; he'd said, "I know where you are. I can see you." He'd told her to hold up one arm, and she'd raised the right, and he'd identified it. He made her do it three more times until there could be no doubt: if she runs, he'll see her. And he'll catch her. She's big and slow, he's small and wiry and fast.

Had he followed her? Or had he been waiting, had he already *known* where . . .

That's too complicated. Her head is pounding, the high sounds have turned into the squeals of tiny pigs, into insect songs. She waves away, like smoke, the certainty that he'd already known where the man lives; the drugstore from which she'd called him was just around the corner. Still, that's nothing, compared to the rest of it, just something to think about later. In the meantime.

In the meantime.

Is it that he doesn't want anyone to see them together, doesn't want anyone to see that she's had help finding the place? But why?

The answer takes its time coming, but when it arrives she knows it's right. Because something bad is going to happen. The kind of thing people ask questions about later.

But it's not as though she has a *choice*. She *has* to go up there. And what could be worse than the way things are now?

She looks at her palm again, at the words she'd written on it only a few minutes earlier, so she'd remember what the Sour Man said. He told her he'd kill her if she forgot, and she used the pen she'd found to write them down.

Two sums of money, both large, one for her and one for him, the word *garage*, an apartment number, and a name. And the word *knife*. The money was what she'd get if she did what she was told, and the knife was what she'd get if she didn't.

But she *couldn't*.

But she has to.

An apartment number, *the* apartment number. On the eighth floor.

The apartment number.

For a light-headed moment, she thinks she'll turn and run, let him catch her, let him kill her. Her fingers have cramped around the railing she's been clinging to while the earth heaved and shuddered beneath her. She's working to loosen her fingers when bright, bright light sweeps over her. She takes an involuntary step back, her arm, with its fingers still clinging to the rail, goes taut like a rope, and she hears the car and watches it go by, angling down the driveway on the other side of the rail as a huge metal door rackets itself open with a squeal that tells her that the door needs to be oiled. She once lived in a house where people seemed to listen all the time, just so they could get angry when she made noise, and she had learned to oil hinges.

And it seems to her that years of her life have come down to this squealing moment, to this choice: which way to run—in, behind the car, or away, to—to what? Into the arms of the Sour Man, into the pincers of his fingernails? Or those dogs?

She doesn't, she tells herself, really believe in that cage full of dogs.

But.

But she has to go in, no matter what.

She ducks beneath the handrail, her back emitting a startled cramp of protest, and then she windmills her arms, unprepared for the slope of the driveway—steeper than it looks—and, as the door begins to rumble its way back down, she leans forward, against the pull of her back, to slip beneath it. Ahead of her, she sees the car's red brake lights brighten and die as it comes to a stop, and she ducks behind the car nearest to her.

She's panting as though she's run a mile, and it feels like something is literally swelling toward explosion in the center of her chest. She has a vision of herself dissolving into tiny pieces and then ballooning outward with the force of the blast, and when it doesn't happen she finds herself wishing that it had. There's a ragged sound in her ears. It takes her a moment to identify it as her own breathing.

A woman laughs, the melody echoing off the hard surfaces of the garage. A car door chunks closed, a sound so solid that, for a moment, it offers her a kind of comfort. There are solid things in the world; it's not *all* wisps of memory and fear and regret and street music.

Without being aware she's doing it, she pats the envelope in her pocket: *one, two*. Maybe later tonight, when this is finished, but then it seems to be inescapably true that this will never be finished. She has no idea how long she has hung suspended there, dangling from that thought like someone at the end of a rope, when she hears a muffled bell and recognizes it: the elevator, announcing its arrival on a distant floor. It will be empty now. Closing her eyes, she feels her way around the car and then, with her eyes half-closed and her head down so she can see only her feet and a bit of the concrete directly ahead of them, she listens to her shoes rasp as she drags them across the hard gray floor toward the elevator. Toward the eighth floor.

16

The Doorbell

THE LOOK MIAOW gives him when she sees the name on the takeout bag in his hand almost makes risking his life in traffic worthwhile. "It's all right," he says, coming into the living room. "Don't get up. This isn't as heavy as it looks."

"Good," she says. "Then you can take it back."

"Any word from your mom?" At the counter, he starts removing the food containers from the bag and laying them out in a finicky order that he thinks will irritate Miaow. He wishes he had bought some flowers. It would have been nice for Rose to find them in her room when she gets back. Why does he always think of these things too late?

"She's *eating*," Miaow says. "Probably someplace good."

"Well, you know, it's just that it's the first time she and the baby—"

"*And* the whole platoon," Miaow says. "She's got the squad with her. And it's *two blocks*. She'll be fine."

"Worrying is part of my job description."

"Mr. Rafferty," Edward says. "Do you think Leslie Howard is hot?"

"Aaahh. I'm more of an Errol Flynn man myself."

"Errol who?"

"Flynn, but don't let it bother you. He's been under the sod since the last ice age. Hope you're hungry, there's a lot of *som tam*."

Edward says, "Oh."

"It's not that he's *hot*," Miaow says. "It's his voice."

"Ahem," Edward says, pronouncing it as it's spelled. "Last time, it was his nose."

"His nose *and* his voice," Miaow says.

"The nose plays a very important role in the production of the voice," Rafferty says. "I can see where you'd get them mixed up."

Edward laughs but cuts it off instantly. "His *nose*," he says, and then he laughs again.

Rafferty says, "Give her a break. It's a very distinctive—"

The doorbell rings.

"She's got a key," Miaow says.

"Maybe the troops dropped her off," Rafferty says. "She's got a baby in her arms, remember?"

"Like Fon would let her come upstairs alone," Miaow says. "Like I'm the only one in the world who can possibly open the door." The bell rings again. "Okay, okay, *okay*."

Rafferty is at the counter laying out utensils and napkins when he hears someone say something that might be, "Miaow," and then he hears Miaow say, "What? Who—who . . ." and then scream, shrill enough to etch glass. The scream turns into a stream of words, "Go away go away go *away*," and the front door slams. Edward says, "Miaow, what's the—" and then Miaow's *bedroom* door slams, so hard he thinks he can feel the floor shake, and from the other side of the door, Miaow is shouting, "Go away, go away, *go away*." He charges into the living room, pushing past Edward, who's shifting from foot to foot, the image of someone who has no idea what to do, and he opens the front door to see a filthy, ragged woman collapsed against the opposite wall, crying her heart out.

Part Two
IT'S A GIRL

17

Perfect

THE CHILD DID not want to come into the world. Perhaps, Hom thought—much later—her daughter had known what was in store for her.

Hom had never given birth, but the process didn't frighten her; it was familiar enough. Her older sisters had borne four children among them, one of them in a hospital many kilometers from their village and three at home. She had seen and heard pain and tears and some screams, but at the end of it all, there was a new soul slipping through the doorway into the world, slick and glistening and howling in protest. All those babies were children now, with no memory of their first appearance in life.

But unlike her sisters, who had been surrounded by friends and relatives who could soften the pain and sometimes perilous passage of birth with familiar faces, reassuring words, and soft, knowing hands, Hom had been forced to abandon her village, leaving behind her friends and her mother and sisters because her mother-in-law had wanted Hom to stay in *her* village, many kilometers away, to contribute to the harvest and the house; to work, it sometimes seemed to Hom, like an animal in a harness. But her sisters, after huddling together out of her hearing, had joined forces, doing what they could to prepare her for the experience and to put things to her in the most reassuring light. They'd even told her to be grateful for all the work her mother-in-law heaped on her because it was important to be active before the child was born, to walk and to work and move as much as possible. This, they said, would make it easier for the child to settle into the womb in the best position, with its head—the heaviest part of it—facing downward. Babies who were born head-first, they said, were the easiest to deliver, and they got their first breath of air early in their passage. In this position, too, it was less likely that the child would become entangled in its cord. Children born in other positions were more likely to have the cord wrap itself around them, sometimes around the neck.

There were malicious forces in places where children were born, including *mae kamlerd*, the spirits of the baby's earlier mothers, which might want to reclaim their child; and there was the delicate matter of the first appearance of a new *khwan*, a soul, just recently assigned to the tiny, squalling body. This was a dangerous moment that could draw ghosts, most of them malicious. The idea that these uncontrollable entities might play a role in what happened during her child's birth made Hom more careful about the things she *could* control, such as helping make sure the baby was in the best position when the time came.

So she had worked as tirelessly and as cheerfully as possible, even though she grew weary as the pregnancy wore on, and her mother-in-law was not an agreeable person. Indeed, her mother-in-law seemed to feel that the entire pregnancy was a ruse to get Hom out of some of the heaviest chores, and as Hom thickened and slowed, the grumbling increased. In bed at night, she had heard her mother-in-law complaining to her son that the woman he married was lazy and weak-willed and that he should have known better than to choose the youngest daughter in a family. They were always pampered, babied too long, as a mother tried to hold on to her last child, tried to feel essential to her daughter's life for a few extra years.

"You just wait," the old lady had said, "she's going to behave like she's the first woman who ever gave birth. She'll make it seem like the most difficult pregnancy in history."

And, in fact, despite all the work that had been demanded of her, Hom was already worried about the child's position. Her oldest sister, one of whose two children had arrived through a very difficult delivery indeed, had showed her how to get a feeling for how and where the baby was positioned in the womb. Where did it kick? If she felt it near her ribs, that meant its head was down and its feet were up, and everything was fine. If she felt the kicks much lower, then she should press against her belly—yes, it would hurt, and if it hurt too much, she should get a midwife to do it for her—trying to feel the hardest part of the baby, the head. *You want the head to be the lowest part of the baby,* she said repeatedly. If it's not there at first, don't worry: babies move around in the womb and most of them will eventually take the right position, the position of someone falling headfirst into a pool, arms at her sides.

But with her sisters miles away, Hom hadn't been sure her assessment—that the child's head felt too high—was correct, and when she asked her mother-in-law to help her confirm the baby's position she'd been told to stop being silly: there was work to do. Babies, she was told, moved around all the time, more, in fact, than Hom did, and there were chores still undone from yesterday.

But her dreams at night were full of babies who wouldn't come at all or who, when they finally emerged and peeked at her over the edge of her pubis, had sly, pale eyes full of a bright, feverish malice. In the worst of the dreams, the baby came out and grew to an enormous size, blocking all the windows and doors, and then slowly turned to look at her and bared long, curved white teeth.

And when, in the waking world, her water broke at last and she was finally put onto a wicker cot, in a room that had tools stored in it, and told to try to keep quiet, her fears proved well-founded: the baby wouldn't come.

The labor went on for hours, racking pains and tooth-grinding spasms as her body tried to push the child out. It went on until even her husband became frightened and suggested getting a midwife from a neighboring village or driving Hom to the nearest hospital. But her husband's mother mocked both notions and kept repeating that babies knew how to be born, that they'd been doing it for centuries, and that she'd had her first one squatting on the footpath between the rice paddies, cut the cord with a penknife, washed the child in the paddy, and gone back to work. Women these days, she said, were weak.

In the end a woman from the village who could endure Hom's cries no longer pushed her way in and ordered Hom's mother-in-law out of the room. Kneading Hom's belly like bread dough, she said, "How long since the last contraction?" and when Hom said she had no idea, the woman said, "Well tell me when you feel one starting." Instantly one seized her and made her gasp, and as she pushed against something inside her that felt bigger and harder and heavier than the room they were in, the woman felt her belly again, not gently, and sat back and said, "It's not sideways. It's bottom-first. If it were sideways we'd have to take you to have a doctor open you to take the baby out, but this way, I think you can do it." She looked at Hom, who was completely lost in a wave of pain, leaned in, and said, "Are you listening to me?"

Hom gasped a yes. "Is this bad?"

"It's not exactly what you want. It's better if it's headfirst, because bottom-first, like your baby is, makes the child thicker, harder to push out. But I've seen babies born this way. One of my sisters' children said hello to the world with her rear end. But here's the thing: you're going to have to help, no lying back and letting the baby do the work. And your mother-in-law and your husband are going to have to help, too. Is that all right with you?"

She had a hard time picturing them helping, but she said, "If it's good for the baby."

"Fine. Just hold still for a minute or two. Push when you feel like you should. Scream if you have to."

Several minutes later, Hom was sitting up, her back against a thin padded mattress, now folded four layers thick, and her mother-in-law was grumbling about the impossibility of washing out the stains and the cost of replacing it. Her husband had hung two lengths of rope from the ceiling beams and tied a loop in the ends that hung just above Hom's head, and then he'd let the village woman position him on the other side of the folded mattress so Hom would have something solid to lean on. When he was settled, the woman, whose name was Amarin, told Hom to bring her knees up to her chest and to hold on to the ropes, lean back against her husband, and push as hard as she could when she felt the next contraction.

By then Hom was covered in sweat and smelled, even to herself, like someone who hadn't bathed in weeks. Her mother-in-law had taken a seat in the doorway, as close to being outside the room as she could while technically being inside, and she looked on disapprovingly as though she planned to write a critical report about the proceedings.

Rising up from deep, deep inside Hom came something that filled her chest and stopped there and then slowly unknotted itself and emerged as a deep, shuddering "*Oohhhhhhh,*" and she collapsed backward against the cushion and her husband's knees, discovering that pulling on the ropes actually *did* lessen the pain. Amarin, her face inches from Hom's pubis, said, "It's going to be fine, you can do this, we can all do it together," but then the pain waned and Hom lay back, gasping, against the firmness of her husband's knees. Much to her surprise, he passed a palm gently across her forehead, wiping away sweat. He asked his mother for a towel, and she got up to get one, leaving the door open behind her.

Like a tide coming back in, the pain reasserted itself, planted a flag in her cervix, and declared itself fully present, and this time the feeling was *different*, alien, something immense passing itself through her pelvis, and she felt her left hip pop out of its socket, but there was no time to think about that because suddenly all of Thailand was tunneling through her from inside, trying to get out, and she pushed down again, and Amarin put her face back *right there*, close enough to see everything, and her mother-in-law came into the room, towel in hand, as the pain simply tore Hom in half, and when the red fuzz that was filling her eyes dissolved, she felt the backs of Amarin's hands pushing her legs even farther apart, and she was saying, "Come on, darling, it's butt-first but it—come *on*, come the rest of the way, come on the rest—" and then Amarin was laughing and wiping her face with her forearm, and Hom's husband and mother-in-law were laughing too, and Amarin said, "She pooped in my face, the little devil, she—she—it's a girl, it's a girl, it's a *girl*. And she's *perfect*."

18

Banana Split

HE'D HAULED THE old woman out of the building as quickly as he could, taking the stairs because he was terrified the elevator doors would open and there would be Rose and Fon and the baby. In the end, he avoids the lobby completely, going all the way down to the garage, and then out to the only place he can think of to take her: the Baskin-Robbins shop where he'd taught the kid behind the counter not to call it Chocolate Mouse. The boy owed him, he figures, and he is certain that no real restaurant will allow her through the door, much less show her to a booth.

The two of them walk without speaking, the silence broken only when she sniffled or blew her nose on the inside of her big, loose white dress. She'd been weeping full-out on the stairs, so this is an improvement; he's never known how to talk to a weeping woman. Still, a talk—however unprepared for it he might be—is obviously unavoidable, and the ice cream parlor is at least neutral territory, and far enough away to give him a little time to attempt to organize his thoughts.

Since she's been studying the pavement as though it were some treacherous alien terrain, full of obstacles and knee-breakers, he's had lots of opportunity to sneak glances at her, to try to peel back the years and the layers of clothes and the dirt and the damage to see whether he can find Miaow in her somewhere. The one thing he has identified is so ephemeral he almost dismisses it: the angle of her neck as she scans the sidewalk ahead. When Miaow first came to live with them, she had kept her face lowered, unwilling to meet people's eyes. He'd been unsure whether it was shyness, shame, or submission, and ultimately decided it was all three, but that the submission was a tactic intended to mislead, because once he got to know her he realized that she was as stubborn as a bloodstain. Looking at the old woman, he halfway believes he sees some kind of connective tissue in this echo, but when she lifts her head, it vanishes. And this is impossibly important, because obviously the first order of business is to verify who she actually is.

One improbability—that someone so old could actually be Miaow's mother—has been rubbed away, one furtive glance at a time. Her stoop, he realizes, is at least partly protective, an attempt to be less conspicuous, to present a smaller target, and, perhaps, to shield from attack the vital organs in her abdomen. Take away the bent back, and it's not difficult to see that her skin might be prematurely wrinkled from endless exposure to the sun, and that the wild swarm of gray hair got its texture from an absolute lack of care and its color from genetics; she's not as old as the hair makes her appear to be. He wonders for a moment whether Miaow will be gray when she's in her late thirties or early forties, or however old the woman actually is.

Halfway to their destination, they pass a sidewalk vendor on Silom who is selling cheap, thin, semitransparent plastic raincoats in anticipation of the wet season. They are ugly but clean, and he buys one in an enervated shade of yellow, the only color she will accept. With it pulled over her clothes and buttoned in place, she's still bulky and messy, and there is nothing he can do about her hair, but at least the coat covers the multiple layers of clothing, and mutes the stains spattered across the outermost layer like a map of countries no one in his right mind would ever visit.

As he pushes the door open, the kid glances up, grins, and sings out, "Chocolate Moose," but then he sees the woman behind Rafferty, and the smile disappears. Before he can protest, Rafferty says, "We need to sit in the back, *all* the way in the back, and talk for a little while. It's important." He pushes a folded five-hundred-baht bill across the counter, and the kid makes it vanish, but he still looks worried.

"If my boss come in," he says, "you tell him I try stop you."

"Do you think he'll come in?"

"No. But I not lucky boy."

"Maybe tonight you will be. Maybe I'll give you some more money."

"Okay. What you want?"

"I don't care. Something chocolate." To the bulky woman, he says, "What about you?"

"Banana split?" she says, and it sounds like a prayer. She looks up at him, her eyes as big as dinner plates, but are they *Miaow's* eyes? "Can I have banana split?"

"Sure."

"*Two* banana?" From her tone, it might be the key to the treasure room.

"Have four, I don't care."

"Two," she says. She has lowered her gaze to the rows of ice cream behind the glass. Her cheeks shine with perspiration, and he realizes, with a tug of guilt, that the raincoat might as well be a portable steam room, and yet she's said nothing, might, in fact, be completely unaware of it. Without looking up at him, she says, "I like banana."

"Good," he says, feeling like an idiot.

"How many scoop for you?" the kid asks him.

"Three, and give her an extra, too."

The kid shakes his head. "Two banana and extra scoop, cannot. Bowl too small."

"Well," Rafferty says, "if that turns out to be the evening's biggest problem, I'll be very surprised."

"Okay," the kid says, with a shrug that has a lot of fatalism behind it, and at that moment, Rafferty's phone rings. He looks at it, fails to recognize the number, and says to the woman, "Come on, let's get out of this guy's way. We can sit back there." He leads her up a couple of steps to a raised area at the rear of the shop and then to a table in the far right corner, partly concealed from the street by the signs flogging the month's special flavors. As she sits, he puts the phone to his ear and says, "Hello?"

"Mr. Rafferty?" A woman's voice.

"You got him. I mean, this is he."

"My, my, *grammar*. I'm Jillian Trelawney, Mr. Campeau's neighbor? The landlady said you might want to talk to me." Definitely an Aussie, vowels that sounded like they were being wrung out by hand.

"And I do," he says, pushing his chair back under the table as the old woman pulls hers up to it. To her, he says, "Just a minute, please," and takes the phone back through the shop and out onto the sidewalk.

"Bad time?" Jillian Trelawney says.

"I'm in the middle of something, but, ummmm . . . yeah, right, sorry. Go ahead."

"Well, I'm not sure how much Ratana, oh, sorry, I mean my landlady, told you, but I don't really know your friend—Bob, isn't it?—I don't know him very well at all, just someone to nod to; he's been, if nothing else, *quiet* most of the time I've been living there. But last night, well, I have to admit that it frightened me. I'm not exactly *compressing* this, am I?"

"No, but it's fine. I'm listening."

"Well, truth be told, I know him a bit better than *that*. When I first got here, and the heat felt like it hated me *personally*, my air-con went out, and that's when it would, isn't it? It wouldn't wait until I was *acclimated*—"

"I've been here nine or ten years now, and I'm nowhere near—"

"Yes, I hear people say that, but I refuse to give up hope. *So*," she says, nattering like a maniac, "Bob bumped into me in the hall—he was out in the morning for a change—and he asked how I was, and I blathered on about the air-con, and he said he could take a look at it. *Well*. Normally, I wouldn't let a perfect stranger, or even a *relative* stranger, into my place, but Ratana *had* said kind things about him, and I thought, well, when if not now, I mean this *is* supposed to be an adventure and he's practically elderly, even if there is something—what's the word?—*raffish* about him."

"He'd love to know you think he's raffish." In the shop, the boy behind the counter is layering what looks like a foot of whipped cream on a banana split and the old lady is sitting back, shoulders slumped, gazing without interest at the top of the table, looking as suspended as someone trapped in amber. Then she raises a hand and used the back of it to scrub at the corners of her eyes.

"So he came in and looked at it, fiddled with something or other, nodded a few times, and said my gezornenstat was all frammelled—probably not his *exact* words, but something impenetrable like that; he said it was a piece of piss to fix, dead easy, and that he had just the thing in his flat and he'd zip right over and fetch it."

"And he did?"

"Well, *yes*, to cut it short just when I was getting into full swing, he did. And half an hour later, the room was miraculously below body temperature and I asked if I could pay him, and he said no, we were *neighbors*, and what were neighbors for? So a few days after that I baked him a little something or other and, truth be told, it was just a *teensy* bit burned, but he quite manfully overlooked that and even returned the dish, conspicuously empty. Am

I talking too much? You have no idea what a thrill it is for me to be speaking English to someone who's not learning it from me."

"No. This is a side of Bob I haven't seen much of."

"Well, yes, he's very much the wounded mystery man, isn't he?"

"Yeah, I guess he is."

"Not the cheeriest joker in the deck, but solid. So, last night—was it really just last night?"

"Far as I know. You're the one who heard it."

A movement from inside the shop draws his eye: the boy, holding up a monstrous banana split and miming carrying it up to the old lady, struggling beneath its weight, and then looking at him with his eyebrows raised. Rafferty nods, and the boy bustles around the counter toward her.

"Well, first I heard a scream of rage or terror or pain, very King-Lear-on-the-heath, just, you know, with a lifetime of *something* that had been all bottled up behind it. And then a kind of high, thin whimpering, could have been him or someone else, I couldn't—"

"Could it have been a woman?"

"Could have been a whooping crane, but whatever it was, it was at the far, far edge of *something*, and then a huge *bang* as an object, or maybe a person, hit the wall between his living room and mine. Knocked down a picture on my side, that's how hard it hit, but it was something I never should have hung in the first place, the very definition of a momentary enthusiasm. And I went all quiet—I mean, I was already quiet, I'd been asleep, but I got even quieter, and then I heard *weeping*. Male or female, I don't know, just a high abandoned sound, wind through leafless trees, a broken heart in the middle of the night. And then *that* stopped, and I just sat there and counted my goosebumps and listened."

"For how long?"

"Four minutes? Five? Time goes all gummy when I'm frightened."

"And you heard what?"

"Nothing much. A little mumbling, then a door slamming, not the front door, so it had to be the bathroom door, these flats are not rich in doors. And then, for a long time, nothing. So I girded my loins, which I'm sure doesn't mean what I think it means—"

"It means to get ready for battle, if you were an ancient Hebrew who wore a floor-length robe and didn't want to trip over your own hem as you were about to brain a Hittite. So they tucked them up—"

"If you're going to pick an enemy of the Hebrews, I've always liked the Girgashites. It's a name with a lot of growl built right into it. You just say, 'I'm a Girgashite,' you've already got a head start. Just make the announcement and watch your enemy flee across the plain."

"So you waited a minute or two and then you girded your loins and . . ."

"Went and knocked."

"And?"

"No answer. I knocked again and said, 'Mr. Campeau? Mr. Campeau, are you all right?' Still no answer. So I stood there for a few minutes, I suppose you could say indecisively, but the truth was that I was terrified and it actually took quite a lot of decisiveness just to stay there. There was nothing, no reply or gunshots or bumps in the night, and after a little while I went back to bed but I didn't sleep until it was almost light. At some point I *think* I heard his door open and close, but I can't be sure. In the morning I knocked again, and then I called Ratana and went to work."

"Does anything else occur to you?"

"Not really, no. If anything, I think I've been overly complete."

"Well, thank you. I'll let you know what I learn, if I learn anything. If he comes home, or if you hear anything at all in that apartment, call me immediately, okay?"

"Promise. Maybe we could meet up sometime. I'll buy you a coldie—sorry, a beer—and I could speak English to someone who understands it."

"Absolutely," Rafferty says. "Soon. Bye." He pockets the phone, feeling like someone from Los Angeles, the global capital of insincere commitments, and then he draws several deep breaths, and goes inside to talk with his guest.

THE BANANA PART of the banana split is gone, and she seems only now to be getting around to the ice cream. His own ice cream, three random variations on the theme of chocolate, is midway down the road to soup, and he's grateful to be able to simulate a little urgency and start spooning it up before he has to begin the conversation. He works it until it feels like a dodge, and then he says, "So. What's your name?"

She says to the sundae, "Hom."

"I'm Poke. Tell me why you knocked on our door."

She looks at him, seemingly bewildered. "*Miaow*."

"And you're Miaow's . . . "

"*Ma*ma," the old woman says, as though it were too obvious to require an answer. "You hear. She *know* me when she see me."

"Well," he says, in Thai, "she didn't exactly say, 'Hi, Mom.'"

She blots her eyes again, using the sides of her index fingers, and replies in Thai. "She was surprised. And . . . and she's angry at me."

"But you think she recognized you."

"Ask her."

"I will." He decides to back off a little. He's operating on assumptions, and he has almost no actual information. Miaow has steadfastly declined to talk about her birth family. "But if she did recognize you, well, it kind of surprises me. That she would, I mean. She was three when—"

"Four," she says, holding up the requisite number of fingers. "Almost five."

Rafferty says, "Aha." Miaow's real age has been a subject of considerable speculation between him and Rose for years, and this information diverts him. "What's her birthday?"

"Twenty-two," she says in Thai. "Twenty-two *Preut sa pa kom.*"

"That's May. Wow, she's a *Gemini?*" Publicly, Rafferty has always scoffed at astrology but that hasn't kept him from classifying Miaow as one of the earth-ruling signs such as Cancer, shared by Alexander the Great and Julius Caesar. Or maybe a Leo, like Genghis Khan. From time to time he catches sight of a little bit of Genghis Khan in Miaow.

"Gemini is the two babies, right?" the woman says in Thai, and then nods. "Yes, Gemini."

"So," he says, "just to focus on this for a moment, she was four when you, um, saw her last, and she was with that gang for three years, maybe a little more, and she's been with us for eight, plus a few months. Wow, that means she's—" He pauses for a second; math is not his strong suit.

"Fifteen," she says in Thai at the same time he says it in English, and then they do it again, each swapping languages for the other's convenience, and he finds himself returning her smile.

But a smile, he thinks, can be misinterpreted, so he retreats from the moment, looks away, and says, "We've been wondering."

"But if you not know birthday," she says in English, "how you can give her happy birthday?"

"Oh," he says, "right. Every New Year we let her choose a date for her birthday. A different day every year. Last year she chose two dates, and told one of them to me and the other to her"—he comes to a screeching halt and says, "to my wife."

The old woman bares a few yellow teeth in a sudden smile. "Yes," she says, nodding. "This is Miaow." And then it's as though she hears what he'd said, and her eyes drop to the table, where she seems to be studying the ruins of her sundae. She unloads a sigh that feels like it will never end and, in English, she says, "Now *she* is mama for Miaow. Your wife."

"Yes," Rafferty says, "yes, she is. For eight years now." But it's an automatic reply; the brief smile she had given him had brought Miaow to mind so strongly and clearly that he might as well have said her name aloud. "But still," he says, fumbling for his point, "you can see why I was surprised you thought she recognized you."

"Baby," she says, "always know her . . ." She breaks off, staring at her plate. "Can I have one more banana?"

"Sure. Just tell him."

"Him . . . him not . . ." She doesn't look up.

"Right, okay." He calls out to the boy for another banana. The boy doesn't seem delighted, but he goes to work.

"All right," he says in English, and then he switches to Thai. "Before we can go any further, I need to know some things." Her eyes come quickly up to him and then drop to the table again. "Assuming you're who you say you are, why did you"—he has no idea what the Thai is for *abandon*—"leave her—leave her alone?"

"Husband make me," she says in English. "Him working, I—I—I working." She licks her lips as he notes the stammer before the statement that she'd been working. "But, but get fired, him and me, we lose our—our room. Him say we . . . we cannot . . . not have money, not . . . have place to live. Not have"—she swallows loudly—"not have . . . nothing . . . for baby."

Out of the corner of his eye, Rafferty sees the boy coming down the length of the counter, carrying a small dish with a banana on it. Rafferty raises an eyebrow and the boy stops dead and then backs up and buries the banana in whipped cream. Then, still looking at Rafferty, he dusts the snowdrifts of whipped cream with powdered chocolate, sighs, and picks up the dish again.

"So," Rafferty says, "you got rid of her."

Her eyes snap up to his, wide and angry. "Not," she says. "Not *get rid* of her. I . . . I wait, I looking where she cannot see me. I looking to see where she—"

"Let me take this in my own order," he says in Thai, speaking over her. "There are things I need to be sure of."

She lowers her head. The gesture is so abject he's instantly ashamed of himself. "Please," he says, "please tell me *how* you left her and *where* you left her." This is information Miaow had never volunteered to him or Rose; her shame at having been wadded up and tossed onto the sidewalk was too deep for her to share with them.

"We want to . . . We want to . . ." She blows out a quart of air and switches to Thai. "We wanted her to be somewhere people would see her. I wanted someone to see her. To *help* her."

"So you put her where?" Although he's seen shimmers of Miaow in her, *everything* depends on her answer to this question.

"A bus bench."

A sudden tight flicker of anger distracts him and sends him in a direction he'd planned to avoid. "And you *tied* her to it."

Whether it's his tone or his words, her reaction startles him. She plants both of her thick, damaged hands on the table, fingers spread so wide that he thinks she might be about to stand up. But she doesn't, and she leaves the hands where they are even when the boy slides the banana, now shrouded in whipped cream and dappled with chocolate, between them. When she raises her eyes to his, there is rage in them. "*Traffic.*" She snaps the word, in Thai, as though she wishes it were solid so she could throw it at his head. "I didn't want her to run into *traffic*. She was still . . . still a baby." And then the rage is gone and she's crying again, and Rafferty feels like kicking himself. That explanation for the twine that tied her to the bench has never occurred to him, and he's ashamed. He's thought for years that it was simply a heartless convenience, to keep her from following them.

As though she's reading his mind, she says, still in Thai, "I could have told her to wait for a few minutes for us to come back, long enough for us to run away, and she would have. She was a *good girl*, she always did what . . . But then what? Sooner or later she would have tried to come after us, she would have run . . . she could have—"

"All right," he says, holding up a hand. It's still horrific, the act of abandoning a child, but ever since he overheard Miaow tell the story to a girl her own age, he's been fixated on the twine. It's been the detail that allowed him to focus on anger, an emotion he can handle, rather than heartbreak. He has no skill with heartbreak. She sniffles and wipes her eyes again. He forces himself to say, "I'm sorry."

In English, she says, "I give her *candy*," and then she simply falls apart, crying helplessly, both hands over her face. Rafferty gets up and flees to the counter and says, "Napkins," and when he's got four or five of them he goes back to the table and sits down. He reaches over and puts a hand on her shoulder.

"She told us about the candy," he says, as she scrubs at her face and blows her nose. At a loss, he withdraws his hand and says, "Eat your banana."

"She *remembers* the candy?" She's blotting her eyes with the heels of her hands.

"She remembers everything. She said it lasted a long time."

"One hour. Maybe two."

"She said it felt longer."

"I know," she says, and then she's weeping again. "Long time, not two hours, long time."

The boy behind the counter looks distressed. He says, "Another banana?"

"No," Rafferty says. To Hom, he says, "Why don't you go to the bathroom? Wash your face, take a little time."

She says fiercely, "I *watching*. I watch until boy come. Cut string, take her. She cannot see me, but I watching. When the boy take her, I follow." She pulls the plastic raincoat open, lifts one of her blouses and scrubs her face with it, then blows her nose into it. The boy's eyebrows are practically at his hairline. He grabs a thick wad of napkins and comes out from behind the counter as the door swings open to admit a Western man with two heavily made-up Patpong women. The boy glances back, says, "Moment," and hurries up the three steps that lead to their table, bearing the napkins in two hands like an offering. "Here," the boy says in Thai, "Here, here, here. Please take these, please."

"Hey," the man calls, "you got salted caramel?"

"One minute," the boy says.

"You can answer from there," the man says. "Don't you even know which—"

Rafferty raises his voice as Hom scours her face with the napkins. "There's no fucking salted caramel, Jack," he says. "Everything else in the world, but no—"

"*Poke*," one of the women says, and he recognizes her: she's been in the apartment a couple of times since the baby was born. Denise or some other Anglo name, pulled out of an old movie or, perhaps, a hat. "Why you're not home?"

The Western man, who has thinning hair drawn back in a dry, autumnal-looking ponytail, gives Rafferty an appraising once-over and says to maybe-Denise, "You *know* this guy?"

"Him marry my friend," maybe-Denise says. "Her have baby now."

Around the wad of napkins, her eyes enormous, Hom says, "You have a *baby?*"

"Your friend pretty?" Ponytail says to maybe-Denise. He's still aiming the dread Stare of Dominance at Poke.

"Number one," says maybe-Denise. "Number one lady in Pat-pong."

"Long time ago," Rafferty says.

"Wow," the Western man says, "you *married* one of these?"

"I don't actually think of her as *one of these*," Rafferty says, feeling his face heat up. "I don't think of *any* of them as *one of these*."

Hom whispers "*You have baby?*" as Ponytail takes a step toward Poke, and the boy cuts between them, saying, "I make ice cream, have ice cream too much, too much. Maybe have what you want. *What* you want?"

Ponytail holds Rafferty's gaze just long enough to feel manly and says, "Salted caramel."

"Not have," the boy says promptly. "Have chocolate, have vanilla, have some kind cherry, have chocolate *moooooose*, have—"

"Shit," Ponytail says, and Rafferty realizes, a bit late, that the man is drunk. Rafferty pushes the table back and gets up, and Hom watches him, looking anxious.

"How about this?" Rafferty says. "How about I buy a double for all of you, since you're with my wife's friend Denise here." He has crossed his fingers for luck as he says the name, and she catches his eye and smiles, putting her head down to hide it from Ponytail. "My pleasure, okay? One American to another."

"I wan' strawberry," Denise says, tugging at Ponytail's sleeve. "*Two* strawberry."

The other woman says, "Chocolate chip. Can I have sprinkle on it?"

Rafferty feels the boy behind the counter looking to him, waiting for a decision. "Sure," he says. To the man, he says, "And what about you?"

"I wanted salted caramel," the man says. He's sulking.

"And I wanted to play professional basketball," Rafferty says, "but look at me. Barely tall enough for miniature golf. Life, it's just one disappointment after another. On the other hand, looks like you've got a nice evening lined up."

"Yeah," the man says, sounding like someone who's having second thoughts. "Guess it does." For the first time, he looks at Hom, and his mouth drops open. Rafferty clears his throat *very* loudly, and the man turns back to the counter. "I'll have . . ." the man says to the boy, "hell, I'll have whatever you think I'd like."

"Okay," the boy says, "for you, triple. You lucky man. I give you special." Two minutes later, they're gone, with a parting smile from Denise as the door closes, and the boy lets out a loud sigh. "Drink too much," he says to the room at large.

As though there has been no interruption, Hom says, looking at him fiercely, "You have baby."

"Less than two weeks now. A boy." He sits down again. "I didn't know what to do when it came. I still don't know what to do."

She leans forward and buries her face in her hands, her elbows on the table. He studies the ravaged profile, seeing bits and pieces of Miaow. She says, without looking up, "You should be happy."

"I *am* happy. I just . . . it's complicated."

"Why?" she says. "You papa. *Mama* do all the work."

"I help," he says, thinking how little he actually does.

She says in Thai, "Two children. Lucky, lucky."

"After all this time," he says, dodging the subject, "how did you find us?"

"I tell you already. Boy who take Miaow," she says without looking up. "I hiding, I watching, watching. I see boy, see him talk her, see him cut string. They go, I go behind, hiding, they talking not see me, but I see where him take her. Him have other boy, other girl—"

"A street gang," Rafferty says. "A bunch of kids. The boy called himself Superman."

"Yes, him bad boy, take thing, fight too much. I see where they sleeping, five boy, two girl. One boy, more old than Miaow, later I know him—I see him before, I see him ask money, ask on street—"

"You mean beg? He begged on the street?"

"Same me," she says. "I do, too."

"So wait, wait. You knew where Miaow was, where the boy was, but—"

She shakes her head. "No. They go. One week more, I go looking but they not same place. Empty. Then, long time, long time not see boy, not . . . not know nothing about Miaow. Think I never see her again. My husband, him . . . him crazy. Pill too much. I run, run somewhere long time."

"Somewhere where?"

She shrugs. "Bangkok. Bangkok wery big. Him not find me."

He says, in Thai, "And you lost Miaow."

"I lost everything," she says, "but only Miaow broke my heart. I thought—I really thought—I would die."

"But still, you found us. How?"

She pauses and closes her eyes, as she's done several times during their conversation, and he realizes she's lost her place in the story. He's trying to think of a way to prompt her when she says, "See same boy again." She rubs her eyes with her palms. "Boy I see ask money in street. See him maybe one week ago, maybe more." She's scratching at the back of her left hand with the nails on the right, scratching hard, and she's already drawn a little blood. He looks away.

"I come Patpong, ask for money on street. Patpong police no good, but some police not take *all* my money, leave me little bit. Some police, him take everything." She's still scratching, and he has to fight the urge to stop her. "So I see boy, same boy I see . . .

begging," she says carefully, sounding it out, and then draws a deep breath and switches to Thai. "He's eighteen, nineteen, now, something like that. He works outside a bar, sending people up the stairs—a bad bar where the ladies dance with no clothes and do bad things for the customers. I saw him and he saw me. He told me he'd seen Miaow in Patpong. She was going into a small bar with a foreign man. I thought, oh, no, Miaow is too young, but he said, no, the man had a wife, a beautiful Thai wife. He said he saw you two or three times more. But never with a lady. You went into the bar alone, you came out alone."

"Must have been . . . what, a year ago?" The only time Rose, who has no fondness for Patpong, has been on the street in years was when she went to the little memorial service at Leon and Toot's a few days after Leon died.

"Maybe a year. I don't know."

"When did he tell you this?"

A shrug. "One week, maybe ten days ago." She's still scratching, and he can't stop himself; he reaches over and puts his fingers on the back of her hand, and instantly she snatches it away and it comes up, fingers curled, a weapon at the ready. He pulls back, and as he does he sees that the palm of the upraised hand, her left, is covered with writing in deep blue, smeared ballpoint ink.

He hears the unmistakable chime that heralds the opening of a door in a 7-Eleven store, which for some reason has become ubiquitous in Bangkok as a phone ringtone. He's glancing over to see whether it's the boy's phone when Hom slips her right hand inside her dress, and it stops. She glances up at him anxiously, as though she's hoping he hadn't heard it, and finds him regarding her.

"My . . . my friend," she says.

"You have a cell phone?"

"Yes," she says with the first anger she's shown. "Have no money, have no room, but have phone. Friend . . . give me."

"So," he says, backing away from the issue of the phone and running straight into the big one, the one that can't be avoided. "We need to talk about Miaow."

Instantly the phone chimes again, and again she silences it. This time she pulls it out, a battered, deeply fingerprinted no-name clone, and turns it off.

His nerve fails him, and he says, "Do you . . . do you want some coffee?"

She shakes her head, looking at the table, and says, "Banana."

Her plate is still heaped with whipped cream and sprinkles, but the banana is gone, leaving a collapsed little tunnel, a bit of dessert archaeology. He calls out, "One banana, plain." To her, he says, "We need to talk about you. You and Miaow. I mean, I don't know what you were thinking, but my wife and I, and Miaow—"

She's shaking her head. "I see," she says. "I hear. She not want me. She, she . . ."

"It was a big shock."

"She never love me again. Love you now."

"Maybe she'll see you later, maybe in a month or two, but now—"

"No. I know. Her not want see me. Never see me. Her want me go away."

"But maybe in a little time—"

"Never."

He finds himself wondering about the writing on her palm, but he can't just abandon the topic, so he says, "Well, then, if you don't think Miaow will . . . will change, what can we do for you? What *do* you want?"

The banana arrives, looking naked and alone on its plate. She doesn't give it a glance. Instead, she takes a breath to say something, blows it out, closes both eyes, and starts over. "Money," she says. "Want money."

19

Banana Rice

THE FIFTH TIME her mother-in-law slapped Miaow, not long after her first birthday, Hom raised her hand in fury, and her mother-in-law took an amazed step back and screamed. Instantly, Hom's arm was seized from behind, and she whirled to find her husband, Daw, standing stone-faced with his own open hand raised and ready to strike. When she backed away from him and turned to comfort Miaow, she saw the gleam of satisfaction in her mother-in-law's eyes.

Her face burning and her throat almost clogged with fury, Hom let her lids drop in submission; she'd learned by then that any display of resentment would only make things worse. She brought her breathing under control, and the three of them endured a tense, precariously balanced silence, enveloped in the scent of the rice on the stove, until Miaow, in a delayed reaction to the slap, began to scream—in pain or rage, Hom was never quite sure which. Ignoring her husband's sharp question and her mother-in-law's reproving *tut tut tut*, Hom stooped down and gathered the crying child to her, pushed her way out of the kitchen, and hurried through the cramped rooms of the house, out into the merciless midday heat.

Much of the village was indoors in sheer self-defense. Even the dogs were quiet, either sleeping or licking themselves with admirable focus as they took shelter in the shaded dust beneath the wooden houses, raised a meter or so against the rainy season's inevitable floods. She smelled food; people had come in from the paddies and fields either to nap or to sit around tables together, talking and joking as they rewarded themselves for the morning's work and strengthened themselves for the afternoon's. Families, people who lived and worked side by side, coming together over the shared sacrament of food.

To Hom, who had come to dread mealtime, the day *stunk* of food.

Straddling her hip, the baby had stopped crying and made the transition to the hiccups that usually followed tears. The hiccups were also a sign that the child was hungry.

The child was always hungry.

Her mother-in-law had insisted, practically from the beginning, that the baby should be weaned as quickly as possible. At first, Hom had thought it was just about the time it took her to breast-feed Miaow, which cut into her time in the paddies, but she soon realized that it was really about control. The relationship between the baby and Hom's breast was the only one in the house the old woman couldn't command, and she had to disrupt it. She had to own it. So Miaow was weaned early—*too* early, according to Hom's own mother's view of things.

Not that Hom had been able to see much of her mother. Somehow, the time was never right for her to go home. There was always some imperative, some emergency, that was manufactured to keep her in her mother-in-law's house. Only in Miaow's fifth month, after Hom subjected her husband to three days of wooden silence, behaving as though she and Miaow were the only people in the world—only after that, and after the first time Daw struck her to bring her back in line—only *then* did her mother-in-law permit her son to take Hom home for an afternoon so her mother could hold the granddaughter she hadn't yet seen. Permission had been given again several months later, but except for that, Hom's mother had heard her granddaughter's voice only on the telephone; Miaow usually protested when her mother's attention was focused elsewhere.

Hom's stomach grumbled, and she knew that the baby was hungry, too, but going in to eat would just start another skirmish. Her husband's mother insisted that Hom overfed Miaow, saying she knew more about babies than Hom did, and that overfeeding her now would make Miaow fat and lazy and useless, "a little lump of grease," she had said, "squatting in the kitchen corner all her life." When the child graduated from the breast to rice gruel, her mother-in-law watched the path of every spoonful of Hom's own rice that was lifted to the baby's lips; several times, she even moved the bowl out of Hom's reach. The old woman had demanded that she look at the big strong man, her son, whom Hom had wisely married, and claimed that even *he*, an active male, hadn't eaten as much as Hom was forcing down Miaow's throat. She'd also suggested that Hom needed that food herself to supply the energy for her day's, and night's, work.

So Miaow was hungry day after day, and fretful about it. Hom had taken to sneaking into the kitchen when her mother-in-law was out, stealing a paddleful of rice, and putting it into a little jar that had once held mashed peaches, which had been Miaow's favorite before they were relegated to the proscribed list. "Fruit is no good for a girl," she'd been told. "It makes them soft and sweet and useless. Girls need to be strong. Women carry the world."

Five times now, the old woman had slapped Miaow, and the baby was only a little past a year old. It wasn't right. Life couldn't be like this. It *couldn't*.

It had never been like this before.

And she knew—her eyes told her, and the neighbors confirmed it almost daily—that Miaow was a beautiful baby, an unusually beautiful baby. She looked very much the way Hom had as an infant, when the old village ladies gathered around her and sighed, and floated prayers heavenward to help her avoid the vengeance of envious female ghosts. As she'd grown older, become a teenager, the village aunties still told Hom what a lovely child she had been. And she *had* been, she knew it; as one of a trio of beautiful sisters, she had heard often when she was growing up that she was the loveliest of the three, that she was the most beautiful girl in the entire village. Even Daw had once told her so. But now she felt like a drab, colorless collection of aging, aching muscles and infrequently washed hair, held together by resentment and sentenced to a life of labor by people who couldn't recognize a beautiful baby when they saw one.

And this was not just wounded vanity on Miaow's behalf. Hom believed that people who were blind to beauty were blind to goodness, *immune* to goodness, because what was beauty but a sign of goodness in a former life? Her husband didn't see the beauty of his own daughter. Neither he nor his terrible mother loved Miaow; and it was clear to her now, despite almost two years of stubborn, stupid refusal to see it, that they didn't love her, either.

She tiptoed as invisibly as possible through the remainder of that day, trying to anticipate her mother-in-law's demands and avoid any additional conflict. She even sidestepped the frequent dinner-table squabble over how much, or how quickly, she was feeding Miaow. Before she went to bed, in the shed she and Miaow shared because the child's middle-of-the-night calls for attention disrupted Daw's sleep, she took half an hour or so to lay out the things she would need, and as she closed her eyes, she commanded herself to wake up at three. The baby often awoke a little after three and wanted company; Hom had trained herself to anticipate the noise and get up in time to have a pacifier in her hand before the child could begin to squall in earnest.

That night, she snapped awake a good four or five minutes before Miaow stirred, and she had on hand something better than the usual pacifier to keep the child quiet: little balls of soft rice, flavored with the overripe bananas that she hung up in their room for just this purpose. The child's relationship with ripe, even browning, bananas—a carefully guarded secret between mother and daughter—was a passionate one: when Miaow ate them, she made low, barely audible moans deep in her throat, so extravagantly satisfied that they sounded almost feral.

While Miaow was adrift on waves of banana bliss, Hom sat at the edge of her cot in the oil-scented, spider-ridden tool room where Miaow had drawn her first breath. Rubbing her hand gently over the center of her chest and willing her heart to stop pounding, Hom *listened* and, without knowing it, counted off the seconds. At last, at the absolute edge of hearing, she isolated the sleep-sounds made by Daw, who somehow snored with his mouth closed. Still, even after she heard it, she hesitated, asking herself questions, answering them, one by one, in the negative, and instinctively popping more banana rice balls into the baby's mouth the moment she had swallowed the previous one.

She released a sigh that felt like it came all the way from her feet. Given the answers to her questions, she couldn't stay here all night long. She couldn't stay here at all. In the end it turned out to be a blessing that she and Miaow had been banished to the shed: the floors of all the other rooms in the old wooden house sang out every time a foot pressed down on them. Within a couple of weeks after her arrival, Hom had learned to map out which rooms people were moving through just by the sounds they made. The floor in the shed, though, was poured concrete, as solid as it was silent, and it was placed only one high, awkward step above the street, so she didn't even have to worry about the stairs, which played melodies of their own.

Before she had gone to bed that evening, she had changed into her lightest and most comfortable clothes and set out her most trustworthy pair of shoes, the only ones without at least one flapping sole to trip her in the dark or one hole just the right size for a snake's fangs. After she slipped into the shoes, she had very little left to do to take the steps that would change her life completely, that would bring an end to the chapter that she'd thought—had even, at one point, *hoped*—would last the rest of her life. All that remained was to take her child and pass through a door that squealed like a ghost in a trap, close it behind her, and start walking.

From a hook on the wall she took down an over-the-shoulder canvas bag she had partly filled with rice from the cooker in the kitchen, and then she surveyed the room one last time. Ugly, lonely, spidery, and smelly as it was, this was where her child had come safely into the world here, and she closed her eyes and said a silent thank-you to the spirits of the room. Carefully, she picked up Miaow, still working happily on her latest rice ball, and seated her in a sort of sling, just a loop of cloth she had cut from her bed-sheet and double-folded for strength. Giving the child another tiny mouthful of the sweet rice to keep her occupied, she held her breath, bent her knees and slipped her arm through the loop in the sling, then straightened slowly so that Miaow was dangling from her left shoulder, the one that didn't have the rice hanging from it. She stood there, congratulating herself on the fit. She'd been careful when she cut it out, but it was still a relief to see that the baby was sitting precisely where she sat when she straddled her mother's hip. This was important, because it meant that she would be able to shift the baby's weight from her shoulder to her hip and back again whenever she grew tired. The sling, now that it had the baby in it, was surprisingly heavy; in spite of the miserly meals she'd been given, Miaow had put on weight, and Hom was facing a long walk.

She said a prayer, a call to the good spirits of the night world she was about to enter. She didn't bother with the bad ones: they would know she was there no matter what she did, and it was useless to try to placate them.

With the fingertip of her right hand resting on the inside of her left wrist, she counted ten heartbeats—not as fast as they might have been—and then she lifted up on the door handle to keep the hinges from squealing, and tugged inward. Immediately, she saw the moon, plump and almost full, floating a few hours above the horizon to the west, waiting for her to follow it into the night. Easing the door closed behind her, she stood perfectly still, listening to the house one last time. No one seemed to be moving inside. With her eyes on the yellowing moon that would guide her, at least at first, she took a deep, deep breath, and said a silent goodbye to the husband, who, whatever else he was, was Miaow's father. Then she lifted her right foot to take the first step of her journey.

20

Twenty Kilometers

SHE COULDN'T MAKE the numbers work.

She was fairly good at math—she had been third-best (out of nine) in her class during her four years of school—but she couldn't make the numbers work. Well, she could make them work in the sense that she could force them to do what they were *supposed* to do, come out to the right totals and everything, but she couldn't persuade them to guarantee that she'd get home safely.

Her village was about twenty relatively flat kilometers away if she took the most direct route, but she *couldn't* take the most direct route because she knew that when they woke up and found that she and Miaow were gone, they'd grab someone's car and look for her, and where would they would look first? Along the most direct route. And the numbers didn't work.

Taking that route, the shorter route, she figured she could make it home in a little less than five hours, moving at a brisk walking speed, say, between four and five kilometers an hour. That would get her there around eight in the morning, which was, unfortunately, about two, two and a half hours after she figured Daw and his mother would wake up and realize that she and Miaow had fled. It was all too easy for her to see herself, exhausted and limping, still several kilometers from her village, while they practically ran her over in a borrowed car.

And, the truth, of course, was that she wouldn't actually be able to walk at anything close to that speed. She had Miaow hanging from her shoulder, which she knew would slow her down, both because of the child's weight and the extra care with which she'd have to take her steps. One stumble in the dark, a little trip that would mean nothing more than a skinned knee to her if she were alone, could be a disaster. If the baby fell, or, even worse, if she fell on the baby, she had no idea what she could do.

So call it six to seven hours.

On the most direct route.

Which she couldn't take.

And how long would the journey take on the other route?

Well, that depended in large part on whether she got lost.

As she did her multiplication and division she was already walking and silently kicking herself for not having gotten up even earlier. The problems with the other route were, first, that she didn't actually know how many kilometers it added to the journey; be conservative, and call it two or three, but it might be six or eight. And second, she didn't *exactly* have it mapped out in her mind. What she had was a relative certainty, based on something several people had said, that the road, or glorified path, that branched south from the main road actually *did* lead to one tiny village, a little dimple of rice paddies on the broad plain, to which she had once walked in a couple of hours from her own village, although she hadn't had to walk back. Some boy had given her and her sister Lawan a ride home because it was getting dark, a sweet, handsome village boy with night-black eyes, but when he laughed he went *hyukk hyukk hyukk*, like, she'd thought, something that lived in a tree. And Lawan and she, sitting in his rattling car, had avoided each other's eyes so they wouldn't burst out laughing themselves. They both knew that once they started to laugh, they wouldn't be able to stop.

Such a sweet boy. Imagine not liking a boy because of the way he laughed.

Imagine not being able to stop laughing.

Imagine laughing.

Her family's village was west of the one she was leaving, which meant that, at the moment, all she had to do was walk toward the setting moon. If she'd been able to strike out along the route she *couldn't* take, she had no question that she could find her way home; she'd traveled it four times now, on the back of Daw's motorcycle, twice in each direction, and once in a car when she took the few things she owned to his mother's house. All she knew for certain about the *other* route was that stretches of it were too narrow for automobiles, that it dipped south, in other words, to her left if she was facing west, and it eventually would lead to Hyukk-Hyukk's village, which she had once walked to, but not from. Years ago.

She almost laughed out loud. What could *possibly* go wrong?

But, on the other hand, she was who she was. She was *Hom*, the prettiest girl in the village, the third-smartest girl in her school, the mother of the world's most perfect baby. She'd made one mistake, that was all; she'd married someone without knowing that his mother was a monster who would eat her son's strength and starve her own grandchild. She hadn't known that, in his mother's presence, her strong-seeming husband would hang his head and stare at the floor like a child caught with a piece of stolen honeycomb.

She had made a mistake, just one wretched mistake, and now she was walking her way out of that mistake.

Her eyes scanning the moonlit ground in front of her, she walked on, looking for stones and holes and revisiting the most recent two years of her life, trying to understand how she could have so badly misread the man she married. Had any of it been her fault? Should she have seen what kind of woman his mother was before marrying into her family? Should she have been more assertive when she first moved into her mother-in-law's house? Should she have known it was time to cut her losses and go, just from the way the woman reacted to the problems that arose during Miaow's birth? Should she have tried to shame Daw into taking a stand? Should she have created alliances in the village? Many of the women there disliked her mother-in-law. Should she have—

But she didn't complete the thought because, in the sling at her hip, Miaow sneezed.

The sound brought Hom back to herself. She reached down into the sling and picked the baby up and held her close, jiggling her up and down a little, a movement Miaow loved, and then Hom realized, looking around, that she didn't exactly know where she was. There was the moon, a little lower than she expected it to be, but still in front of her, where it should be. Here was the rutted, uneven road, and back there, behind her, was the village. But how long had she been walking? Half an hour? An hour? Could she have passed, without seeing it, the branch to the left, to the south, that would take her to Hyukk-Hyukk's village? Could she *already* be trapped on the straight route, the direct route, where sooner or later they'd come rattling up behind her in some old car?

No, she decided. Life was not that cruel. Well, maybe it *was* that cruel, but it should have used up its cruelty toward her for the time being, after all she and her baby had been through in that woman's house. Hom believed she was a good person; she should trust her karma—which would surely not have abandoned her at such a point in her life—and keep walking. The alternative, turning around, would eventually lead her back to the town she was fleeing. Things would be fine, she told herself, if she just kept going; the branch that led southward was still ahead of her, it had to be.

She was certain of it.

She put Miaow on her hip, one arm under the child's bottom, and used her free hand to fish from her pocket the next-to-last of the banana rice balls, which she popped into Miaow's mouth. Almost immediately she was rewarded by a little moan of pleasure.

With Miaow moaning happily at her hip, Hom put her faith in the fairness of the world and walked on.

ALL THE PROMISES.

She was getting tired now, the moon was nearly down, and she wasn't looking forward to the deepening of the darkness. The Thai night is full of ghosts, most of which are merciless and on the verge of starvation all the time. On the other hand, there was one good bit of news: she'd come upon the branch to the left and she'd followed it. So far, it seemed to be taking her in the right direction. But the moon *was* going down.

She was again carrying Miaow, who had taken the regular rhythm of her walking as a kind of rocking and had fallen fast asleep in her arms. It was almost too much to hope for, her baby being this quiet as they moved through the darkness. Of all the ghosts that prowl the Thai night, the one she most feared was the ravenous Krasue, with her floating head surrounded by ribbon-like intestines, who shuffled off her ordinary-looking daytime body and took to the air at night to seek newborn children or pregnant women to devour. Hom knew that there was no way to escape Krasue if she came for them, and she was putting her faith in her knowledge that she was not pregnant and her slightly shaky conviction that Miaow no longer qualified as a newborn, although she had no idea how Krasue defined that term. With that uncertainty suddenly glaring at her, all her anxiety at being on the wrong road and being overtaken by her husband began to feel almost trivial.

But Miaow was still asleep, so at least there was that.

The road had dwindled and roughened. It was too narrow and too bumpy to be called a real road, and too wide to be a path. She remained in its center as best she could, staying away from the vegetation on either side. For one thing, dark as it was getting on the track she was following as the moon sank, it was even darker beneath the canopy of trees and vines, and she felt instinctively that the forest spirits were most likely to be *in there*, away from the powdery stretch of stars that would help her stay on the road when the moon finally disappeared, which would probably happen in the next half hour or so. Soon enough, though, the sky behind her would begin to pale. All she needed to do was stay beneath the stars until the new day arrived.

Don't think about Krasue.

So she followed the stars, lost in her thoughts and her regrets, looking from the heavens to the ground in front of her, searching always for the thing that could trip her. She was sure she could fall in a way that would keep Miaow safe from harm, but even so, she was terrified at the thought of the cries of alarm the child would send up. They would broadcast an invitation into the night, rippling outward from them in a circle like the one made by a stone dropped in water, a call to the starving spirits.

Do *not* think about the spirits.

All the promises. He had made so many promises. They were going to stay with his mother just until the baby was old enough to travel, and he had described to her many times their journey to a different world, to Bangkok, on one of the fast trains, so smooth and silent, he said, that you have to look out the window to make sure you're really moving. And the seats were so clean, so soft, that people slept through the trip instead of looking out the windows as the world streaked by. He had said that Bangkok was so big that you traveled through its outskirts a full hour, even at that speed, before you reached its center.

And he had friends there, he'd said, who would help them. He'd talked about the man who had gotten rich running a restaurant that served *their* food, Isaan food, and how that man would help them find a place to stay, a place that would be perfect for Miaow to grow up in, how he would find jobs for them—for him first, until Miaow was old enough to be left with someone, and after that, for Hom, too—jobs that paid real money, money enough to send some home to her own mother and father. She could *help her mother and father.*

She could get away from the endless drudgery, the endless sweat, the same faces, the net of gossip, the whine of the mosquitoes, the sameness of the landscape, the sense that she was missing everything that was going on in the real world, where *real* people lived. Life, she was sure, was supposed to be a banquet, and she had been sentenced to a lifetime of thin gruel, one flavorless meal after another, until she died.

She had seen only three villages in her life: her own, her husband's, and the one that Hyukk-Hyukk lived in. You could walk from one end to the other of any of them in less than ten minutes and see nothing interesting enough to slow you down; just peeling, run-down houses, owned by people everyone knew. A few dusty little businesses, run by the same people. A few spaces to park motorbikes. Ugly black electrical cables dividing up the sky into straight lines. Around each village, the flat paddies, stretching away in all directions. She was young, she was strong, she was pretty, she was, she believed, reasonably smart. And she was living in a place where the only thing on that list that mattered was that she was strong. The same thing people admired in a water buffalo.

Oh, yes, and she'd been told she had a *wide pelvis*, which, she supposed, meant that she could bring other water buffalo into the world. That's what she had been in her marriage: a water buffalo. She lowered her head and whispered to Miaow, "My little water buffalo." Miaow made a sharp sucking sound with her mouth, although she'd been weaned for months and months, and the sound frightened Hom, stopped her where she was, and set her to scanning the trees, trying to penetrate the deep gloom of the landscape, and realizing that, in fact, it wasn't all that gloomy. While she'd been trudging along and chasing her thoughts, the sky had gone from black to a deep gray, lightest behind her, to the east. The lace of the trees had begun to appear; in a few minutes, she'd be casting a shadow. The night was over.

Precisely at that moment, Miaow let out a whimper, practically the first real noise she'd made in the three hours or so that they'd been walking. She had *waited* to cry, waited until the evil spirits had fled with the night. She'd waited until they were safe.

"Best baby in the world," Hom said. "I will never, ever leave you."

21

Wherever That Was Now

As the day warmed and brightened and the spirit world receded, drawn away on the tide of the darkness, the things that had kept her moving—anger at first, when she stepped out of the house, replaced by uncertainty as she looked for the turnoff to the longer route, and then fear as she picked her way through the ghost-ridden forest—turned to an uneasy mixture of eagerness and doubt. She was reasonably certain that she was only a few kilometers from Hyukk-Hyukk's village, and for all she knew, he was still there, with his sweet, beautiful midnight eyes and his stupid laugh, and probably that same clattering car, held together with tape and wire, with a passenger door that he'd had to tie closed with a length of rope, knotted around the posts of two missing windows.

He had liked her, she'd known it. Although her sister Lawan, the flirt in the family, had squeezed into the middle, between her and Hyukk-Hyukk, he'd leaned past Lawan several times to talk to Hom, and, a few kilometers into the trip, he'd tilted the rearview mirror so they could see each other in it. When he did that, Lawan had pinched Hom's thigh, hard. Hom had let out a little yip, and Hyukk-Hyukk had asked if something was wrong, and she'd said, no, no, it was just that he was such a good driver. She'd met his eyes in the mirror then, seeing that he'd gone scarlet and that Lawan was glaring straight through the windshield like some ancient queen being taken to the place where her head would be cut off. Hom had burst into laughter and heard the answering *hyukk-hyukk*, and then Lawan had begun to giggle, too, and for a few kilometers the world had been perfect. They were young, they were beautiful, they were free, and even that awful car, with its broken windows and the occasional *bang* it let out from the exhaust, as though it was practicing for a *real* explosion, was part of the story, a story that could have ended in any of a dozen ways, all of them happy.

Instead—she cut the thought short as though with a pair of shears, maybe the old but amazingly sharp ones their mother used when she made clothes. She was here, she had survived the forest, she was almost home, she had the world's best baby.

And there it was, wasn't it?

When she saw Hyukk-Hyukk and his midnight-black eyes again, *if* she saw him again, she'd be carrying a baby. That was, of course, a completely different story. Not so many possible endings, not so many of them happy. He could be married, she suddenly thought, surprised at the pang of regret that accompanied the notion. She'd barely known him. It had been years ago. She was married. She was *carrying a baby*.

She was in a new world, one with no clearly marked exit.

What had she done to her life?

This was, she supposed, what her mother had meant when she talked about growing up, that mysterious stage of life when she would have *responsibilities*, when people would *depend upon her*, when she could no longer claim *not to know better*. Now, she supposed, she knew better, and what she had learned was that some doors, when closed, could not be reopened, and that the doors that locked most permanently of all were the ones between you and the times when you were happiest. The surprise, it turned out, about knowing better was that it was mostly for the worst. Time only moved in one direction. It moved away from when you were happiest, and it dragged you with it.

So the boy might still be in the village, he might still have the world's darkest eyes, but she was no longer someone who could catch those eyes in a rearview mirror and ask herself, even lightly, whether he was her future. The future was here, and in it she was a woman with a child and a husband and a mother-in-law. She was a woman who hadn't laughed in months and who seemed to have lost the map to anyplace where she could laugh.

On the other hand, here was Miaow, this warm, shifting weight in her arms, with eyes that were seeing everything for the first time, dropped like a stone into a world that had no place set aside for her, that could roll over her and crush her and move on without slowing, this child she had caught as it fell into life, and whose diaper, she suddenly realized, stank to heaven and who, Hom knew, had the power to break her heart in whole new ways, ways she had never dreamed of before. And to whom she was, for the present, everything.

And so, in the end, when she saw the village, *his* village, she skirted it, head down like someone who had stolen something there long ago and was afraid she'd be recognized. Once she was safely on the other side, she drew the deepest breath of her life, kissed her smelly child's forehead and struck out for home, whatever and wherever that was now.

22

The Ticket

OF COURSE, AFTER a few days, he came for her.

She'd felt, during that time, like an intruder in her own house, even though her mother had melted over the baby, and her sisters had briefly abandoned their own husbands to come see her and to coo about Miaow, how she had Hom's father's coal-black eyes and the little dimple in the center of his chin that they'd always teased him about. The dimple, as it happened, would disappear sometime during Miaow's early childhood, but that, combined with her black eyes, had won her grandfather's heart. He was a man who had sired nothing but daughters, all of whom resembled the beauty he had married; and Miaow, even though she was a girl, had delighted him by paying him the long-delayed courtesy of looking like his side of the family.

The village grannies had streamed in to pay their respects and had made a point, in response to whispered instructions from Hom's mother, of complimenting Hom's father on his strength and vigor, planting his resemblance across the leap of a whole generation. And here, in this house and this village, there was no reluctance to tell Hom how beautiful the baby was, even if the praises were whispered to avoid provoking the envy of the spirits. The story of Miaow's magical silence during their passage through that long dark night was shared and marveled over, and it marked her, many believed (or said that they believed), as an exceptional child, one with potent spirit guardians.

Also expressed—at least, by those who were unaware that Hom could hear them though the house's thin walls—was a certain disapproval that she had abandoned her husband after such a relatively short time. She had answered their questions honestly: no, he had not been a drunkard; no, he hadn't actually beaten her, just a few slaps (and some of the women gave tiny nods of recognition); no, he hadn't appeared to be a butterfly, flitting from woman to woman. So he had a difficult mother. At this piece of information, most of the married women glanced at the other married women. Whose mother-in-law *wasn't* difficult? Many of them, in fact, had become difficult mothers-in-law themselves and were aware, perhaps even a little proud, of the fact. Who among them had a son who had chosen a girl who was worthy of him? And even if she *was* worthy of him, what did she know about life, about marriage, about the superior wisdom, the breadth of experience, of mothers-in-law?

Hom, they whispered (although not quietly enough, in that small house), had been the baby of her family, the spoiled one, the willful one who had always demanded her own way and the too-pretty one who usually got it. Her mother-in-law, they agreed, was probably simply set in her ways; the newly married couple was, after all, living in her house, which spoke well of Hom's husband. He had not abandoned his widowed mother. How bad could she be, asked these women (whose greatest fear was being left alone and penniless) if her son had stayed beside her to protect and care for her in her old age? On the whole, many of them thought—remembering the first year or so with their own daughters-in-law—there were at *least* two sides to every story.

So, in the familiar room she had reclaimed (which seemed smaller now than she had remembered), Hom heard some of this, heard her own mother agree that Hom had always wanted things her way. Hearing those words, she hugged Miaow so hard that the baby cried out, and waited for the knock at the door, the one she dreaded to hear.

When it came, at dusk on her twelfth evening there, she was asleep beside Miaow after an active day. Snatched from a good dream, shaken awake by her mother to learn that real life had just shouldered its way in, she told her mother not to let Daw in but to keep him at the door while she put on clean clothes and threw water in her face, not to clean it but to sharpen her wits, bring her the rest of the way back from her dream.

Her father stood aside when he heard her coming, but Daw did not come in. He had even, she saw, politely bent his back a little so he didn't tower over her father quite so much. He had combed his hair, put on his best shirt, making him look more like someone who had come courting than a man intent on reclaiming a wayward wife. And, rather than barging into the house, he asked Hom's father whether he and Hom could go for a short walk and talk outside. He had bothered them too much already, he said. Would her father consent?

Hom realized she was staring at him and lowered her eyes. He'd never behaved so deferentially, and she didn't want him to see her confusion.

"She's not only my daughter, now," her father said. "She's your wife. I think you should ask her."

"I want my father to hear what you say," Hom said. She still hadn't met his eyes,

Her father said, "This is between you and your husband." But he stayed where he was.

Daw took a step forward, just inside the doorframe, and startled her by saying, "*Yoot duang jai*," or "dearest heart," which he hadn't called her since the day she said she'd marry him. Even her father's eyebrows went up. "Please? We can stay close enough so your father can see us."

Her father asked her, "Daughter?"

Hom said, "How far away is your motorbike?"

"I borrowed a car." He pointed down the street, at a battered and peeling Honda with a cracked windshield, four houses away. "I parked it there. I thought it would make you more comfortable if it wasn't so close."

This was, for an instant, anyway, the Daw she'd thought she had married. When she met him, when he first rode his motorcycle into her village to see the girl people said was so beautiful, one of the first things Hom had liked about him was his name, which meant *bright shining star*. It hadn't hurt his cause that he was strikingly handsome and that a couple of other girls in the village got a little silly about him, and that even one of her own sisters (already married) had stood stock-still, watching as he approached the house and said, "Hmmmmmmm," in the precise tone their mother used when she saw something in the market that she really wanted.

And, back then, he'd shown her a kind of gentleness that went with his name and that set him apart from the boys in the neighborhood, who seemed to take it for granted that she'd eventually fall into one local set of calloused hands or another, and who regarded the competition as a sort of sporting event in which she was the trophy. She'd seen enough trophies won to know that their value faded the moment they were put on the shelf.

So he seemed to value her, and—another advantage—she hadn't had to watch him grow up, through baby teeth and plump cheeks to acne, peach fuzz, and an Adam's apple; he wasn't someone whose jokes she had heard a hundred times; he wasn't bone-wearyingly familiar, like the village she wanted so deeply to leave. That was perhaps the best thing: in addition to his beauty and his bright new shininess and the luster of his name, he was a ticket to some-where else—even somewhere, he hinted, as unthinkable, as exotic, as Bangkok.

"There's the bench," Hom said, pointing at a sagging, splinter-filled seat that her father had built long before she was born. It was only a few meters from the door. "We can sit there."

Daw stood aside to let her pass, and Hom squeezed past her father and down the step, into the deepening evening. Instantly, mosquitoes whined at her, but she got bitten much less than most people while mosquitoes seemed to regard Daw as a gourmet meal, so she allowed herself a tiny twinge of satisfaction and took a place on the end of the bench closer to the house. Since the ground sloped downward away from the front door, it would lessen the difference in their height, too. In the house, Miaow began to cry.

"I only have a few minutes," Hom said.

"She sounds healthy," Daw said.

"Yes, she's getting enough to eat now."

He slapped at his neck and waved his hand in the air to dispel the friends of the one he had killed, and said, "I came to say I'm sorry."

"Well," she said. "Thank you for that."

"My mother is not an easy person. She used to be different, but life has not been kind to her."

"That's not a reason," Hom said, "to take it out on everyone else."

"No, no, it isn't. And I'm sorry I didn't take your side more often."

"It wasn't my side," Hom said. "It was Miaow's."

In the doorway, her father cleared his throat.

"I want us to start over," Daw said, slapping his neck again. "In Bangkok."

This wasn't what she'd expected. On the other hand, it wasn't like she hadn't heard it already. With her father behind her and her mother-in-law some twenty kilometers away, she felt she could safely challenge him. "You said that before, and we never—"

"Here." He reached into his shirt pocket and pulled out two long rectangles of tan paper with green print on them. Passing his index finger under the line that read *Bangkok,* he said, "This is the fast train, supposed to be nine and a half hours. It's more expensive, but for you and Miaow, it's worth it. The slow one can take seventeen or eighteen, stops everywhere." He pointed at the date. "Five days from now."

She felt a flare of irritation. "How do you know I'll go? Maybe you wasted your money."

"I can get it back," he said, and she dropped her eyes to hide the sudden and surprising wave of disappointment.

"But I don't want to give it back." He took her hand and opened it and put the tickets inside. "What I want to do is keep my promise. I want to give you a new life. Away from this village, from my village. From my mother."

Her father cleared his throat again, and Hom knew that it was a prompt. When all was said and done, this was no longer her home. Her parents were past babies, past drama, past conflict. They wanted, as her father had said to her, to hold each other's hands as the sun set. And she was in the way here.

Daw rested a finger, so lightly she barely felt it, on the hand with the ticket in it. "I'm giving these to you. Both of them. That way, you'll know that I meant it, even if you decide not to go with me." He looked at her, lowering his head so he could see her eyes, and said, "I might ask for mine back, though. But you . . . you keep yours one way or the other."

In the house, Miaow, who had stopped crying, began again, and Daw stood and extended his hands to help Hom get up. After a moment, she took them and rose to her feet, avoiding looking at him. "I want to see her," he said. "I've missed her. Is it all right with you," he called to her father, "for me to go in and look at the baby for a minute or two?"

"Fine with me," her father said. "What about you, daughter?"

"Ummmm," she said, trying to think of a reason to say no. "I guess so." Daw took a step forward, and she put a hand, fingers spread, in the center of his chest. It took no pressure to bring him to a halt. "I'll lead you in," she said. "She hasn't seen you in a while."

Something flinty kindled in his eyes, but then it passed and he said, "Good idea. I wouldn't want to frighten her."

So, with her heart thundering in her chest, she led him in, past Hom's mother and two of the village grannies, eyebrows raised almost to their hairlines, and past them into the tiny hallway that led to the room she grew up in, which she had been sharing with Miaow. Behind them, one of the grannies whispered a short, sharp remark and the other women laughed, and she knew it was something earthy about how handsome Daw was. As long as she'd known him, older women had all but patted their chests, as though they needed help breathing, when they saw him. Even the women in his own village, the ones who didn't particularly like him, had to admit he was a good-looking man. One of them, without knowing that Hom could hear her, said it was *like gold-plating shit*. She'd been crestfallen when Hom burst into laughter, but then the two of them had locked eyes and giggled until they had to hold each other up.

When they came into the room, Miaow stretched her arms out toward her mother, still crying, but Daw stepped up to the bed and picked the baby up, holding her to his chest and bouncing her up and down a little. Miaow stopped crying, and her eyes were enormous as she looked up at her father's face. "There, there, there, there," Daw said, "everything is all right. And what a pretty, pretty baby you are." To Hom, he said, "She's *so* pretty."

This was new territory. What she *wanted* to do was take the baby away from him, but instead she tilted her head to the left and looked from Miaow to Daw, suddenly noticing something she had never seen before. In the baby's upper lip and the curve of her chin, there was an echo of Daw's mother.

"She's beautiful," Hom said, holding out her hands. He gave her the baby, but Miaow's eyes stayed on Daw's face.

"The tickets are for five days from today," he said again. "I hope you'll come with me. If I haven't heard from you on the day before, I'll stop by and get mine."

"Here," she said, handing one of them to him. "If I don't go, this will spare you the trip."

23

But Together

BUT IT WASN'T the fast train, after all. It took sixteen hours. It stopped in places where Hom didn't even see a village. The promised luxurious seats were actually cramped benches that amplified every uneven join in the tracks, and the jolts and the noise kept Miaow up, waving her fists and squalling, for much of the trip.

And it *reeked* of shit. When she went into the bathroom she understood why: there were *farang* on the train, and the only place to move your bowels was a Thai squat toilet. From the look of the floor, many *farang*, some of whom had probably just eaten the spiciest food of their lives, had been squatting with nothing to hold on to when the train suddenly lurched, and they'd had to duckwalk, mid-function, to get back to the hole.

For the first few hours Daw made excuses, saying that he'd saved money with the cheaper tickets and that they'd need it in Bangkok to make sure they could afford a place that would be safe for Miaow, and that Hom would see, things would be fine once they got there: he had friends, and the man with the restaurant would steer them to good jobs. But the enormity of the lie about the train—the very first thing he'd promised her about their journey—filled her with a kind of dread, and she stopped listening. After a while he seemed to understand that, because he got up and navigated the corridor between the seats as the train swayed until he was out of sight. When he came back he had a pleasant-looking woman dressed in the train worker's uniform with him. He introduced her to Hom as *Khun* Siriporn and explained that from then on, all Hom had to do when she needed the bathroom or had to change Miaow's diaper was to go up through two cars and into the third, and *Khun* Siriporn would take her to a better bathroom. *Khun* Siriporn had nodded agreement, although Hom thought she saw disappointment in the woman's eyes at the revelation that the favor Daw needed was for his wife and child. Still, she had said yes and she rose to the occasion by giving Hom the name of the other attendant who would be up there if she, Siriporn, was on a break or had been called elsewhere. From then on, when another stop was announced, Daw would take Miaow and walk up and down with her until the train was in motion again. Often, Siriporn would drift in during the stops, and when the cars were in motion again, Daw and Siriporn would walk back up the aisle and into the forward cars, talking like people who had known each other for years, his fingers touching the crook of her elbow as though he were the one who'd been on trains half his life, and she the one who might need steadying.

When he came back he had a sandwich for Hom on very white, very soft bread with some kind of meat in it, a banana for Miaow, and a glass of something that smelled like the stuff her father drank on weekends. A little later, he got up and went into the forward car, as though the rules simply didn't apply to him, and returned with another drink. Hom watched him slip into a doze, head back, mouth open. Not so handsome at the moment, but still better-looking than any of the boys she'd grown up with. She watched him sleep for what felt like a long time, and something cold and heavy seemed slowly to replace her heart. At one point she wanted to get up and move around to dispel the sensation, and she was startled to find his fingers wrapped around her wrist before she'd even slipped past him and into the aisle.

"I just want to walk a little," she said.

"The train might make a sudden turn," he said. "I'll take the baby."

She was amazed at how little she wanted to hand Miaow to him, but she did it, and for the next thirty or forty minutes she paced the length of the car, watching Miaow sleep at his chest, watching his gaze follow her beneath his half-closed eyelids. They barely spoke for the rest of the journey.

SHE SMELLED BANGKOK long before she saw it. It smelled like trucks.

He was asleep, or so it seemed. He slept much more lightly than she did. Twice in the night when she needed to go to the bathroom, once to change Miaow and once for herself, his eyes opened the moment she stirred. Both times, he insisted on accompanying them, waiting outside the bathroom until they were done, and then following them back to their seats, where he would—it seemed—instantly fall asleep, only to open his eyes whenever she changed her position.

She supposed she could persuade herself that he was worried about them.

When she looked out the window after spoon-feeding Miaow most of her remaining food, the black, empty countryside had given way to lights. They were in motion everywhere, some high in the air, or rather, as it turned out, on roads magically hung ten meters above the ground, and other lights were taking long downward slopes to, she supposed, an airport. Some of the lights took the form of pale rectangles, the windows of the poor-looking houses and low, cheaply built structures along the tracks, glowing even at this hour, which must have been a little before five in the morning. People who got up early or went to bed late. People who, for all she knew, stayed up all night. Rhythms must be different in the city, she thought, than they were in the countryside.

The buildings grew closer together and higher. The sky brightened. The train began to slow. She couldn't open her window to look ahead and see what was coming, but whatever it was, it let out a lot of light.

Whatever it was—good *or* bad, she supposed—it was her new life.

The moment the train stopped, Miaow began to cry.

THE NICE PLACE to live turned out to have a dirt floor beneath three walls of plastic sheeting stretched over rotted wooden beams in an inconceivably filthy, rat-infested slum built on a downward slope near the port. They would share the space, he said, with three other families in eight-hour shifts. Food was cooked, or at least warmed, on a tiny Sterno stove positioned dead center on the dirt floor to keep the heat away from the plastic walls. The crib, which apparently belonged to one of the other families, had a wire mesh cover stretched across the open top to keep the rats off the baby. Never had she been expected to be grateful for something so horrifying. Her first night there, she never closed her eyes.

The Isaan restaurant, which they found after a long roundabout search several days after they arrived, turned out to be a cramped, smoky place run by an irritable little man who actually sighed at them the first time he saw them. The sigh sounded to her like exhaustion. On the other hand, they left with two white plastic bags of food that was so good that Hom burst into tears at the first mouthful: it took her straight back home and into her mother's kitchen, which now felt thousands of miles away. While Daw was in the restaurant's bathroom (and for quite a while; it hadn't escaped her that he had only once left her alone in the hut to use

the community latrine, and she wasn't sure whether it was to protect her or to keep her from running away) the restaurant owner
had changed his tone somewhat, had grown more gentle. She
would, he said, have to be strong. She was in for a difficult, possibly
dangerous, often dirty experience, but thousands of people had gone
through the ordeal just in the time he personally had been in
Bangkok, and most of them had survived, had moved on to jobs and
families and apartments. "Not palaces," he said, "but clean—or at
least as clean as they make them—and safe. Doors you can lock,
although Bangkok isn't all that terrible. People do steal, though,
they do that everywhere I've been." He looked out the window at
the street. "The people who have been here the shortest time
have the best hearts," he said. "The city changes people. Maybe all
cities do. If you really need to trust someone, it might be better to
trust someone who hasn't been here too long." He drew a breath
and was about to say something else, she thought, but then he
glanced past her and she realized that Daw was standing behind her,
having come out of the bathroom without making a sound.

After they left, she followed Daw along the sidewalk of an
impossibly crowded street called Silom, and she realized that she
was seeing more people in a single block, just on her side of the
street, than lived in her entire village. Most of the passersby
avoided her eyes; over the course of a long, jammed block, she got
only three or four nods or smiles. It was enough to make her feel
like a ghost; even with Daw walking beside her she felt alone in a
whole new way. And it wasn't just the males or the older people.
Even the girls her own age seemed to have walls around them; girl
after girl looked at no one, kept her gaze unfocused, went past her
as though she were invisible. If one of them *did* look at her, she
seemed to be judging Hom's clothes, her hair, her lack of makeup,
possibly evaluating her as competition.

Suddenly, a tall, thin woman stopped right in front of Hom,

clasped her hands at the level of her heart, and said, "Oh, what a *beautiful* baby, she's *perfect*." The woman put out a very long finger with a manicure that had probably cost more than all the clothes Hom owned put together, and Miaow reached out and grabbed the finger and laughed, and the tall woman said, "Oh, my GOD, what an *angel*, just *look* at those eyes," and from nowhere Daw appeared, knocking the woman's hand away and saying, "Get away from her, get away. *Tutsii! Tutsii!*"

The woman backed away, saying to Daw, "You're pretty, darling, but you're stupid," and to Hom, "Sorry, sweetie. Beautiful baby. Looks like you, thank God," and then she flipped her hair at Daw. To Hom, as she walked away, she said, "You can do better, *teerak*. You're a beautiful girl."

"Ladyboy," Daw said, almost spitting it as he watched her go. The woman glanced back and exaggerated the swing of her hips. "*Dirty*. They steal things. He—he sleeps with men."

"He? But he's—I mean, she's—"

"No, no. It's a man. There are lots of them here. *Farang* men like them. He's just a whore."

"He thought Miaow was beautiful," she said, suddenly resentful.

"They steal," he repeated. "They come here, to this street, to . . ." He let the thought trail off.

She peered at the street that had opened up to their left, short, straight, drab, ordinary enough except for the night market being built down its center, and then a neon sign came on, followed by another, and she said, "Oh. *I* know about this place. A girl in our village came down here, and—"

"Girls from all over Thailand come down here," he said sourly. "Boys, too."

"The girl in our village, the one who came here, she married a *farang* she met here and now she lives someplace cold and sends her parents clocks and things. Let's go look at—"

He said, "No" and took her arm.

"*Stop* that," she said, tugging her arm free. "I'm here with you, I'm your daughter's mother, but I'm not your slave. I wouldn't take it at your mother's house, and I won't take it here."

He said, "You're my wife."

"Well," she said, "I could also say you're my husband. It doesn't mean we own each other."

"People *said* you were too pretty," he said. "They told me you were spoiled. But what's done is done. You're going to have to listen to me. You don't know this place. People here will steal from you. They'll hurt you. That *kathoey* could have cut you, she could have picked your pocket—"

Her cheeks felt hot enough to fry an egg on. "There's nothing in my pocket. You haven't given me anything to *put* in it."

Men were going past them now, mostly alone, headed up the little street where the lights were coming on. They were focused on where they were going and paid no attention to her and Daw. "I'm going to go look at this," she said. "You can come with me or not, I don't care."

"You could never find your way home."

"*Home?*" she said, not knowing whether to laugh or cry. "You call that home?"

He said, "Stop. Please stop." And his tone did in fact stop her, cut her off before she could let out everything she'd been holding in since the moment she saw the inside of the train car and knew she'd been lied to. He didn't sound angry or assertive. He sounded tired. Much more surprising, he sounded sad. "Listen to me. Please. We're married. We have a child. You've come with me to a big city where you don't know anyone. You're angry with me because the place we're staying in is filthy and probably dangerous, but I promise to protect you. I'll do my best to protect you. You heard the man in the restaurant. *Everybody* starts like this. Within a week, I promise you, I'll have a job. *You'll* have a job—"

"How can I have a job? Miaow—"

"I have the names of some women who take care of babies while their mothers work."

"I'm not giving—"

"You can talk to the women. You can talk to the mothers whose kids they take care of. It's going to be harder for me to get a job than it is for you. I could get you a job tomorrow, folding clothes in a laundry that takes care of some of the big hotels. I already know who to call. Long work, but not hard. Lots of women to talk to. I'm going to have to get a bottom-level job, probably in building, lifting things, moving them around. Sometimes the men who hire workers make them work for a week or two and then fire them without paying them. So here's the truth. It's going to be hard."

"I'm not giving Miaow—"

"Meet the woman first. I have three names, you can meet all of them. Bangkok is full of mothers who are working and have to let someone take care of the babies. It'll cost something, but she'll be someplace clean and safe. You'll have a job, it'll help, it'll help us get our feet under us until things get better. It'll give us time to learn more about living here. *Everybody* starts this way, Hom. We can do this, but only if we do it together. We can't go back to the village now. Your parents want to be alone, the only place I have is with my mother—I know, I know, you don't have to say it. I feel the same way. We're here, now. We came here together. Together, I think we can do it. I know we can. But *together*."

In the entire nineteen years of her life, no one had ever told her she was essential to something important. No one had ever said that his success or failure could depend on her. There was Miaow, of course; every baby depends on its mother, but to be the key to an adult's life, especially an adult who seemed, at times, anyway, to love her . . . well, that was something completely new. And it was Daw who needed her help. Looking at him now, she saw more of the boy she'd thought she'd been marrying and less of the martinet he had become at his mother's house. It felt, at that moment, as though that boy had returned.

She said, "Tomorrow. We'll meet them tomorrow."

He lowered his eyes to the sidewalk, and she thought for a moment that he was embarrassed that she had seen how much her agreement meant to him, but when he looked back up, his eyes were clear and calm. "So," he said, indicating the street with a wave of his hand, "do you still want to take a walk?"

She turned away to see more men, all *farang* except for a few who could have been Japanese or Chinese, most of them middle-aged, many of them overweight and unattractive, most of them alone, and she saw the girls waving them in from the doorways, and she thought how sad it was that the men didn't have wives they could work with to build something strong, and how unhappy the girls' lives probably were, and she said, "No. Let's go home."

In the years that followed, she would ask herself why she hadn't just found a way to kill all three of them, right then and there. And she would ask it again and again and again.

24

Smelled Pretty Much Like Hers

ON MIAOW'S SECOND birthday, Hom persuaded Daw to spend a little of their rapidly dwindling savings on something to commemorate the day. She'd already located the photographer, who had a little shop, so inconspicuous she'd walked past it twice looking for it. Its dusty, unlit windows were full of pictures of brides, so faded they looked like ghosts, and they'd startled her so that she'd slowed for a moment to get up the courage to go in. The photographer was old and bent, and his hands shook so badly she wondered how he could hold the camera still, but when she'd bathed Miaow and washed her hair and slicked it down and they were finally sitting there in front of a huge white sheet of paper, she'd seen that the camera was a big wooden box with legs and that he clicked it to take the pictures with something he held in his hand.

And the pictures had been beautiful. She could afford only two prints, in the smallest and cheapest size. She'd sent one to her mother and kept the other in a small zippered bag with an elephant embroidered on it that she'd been given on her sixteenth birthday. In it she kept her state identity card, a photograph of her mother, and whatever small amount of money she had. Instinctively, she rarely brought it out in front of Daw.

By the time they went to the photographer's studio, they had been living for several months in a sagging, creaking former hotel, a tinder-dry potential bonfire that, thanks to a series of well-placed bribes, no longer officially existed; it was shown on the city records as having been demolished. The owner, who had paid the bribes for its imaginary demolition, was a developer who had for some time been buying every structure on three narrow, obscure *sois* that intersected in the middle, like the horizontal cross-bar in a capital H. Once he owned everything on all three *sois*, he bribed his friends in the city government to get those structures condemned as well, and then he paid another round of bribes to begin actual demolition. Only then, when all three *sois* were depopulated and reduced to rubble, would he announce his grand project and wait for open palms to be extended by the officials who would have to approve it. He had seen the future, and it was shopping malls. It was a low-risk game because he was displacing only the poor, who had nothing to drop into those perpetually outstretched government palms.

In the meantime, the nonexistent hotel was now a nonexistent boarding house, of sorts: one family to a room, at least theoretically. One working bathroom—which is to say, actually connected to the plumbing—for each floor, no electricity in the rooms, and no cooking allowed on the premises, a restriction everyone got around with canisters of propane and portable grills. In order to make the fiction that the building was empty sufficiently plausible to let the beat cops deny they'd been bribed, all the windows on the three sides visible from the street had been nailed closed and thickly painted over, and the front entrance was barred and chained behind big signs that said CLOSED and NO ADMITTANCE. The tenants came and went through a rear door that was still labeled EMPLOYEES ONLY in Thai and opened into what had been the hotel's kitchen. Beyond that lay the lobby, and both of these big areas were now home to the place's cheapest living spaces, a maze of rectangular compartments divided by pieces of rough-cut, splinter-bristling, shoulder-high plywood. On the bright side, relatively speaking, there were three bathrooms on the ground floor, and they all worked.

Daw and Hom had moved out of the harbor slum and into one of the plywood spaces with the first paycheck Hom earned in her new job. She was working for a company that laundered and dry-cleaned the clothes that belonged to the guests of the most expensive hotels in the city. The first time she emptied one of the big drawstring bags onto the table, she'd been dazzled. These were the kind of clothes she had seen on television, the kind of clothes the Queen might have in her closets. Fairy-tale clothes, movie star clothes. Beautiful as they were, her first revelation, as she sorted the garments into piles, as she'd been told to, was that the rich and beautiful perspired, too; and that, under the perfume, their sweat smelled pretty much like hers.

That first morning she was worrying about Miaow, from whom she had never been separated, when a supervisor snatched a garment out of her hand and slapped her, bringing her present in a neck-snapping instant that had her blinking tears from her eyes. In the supervisor's other hand was the item of clothing she had seized—a silk dress, light as a cobweb. Hom had been in the act of putting it into the wrong bag, the bag that would send it to the laundry rather than the dry cleaner.

"Did you *ask* me?" the supervisor demanded. "What was the rule?"

Hom had a hand pressed to her burning cheek. "Ask about anything that I'm not sure should be dry cleaned."

"You would have to work for two or three weeks to pay for this," the supervisor said. "And the moment you paid it off you would have been fired. I would have *already* been fired for letting you make the mistake. Take your hand away, I didn't hit you that hard. What were you *thinking* about?"

"My baby."

"This job is *for* your baby," the supervisor said. "If you put him with one of the women the other mothers here use, he'll be fine."

"She," Hom said.

"Really." The supervisor cocked her head and regarded Hom. "Does she look like you?"

"Mostly."

"Must be very pretty."

She felt herself blush. "I think so."

"Well, you're taking care of her now by working here. You're going to give her a better life. So keep your eyes open, pay attention." She glanced around the room, which had a dozen women in it, each sitting alone and silent at a huge table, sorting clothes. "Listen," she said in a low voice, "the way you look . . . well, I could put you someplace where you'd make a lot more money."

"No, thank you," Hom said instantly.

"More in a night than you'd earn in two or three weeks here."

"No, thank you."

The supervisor straightened, brushed her white cotton apron with both hands, and did another quick survey of the room. "Well, keep it in mind."

That night, when Daw asked her about her first day of work, she didn't tell him about the supervisor's suggestion.

BY HER EIGHTH month on the job she had been given a small raise and she and Daw were in their fourth room in the nonexistent hotel, one on the side of the building that did not face the street, up on the third floor. They'd been waiting for that room because Hom had made friends with the family that had it when they moved in, and the man had been able to pry the windows free and set them on metal runners that allowed him to slide them up and down. He'd also tacked porous black cloth over the inside of the windows. They could be opened only at night when candles or lanterns were not lighted. But to Hom the darkness felt like a small price to pay. The movement of relatively fresh, relatively cool night air felt like a great luxury, and the sound of rain was pure music. The rain and Miaow were the things that made her happiest.

Daw couldn't find, or keep, a steady job. He had worked construction for a few weeks at a time, being fired—he said—on payday, sent away with only part of what he'd been promised and warned that he'd be beaten half to death and charged with stealing if he ever came back. Hom had asked the women at work if they'd ever heard of such a thing, and some of them said yes, that it was one way the contractors made extra money: hiring new workers, underpaying them, and then letting them go and pocketing the rest of their salary.

When she heard that, she felt a wash of shame at having doubted Daw—because she had—and a wave of sympathy at how humiliating it must feel to be cheated, to be treated like someone so low he could be stolen from with impunity. Back in his village, he had been *someone*. Here, he was just another country boy who could be exploited by anyone with a solid job and a few thousand baht.

But. He was getting money from *somewhere*, she knew that. He was drinking; she smelled it on him most nights, and once or twice a week he came home too drunk even to pretend. She herself didn't drink, but she wasn't unworldly enough to think alcohol was free. She hated the drinking, in part because it meant he was hiding money from her, but also because it frightened her. She kept quiet and watched him out of the corners of her eyes on those nights; the room was small and his mood was unpredictable. Nor was she the only one to sense that something was wrong. Miaow was becoming, Hom thought, an extremely attentive child, usually quiet but constantly aware of where everyone was in the room, especially her father. When she wasn't beside Hom—Daw often didn't want Miaow on the thin mattress they shared—Miaow always managed to turn herself so she was facing her father, like a more fearful version of one of those flowers that keeps its face to the sun all day long.

When Daw was drunk, Miaow sometimes whimpered, a high, wispy little sound like a dog might make if she'd been locked in an empty room. She only stopped when Hom picked her up, and sometimes not until they'd left the room so they could go back and forth in the dim corridor. She usually fell asleep when Hom took her out there.

But at least she didn't worry about the baby in the daytime. At seven-thirty every morning she dropped Miaow off at the house of a woman who called herself Sonya—not a Thai name, although she was Thai—and picked her up a little after seven at night. Sonya was a tall, too-thin woman with hair dyed a violent red who seemed to be constantly in motion, almost unnaturally energetic. Hom had been uncertain about her at first, but she was obviously good with the six or seven babies she always seemed to have on hand. She lived in a big one-room apartment that she'd made over as a sort of baby park with soft carpet and foam-rubber pads everywhere, and plush toys and rattles scattered here and there. She kept the floor very clean and she was always moving the toys as far as possible from the children. "Make them crawl," Sonya said. "If I don't keep them moving, if they're asleep all day, they'll keep their parents awake all night." Hom felt welcome at Sonya's, often more than she did in their room in the not-hotel. She took to leaving Daw snoring in the room while the night sky was just going pale so she could arrive at Sonya's an hour or so early and the two of them could talk, joined sometimes by other young women, village girls, most of them, whose children also needed looking after and who apparently didn't yet know many people in Bangkok. One morning, about a week after Hom started dropping Miaow off early, Sonya asked if Hom would like her to speak to the baby in English some of the time.

"You speak English?" Hom asked.

"Little bit," Sonya said, in English. "Have American boyfriend before."

Hom's English was sparse, but "American" and "boyfriend" were within her zone. Sonya suddenly seemed more worldly, even a little more glamorous. She wasn't skinny, Hom thought, she was *slender*. She decided not to think about how and where Sonya had met her American. "I'd love that," she said. "It will make her smarter. Will it cost me extra?"

"I shouldn't tell you this," Sonya said, "but I'd take care of Miaow for free. She's the best baby of them all. No, it won't cost you anything."

Warm with pride, Hom said, "Do you do this for all the babies?"

"No. Right now, only Miaow." Sonya put a hand on Hom's forearm and leaned toward her, a gesture that had something confidential in it, a gesture that reminded Hom of her village friends. "Let me tell you something. My mother, who's dead now, could sometimes see the future. Not always, not whenever she wanted to, but sometimes. When I was eight she told me that I would be with a *farang* man and that he would make me unhappy but he would not be a bad man. All that happened."

"And you can do this, too? See these things?"

"Not like my mother could. I get pictures sometimes, just when I wake up in the morning. It's like I can see an album full of photographs before they've been taken. Sometimes I hear things, too. Voices. I heard my American boyfriend telling me he had died in America more than a week before someone said it was true."

Hom said, "I'm sorry."

"No, it was long after we broke up. But he was a good man, I wasn't surprised that he'd come to tell me."

"And you can see something for Miaow?"

"Mostly hearing. When I look at her, sometimes I hear English, like there might be someone important in her life who speaks English. My English is not good enough to teach her, *really* teach her, not even good enough to understand everything that I hear being said to her. I just think it would be good for me to say English words to her sometimes. *Hello, how are you, you are very pretty baby.* That's all."

Her heart suddenly feeling twice its normal size, Hom said, "I think it would be wonderful. Maybe someday she'll go to America."

SHE WORKED HARD, she paid attention, and she did well at the job. After a few months, the supervisor, once so brusque, smiled at her every morning and said, "Hello, *Phuhying thi na rak*" or "pretty one." Several times she asked Hom to work beside some terrified new girl, usually just down from the country, for her first day or two at the sorting tables, to help her get used to things. The girls she helped thought of her as a friend. For most of them, Hom was the first person in Bangkok who had been nice to them, who had extended a hand in any way. In the three brief break periods they were given each day, these women sat with her. They shared their food and their stories. Other women, women who had been there longer, heard the laughter and the babble of talk, saw the food changing hands, and began to join them. Even the supervisor sat with them occasionally, offering motherly advice from a chair that seemed to be a foot higher than theirs even though it was exactly the same size. Among the newcomers, Hom felt like a worldly-wise Bangkok veteran who knew how things worked. Among the older women, she still mostly listened, taking in the things they said, laughing at their jokes, and storing away whatever seemed to be useful. Several times each week, four or five of the women would go for a quick, cheap meal at the end of the day, and Hom was surprised to find that they always invited her, although she rarely went at first, eager to get back to Miaow and figure something out for Daw's dinner.

Still, she was, she realized, making friends. At first, she wasn't quite sure how to cope with it. These were the first real friends she'd made since her marriage. In Daw's village there had been two women she'd liked and could laugh with, but she'd been wary of sharing her problems with them, afraid her confidences would find their way back to her mother-in-law. She had begun to think of marriage and motherhood as the new geography of her life, a friendless geography. But now there were women who said hello to her, who joked with her, who wanted her to go out with them. Her life began to feel bigger and more real, now that there were people in it.

But she could only go out with them occasionally and for a short time, because she had to make the side trip to pick up Miaow at Sonya's, and she never knew when Daw might get home. Sometimes she'd find him waiting, the air ropy with cigarette smoke, and a pile of butts in the soup can he used as an ashtray, and sometimes he wouldn't come home until long after Miaow was asleep, after Hom had covered the food she had made and curled up beside her daughter. On the nights when he was late, he was usually half-drunk, and the drink seemed to make him resentful of the bond between her and Miaow, resentful that they were still living mostly on her money in spite of his efforts to find work. The days when he most felt like a failure were the days when he would come home angriest, and on those days there was a wall around him that she couldn't penetrate. He had underestimated Bangkok; he had thought he'd be accepted there as he had been in his village. He'd assured her that he could care for them all, and now he couldn't even pay for the cheap, terrible little room they slept in. It took nothing to set him off on those nights: what she'd made for dinner, the fact that she hadn't waited to eat with him and the food was cold, or the fact that she *had* waited and the food wasn't ready. The anger was already in him, circulating with his blood, eager to burst out. And when he'd drunk too much, he *wanted* something he could hang it on, some excuse to take it all out on her.

Three times, he slapped her. Each time, Miaow started to scream the instant she heard the sound, and Hom had to get between him and the baby because the screams redirected his anger at Miaow, or, as Hom said on the third night, *the smallest person in the room*. That had sent him out again, spiraling back into the night, even though it was pouring, slamming the door so hard it was probably heard by everyone on their floor and the one above them, and he hadn't come back until the following evening. When he finally arrived, he ignored her, ignored the food she had made, ignored Miaow, who had tottered to the most distant corner of the room. He lay down on the mat with his back to her, and she caught a whiff of perfume.

THAT NIGHT, AS he snored beside her, she decided to make a point: she would let him see what it would be like to be alone. She wouldn't be there when he got home, unless he came in very late. There would be no one to smile and say hello, there would be no food waiting for him. There hadn't been a night since they left his mother's house that she hadn't cooked for him. Even in the awful little hut down near the port she'd always found a way to make a meal, no matter how sparse.

But the following night, she went after work to a sidewalk food stall, bought the smallest portion the man sold, and ate standing

up, leaning against the warm wall of a building and watching
the city flow past. By then she was accustomed to the crowds; the
people no longer looked as grim or as much alike to her as they
had when she first arrived. Several women felt her gaze and
nodded to her. In those first months, she had felt invisible.

When the food was gone she carefully put the paper plate and
the plastic utensils into a trash barrel beside the vendor's cart,
treating the city with the same respect she had shown to her village, and then, struck by the thought, she took another, slower,
look around. It was true. Bangkok no longer felt alien to her. It
had become her new village, even if it hadn't become Daw's.

For a moment, that realization softened her heart; he was mis-
erably unhappy and he had no idea how to deal with it. She asked
herself whether she should give up on her plan for the evening
and just go home. But then she remembered the slaps and the
perfume.

So now, joining the flow of people on the sidewalk, she headed
for Sonya's apartment to retrieve Miaow. Without thinking about
it, she checked her purse for the half sandwich—avocado on soft
white bread—that she'd made for the child that morning. Miaow
hadn't yet developed a taste for spicy food, but she loved the
blandness of avocados, and Western-style white bread was easiest
for her to chew and swallow. A quick detour into a 7-Eleven got
her a small jar of chocolate pudding and a plastic spoon. Feeling
guilty about the pudding, she also bought an orange, even though
Miaow had no real affection for fruit other than bananas. When
Sonya opened the door, Miaow looked up at Hom from the floor,
beamed, and said, "Hello," which drove Hom a surprised step or
two back and made Sonya practically collapse in laughter. Hom
said hello back and Miaow said hello again, and the two of them
traded hellos for a minute or two until Sonya said, "I'll do something this week to move this conversation along." She bent down

and picked Miaow up with a huge grunt that made Miaow laugh and handed her to Hom, saying, "You take care of my favorite pupil." Hom bounced the child in her arms—getting heavy now, more than eleven kilos—and carried her down the stairs, ignoring Miaow's protests. Stairs were one of her favorite things, but the ones in Sonya's building were too steep and the risers were too high. Once they were back on the street she put Miaow down and took her hand. Instead of heading in the direction of home, she led her to Lumphini Park.

She hadn't spent any time in the park although it was fairly close to her work and to Sonya's place, and she'd never before seen anything quite so lush. Dusk was gathering itself and thickening into darkness, especially beneath the largest trees, and she was nervous about going too far in. She chose a bench at the foot of a small tree that let her look down over the long green sweep to the little lake, and after she took it in for a few moments, she gave Miaow her sandwich. The avocado made the child so happy she grunted as she ate it. Lights were going on in the buildings on the far side of the park, and the reflections flowed and rippled across the surface of the lake. For the first time in what felt like months, Hom relaxed almost completely, and the sigh she released was loud enough to stop Miaow in mid-swallow and start her coughing.

Hom got up, laid a paper napkin over her shoulder, and bounced the child up and down, feeling the pull down low in her own back; she wouldn't be able to do that much longer. She thumped Miaow between her shoulder blades for a few moments and then, with a little frisson of panic, lower down until the choking resolved into hiccups. She listened to Miaow and tried to make a hiccup sound of her own at exactly the same time the child did, and when she succeeded, Miaow's eyes went enormous and her mouth opened so wide that Hom began to laugh. Still laughing, she walked in a tight circle, patting her daughter's back until Miaow began to kick her legs and say, "Down." She ran in slow motion, letting the child chase her around the bench until she collapsed, fanning her face with her hand and exaggerating her panting, and Miaow, shrugging off Hom's help, clambered onto the bench beside her and put her head in her mother's lap and they let out simultaneous sighs. Miaow laughed again, at nothing, and Hom looked at the lights dancing on the water and, for a long moment, life was perfect. The elation lasted for a companionable hour or so, until Hom started to walk her child toward the place where she could catch the bus for home. The moment they took their seats on the bus, Miaow fell asleep.

When they had climbed the stairs to their floor, Hom slowed and picked Miaow up, saying, "Shhhh." In his never-ending effort to reduce costs, the building's owner had removed the bulbs from two of every three of the corridor's overhead lights, so she could see the pale strip beneath the door of their room all the way from the stair landing. She was surprised by how disappointed she felt. For a long moment she listened to her own heartbeat as she debated turning around and going back down the stairs. Instantly, she had a plan: drop Miaow with Sonya and ask her to recommend the cheapest hotel she knew of. That way, even if the hotel was rat-infested and bug-ridden, she would know the baby was safe with Sonya. Better still, maybe Sonya would let Hom sleep there, too, just for that night or for a few nights, on that clean, soft floor.

This is a daydream, she thought. *I can't do any of it until I've had more time to plan it, to find a new job, or he'll be waiting for me when I get off work. He even knows where Sonya's place is.* And behind the practical issues rose a wave of doubt. Maybe she wasn't being fair to him. He was much unhappier than she was. He was the one who couldn't get a job. If she left, she'd have Miaow; he was the one who would be alone.

Maybe. That perfume: maybe he wouldn't be alone at all. The money for the liquor: maybe he already had a job. *Maybe.*

And everything she owned in the world was inside that room. Shifting Miaow to her left arm, surprised yet again by the child's weight, she walked slowly down the hall and then, positioning herself to go through the door right shoulder first so she'd be between him and the child, she slipped the key into the lock and turned it.

There was only one light on, the little one on her side of the sleeping mat. He was lying on his back with both their pillows beneath his head, reading a comic book with the pages tilted toward the light. She stood there, still in the doorway, looking at him, and he put down the comic, lowered his head, and asked her forgiveness. Then he asked again. Miaow whimpered as they went into the room, but she put the child down and went to him, allowing him to wrap his arms around her. He was shaking as though he was cold.

25

Something Coiled About It

DAW FINALLY LANDED a job with a moving company, lugging large items from one place to another. The firm specialized in relocations within Bangkok, so he was rarely gone overnight, which she viewed as a mixed blessing. But the family's clock was now completely at the mercy of his job: sometimes he had to be up and out by 5 A.M., and quitting time depended on how much they had to move, and how hard it was to get stuff out of the old place and into the new place. Occasionally, they did two jobs in a single day, and on those days he didn't get home until midnight or even later. On those nights, he said, "the boys" would go out for a drink or two, and he always came home reeking of alcohol. Occasionally, one of the "boys" apparently wore perfume, because those were the nights she was most likely to smell a florid, over-sweet, probably cheap, scent. At first this sign of betrayal hit her like an elbow in the ribs, but week by week and month by month she realized that the landscape of the relationship was changing on the most basic levels. She and Daw, she thought, were less and less like lovers and more like business partners, united primarily by the need to keep the unit of three afloat from day to day. They rarely made love now. Miaow had a kind of emotional barometer that sensed when her mother's focus was primarily on Daw, and she didn't hesitate to demand attention at those times. Then, too, Daw was usually tired from his work, she was usually tired from *her* work, and, of course, there were those perfumes. It got to the point where her reaction to the colognes and the toilet waters and the powdery fragrance of makeup felt so little like jealousy it was hard to call it that. In time, she had to admit it was more like hurt feelings.

And she learned, more or less, to ignore it. They were polite, even occasionally affectionate, with each other, more focused than before on the challenge of surviving in the city. She tended to Miaow when she could and got her to and from Sonya's when she couldn't; and as she and Daw dealt with the small but insistent demands of daily life, the amount of energy they had for each other waned, and with it went much of the tension between them.

On one hand, Hom welcomed the easing of the drama, but on the other, it soon began to feel to her that the drama had become the primary emotion in the relationship, the only energy they shared. Its decline left her feeling not closer to him but more remote. And as they grew farther apart, going from lovers to spouses to parents to, she supposed, collaborators in the enterprise of staying alive, she invested even more of her heart in Miaow.

But she was still a young woman, energetic and curious, and even during the rare intervals of affection between her and Daw, she felt like the horizon that once seemed so vast and full of possibility had shrunk practically to the tip of her nose. She was trapped in a cycle: small room; moody, often distant husband; a child who, at three, intermittently delighted and exhausted her; and the dull, unchanging routine of work. Life was as monotonous and as predictable as a drumbeat. Even her new friends, who had so engaged her at first, soon began to oppress her. They were unattached, they were having adventures in the big city; they talked about the men—alternately good and appalling—who seemed to drift in and out of their lives. They made jokes and laughed until the tears came. Hom couldn't remember the last time she'd made a joke, or even felt like making one. Compared to them, she was an obscure, colorless satellite caught in a tiny orbit around her husband and her child. As a small, lifeless moon, she could barely remember how it had felt to be the planet around which things revolved. How it felt to be the person who *mattered*.

Primarily, she supposed, she felt foolish. She had believed him and believed him and believed him: when he said he loved her, when he promised to be a good husband, when he came to make amends after she escaped his mother's house. She had believed him about the fast train, and the optimistic picture he had painted of how they would find their feet in Bangkok. She had believed that she and Miaow would be safe with him. Worst of all, she had believed that their marriage would be a world inhabited solely by the two of them, and then the three of them. Not that there would never be problems, but that the problems would be *shared*. The problems might prove to be difficult to solve, but they would be theirs alone, and she had believed that love would bring them through. Because that, she had thought, was what marriage *was*. It was a shelter they would share: the three of them on the inside, caring for each other, and, out there, everyone else.

But perfume. Perfume meant he had told the biggest lie of all.

Her sense of betrayal was more about trust than it was about sex. They had made love much less since Miaow was conceived. He had been nervous at first that it might not be good for the child she was carrying, and then his interest waned as her belly thickened. After the birth, he gave her the time she needed to recover, and then more time, until she asked about it, and he said he was ashamed to go to bed with her in his mother's house. In the early months of their marriage, Hom had been noisy in her enthusiasm, and they both knew that his mother could hear her. And now, being jammed into a tiny, thin-walled room with their daughter only a few feet away wasn't really conducive to spontaneous affection, either. On the few occasions now when they *did* make love, she could see that he interpreted her silence as a lack of enthusiasm, which, in part, it was. He might not, she thought, have wanted her often, but he wanted to believe that he still had the old magic. So he sulked.

And he had struck her. She had known since her early teens that some men occasionally hit their wives; it was no secret in her village that some marriages were much worse than that. The occasional infrequent slap, while it was nothing for either partner to be proud of, didn't necessarily mean that the marriage was over. Men, she had been told, were like that sometimes. Men drank too much sometimes. The women whose husbands never raised a hand to them kept silent to avoid isolating or shaming the ones who were less fortunate.

But she hadn't thought it would happen to her.

So, all that, and perfume, too.

Marooned on icebergs of resentment and disappointment, she and Daw floated apart.

BUT THEN THERE was an opening in the clouds, and Hom, at least momentarily, caught a glimpse of freedom. She would no longer be imprisoned twelve to fourteen hours a day at work and in the increasingly oppressive room she shared with Daw and Miaow. Sonya moved into a new two-room apartment and hired a helper, so it was possible for Hom to leave Miaow with her much later than before, until ten in the evening or even eleven. Instead of waiting in the tiny room, empty until Daw finally decided to come home, Hom had her evenings to do whatever she wanted. She began to go out four or five times a week with her circle of friends from work. The restaurant they favored was a little dump not far from the Isaan place where she and Daw had gone when they first arrived in Bangkok. The food was acceptable and the beer was cheap, and they began to assemble in groups of five or six, shoehorned into a booth for four, carrying on several conversations at the same time and elbowing each other every time the place's newest employee, a tall, willowy young man named Chai, emerged from his usual station in the kitchen—he was an apprentice cook—to deliver food to some customer when the waitresses were overextended.

The waitresses were often overextended, and over the course of a few weeks Chai was pressed into service often enough that he began to call the women in the booth by name, although it was Hom's name he memorized first, blushing when he said it. Hom found herself thinking, *What a country boy,* and was surprised to realize it wasn't an insult. One night, one of the women looked at the full tables and said, "Maybe I should work here," and two days after that Hom spoke to the manager and was given a short four-hour shift waiting tables during the busiest period of the evening. She felt a little guilty about leaving Miaow with Sonya's helper, but the money—especially the nightly tips—felt good in her pocket. She began to hide the tips in the bottom of the bag she used for dirty laundry, someplace Daw would never look, and she told herself she could save it there until she could afford a place of her own. Although the idea startled and even frightened her when it made its first appearance, as the days passed it blossomed before her: just her and Miaow, no fights, no sulking, no irregular hours, no perfume. A closed partnership of two. The fact that she was taking action lightened her heart. She even felt, on occasion, affection, of a newly remote kind, for Daw.

She was, it turned out, a first-rate waitress. She remembered customers' preferences and, if they told her their names, she remembered those as well. Generally speaking, she liked most people until they gave her reason to change her mind, so smiling was easy. Her tips grew at such a rate that she began to share them with the people who worked in the kitchen. And, slowly, she and Chai made friends.

He was lonely. He was homesick. He was the oldest of three boys and he had come down to Bangkok with the assignment not only to earn his keep and send something home, but to prepare for his brothers to come down as well. As handsome as he was, he seemed completely unconscious of it, while at the same time Hom's beauty seemed, at first, to intimidate him. Before they got to know each other she'd sometimes feel his stare from across the room, or one of the girls would nudge her and say, "Fish alert," and she'd look up to see Chai gaping at her with his mouth open as wide as tilapia some Isaan rice farmers raised in their paddies.

After two or three weeks the looks had become mutual and Hom stopped hurrying out to pick up Miaow the moment the dinner rush was over, sitting instead in one of the empty booths with a glass of juice or, if she was feeling reckless, a beer. On the nights she wasn't working, when things got really slow, Chai would come out, usually with a little treat he'd made for her, and sit, as far away as possible while still having both buttocks on the cushions of the booth. He talked to her about his family and his brothers and his ambition to own a restaurant of his own someday, and she listened. He asked her questions, and then *he* listened, although her answers weren't completely honest: she edited out both Daw and, with an intense pang of guilt, Miaow.

She had been with only one boy in her life, and he had been transformed into a sullen, untrustworthy, inarticulate stranger who had apparently come to prefer other women to her. Chai was young, he was sweet, he was easy to talk to. She could still smell the village on him—slow, warm, dusty—and it reassured her. Occasionally, when there were no customers, they clocked out early and he took her someplace nearby for a drink, beer for both of them. She stayed with him, one eye on the wall clock, until she had to run to get Miaow in time. Twice, Sonya was on the verge of going to bed, and treated Hom to a raised eyebrow that was both a comment and an invitation to share, but Hom just thanked her, apologized for being late and hurried out. The second time, Sonya said, "If you keep this up, you're going to get here one night after I've locked up, and you're going to have to leave Miaow here all night. Not easy to explain to your husband."

Hom had said, "He won't even notice," in a tone Sonya had never heard before, and from then on she and Sonya weren't quite so close.

The next night, Chai asked her to go out again, and she declined. But she knew that the door was there, any time she wanted to go through it. Her world got a little bigger. At any time she chose, she knew, she could say yes and then yes again, and Daw would no longer be the only man with whom she had made love. The possibility hung there in front of her, glittering faintly. Of course, Chai still didn't know about Miaow.

AFTER A COUPLE of months on the new job, as she and Chai continued to warm their hands at the fire of their potential, she realized that Daw had adjusted to her schedule and that he was now coming home later and later every night, sometimes at one or two, even when he had to get up at the crack of dawn, and she noticed that he had a new kind of energy, speedy, edgy, and somehow brittle. One night, hanging up the pants he had left on the floor, she found six small white pills mixed in with his change. She put them in a neat stack on the little shelf she'd built above the metal bar from which they hung their clothes, and in the morning she asked him about them.

"They're great," he said. "Even on the hardest days, I don't get tired. Don't need to eat as much, either."

She had been gaining weight, what with her after-dinner dinners with the boy from the restaurant, and she asked if he thought she could try one.

"Sure," he said, "but let me cut it in half for you. You're not as big as I am, and half will be plenty."

When she went to work that day, she seemed to feel the little tablet in the pocket of her jeans, emitting a kind of warm buzz, even through the square of toilet paper into which she'd folded it. Since her morning energy was always high, she decided to take it after lunch, thinking it would get her through her shift at the restaurant and keep her from yawning in Chai's face if they went out afterward. But when it came time, she hesitated. She went to the bathroom and took it out, unwrapped it, and studied it. It was small and white and as clean-looking, as safe-looking, as an aspirin, but reassuringly smaller. She licked her finger, touched the tablet, and then tasted it. A little bitter, but no more so than aspirin. Still, she sensed something *coiled* about it, something that made her think it might be bigger than it looked, and she folded it up in its paper wrapping again and put it back in her pocket.

That night she told the boy in the restaurant that she was sleepy and had to go home. When she picked up Miaow early, she was feeling virtuous and committed, and on her way home she stopped and bought Daw a treat, a little cellophane-wrapped box of spicy tamarind candy that he loved. That night, he got back after midnight, walking into things as he came in and absolutely stinking of something that someone had probably thought smelled like flowers.

She lay still, pretending to be asleep and counting her heartbeats as he fumbled through undressing and getting into bed. When he put his head on the pillow his cheekbone hit the corner of the candy box and he said, "Shit," and threw it across the room without looking at it. It took him no time to begin snoring, but she lay awake until it began to get light, vacillating between fury and despair. She finally fell asleep by focusing on the sound of Miaow's breathing.

Time stuttered onward, five days of working at a job and a half and grumbling about it, followed by two days spent wishing she were back at work. She took the half pill two days after he gave it to her, just before the lunch break in the sorting room, and was amazed at how the time at work seemed to fly past, how *interesting* everyone was, how much she—who had always been shy—had to say to them and how quickly the words came. She asked him for another and then two more, continuing to break them in half, although when she took the third one he gave her, she swallowed both halves and was dazzled by her energy and how well-disposed she felt to everyone. Daw had taken to coming and going as he pleased, not getting home some nights until two or even three in the morning, then dragging himself out of bed in the morning, taking a pill, and then bouncing off to work. By now the sleeping mat smelled like a bag full of makeup, even when he wasn't home. He was working some weekend days now (or said he was) and for the first time, there was money in the house. He bristled with energy, although his memory was a little spotty, and he always had bills in his pockets. She could see the change in both his finances and his confidence; his hair was neatly cut again, and he was shaving every other day in the bowl of water he filled up from the bath at the end of the hallway and then left in the middle of the floor, right where she'd trip over it later and have to spend five or ten minutes mopping up and wringing the cloths out through the window that wasn't supposed to be open. She'd stopped worrying about the window, thinking that now, with him working and her doing almost two full jobs, they had enough to get a *real* place to live. She entertained the idea several times before she realized that she was no longer thinking seriously about leaving him.

Things had been easier since they began taking the pills. They fought less often, in part because they seemed increasingly to inhabit separate worlds, coming together and separating without the collisions that had made things so difficult. And, if she had to admit the truth to herself, she had long spent her bag of tip money to buy her own pills, and her new tips went as fast as she earned them.

Because by that time she had her own source, a kitchen worker in the restaurant who gave her a discount (he said) for being so nice to everyone. Weeks later, she learned he told everyone that, and that, in fact, charged some of the others less, but she didn't care: the pills got her through the day's work, and the night's too. She told herself she was taking them on a reasonable schedule: a half around lunchtime to pick her up in the long hot afternoons at the sorting table, a whole one just before her shift was over to propel her through the hours she spent on her feet at the restaurant. But on the nights when Daw awoke her when he came in, making it more difficult to drag herself out of bed, she began to take a half within a few minutes of getting up, telling herself she'd skip the one before lunch. She usually took it anyway.

And, as she continued to see Chai and it grew more and more difficult to edit Daw and Miaow out of the version of her life she shared with him, she found a new benefit to the pills: they heightened her interest in him; they helped her ask the questions he wanted to be asked. Sweet as he was, like most men, she decided, he was happiest when he was talking about himself.

And when he finally asked her to go home with him, the pills came to the rescue again; difficult as it had usually been for her to tell a lie, it required no effort for her to sweep aside the fact that she had to pick up Miaow and to say, without even a brief pause to improvise, that her morning shift had changed and she had to be at the sorting table an hour earlier than before. She promised herself she'd tell him about Miaow sooner or later, when and if it seemed necessary. As she walked toward Sonya's, she also reminded herself that she had no intention of going to bed with him. Still, it had been reassuring to be asked. She'd been seeing a different woman in the mirror lately, older and more tired-looking, and thinner too; the bones of her face were emerging with new and unflattering clarity.

That, she knew, was because she'd been having trouble sleeping, and when she mentioned it to the kitchen worker who sold her the little white pills, he said he had something for that, too, and sure enough, they put her out in a matter of minutes and she slept deeply and dreamlessly.

One night, in fact, Daw had to elbow her awake to tell her that Miaow was crying in her sleep. She felt a flare of resentment toward him for not dealing with it himself, and when she shook Miaow awake she might not have been as gentle as she usually was, because Miaow let out a bewildered yelp and rolled away from her. She took the child in her arms and rocked her back to sleep, but there was an infinitesimal stone of resentment in the center of her chest. In the morning she remembered none of it, and was surprised when Daw told her what had happened. Doubted it, in fact, until she saw something new in the way Miaow looked at her.

She hadn't written or called home for weeks and weeks.

26

Day by Day

DAY BY DAY, night by night, pill by pill. Not so much difference for the two of them now between day and night. Miaow, though, Miaow still slept all night.

With their increased income, they moved into what had been called a "suite" when the hotel was still a hotel: double the price, two rooms rather than one, with its own functioning toilet, one that could actually be flushed, although the shut-off valve to the shower was, like the one in their old room, welded closed. Still, they could run the water in the little bathroom sink to wash underwear and Miaow's clothes and even soak cloths and use them to clean themselves in a perfunctory manner, a quick, approximate sponge bath rather than the showers and the lengthy baths she had always loved. But now the wet cloth satisfied her. Despite the fact that they were much closer than before to the floor's one functional shower, they rarely made use of it.

But the most important thing about the suite was that it gave her a room of her own; she had argued for the necessity of her having the inner room so he could come and go without waking her. No more having to get Miaow back to sleep when he stumbled in at three in the morning and no more (although she didn't say it) having to smell the perfume of the week. By making her pills last longer for a couple of weeks she had bought a cheap but perfume-free sleeping mat and a separate, smaller one for Miaow, and she'd put them right next to each other. But that hadn't been such a good idea after all. After a few weeks, when she realized her increasingly eccentric sleep patterns were keeping the child up, she'd created a space between the mats and put a rolled-up blanket between them. Separated even so modestly, Miaow seemed less sensitive to whether her mother was asleep.

As the months sped by, she discovered another benefit to having a space of her own. She didn't have to share her pills with Daw; they were all hers. She was becoming more accustomed to the various tablets and capsules and more expert in their use, and she found that she was also growing possessive of her experiences with them. She didn't *want* Daw in there, staring at her, monitoring her intake, asking what she was feeling, making her talk about it. He could go on forever about what the pills did to him, how they made him feel, making suggestions to her, everything from optimum dosages to mixing cocktails, for what seemed like hours on end. She was doing just fine without all that *sharing*, and she wanted own her experiences, she wanted to keep them to herself; they were, after all, all hers.

Over the following weeks and months, as the pills carved their way into her rhythms, she began to see the hours of darkness differently. She came to regard as wasted much of the time she had previously abandoned to sleep. By postponing swallowing the sleeper sleep until three or four in the morning, she could set her own rhythms, choose her own projects. For one thing, she could clean; she had taken to wiping down the floor and the walls, at least as high as she could reach, with a damp cloth, turning it until it was gray on all sides and then rinsing it out, repeating until she was done. She could do this almost nightly and still feel like she was falling behind. She could organize her clothes for the week, laying out five sets of T-shirts and jeans, which she would cover partially with the long buttoned jacket she wore at the sorting table and removed to eat in the restaurant. She could mend things, both hers and Miaow's, spotting an area of wear and reinforcing it before it could give way, re-patching the patches. She bought new buttons for her blouses, snipped off the old ones, and replaced them. She bought a stiff brush so she could clean out the stuff that got wedged into the tread of her shoes. Everywhere she looked, she saw something that needed to be done. One night she came home with a tablet of lined yellow paper and began to write down her thoughts, which evolved into the story of her life, told in no particular order. She illustrated it with line drawings, taking it with her in her purse each day so Daw couldn't read it if he came home early, which he never did. She bought a second tablet and wrote dozens of letters she never sent, to her parents, her sisters, and her friends from the village. The night-time hours were, if anything, too short.

One night, when she'd run out of things to do, having been aware for the first hour or two of Miaow's gaze, she gave up and swallowed a sleeper—actually a sleeper and a half—and drifted most of the way to the cliff she always fell over now when she went to sleep, but instead, abruptly, she sat up. The suite had rats, and she'd suddenly envisioned a new kind of rat trap, one that couldn't snap shut on her daughter's fingers. Within minutes she had created it: a bread knife with a dab of Miaow's peanut butter on its tip, balanced on the edge of the built-in four-drawer storage unit. The knife was positioned over a wastebasket, and several times in the first two or three weeks she'd been awakened by the knife racketing into the basket and the rat running feverish laps at its bottom. Daw had forced open a window in both rooms—nothing as crafty as in their old room—and she just dumped the rat out the window. Eventually, she made a trap for Daw's room, too.

She was learning that, with the pills, nothing stayed the same for long. As the sleepers lost their potency, she upped the dose and noticed a fundamental change in her usual nightly dance with sleep. Where in the past, before the pills, she had drifted slowly into dreams and then snapped awake in the morning, ready to go, she now fell asleep without any transition, completely and abruptly. And waking, instead of being a gentle swim into the morning light, had become an ordeal. After several days when she slept through the alarm and had to be awakened by Miaow, hungry for breakfast, tugging at her finger, she took to putting one of the white pills on the floor beside her bed and setting the alarm an hour early so she could roll over, take the pill dry-mouthed, and drop off again until she abruptly snapped back to life, often ahead of time, surfacing instantly with her foot tapping and a list of chores and errands assembling itself in her head. Jump up, check the other room to see whether Daw was asleep, had already left, or (possibly) hadn't come home at all. Make a quick breakfast for either two or three, depending. Wash face, scrub under arms, wash Miaow's face and hands, get dressed, argue with Miaow about which T-shirt she would wear that day, and bundle her out the door.

Her relationship with Sonya had become businesslike and even chilly. In the morning, Hom darted in and out like a humming-bird, always running late, and Sonya no longer talked with her about teaching Miaow English or, actually, about much of anything. The evening visit was equally truncated. Hom would nip in with minutes to spare, wake the child from her napping place on the floor, take her hand—she had become far too heavy to carry comfortably—and lead her down the stairs, occasionally hurrying her even though she knew Miaow was proud of going down without help and enjoyed prolonging it. Sometimes when Hom appeared at Sonya's, Miaow would cry as though she were unwilling to go. Once or twice she stretched her arms toward Sonya's helper, as though she wanted to stay there.

And, in fact, it seemed to Hom that Miaow's terrible twos hadn't eased much when she had turned three, or even now, as she approached her fourth birthday. She was querulous, insistent, demanding. She eyed her mother at times as though she were a stranger. Sometimes when they were alone in the room that belonged to just them, Miaow would fold herself into a corner and talk under her breath to the two rag dolls she'd had since she was in her crib. She kept her face toward the floor, moving the dolls from one side to the other as though they were playing with each other, maintaining an inaudible dialogue under her breath. It didn't take much to start her crying, and she went into a rage if Hom took the dolls away—even if she just wanted the child to eat. And when they were sitting on the floor together, eating, Miaow often whispered to the dolls rather than engaging with her mother.

Miaow's new distance angered Hom; wasn't she working herself half to death for the benefit of her child? What was wrong with Miaow? What happened to the cheerful child who smiled at her all the time, the quick learner who sometimes startled both her and Daw with her English words? Where was the little girl who had turned to her for everything, who cried for her the moment someone else, even her father, picked her up? Now she seemed happier with Sonya and Sonya's not-very-intelligent assistant than she was with her own mother.

And it seemed to her, during the times she was thinking about Miaow, that it was all she did: she felt like she was preoccupied with Miaow night and day. She had invented the *rat trap* just for her. Wasn't that love?

There were times when an unwelcome notion peeked through at her: Were the pills to blame? But how could she do without them, how could she power through it all, her fifteen-hour work-days, her loneliness, her unsatisfactory, unfaithful husband, all of it? She decided several times to stop taking the pills, but after a few sleepless nights and a few endless, exhausting days, they always waved at her from her peripheral vision, calling her back to them. Several times, when she found herself taking a little extra—another quarter or half, or perhaps more—for the same effect, Daw came home, bursting with energy, with something new, something that lasted longer and gave him more energy—so, he said, he could take less, work harder, work longer. Once again Hom began cautiously, by halving them, and once again that lasted only for a couple of weeks until she graduated to just popping the whole thing, or, occasionally, two. They *were* stronger, they seemed to make her faster, clearer, more incisive, better at her job in the restaurant.

They cost more, too.

She had begun to notice that her days, vivid as they were when she was living them, were getting more difficult to remember. Sometime she couldn't recall what she'd done the previous day, sometimes she remembered an event as having happened on a day when it logically could not have. Once she got dressed and went to work to find the restaurant fully staffed; it was Sunday, the one day she didn't work. She went back and got Miaow so she wouldn't have to pay Sonya for a whole day, feeling the curious gaze of Sonya's newest helper, the one who worked weekends.

And then, on the eighth or ninth morning that she straggled into the sorting room too late, the supervisor took her aside and told her she was concerned about her. Maybe, she said, Hom was trying to do too much, but whether that was the issue or not, it was obvious that something was wrong. She was late as often as she was on time, she seemed jumpy and quarrelsome, and she had recently made several mistakes, sorting errors that would have cost the business a lot of money, or even an account, if a new girl, one of the ones Hom had trained, hadn't spotted them at the last moment and called them to the supervisor's attention. "What I want you to do," the supervisor said, looking at Hom very closely, "is take a few weeks' vacation. Think about things," she said. "Get some rest, you look tired. If you still want to be here when things have settled down, you come talk to me, and we'll work something out."

Then she had reached into her pocket and pressed into Hom's hand a small wad of bills, the exact pay for the three days she'd worked that week. Not until Hom was on the sidewalk did she realize that her firing had been planned. The supervisor had precisely the right amount of money in her pocket. The new girl, the one who reported the mistakes, had been sitting at Hom's table. She never glanced up the whole time Hom was there.

As she stood perfectly still on the sidewalk, the wave of shame almost swept her off her feet.

ON THE FOLLOWING Saturday, the day that Hom worked a full day-shift at the restaurant, she came home to learn that their rent had been doubled. Daw had been there when the rent collector knocked on the door to get the money and give him the news, and when he protested, the collector gave him two days to move out if he didn't like it. There were a lot of people who wanted the room, he said. Stay and pay, or go, the management didn't care which. That night, shortly after Hom got home, Daw came in from wherever he'd been, sober and fragrance-free, to report the conversation.

"And I'm not getting as much work as I was," he said. "One of the men who ran the company split off and started his own outfit, so now there's only about half as much work."

"Really," she said. "I'd think you'd be home more."

"I'm out every day, looking for something new," he said. "Now that you got yourself fired, I need to make more. Great timing, by the way."

They were in the front room, Daw's room. She'd only gotten home around six-thirty, half an hour before he came in, and when she heard the front door open she'd left Miaow in the inner room. Now, perhaps hearing the anger in their voices, she began to call for Hom.

"Mommy," she said. "Mommy?"

"Take care of her," Daw said. "Then make something to eat."

"I had no way of knowing you were going to be here," Hom said. "You're never here at this hour. I haven't got anything you'd want."

"What about you? What about the kid?"

"I ate at the restaurant. I can just heat some soup for her."

"I don't want soup."

Hom got up. "I wasn't offering you any."

"Sit *down*," Daw said.

Hom said, "Go out and get something that you—"

As she turned away, Daw grabbed her wrist and yanked her back, so hard that she stumbled and went down sideways onto the chair, hard enough for it to start to go over backward, but he slammed his forearm down on her knees and brought the chair's front legs back to the ground.

From the other room, Miaow called, "*Mommy*." She sounded anxious.

"You've got money in your pocket," Daw said. "You got tipped all day long. Go out and get me something right now. *Tom yam goong* and *phad kaprao*. And get them back here while they're still hot."

Hom said, "Tell one of your girlfriends to—" but he slapped her in mid-word. She sat, stunned and glaring at him, barely hearing Miaow crying from the inner room, and then, slowly, she stood up.

"If you *ever* do that again," she said, "that will be the end. It will be the last time you ever see me. If you don't believe it, hit me right now. Come on, do it."

Miaow said, "*Mommy*," again.

To her surprise, Daw stretched an arm toward her. She pulled back the hand that was nearer to him, and he leaned forward and took the other one. She started to withdraw it, but he covered it with both of his, gently, and she stopped resisting. For the first time in months, they looked into each other's eyes.

Finally, he said, "I'm sorry." His glance skittered down to the floor and came back up again. "I'm worried and, I don't know, frightened." He closed his eyes, and when he opened them again he said, "Maybe it's the pills."

Something inside her clenched itself tight, but she pushed it away. She looked at him, registering the changes in his face: heavier, more blunt, less finely formed. Older. She sat back down. "Do you think so?"

He said, "Are you happy?"

"No," she said, biting back what she wanted to say about his absence, the perfume, the other women. He had come to her, and the least she could do was listen.

"Let's try it," he said. "Let's throw them away, all of them."

Miaow called out again, and this time, Hom said, "Just a minute, sweetheart. I'll be right there."

Daw said, "Can we do this?"

"Why would I—" she said, and then she abandoned the sentence and sat completely still. She was looking at her lap but she could feel his eyes on her. "I mean, it's not . . ."

Miaow called her again, obviously on the verge of tears.

"It's up to you," he said. "But I'm going to do it. *Try* to do it."

Hom felt a feathery little ball of panic in her chest. She had to breathe around it. She said, "I don't know, I mean, I'm not—"

There was something rising in her throat, and she swallowed it once and then again, and when she could speak, she said, "When? Where?"

"Now. In the sink. We'll throw them in and run water over them." He got up and went to his drawer and pulled out a cloth bag with a knot at the top. He held it up to her, eyebrows raised. "Yes or no?"

In the moment it took her to find an answer, she had the sensation of something heavy rising up from inside her and escaping into the room; the light seemed just a tiny bit sharper, and she had a sense that it was a long time since she'd taken a really deep breath, the kind that relaxed her all the way to her toes. She shook her head to clear all that away, and said, "Yes." Then she was up and hurrying into her room. Miaow was sitting with her back against the wall, one rag doll clenched tightly in each hand, looking up at her. "Just a minute, sweetheart," she said. "Everything's fine," and then she went into the little bathroom, feeling like she was walking up a steep hill, lifted the lid of the toilet's water tank, and peeled away the Ziplock bag she had taped to its underside. Trying not to look at it, trying not to register the familiar shapes and colors. She turned to see Daw looking at her, and, a good two meters behind him and peering around his legs, Miaow.

"Honey," she said to her daughter, "go over to your dollies for a few minutes. Your daddy and I have something to do." She stepped to the sink and started the water flowing.

"Plug it up," Daw said.

She put the plug in the drain and said, "You're sure about this?"

"I'll *show* you," he said, and he loosened the drawstring on his bag and turned it upside down over the sink.

Hom watched the pills spill into the water. There were a lot of them, and several were new to her, and she felt a quick current of resentment: he'd been *keeping* them from her. But she swallowed the emotion—something she'd grown used to doing—and exhaled heavily, stepping back a little to avoid getting splashed as he shook the bag empty and dropped it to the floor, and then put his hand in the water and began to stir it. While his attention was on the sink, she worried open the Ziploc and fished out a couple of clean-looking white uppers. She'd eased two of them out and into her palm as he turned to her, and she felt the instant blush of someone caught in something furtive, so she handed them over and went to work on the others, feeling the familiar shapes and weight as she worked them free and passed them on. When the bag was empty, nothing in it but the dust the pills had left behind, she held it upside down in front of him, and he nodded.

She had thought the pills would dissolve quickly, the way she envisioned them doing in her stomach, but they stubbornly retained their shapes as Daw stirred the water with his hands. The colored ones were tinting the water around them, but none of them seemed to be shrinking.

"Wish we had hot water," Daw said. "That would speed it up."

"Maybe we should just leave them," she said. "Let them fall apart on their own."

He startled her by laughing, although there was no amusement in it. "Might not be a good idea. I might be in here in two minutes with a couple of straws."

To her surprise, she laughed too. She couldn't remember the last time they'd laughed together.

He had big, flat hands, like paddles, and he was stirring hard enough and fast enough that water occasionally slopped over the edge of the basin. He leaned down, a little closer to the water's surface. "Here they go," he said, and, sure enough, some of them were disintegrating, leaving smoky little trails behind. She stepped closer without being aware that she had done it, and they stood, shoulders touching, watching the whirlpool until he pulled the plug and let the water, not so clear now, drain away into the dark pipes, unrecoverable. When it was gone he took his cloth bag, ran water over it, and mopped the basin several times, rinsing the bag and wringing it out each time until he apparently felt the basin was clean. He licked an index finger, passed it over the porcelain, and licked it again. Then he nodded. "Done."

He turned and opened his arms to her, and without a moment's thought she stepped into them and felt them close around her. "Miaow?" she said. "Can you come here for a hug?"

They all went out to dinner for the first time in months, and then went for ice cream. Daw told Miaow she could have anything she wanted, and she said she wanted three flavors: banana, banana, and banana.

27

A Sparkling Little Bouquet

IT LASTED ALMOST two weeks, two endless, itchy, irritable, bite-the-tongue-and-breathe-deeply weeks during which she found herself sidestepping sudden flares of anger as she would puddles on the sidewalk. On the thirteenth day—at a time when, before the supervisor let her go, she would have been at the sorting table, thinking about lunch—she was instead (she told herself) straightening Daw's room, and, naturally, that meant that she had to hang up his trousers. He had four pairs, all jeans, and the three he wasn't wearing were—in the order in which she spotted them—crumpled on the floor, wadded up on top of his drawer unit, and dangling from a coat hanger he'd slipped through a belt loop. That was the one, she decided, he'd thought she'd be least likely to handle.

That was the one with the pills in the pocket.

A sparkling little bouquet. Five, in all. Two of the tidy, immaculate white speedies that had gotten her started in the first place, one sleeper, one she couldn't identify, and an orange tablet she recognized as *yaa baa*, which she hadn't yet tried. The guy who worked in the kitchen and sold her most of her pills had told her not to mess with it until she knew she could either be alone for a few hours or in the company of people she trusted who had taken it before. "It's a big one," he'd said. "You want to be a little careful at first."

For a moment Hom was startled by how deeply the discovery of Daw's deception upset her, how sad it made her feel. Then she felt a surge of anger that he was keeping the pills from her, followed by a sudden impulse to get revenge by swallowing all five at once and seeing where they would take her. But no, he'd be furious; he might even hit her, and, anyway, she had to go pick up Miaow pretty soon. At the notion of going out, a little insect hidden somewhere in her mind rubbed its long legs together in anticipation. Once she was out, she could get her own. The energy churned inside her. She put the pills back, took a quick look through the window, saw that it was drizzling and that it might be a prelude to something more dramatic, and grabbed an umbrella. At the last moment, she remembered to get a little rain cape for Miaow.

First, a stop at the restaurant for a quick buy from the guy in the kitchen (and a nod and smile for Chai) and then, with the pills secure in the pocket of her jeans, a quick swing by Sonya's for the child. She could wait to take the uppers until tomorrow morning, she thought, but she'd sleep like the dead that night.

AND SHE DID, that night and the nights that followed. With the weeks blurring into months, with no one tracking the time, she and Daw became silent partners, never acknowledging in so many words they were both complicit, that they had chosen their path together. There was a new feeling of freedom about it, a sort of mutual abandon, something like a shared commitment. They no longer hid their pills from each other. They sat together through long nights, bristling with words and ideas, laughing and talking over one another, launching themselves into new experiences as they never had before, comparing notes on the pills, developing a connoisseur's vocabulary. When things went bad, they eased each other through it. They were, Hom discovered, closer than they'd even been. He became the scout, discovering and bringing home new adventures, especially new painkillers, and she chipped in, sometimes with money scooped from the register at the restaurant because they were spending almost as much as they were earning.

They could no longer afford to keep Miaow at Sonya's, so she was home all day and all night, "underfoot," as Daw sometimes complained. Sensing that she was excluded from something she didn't understand, Miaow located and claimed the empty corners of the apartment's two rooms, the spaces her parents never used.

As her mother and father formed a new, overenergetic team, Miaow withdrew even more deeply into herself, more silent with every passing month and season. Largely unobserved, she grew taller and more slender, her plump baby features giving way to a distinct, and even striking, face, although it was usually tilted downward, toward the floor. She became comfortable, or so it seemed, with her invisibility. Being alone, occupying her solitary corners became her obvious preference. She backed away from hugs, avoided eye contact, and often answered questions in a whisper, as though making more noise than that would draw attention to her or, perhaps, prolong the interaction. Or, as Hom sometimes realized with a squeeze of pain around her heart, make her or Daw angry.

For company, Miaow clung to the tatters that were all that remained of her two rag dolls, and she spent much of her time in the back room with them, engaged in a murmured three-way dialogue, improvising plays in which she assigned all of them, including herself, names and clearly defined roles. The plays were usually about things she had seen and done, and sometimes the dolls had the names of people she had met: Sonya and her helper or kids who had been staying at Sonya's when Miaow did. Miaow used a different voice or whisper for each person, and the characters weren't limited to the dolls; she would invent spirited exchanges between windows and doors or among dinner utensils. Whatever the play of the moment, it ceased the instant the door was opened and the spell shattered. She usually hid the remnants of the dolls behind her, as though she thought they might be taken away.

Slowly, she grew an invisible shell. She obviously dreaded Hom's occasional seizures of guilt, almost operatic in their intensity; she often talked softly to herself as Hom promised her that everything would change. She usually had to be asked a question twice before she would answer, and when she did, it was often a monosyllable, barely audible.

As Miaow sealed herself off and floated into her whisper world, Hom fretted. With no day job except for her full-day waitress shift on Saturday, and the ever-increasing cost of the pills, she found herself missing the hours at the sorting table, not solely because of the money, but also because she felt trapped in the apartment day after day with no one who understood her state of mind. She chafed at her solitude even when she was caught up in the wind-tunnel energy of an amphetamine project or luxuriating in the trapped-in-amber languor of the pain pills. In between those high points, she was bored and resentful or jittery and short-tempered, staring out the window and at the ugly *soi*, wishing she were down there or, really, anywhere. But, she told herself, there was nothing she could do; she was stuck there, with a child who barely acknowledged her, who *rejected* her, until Daw got back, which he usually did just before she had to leave for the restaurant. It became more and more important for her to get to work on time; she wasn't as polite and patient with customers as she had been, and she knew she was no longer the management's pet waitress.

Even Chai was gone. He'd found a better job, cooking at a nicer restaurant. He had come by to see her three times, the two of them sitting in their old booth, but it was clear that the attraction between them had evaporated, at least on his part. Several times, halfway through a long and—she thought—interesting answer to one of his questions, she saw his brow furrow, and she realized that he had lost her thread. And, at least once, so had she; when this happened he looked at her as if he wasn't quite sure who she was. So he stopped coming. The girls from her old job had stopped coming, too, for some reason and so, other than the money, she no longer had any cause to look forward to the restaurant. In fact, the only thing it had to recommend it was that it wasn't the apartment, where time often felt as thick and slow as sludge.

When Daw was late coming home, which wasn't as frequent as it had once been, she towed Miaow down the hall to a single room occupied by a thin, tired-looking woman with two small children of her own. Each time, Hom gave her a few baht and a promise that Daw would be home in an hour or two, which he generally was. Occasionally, though, he came in later, or he neglected to retrieve Miaow, and that always cost Hom a little extra and sometimes led to a sharp exchange with the woman, whose children kept baby hours, up with the sun.

As the days folded into each other, sometimes quickly, sometimes agonizingly slowly, Hom's world often seemed to be encased in thin glass that shone with a hard, sugary glitter, accompanied by the sense—especially when she was on the pills' downslope— that everything around her was breakable. She sometimes envisioned herself rapping her knuckles on the air in front of her and watching the cracks spread in all directions. Often she would suddenly come to herself, not quite sure what she'd been doing, as though she'd been sleepwalking. When that happened there was usually a bolt of panic as she tried to put together the pieces of the time she'd lost, tried to find the thread of whatever activity had taken her to where she was standing or sitting. In these moments she felt entirely adrift. There seemed to be nothing to connect her either to the girl she had been in the village or to the child sitting silently in the corner.

Increasingly often, she woke in the middle of the night, when the speed that had pushed her through the day had faded away and been replaced by the soft cushion of the sleeping pills or the pain medication. At those moments, undistracted by the scattering of her energy, she would realize, as though it were a new discovery, how little attention she had been paying to Miaow. *I could have taken her out today,* she would think. *She won't be this age forever. She won't always want to be with me. By the time I was seven or eight, I didn't want to be with my mother. Anybody was more interesting than my mother.* And the next day, she might or might not remember her resolution, but if she did and if the weather was dry and if nothing more pressing claimed her attention, she would take her daughter out. But Miaow dragged her feet, looking at the ground and lagging behind much of the time, as though she wanted to turn around and go home, so Hom would abandon the plan.

In fact, she felt as though Miaow had shut her out. When all three of them were together, Miaow stayed in the other room, and when she was with them—at mealtimes, mostly—she usually seemed to be pretending to be alone. When they caught her gazing at one or both of them, she looked away, as though she'd been doing something she shouldn't. She kept her eyes on the floor or, if they hadn't taken them away from her so she could eat, on the dirty remnants of her rag dolls. Often, Hom had to address her two or three times to get a response. When Miaow did engage with them she was demanding and querulous, resistant to requests or orders, and often burst into tears over nothing, or so it seemed to Hom. Once, when Miaow was being fractious and Hom was trying to quiet her to prevent Daw from losing his temper, she remembered the silent baby she had carried through the forest, and when that image came to mind she sat beside Miaow and wept. Her tears frightened Miaow, who backed away, crablike.

It wasn't as though she didn't realize, at unpredictable, scattered times, that she needed to change the way she was living. Sometimes when she woke in the morning—in the bright, quiet interlude before the day picked her up and had its way with her— she found herself remembering her sisters: how close they had been and how their mother was always there, almost, at times, a fourth sister. She was there even (and, often, especially) when they wanted her to leave them alone, leave them to make their own mistakes: to stay out long after dark and get devoured by mosquitoes; to jump into the paddy at night and catch cold; to break an arm, as Hom had done when she was twelve; and, in one instance, to be chased right up to the front door by an unknown man who might have been crazy. Her childhood had been loud, it had often been disorderly, but it had never been lonely. The village had laughed about Hom's mother's attempts to manage her rambunctious gaggle of girls, jokingly predicting dire futures for them and calling the sisters *the terrorists*; but there had been a kind of *glue* there, holding them together when they were fighting with each other.

She had expected to feel that glue between her and Miaow. Even when Hom's own mother was at her angriest or most distracted, it was impossible not to feel the warmth of her love for her daughters. As much as Hom wanted to believe that the distance between her and Miaow was at least partly Miaow's fault—that Hom had simply given birth to an unemotional child—she could only believe it when the pills were at work. In the moments when they had no claim on her, she was defenseless against the icy waves of guilt she felt. Very occasionally she would surface from sleep in the middle of the night to hear Miaow's slow, even breathing two or three feet away, and she would roll over and light the candle to look down at her sleeping child. It was always the same reaction, a kind of amazement at the perfection of the thick lashes, the fine, fragile sculpture of her nostrils, the flawless-ness of her skin; and then, as she watched, the image of Hom's mother or of her oldest sister, who most resembled their mother, would float up through the landscape of Miaow's face and estab-lish itself there. When that happened, a kind of heaviness would declare itself in Hom's chest and spread rapidly outward, as sudden and unexpected as a flock of birds erupting from a thicket, and sometimes Hom would begin to weep. And when she did, Miaow would open her eyes slowly and, without rolling over or looking away, scoot farther from her mother, until she was at the edge of the candlelight. As long as Hom remained awake, Miaow's eyes would be open.

Each time, the sleeping pill would eventually pull Hom down again, but the memory was always vivid when she woke the next day. Those were the mornings on which she was most likely to promise herself that she would change the way she was living.

And she meant it, every time. But always, by midday, when the morning cocktail of pills was doing its work, she would find herself mentally counting the ones that remained and, eventually, checking the bag to make sure.

As money got tighter, Hom tried to impose a kind of disci-pline on how much went to her habit and Daw's, jamming a small fistful of baht into the hip pocket of her jeans after she was paid at the restaurant and limiting herself, in her dealings with her suppliers—she had several by then—to the money she carried up front. Three or four times, always promising silently to make it up next time, she augmented her salary by palming some of the tips she was supposed to share with the staff, and twice, when a customer was too drunk, she thought, to count his change, she short-changed them. One of them privately shamed her the next evening by pushing over to her, just before he left, the precise amount she had stolen. She stood beside the table as the door closed behind him, her face burning. The fear she felt about the thefts was unpleasant, but it was nothing compared to the tamped-down, pressurized panic that filled her when the plastic bags were almost empty.

Even with the occasional theft and her attempts to limit her spending, she and Daw had less money every week. Daw's pay from the moving company was shrinking, and he was complaining about the way he was being treated. This meant that additional weight fell on her to come home with the essentials, the mixed bag of speed, painkillers, and sleepers that got them from one day to the next. Painkillers had become her favorite of them all. They wrapped her in cotton, dulled the edges of her fears and her worries, lessened the shock she felt when she looked at the gaunt, sharp-featured woman in the mirror, and silenced the nagging voice inside her that told her it wasn't enough to stop *sometime in the future*; she had to stop *now*. *They* had to stop now.

One night she came home, tired out and shaky, to find, yet again, that Daw hadn't returned and that Miaow was still with the woman up the hall. She felt a hot bloom of fury; she had only a few baht left. When the woman opened the door, Hom saw Miaow on the floor across the room and was astonished to realize—as though it had all taken place while she wasn't looking—how much her daughter had grown. Miaow was laughing as she played with the babies, one of whom was a toddler, while the other had obviously just mastered crawling. When the woman shook her head, as though in rejection of whatever excuse Hom was going to make, Hom gave her a look that drove her back a step, blinking like someone who had been slapped. At that moment the spell was broken; whether it was the woman's sudden movement or a delayed recognition that the door had opened, Miaow glanced up at them, and as Hom watched, the happiness drained from her child's face and was replaced by the closed, inward-looking expression Hom had grown used to. The woman reached over and curled Hom's fingers back over the money and said, "I just wanted to say that you don't have to pay me. Miaow is such a delight, and my kids love her so much. I feel like I should be paying you." Miaow's eyes had gone to the woman as she spoke, but the moment she felt Hom's gaze she looked back down at the floor. Then, so slowly she might have weighed a hundred kilos, Miaow got up.

Hom followed her down the hall until they reached their door. As Hom unlocked it, she put her hand on Miaow's shoulder, but Miaow shrugged it off, went into the back room, and closed the door behind her. Hom didn't even know she was weeping until she saw the room swimming in front of her. She stood there, hand over her mouth, looking at the closed door and trying to decide what she should say, how to begin. If she could only find the first five or six words, the *exactly right* words, she was certain, all the rest would come to her. In the end, she dried her face, filched a Korean imitation of Oxycontin from her husband's stash, and sat on the couch to wait for him to come home. By the time he did, she didn't feel quite so bad.

Two weeks later, Daw was fired from his job.

28

Shiny New Brass Locks

He jolted her awake by banging open the door to the back room, raging, about two hours after he'd left for work. He had four days' pay in his pocket, and he'd had to threaten his boss with physical harm to get that. They claimed he'd stolen something, which, he said, he hadn't. Hom was startled by the fear behind his rage; he'd never seemed frightened of anything before.

It took an hour or two of listening, encouraging, even cajoling, to get him to the point where he could stay on topic long enough to tell her *all* the bad news: they'd fired him the moment he came through the door, and the head of the company, whom he'd never even seen before, had been there in a fancy silk shirt to promise him that they would tell competing companies that he was a thief if any of them asked for a reference. Moving was the only job he'd ever had in Bangkok, and it was closed to him now.

The two of them were so wrapped up in their problem that neither of them had given Miaow a second thought. Only after Hom managed to sit Daw down so she could fix him something to eat did she realize Miaow was no longer in the back room. Hom checked the barely functional bathroom, and then, feeling stupid, she looked again at the corners her daughter had claimed as hers. Not until then did she feel the stab of panic, a tangle of snakes low down in her stomach.

Back in the living room, she had to draw a couple of deep breaths before she said, "She's gone."

"Don't be silly," Daw said. "Where could she go?"

Before he'd finished the question, Hom knew where she had gone. Halfway to the front door, she heard the knocking. She opened it to see the thin woman from down the hall. The woman, whose name Hom couldn't remember, had Miaow's hand in hers, but her arm was stretched nearly straight by the weight of Miaow's reluctance; she was hanging back, *dawdling,* as Hom's mother would have said, as though pulled by the gravitational force of the woman's apartment. Her eyes were on the floor, her face rigid with resistance.

"I'm so sorry," Hom said, but the woman wasn't looking at her. She was staring past her at the front room, and Hom realized that for weeks, perhaps months, things had been left wherever they fell or were dropped; clothes were everywhere, plastic plates and paper napkins littered the floor, and the small wooden chair that she used to sit in when she was sewing lay on its side as it had ever since Daw walked into it in the dark. "We were, ummm, we were searching for something," she said, feeling shame heat her face and just barely not stammering. "Thank you for, for bringing her back."

With no conviction in her voice, the woman said, "I knew you'd be worried." To Miaow, she said, "Here you are, sweetie. Maybe your mom will bring you back down again." She released Miaow's hand and gently pushed her to the doorway. Miaow went through it, sidestepping her mother, avoiding her father's eyes, and closed the door to the back room behind her.

"It's a difficult age," Hom said.

The woman said, "I'm sure," peered at Daw with evident curiosity, said, "I've got to get back to my kids," and went back down the hall. Hom closed her door more forcefully than was necessary.

Behind her, she heard Daw start for the back room, and she said sharply, without even turning to him, "Leave her alone."

THE NEXT DAY, having forgotten that he'd denied stealing anything, Daw showed Hom a pair of cuff links, circles of polished black stone, each with a tiny diamond at its center. That afternoon he sold them for more money than he'd made in a month at any time since they'd come to Bangkok, but in what seemed like no time—certainly no more than a week or two—the money was gone. Hom's mother had always said that bad fortune never came in small doses, and at the end of the same week Hom erupted in anger at a customer in the restaurant and was sent home for good with her week's pay and her tips, which she declined to share with her coworkers.

And there they were: they had no income and they had spent what money they had.

A few days later—neither of them could have said how many—the man who came in the morning to collect the rent learned they didn't have it, looked at the rooms, and gave them four days to get out. If they weren't gone by then, he would have them carried down to the street; and, he added, noticing the open window, their belongings would be thrown down after them.

That night she and Daw, fueled by the little white ones, made feverish plans for putting things together again. At eleven or thereabouts he went out and came back with two cheap bottles of wine, and when Hom woke up late the next morning, her head hammering, she lay motionless on the bare floor of the front room, where she had never slept before, trying to remember if they had really discussed what she thought they had discussed, and what had happened afterward. And then, when she rolled over, the grit of dried mud on her arms and legs brought it back, like something enormous surfacing out of dark water, and she let out a scream that woke Daw.

He had begun by talking about money. Neither of them had a job or any prospect of getting one. They had eaten virtually all their food and had only a few days left in the not-hotel. As much as she had hated the little shack down near the harbor, she'd immediately raised the notion that they could return to it; after all, if they'd fought their way out of it once, they could do it again. But no, Daw had said, it was impossible; he'd checked it after he was fired, and it was taken. He'd also, he said, gone to talk to the man in the Isaan restaurant, but the man had nothing to suggest; there had been a flood of villagers into the city as the price of rice dropped. He had, Daw said, been rude to him. There seemed to be no way around it: until they had put things back together, they were going to be sleeping in the street.

She had sat back, absorbing that, but he wasn't finished. It would be dangerous, he said. Some of the people on the sidewalks were desperate, some of them crazy, all of them impoverished, and most of them eager to steal whatever they could get away with, even if people got hurt. Homeless people were murdered from time to time.

As dangerous as it would be for them, he said, it would be much more so for Miaow. Children were assaulted on the street, and whatever they had, no matter how little, was taken from them. Sometimes a child was simply stolen; a car would stop and men would jump out and carry the child away to be sold into slavery or into child brothels. Some of the brothels were in foreign countries, Arab countries, where, people said, the captives could simply be disposed of when it was no longer profitable to feed them.

He said, "I think you need to go north and take her with you."

At this point, Hom had jumped to her feet and run from the

room into the corridor, hands over her ears, forgetting that it was raining. She'd stumbled down the stairway and out into the empty *soi*, not even feeling the drizzle needling her face. With no destination, just abandoning herself to the need to run away from *everything*, she splashed down the *soi* toward nothing, not realizing she'd clapped her hands over her ears again until her feet went out from under her in a mud slick and she couldn't get her arms down quickly enough to break her fall. She'd sat there, cold, filthy, and wet, listening to her teeth chatter as she shivered, shocked into sobriety, and then she had wailed. Suddenly the awful little rooms she had either disliked or taken for granted seemed almost palatial: they had walls and a roof and a window they could open, they had a door they could lock behind them. They had kept all of them—they had kept *Miaow*—safe. And the truth was inescapable: they only had a few more days there, and nowhere to go.

She *couldn't* go home. Home was no longer there. Her father had died a year and a half ago, and two weeks later there had been a knock at the door and her mother had learned that the house and the paddies, like so many that had belonged to the nation's rice growers—the real producers of much of the country's wealth—had been mortgaged to one of the big millers, who kept the price of unmilled rice low and advanced the farmers loans in full knowledge that it was the cheapest way to steal the land.

And her parents had made a grave mistake in not continuing to have children until they produced a boy. To a poor family, boys were security. Boys were the future. When a couple was too old to work, it was their sons' duty as good Buddhists to care for them. The obligation of a girl, though, was to care for her *husband's* parents. Her sisters all lived with their husbands or their husbands' parents now, and her mother was shuttled among them, an inconvenient guest. Her sisters' husbands were from poor families, just like hers; two of them didn't even own the land on which they lived. There was no room for her and Miaow there. The only thing she could think of, and it filled her with despair, not just for herself but also for Miaow, was returning to her mother-in-law's house, the place she had sworn Miaow would never go back to. And now it would be even worse: she had defied the old woman and they would be returning as supplicants.

When she came back—hours later, it seemed to her, although it couldn't have been—dripping water everywhere and tracking mud into the front room, Daw was sitting right where she had left him. He would not return to his mother's house, he said. They weren't wanted there. And they couldn't take Miaow into the street, they couldn't put her through it. What they needed to do was give her a better chance with someone else, maybe only temporarily. It was the only thing that was fair to her. It was for the child's sake.

He'd obviously been thinking about it. She could do it, he said. She could be completely in charge. They would take Miaow someplace where there were a lot of people and leave her there, but actually keep watch. Hom could pretend to go away and then come back and hide herself to see who tried to take the child, if anyone did. If it looked wrong to her, if the people looked dangerous, she could run out and claim her and then try again the next day. If the people seemed all right, she could follow them to see where they lived. In a few weeks or a month, when they were on their feet again, she could go and reclaim their daughter. He promised, they'd get her back.

It was unthinkable. But.

There was nowhere for them to go. No place with her family up north, no place in Bangkok. And suddenly she realized that there were—there *might* be—two places where Miaow could be safe for a short time, as long as it would take to get a job, any kind of job. And if it wasn't enough to support the three of them, well, then it would still support her and Miaow.

Daw had been staring at the floor since he'd proposed his solution, and he didn't look up as she rose and went through the door to the back room and into the bathroom, avoiding looking at the place where Miaow slept. She scrubbed the mud from her hands and washed her face, groping with her eyes closed for the old T-shirt that served as a towel. When she opened her eyes, she was facing the mirror, and the woman she saw there looked abraded, chipped away, like she had stood for a long time facing down a sandstorm. Some of the prettiness she had taken for granted was still there, but the bones of her face were too evident and her skin, once so smooth, was mottled here and there with blemishes, a kind of acne that she knew was a gift of the meth. *Makeup*, she thought, *I can cover it with makeup*. Pull the dry hair back in a ponytail, use a little water to create spiky bangs to cover some of the bumps on my forehead. Lipstick, a little rouge. She could look like someone who some kind of business might want to hire. Whatever the job was, she would snap at it. It was the key to keeping her child, or—if need be—to getting her back.

She mopped her face again, pulled off her wet clothes, and went into the small bedroom, where she lay down and put an arm around Miaow. She wasn't aware that she was sobbing until Miaow, slowly and carefully, extricated herself, went into the corner where the remnants of the rag dolls were, and lay down with her back to her mother.

All that night and the next day, Hom ransacked her mind for ways around the future Daw had presented to her. In the end it came down to two concrete issues: a safe, temporary home for Miaow, and some source of income. It seemed to her, as she paced the rooms through the day and into the evening, that Daw was responsible for everything that had gone wrong. He'd lied to her about how life would be in Bangkok, he'd been the one who brought the drugs into their lives, and he'd been the one who stole the cuff links and had been spotted. And there had been the perfumes and the fabrications about the evenings with "the guys." The only thing that mattered to her at this point was Miaow; her first responsibility had to be her daughter. She got up and took a sleeper, and by the time she drifted off, she had a simple plan for the new day.

But the sleeper tricked her, cheated her out of the early start she'd imagined. It was almost noon by the time she was dressed and made up and ready to leave Miaow with Daw, telling him she was going to see about a new job, which, at least, had the virtue of being true. Even with such a late start, she was disappointed by 2 P.M.

At her very first stop, the woman down the hall said no, she couldn't accept the responsibility of taking Miaow, even if it was only for a week or so. An occasional afternoon or an hour or two in the evening was no problem, but no longer. There were days she could barely handle her own kids. She was still apologizing when Hom stepped back into the hallway and closed the door behind her.

Sonya's expression when Hom stepped through the door told her all she needed to know. Before she could even begin to ask, Sonya said, "You're too thin. You look exhausted. You've got to stop, for your daughter's sake, even if you don't care about yourself. Do you *ever* think about your kid?" Hom bit back a dozen responses, took a long, slow breath, and asked whether she could leave Miaow for a week or two, saying she'd pay double.

She was barely allowed to finish. "You must be joking," Sonya said. "First, she's too old to stay here now, and second, how do I know I'd ever see you again? Honestly, honey, you've got to get your life under control." By that point, half a dozen kids, all younger than Miaow, were listening, fascinated, and Sonya said, "I've got to see to these kids. Come back when you're yourself again."

In the street, Hom steadied herself with one hand on the building's warm wall, as she trembled from head to foot and willed herself not to weep. She couldn't ruin her makeup. At the moment, the most important thing in the world was not ruining her makeup. When she had stopped shaking and her breath was more measured, more dependable, when she was sure she had her voice under control, she set out on the walk she had made hundreds of times, back when she took the stability of her life for granted. All the worries she'd had then, all the resentments: all nonsense. She had been happy then, compared to now. As much as she disliked her mother-in-law when they lived in that cold, creaky house, she had been happy in her relationship with her daughter. Terrified as she had been in the forest, there had been a part of her that was thrilled by the adventure. If she was ever happy again, she promised herself, she wouldn't let it slip by. She'd say a thank-you prayer every morning.

Most of the women in the sorting room were unfamiliar to her, although the one she blamed for her firing glanced up when Hom came in, froze for a moment, and then went back to work. Across the room, the supervisor was peering at her, her mouth partly open, and then she stood up, as though she had to defend her territory.

But before she could say a word, Hom said, "When I came to work here, you said you knew someplace else I could go, where I'd earn more money." The supervisor held up a hand and said, "Not here," and then she led Hom into the hallway. When she'd finished giving her the information, she added, "Tell them I sent you."

"Really," Hom said, her voice rasping with unexpected fury. "Do they pay you?"

Stepping back and opening the door to the workroom, the supervisor said, "If they take you. The way you're looking, I'm not sure they will."

It was a massage parlor above a barber shop in Patpong. She had expected something along those lines, but she still stood on the sidewalk looking at the door for a few minutes before she pushed through it and climbed the stairs, every step feeling a meter high. The man who opened the door at the top of the stairs was little and balding and long nosed, and Hom immediately thought of a weasel. She gave him the supervisor's name, and he looked her up and down in silence and then led her to a window-less little room, reeking of rubbing alcohol and men's feet, empty but for a massage table and a clothes tree in one corner. He said, "Got a regular here, and his usual girl is out with the monthlies, so you get an audition. Take good care of him." He opened a little cupboard at one end of the room and pulled out a white sleeveless top and white shorts. "Put these on. You can shove stuff in here."

Hom was shaking when the man came in. Her mouth was almost too dry to say hello, but he nodded and smiled at her and said, "Don't worry, honey, we'll make this quick." It didn't feel quick to *her*, though, and she was amazed later to realize he was in the room only about twenty minutes, but he seemed satisfied, and as he left, he tipped her ten dollars in American money. She sat on the table, crying, until the boss came in and said, "You did okay, but I can't have a lot of crying, understand? It fucks with the customers' fantasies. You want to do another one?"

She waved it off and asked if she could come back the next day.

"You can work a few hours, see whether you can take it. Normally, I wouldn't give you short hours like that, but Tik has her period and you can take up part of the slack in the next couple of days. When you start regular, though—if you do—it'll be the full shift, all twelve hours. Think you can handle it?"

Hom said, "I won't cry again, I promise."

When she left, her legs still feeling a little wobbly on the stairs, she had her tip folded into her underpants. She had no intention of sharing it with Daw. For one thing, she'd have to explain how she got it, and she knew instinctively that he'd beat her, and—possibly even worse—he'd make it about him: it would be *his* final humiliation, not hers. And anyway, she'd already created a kind of border in her mind, an almost tangible line between where she was now and where she would be when it was just the two of them, just her and Miaow. This money was her first step across that line; it was earmarked as partial payment on a place where she and Miaow would live.

She was cursing herself for having wasted the first day. The second was gone now, which meant that she had only one more before they would be evicted. She needed to have a new place secured and a deposit paid. At home, she stood in line in the hallway for the shower and then stayed under the spray of water so long that someone started banging on the door. When she came out she told Daw she had a headache and spent most of the rest of the day in bed, which drove Miaow into the bathroom.

She worked four hours the next day and collected another seventeen dollars in tips—both her customers were Americans—and when she left she asked the weasel-faced manager when she'd get her salary. He said that *if* she worked out, the girls were paid every Saturday. For a moment she thought her legs would go loose beneath her, but she leaned against the counter and made herself smile. "I'll work out," she said, and then she joined the other waiting women. One of them had told Hom there might be a room available in the place where she stayed. A second woman volunteered another address, but the others all seemed to be sleeping on the massage tables. So she had two leads. And one day before she would need to move into one of them.

But unless one of them was the cheapest place in the world and required no guarantee, she still wouldn't be able to move in until she was paid on Saturday, probably *late* on Saturday. And this was Tuesday. She did the math in her head over and over while she worked on the customers and they worked on her. She'd taken an upper to make the time go faster and to help her talk to the men (one of them did want to talk) but even with the speed's help, she could find no way to earn enough money to make an advance payment on a place before they were thrown out of the not-hotel. And then there were *four days* after that, as non-negotiable as a concrete wall—Wednesday, Thursday, Friday, and most of Saturday—before she'd be have the money to pay for a place. It might as well have been a year.

She'd even asked Weasel-face whether Miaow could sleep there, with her, on a table. He'd said that she, Hom, could, if need be, but not Miaow. "Not for all the money in the world," he said. "A kid in a place like this? All we'd need is one cop, and I'd be in jail for ten years."

For now, all she could do was look at the progress she'd made. Four days from now she would enter a new world. She and Miaow would have a place of their own. She'd find someone to take care of the child while she was working; in less than a year, Miaow would be in school during the day.

Hom would quit the pills and stay away from them. She would be good. She *knew* she could.

In the meantime, she had two possible rooms to look at.

The first rooming house was full and no one was scheduled to leave anytime soon. To find the second, she had to go to a neighborhood she didn't know, and when she found the place it turned out to be a run-down wooden structure with a sagging roof and bars on the windows, and an electric lock on the door: she pushed a button and waited until someone came and lifted the curtain on the inside of the door. Then there was a buzz and a click, and the door opened into a small room with scuffed linoleum floors and a battered counter at the far end. The place smelled of mold. The woman behind the counter said they were full, but that a room would open up in a few days. Her heart pounding, Hom said, "Can I leave you a deposit?" She hadn't even asked to see the room.

The clerk, a plump-cheeked, dark-skinned woman in her mid-forties, had strands of silver in her hair and, Hom thought, kind eyes. She said, "How much of a deposit?"

"Twenty-seven dollars, US?"

The clerk shook her head. "Tell you what, sweetie. Give me twenty and keep the rest. That'll cover two nights when the room opens up. If you want to reserve long-term—you do want to reserve long-term, right?"

"Yes." The rate was almost what they'd been paying at the not-hotel, but she had no time to argue. She could always move later.

"Well, then, bring me another twenty in a day or two. If the room's open by then, and if you've got another fifty to protect the owners in case you skip ahead of your scheduled time, you can move right in. If not, I'll hold it for a week. Either way, you'll be marked down as a long-term resident. After you stay a month, if you've paid on time, it'll go down to eight dollars a night." She put both hands on the counter and leaned very slightly in Hom's direction. "You're going to be able to pay the rent, right? You have a job?"

Hom said, "Yes," feeling her face go hot with shame.

"Hospitality industry?" the woman said. "We've got a lot of girls in the hospitality industry here."

"What about a baby?"

"Sorry," the woman said. "I didn't hear you."

Hom said, "What I said was—"

"You can say it a hundred times and I won't hear it. It'll raise the room rate to ten per night, which means a bigger deposit, and I'm not sure you have a bigger deposit. But will you be able to cover eight a night when you move in? Does the baby cry?"

"Yes, I can cover it," Hom said, "and no, she won't cry. She is bigger now."

"I'm Kanda," the woman said, tearing a stub out of a little book. "If she doesn't cry, she's your little secret until the owners find out. This is your receipt to put the place on hold. Bring me another twenty and the fifty-dollar deposit in a day or two, and I'll give you one for a long-term stay. From then on, you can pay by the week."

"Oh," Hom said, and then she was crying. Kanda put up a hand and started to say something, but Hom bent slightly at the waist and gave her a *wai* so high her elbows were practically level with her eyes.

"Please," Kanda said. "Please."

"Thank you, thank you, thank you," Hom was saying as she backed out of the room.

In the street she dried her eyes, smearing her eye makeup all over her face, and considered. She had a job, and she had no right to be ashamed of it; it was her path to keeping her child. She had a place to stay that would open up in a few days, maybe three or four or five. She had the room. She would have the money to pay for it. She had everything but time.

Nor did she have the physical or emotional strength that night to defy Daw, who sat in the front room on their last night there, surrounded by the bags that the two of them were never going to be able to carry, whispering furiously that if she insisted on keeping Miaow instead of cooperating with his plan, he'd cut them both loose, leave them to cope alone. He didn't *want* to, he said, but he wasn't going to be able to be with them to protect them most of the time because he needed to be free to find work, and that was going to be difficult; his only experience was in moving, and that was closed to him. Unless she thought she could protect Miaow alone and without his help, they would have to follow his plan.

One by one, he ticked off what he called *the safety features*: he had chosen a place near nice stores, even around the corner from one of the big new malls, so the people there would probably be high-class, not likely to steal a child to sell her or make her into a house slave. They would be right there, hidden, keeping watch. If the people looked wrong to her—looked wrong to both of them—he promised to run in and break it up. They could take Miaow someplace else; he'd chosen a second place, too. She sat, lips pressed tight against everything she wanted to say, and watched as he transformed himself into the person he had probably always been, the spoiled, too-handsome mother's boy who took it for granted that he would get his way, who thought of no one but himself.

She let him talk, hugging her secret to her: she had found a job and a place to live. She just needed a few days she wasn't going to be given. She was, she was surprised to find, afraid to tell him about the job. He would demand that she give it up. He might hit her. And she couldn't, she *wouldn't*, give up the job. She had no alternative, and he had none to suggest.

Or even worse, he might nod and accept it. Even though she was almost certain they were finished, she couldn't bear the idea that he would let her be a whore to solve the problems that he had, in her opinion, created. So she sat mutely, exhausted almost beyond feeling, until he had run out of arguments, and then she went into the bathroom and dry-swallowed one of her last remaining sleepers. She didn't expect it to work, but when she lay down, with Miaow all the way across the room, practically pressed against the wall, the drug opened beneath her like a deep cave, and she fell right in.

In the middle of the night she was snapped awake by a thought, so complete she might have been puzzling over it for days. To Daw, Miaow was competition. All the love she gave Miaow was love he believed was rightfully his. His mother had given him all her love, all her attention; why didn't his wife?

She was still awake when she heard him moving around in the front room. It was seven, three hours before the deadline to empty the apartment of everything they wanted to keep. Miaow said nothing as they dressed, looking from one of them to the other, clearly aware that something unusual was happening, but when Daw told Hom to wash the child's face, Miaow said, "I'll do it." By a little before eight, they were out and walking.

No one spoke. They walked single file, Daw in front, Hom bringing up the rear, and Miaow in between. Miaow never looked left or right, never said a word. Daw only spoke to direct them to turn right or left or to wait to cross the street. Hom spent the time counting, alternating between counting her steps and the pounding of her heart, which was so heavy she could see her T-shirt moving when she looked down. When she saw that, she looked straight ahead again and went back to counting steps.

It took some time, although Hom couldn't have said whether it was ten minutes or an hour, before Daw stopped and said, "Over there."

They stood at the edge of a wide street with big stores, their windows still dark, stretching left and right. Directly opposite them was a bus stop with a heavy concrete bench: a flat seat with three upright beams, also concrete, that supported the bench back. Daw waited for a break in the traffic and led them across.

When they got there, Miaow looked around and said, "Why are we here?"

"You're going to wait here a little while," Daw said, taking something out of his pocket, the twine Hom had insisted on the previous evening; as much as she didn't want to abandon the child, to leave her to strangers, she was even more frightened that Miaow would chase them, running straight into traffic. But when she saw the twine in Daw's hand, her legs weakened beneath her. She said, "Daw."

But he just looked at her and said, "We've *talked* about this. It's better for her. And if it looks wrong, we can stop it the minute it happens. If we're settled in a few days, a week or two, we can put everything back together."

"Four days," Hom said, unaware that she'd said it out loud.

"Sure, sure," Daw said without looking up. "Four days." He took Miaow's hand and tied the twine around it while she looked up at him, expressionless. Then he tied it to the nearest of the uprights that supported the back of the bench, giving her a little less than a meter of slack. "See?" he said. "You can sit down and everything."

Hom was weeping openly by the time Daw backed away from Miaow. She took from her pocket one of the all-day candies Miaow loved and held it out, saying, "Here, sweetie. By the time you finish this, everything will be all right."

Miaow gazed at her, not the candy, for an unmeasurable amount of time, and then she took it in her free hand. She looked from one of them to the other and said, "You don't want me anymore."

"You just wait here," Daw said. "Someone will come get you pretty soon."

Miaow put the candy into her mouth. Around it, she said, "I don't want you, either."

"IT'S JUST A few days," Daw hissed into Hom's ear as he pulled her away. Miaow said nothing as they stepped down into the road and navigated the traffic. When they were on the other side, Hom looked back and saw that Miaow had sat on the very end of the bench, sideways so that her left shoulder was against the bench back, and she was picking at her left wrist. She was, Hom realized, ashamed of the string. She was trying to undo the knot or, failing that, to hide it. She felt a sudden surge of pride.

"Go half a block your left," Daw said. "There's a truck parked there. She won't see you from there. When somebody cuts the string, unless it's a cop, you can follow them."

"You said you were going to wait with me."

"Don't be silly," he said. "*Somebody's* got to get our stuff out before it all gets tossed. They won't just throw it out the window, they'll pick over it first, take anything that's worth any money. You want to give away everything we own?"

"We're *already* giving away everything we own," she said. She looked back. Miaow was sitting on the bench as though she had all the time in the world, looking in the opposite direction. But then she raised her free arm and wiped her face with it.

"Just a few days," Daw said. "Just don't screw it up when you follow them."

Hom said, "I hate you," but he was already walking away.

He was right; the truck gave her a nice big space where she could keep an eye on the bus stop, at least during the intervals of relatively light traffic. Miaow mostly sat still, her eyes on her lap. People came and went. Some of them, mostly the ones who waited for the bus and had time to notice the child, talked to her, but the conversations were short and no one tried to take her or went for the police. She kept the string out of sight.

After a few hours, the truck driver got in and drove away, and Hom realized she badly needed to go to the bathroom. The stores had opened, and she went into the nearest one, panicking during the first few moments that Miaow was out of her sight. She found the bathroom and relieved herself, taking a few extra seconds to splash enough water on her face to wash away the sweat and the tear tracks. When she was done she hurried back outside to discover that another truck had pulled into the space, and this time she saw the sign that said LOADING ZONE.

The next truck came a few hours later, or so it seemed to Hom, and she asked the driver what time it was. It was past noon. The sidewalks were busy now, people with money looking for places to spend it. Most of them were adults, but as the afternoon wore on, there were more and more children, and Hom realized that school must have let out. Some of the children slowed when they saw Miaow, but she ignored them and kept the twine out of sight. Lines for buses formed and re-formed. Some people talked to Miaow as they waited, but most of them either chatted among themselves or craned down the street, looking for the bus. Miaow seemed to have retreated into herself. Much of the time she looked down at her lap.

Two more trucks came and went and the day grew cooler. Hom had gone to the bathroom one more time, and all she could think of was how badly Miaow must have to go. Shadows grew longer and then it was getting dark. At one point, when no one was near Miaow, a big brown dog trotted past the bench, stop, stopped, and turned around to look at her. Tail wagging so hard it almost wobbled, the dog approached her, and Hom cheered up for a second; her village had been full of big, dumb happy dogs who seemed to live only for meals and romps, but Miaow looked panicked. She'd never really been around dogs. The dog spread its front legs and lowered its chest almost to the pavement, dog language for *let's play*, but Miaow got up, tugging at the twine around her wrist, and edged around the end of the bench until it was between her and the dog. The dog sat, clearly disappointed, and then trotted off. Miaow sat on the bench again and wiped her eyes with her free hand, and Hom realized that she was crying, too.

That was it. Hom started out from between the trucks, getting an indignant honk from a passing car. When she looked back down the street, she saw that a boy, perhaps twelve or thirteen years old, had stopped to talk to Miaow. From what she could see, he was a nice-looking boy even though his clothes were dirty, and Miaow, who rarely spoke to other children, even at Sonya's, seemed to be responding to him. After a few minutes he must have asked her a question because she nodded assent, and the boy pulled out a small knife and cut the twine; after a few more words, the two of them set off together, coming toward her but on the other side of the street. She ducked to the far side of the truck until they were well past her and then plunged into traffic, ignoring the horns and the squeal of brakes and dodging between cars to get to their side of the street. Staying a block or so behind them, she followed for almost an hour.

It was fully dark when the boy turned down a narrow, down-ward-sloping *soi* that led to a "number hotel," one of many that specialized in accommodating people who were having discreet affairs; the garage was at street level, and the moment the customers pulled in, an attendant lowered a black curtain behind their car to conceal their license plate and to allow the couple to proceed unseen up the stairs to the second floor, where the rooms were. This one had evidently gone out of business because the rooms were all dark, but the big garage doors were standing wide open, one of them off its hinges. The light from a few flashlights and a small fire in a can revealed five or six other kids there, mostly older than Miaow, who gathered around her and the boy. One of them, a girl, immediately gave her half a mango. Concealed by the darkness, Hom watched the children sit in a circle as Miaow ate. They looked at her curiously but not antagonistically, obviously asking her questions. At one point, the boy pulled something from his pocket that was almost certainly the twine he'd cut from Miaow's wrist, and this produced some knowing nods and chatter. A few minutes later there was a burst of laughter loud enough to reach Hom's ears, and she told herself that she had heard Miaow's laugh among them.

When she left to go wherever she was going—as it turned out, to a park bench to sleep—Hom felt almost happy. They were just kids, a gang of kids, and the boy who set Miaow free seemed to be in charge. Instead of fearing him, the other kids seemed to like him. She could find the place easily. Payday was Saturday, and it would be more than she'd ever made at the restaurant. In the meantime, starting the next day, she could sleep on a table at the massage parlor, and Sunday she could pay for the room and then go retrieve Miaow. All she had to do was to work for a few days, stay away from anyplace Daw might be, and get paid. Then she could retrieve her daughter and move with her into the room she'd reserved. She could find someone new to take care of Miaow while she worked; it was almost time for her to start going to school, anyway. They would have a new life, a life together. She would stop the pills. The two of them would love each other again. It would be much easier, she was certain, to get Miaow back from a bunch of kids than from adults who might want to keep her or even report Hom for abandoning her. This was the best possible situation. Walking away, she was almost content with her plan.

But when she went back on Sunday, rent and meal money in hand, the doors to the garage were closed and repaired, and equipped with shiny new brass locks. The kids were gone.

Part Three
THE UNRAVELING

29

Boss of Him

WHAT SHE WANTS, it turns out, is one hundred thousand baht.

Rafferty actually laughs when he finally pries the answer out of her. They've left the ice cream shop and are wandering along Silom, heading away from Patpong and the apartment. Silom is, as always, bumper-to-bumper, and the sky train, which seems to be working this week, rackets by from time to time, some thirty feet above the street, looking to Rafferty like a captive spacecraft that's been let out for its nightly run. It's dragging its noise past them when she names the sum, and he has to ask her to repeat it, and then he stops walking and laughs.

She says, "What funny?"

"If I had a hundred thousand baht," he says, "do you think I'd be wearing these shoes?"

She glances down at a pair of running shoes whose running days are a faded memory. There's a hole over his right big toe, and one of the laces, which broke at some point in the distant past, has been tied back together in a way that leaves a long loose end over which he occasionally trips.

"Some *farang* crazy," she says. "Have rich, look poor."

"Well, I'm not crazy, just broke. Not broke like *you* were, but I have no idea why you think I can find one hundred thousand baht."

She says, "He told—" and does everything but slap her hand

over her mouth. She lets the syllables degenerate into a mumble and backs away from him, coming so close to the edge of the curb that he makes a grab, wrapping his arm around her waist to keep her from pitching backward into the traffic. He's off balance, too, and for a moment it feels to him that they might both go over, but then she's pushing and he's pulling, and after an unpleasantly elastic moment, they're standing upright, facing each other, and she's laughing.

But it ends as quickly as it begins, and her face assumes its usual aspect, withdrawn and unfocused, more interested in the sidewalk than anything else, her mouth tight, lips pressed together so hard they almost disappear.

"*Who* said?" Poke asks. He backs away to give her a little space, half fearing that she'll go off the edge of the curb again. He's kicking himself for leaving the ice cream parlor, but the place had suddenly filled up, and he didn't want to talk about money with people sitting four feet away and listening for all they were worth. She's still looking at the pavement, so he puts a hand down, in the center of her field of vision, and wiggles his fingers. He says, "You don't want to talk about the money?"

After a moment so long he thinks she might not have heard him, she says, "You not have."

"I haven't got a hundred thousand, no, but I've got some."

She says, "No good."

"So what you're telling me is that it's a hundred thousand or nothing, is that it?" She shakes her head but says nothing, and he says, in Thai, "I actually do want to help you."

"One hundred."

"Haven't got it. *Who* wanted it?"

She shrugs like someone who's given up. "Sour man."

He repeats it in English to make sure he heard it correctly. "The Sour Man? Who is the Sour Man?"

"Man," she says.

"I got that far. Is he the kid who was in Superman's gang, the one who told you he'd seen her?"

"No," she says. "Boss of him." She chews her lower lip and looks over his shoulder, as though she's hoping for rescue from the conversation.

"And this boss, this Sour Man, wants you to ask me for a hundred thousand baht."

She shakes her head, but he's pretty sure that it means she won't discuss him.

"Are you afraid of him?"

A group of Japanese men has come down the street, red-faced and laughing—probably after an evening in the bars of Thaniya Plaza—bobbing their heads politely at people who catch their eye. One of them sees Hom and slows to stare at her, and the one behind him bumps into his back. Behind *him*, a young Thai man extends his left hand in an unusual position and starts to brush the Japanese man's shoulder with his own as he passes, but Hom yells, loudly enough to take Rafferty a step back, "*Thief!*" Instantly, every Thai within sight is looking in their direction and the pickpocket is hurrying past his intended victim. The Japanese proceed on their way, undisturbed.

"Well," Rafferty says in Thai. "You've got an eye."

"No good," Hom says. She makes finger-scissors with her right hand and mimes slipping them into something while, with her other hand, she bumps Rafferty's shoulder. "See?" she says. "You feel"—she bumps his shoulder again—"*this*, but not this." She mimes closing the fingers on something and lifting it straight up. "Later, you, *ohmigod, I lose wallet*. Boy no good."

"Do you know him?"

"I see. I see many many."

"So, the Sour Man."

She says, "No."

"Okay, fine."

She's started to move away from him, so casually that she might have forgotten he was there. "Wait," he says. "You do want money, don't you?" He knows it's futile, he knows it won't really help her, she'll either lose it or it will be stolen, probably by the Sour Man, whoever that is, but she *is* Miaow's mother. He's got to do *something*.

She stops, but she doesn't turn back. He has to follow her and step in front of her again. "I can give you twenty thousand baht."

"Cannot," she says, "no good," and she turns away again. He puts a hand on her shoulder, stopping her. "Okay, thirty." He's speaking Thai. "But that's it, for now, anyway. We don't have much money right now, and the"—he'd been going to say *baby*, but it seems enormously inappropriate, so he says, "expenses are high, the rent is due . . ."

At the word *rent*, she nods.

"I have money coming in a few months. That's how writers get paid, mostly: twice a year. I'll probably never be able to give you a hundred thousand, but I can give you some from time to time." Her eyes are fixed on his chest, as though eye contact might break the spell. "I want to help you. Just not all at once. You take the money I'll give you tonight, and then go away. When I can give you more, in a few months, I'll call you, and—"

She's shaking her head. "Cannot. Cannot call. Not my phone. Phone of friend."

"Okay," he says, and he fishes around in his hip pocket until he comes up with his wallet. Her eyes go to it, and, knowing it will be a disappointment, he works out one of his business cards. "My phone number," he says in Thai. "If you need to talk to me."

She looks up at him as though he's suddenly begun to speak an improvised language of his own. Then she reaches out and takes the front of his shirt between her thumb and index finger and, with a quick look behind her, pushes him back until his shoulders are touching the dark window of what seemed, as he craned for a glimpse of it, to be a shoe store. When he can go no farther, she says, "*Talk* to you?"

"I'm going to give you money tonight," he says. "Twenty—no, thirty—thousand. I know you want, or someone wants, more, but you're not going to get it. Without Miaow, my life would be—well, I'd be a lot less happy. So I owe you, I want to help you." She seems to be looking through the window behind him, so he says, "Are you listening?"

"Yes," she says, her eyes still on the dark window or, he thinks, perhaps scanning the reflection of the street behind her.

"I'm giving you this card so that, if you need to talk to me, if that man takes it all or gives you trouble, you can call. I don't want you to follow Miaow or come to the apartment again. If you ring the doorbell again, I'll have to call the police. Do you understand?"

She's still looking at the window, but she nods.

"Just so we're clear . . . will you please look at me for a minute?" When she does, he says, "I'm giving you thirty thousand now, tonight. That should be enough for you to get a place to stay, get some time off the street. If you need a little more, and I mean a *little*, you can call me. In about three months, I'll get some more money, and if you call I'll probably be able to give you some. But you stay away from Miaow. I'll talk to her, and if she ever wants to meet you, I'll let you know when you call. I *will* talk to her. Okay?"

She nods, looking at his chest.

"But you have to do one thing for me. You have to tell me how you found us. The house, I mean, I know how you knew we'd been on Silom, but how did you find the house?"

She's chewing on her lower lip so hard he expects it to bleed, but she says, "Sour Man."

"The Sour Man—what? Told you where we live and that we had Miaow, and—"

"No." She looks over his head and blinks several times so hard he thinks she might have something in her eye, and then she says, in Thai this time, "No. Some days ago, maybe a week or maybe two, he showed me a picture of you and said he would pay me one hundred baht every day I followed you until I found your house. He showed me the bar where you took Miaow. So I tried to follow you, but sometimes I forgot or you didn't come, but he gave me money every day and told me to keep trying. And he hurt me."

"Hurt you."

"My ear," she said. "Never mind, it doesn't hurt now."

"Why didn't he follow me himself?"

"I don't know. If I asked questions, he hurt me."

"Then, then—wait a minute. Then you didn't know we had Miaow?"

"No, I knew Miaow was with a man who came to Patpong sometimes, but I didn't know it was you."

He steps back without being aware he's doing it and then, for lack of anything better, goes to stand beside her. Both of them are leaning against the window, looking at the sidewalk. It feels almost companionable to him. "So, when she opened that door . . ."

"I didn't *want* to knock on your door. I wanted to go home. I was standing out where the cars go in and out, under your building, and he told me about . . . on the phone, he told me. And he told me one, umm, one hundred—" She holds up her left hand, and among the scribbles he can make out the number. "And it was Miaow," she says.

"So," he says, partly to hear it out loud, "the money's for *him*. I mean, *you're* not actually asking us for—"

"No. For him."

"He figures I'm rich enough to pay you a hundred thousand baht because you're Miaow's mother. Because why? Because I'd be afraid you'd try to take her? Because—" He breaks off and then nods. "Yeah, whatever is going on in your life, you're her mother and I'm a foreigner." He sees her looking down at his left foot and realizes he's tapping it, fast, on the pavement. "So," he says, "if you had thirty thousand baht could you go someplace he couldn't find you?"

It takes her a few seconds, but then she says, "Yes."

"Then fuck him," Rafferty says. "Let's go get your money."

IT'S ALMOST MIDNIGHT when he opens the apartment door and eases it closed. The living room and the kitchen are empty and dark, but there's a strip of light beneath Miaow's door. He looks at it for a minute or three, trying to figure out how he can frame what's just happened, and then he gives up and decides he'll sleep on it, assuming the couch will allow it, and that's when he sees there's also light beneath the door to the room Rose currently shares with, ummm, Frank. Not wanting to wake the baby or alert Miaow that he's home—he's nowhere *near* ready for that conversation—he knocks in a feathery fashion on the door to the bedroom. It opens almost immediately, and Rose, smelling of the lemon soap she favors, wraps her arms around him. To his total surprise, he begins to cry. It's silent, but it's weeping.

Rose pulls him into the room and closes the door. She says, in a whisper, "Not you, too. I go out one time, the world ends."

"I'm just happy to be home. With you. Someplace safe." He sniffles.

She leans toward him and wipes away the dampness beneath his eyes. She whispers, "Well, just be glad you weren't here. If you had been, you might have gone someplace else."

He starts to sniffle again but cuts it off and swallows instead. "Miaow?"

"I've *never* seen her like that. She was everything no one ever wants to be. She was frightened, heartbroken, embarrassed, even guilty. But mostly, I think, she was embarrassed. Wanted us to move tomorrow, wanted poor Edward to go away, wanted—"

"Edward didn't even see her." He backs away to sniff again and decides he's missed a bet all these years by not whispering in her ear. It's intimate in a new way, and it gives him an opportunity to inhale her various fragrances without looking like an eager dog.

"Yes, he did," she says. She tows him to the foot of the bed and they both sit. With her lips practically touching his ear, she says, "He went to the door and looked out while you were walking her to the stairs. Fon and I saw him as we got off the elevator. The door to the stairs was just closing. I was carrying the baby, and we waved to Edward to hold the door open, and that's when Miaow, who had apparently hidden in her room, came out and caught him looking down the hall. She acted crazy, like she wanted to kill him. We were trying to get through the door and she was actually trying to push him out into the hall."

"Poor baby."

"Which one?" Rose asks.

"Well . . ." He hadn't expected the question. "Miaow."

She pulls away and gives him a look that he hasn't seen often, and it's not admiring. "Really? That's what you think?"

"Oh, well," he says, backing off instantly. "She'd had a shock, and—"

"Fon ripped her to pieces, with Edward right there. Called her a heartless little snob, asked what it had to do with *her* if her mother was poor and homeless, asked whether she was embarrassed by me and by her—I mean, Fon—because we were prostitutes, after all, what about *that*? This was in Thai and pretty fast, so Edward didn't get it, but Miaow went as white as a sheet and Fon asked whether *any* of us were good enough for her, said maybe she should apply for adoption by the royal family—"

Rafferty laughs out loud and then covers his mouth and looks over at the crib. The baby hasn't even taken his thumb out of his mouth.

"He's dead to the world," Rose says. "First there was the restaurant, with all the people in Thailand, and half of them coming by for a closer look at him. The people have spoken, by the way. He's a pretty baby."

"How could he not be?"

"And then he comes home to a room where people are doing practically everything except shooting each other, and now it's official. He's his father's son. People crying and screaming at each other. It was bad enough to bring old Mrs. Pongsiri down the hall to see if anyone needed help, and she's as deaf as a tree. And Frank is just all big eyes, taking it in, staring at whoever is screaming the loudest. Looking like he wanted to get in and break it up."

He says, "Put your lips closer to my ear."

"Not yet," she says. "But in a couple of weeks I'm going to take about five years off your life. On this very bed."

"Promise? I'm going to start crossing off days on the calendar."

She takes his hair in her fist and pulls as she falls all the way back until her head is on the pillow, and he follows. When they're side by side, looking at the ceiling, she says, "So our daughter is a snob, poor thing. How was she?"

"You mean Miaow's mother?"

"Of course, I mean mom. That's who you've been with, right?"

"Sad. Dirty. Broken. Abandoned. Lost, hopeless. And, after Miaow's reaction tonight, heartbroken all over again."

"Living on the street. Begging?"

"When the cops will let her keep it."

"Fuckers," Rose says in English. "What did she want?"

"Well, at first I thought she wanted to see Miaow, and I'm sure she did. Miaow's reaction turned her inside out. And yes, if that's the real question, she wanted money, but it wasn't actually for herself." Rose is silent, turning her head to look at him when he tells her about the Sour Man and the kid from Superman's old gang. "She was being used. She had no idea she was going to see Miaow until about three minutes before that door opened."

"She still abandoned her daughter. Did you give her any?"

"Um," he said.

"How much?"

"Well, she was told to ask for a hundred thousand."

"How *much*?" Rose says again.

"Not so much. Enough to get her away from the guy who—"

"Forty? Fifty?"

"Are you kidding? Forty or fifty? *Please.*"

"How much?"

"Thirty." She pulls back far enough to look at his eyes, and he says, "Thousand."

The silence is so thick it feels gelatinous. Rose says, "So, if she had asked for two hundred thousand would you have given her sixty?"

"No. Don't be silly."

"Oh, *I'm* being silly. Well, then, why wouldn't you have given her sixty?"

"Because we don't have sixty. I mean, not where I can get it without—"

Rose says something under her breath in Thai, too fast for him to catch, and then asks, "And are you going to give her more?"

Poke says, "No?"

"Good guess," she says. When he doesn't reply, she says, "We have a baby now, Poke. *That* one, over there. The one in the crib.

Sometimes I feel like I'm the only one in the house who remembers that he's here. Babies get sick. Babies cost money. This woman abandoned her own child—"

"It wasn't exactly the way we thought it was."

She props herself up on one elbow. "No, I'm sure it wasn't. She's had years to invent new stories. She probably even believes them."

"I believe her."

"You have a big fat soft heart. There's nothing you won't believe. It's one of the reasons I married you."

"But."

"But you and Miaow and Frank and I are what matter now. This woman could drain you for—"

"I'm *worried* about her."

"Worry about us."

"I'm frightened for her. And whoever she is now, she used to be Miaow's mother."

Rose says, "I don't believe this."

Maybe it's the tension that's been building in him since the moment Miaow screamed, but he says, "I can't help what you believe or don't believe."

Rose regards him with her mouth slightly open as though she thinks she misheard him. Rafferty is about to apologize when Frank begins to whimper in his crib.

"I've got to take care of this," Rose says, getting up. The temperature in the room has plummeted.

"Can I help?"

"Sure, you can," she says with her back to him. "You can remember who you're supposed to be taking care of. I can handle the baby, which is a good thing, considering how often members of the baby's own family volunteer to help, but you've got to take care of the rest of us. And one of the things that means is not giving away our money." She's bending down to pick up Frank, who has turned up the volume.

Rafferty rolls off the bed. "I *am* sorry. We can talk tomorrow. Or in a few minutes, when Frank's asleep again, if you want."

Bouncing Frank up and down in her arms, Rose says, "About what?" and the words might as well be etched in ice. Rafferty hasn't heard this tone often from Rose. He leaves the room and quietly closes the door.

Since he's right there, he checks Miaow's door again, sees that the light is still on, looks at his watch, and very, *very* softly, knocks.

And hears, "Go away."

So he turns around and wanders aimlessly into the living room, where he stops, shifting from foot to foot as he wonders how to make things right and where to begin, and finds himself gazing down at the couch.

Like so much else in his life, it looks lumpy.

30

Whatever It Is

SHE HADN'T INTENDED to go back to the park. What she *had* intended to do was to fold the money as tightly as possible, wedge it beneath her innermost layer of clothing, choose a direction at random, and walk until daylight. For the second time, it seems to her, she is walking through the night to a new life.

Maybe *this* new life, which she isn't even trying to envision beyond the notion of a long bath and a real bed, will be the one that works, the one that will let her live like a human being again.

He had been a surprise, the man who Miaow lived with now. Except for the men in the massage parlor, she'd never really talked with a *farang* for any length of time. Most of the men whom she met on the table were sad and kind of lost in spite of their money and their passports and their white skin, people who had everything except some notion about what to do with it. They climbed the stairs and went into the room not even knowing who would be waiting there, as though the massage tables and the girls were interchangeable, one pretty much like the others. They came in, they either chatted easily or talked in nervous fits and starts, or stayed silent while she did what they wanted her to do, and then they tipped her, most of them, and left. Not many of them requested her again, even though they all asked her what her name was the first time. She made up a non-Thai name she thought they would remember, Star, but while most of the other girls had customers coming back and asking for them by name, few asked for her.

For the first month or two, she'd slept on the table where she worked; she didn't have the heart to move into the place she'd chosen for Miaow and her. She rarely even went down the stairs to the street, except to buy pills—in part because she was worried about running into her husband—until it became obvious to everyone that she wasn't going to be one of the parlor's top attractions, pretty though she was, and they told her she could keep working there but she'd have to find another place to stay. That turned out to be several steps down from the place where Kanda had been so sweet to her, a tiny, filthy room that she shared with an absolutely gigantic and fearless rat that she called Daw. "I'm home, Daw," she'd announce when she came in, and it wouldn't even run for its hole at the base of the wall. When she left in the morning, she put out a bowl of water and told him she hoped he'd have a good day.

After most of a year they fired her because (if she's being honest with herself) the pills, especially the pain pills, got out of hand again and she started showing up late or not at all, and some customers complained about her. Several of them said she was obviously using drugs. Without the money she'd been earning she'd had to give up the little room and Daw, too. She'd grown fond of Daw, but *come on,* she'd asked herself, *who takes a rat with her?* And anyway, he had a good deal where he was: regular crumbs on the floor, cozy hole in the wall, no cats. She hoped the next person who lived in the room would be kind to him.

The human Daw had gone home to his mother's house, she had learned in a letter from her sister, and had found a new wife. Hom's only reaction when she read the letter was to wish the new one better luck than she had enjoyed. Between the mother-in-law and Daw's pills, she would need it.

She hasn't thought about Daw in years.

Three or four years after she'd lost Miaow, she saw one of the kids from the gang who had taken her in, and he said that Miaow had been loaned to one of the adult gangs who put kids on the sidewalk to sell things to tourists. He'd told Hom which sidewalks, but by then she was sleeping on the streets, mostly under bridges, just as Daw had said they would. Her memory had begun to stutter and the world had gotten foggier and foggier. There was no way she could take care of a child. She could barely take care of herself. Miaow was probably better off on her own. And it struck her, just then, that her memory had been better since the boy in Patpong told her that he'd seen Miaow and that she apparently had a family. She thinks, *Maybe I just needed something worth remembering.* Instantly, she has a picture of herself, scrubbed clean and pill-free, meeting her daughter again: some tears, a hug, some kind of promise for the future. In that instant she makes a decision. She reaches into her shirt pocket, takes out the fold of paper with the pills in it. Then she drops them to the pavement and grinds them to powder under her heel.

She looks around. Where is she? Oh, right, she's here. Pretty much where she'd decided not to go.

It's got to be almost 1 A.M. What she should do, she thinks again, trying to convince herself, is turn around and go in the other direction, *any* other direction, just keep the park at her back until she can vanish into some poor area of Bangkok miles from here.

But look where she is. At the same time that she's been commanding herself to disappear from Patpong—from this whole part of the city—another voice has been arguing that the Sour Man has no idea where she sleeps; she's only seen him in Patpong, and that applies, too, to the boy who brought her to the Sour Man's attention. Even if they know, or guess, that she sleeps in Lumphini some nights, Lumphini is big.

And she's only going to be there a minute or two. In, dig, out. She *needs* to do this.

Looking around, she decides that she can take advantage of the fact that she and the *farang*, in going from ATM to ATM, had strayed far from her usual route. She decides to circle even farther around the park and come in from a completely new direction. In a matter of minutes its relative darkness looms up in front of her. There's a bit of broken fence, low enough for her to climb, nearby. She's been looking behind her all evening, ever since she and the *farang* set off for the ice cream place. No one seems to be following. She grabs a deep breath and walks quickly to the sagging fence and then into the trees. She sticks to the trees wherever she can, avoiding the open spaces, keeping well back from the edge of the lake. She stumbles a couple of times; she knows every obstacle and awkward step on her usual route, but this isn't that path, and she swears sharply once as she almost goes down.

One minute. That's all she needs, one minute at most, and she'll be gone, as though the world swallowed her up.

The phone in her pocket vibrates.

It hasn't buzzed since they left the first ATM. But it's buzzing now. What does that mean?

Instantly, she envisions the Sour Man pacing the dark Patpong sidewalk between Silom and Surawong, swearing with every step, waiting for her. He must be furious by now.

The image energizes her. Get this errand done and *get out of here*. She moves faster now, not quite so worried about silence, and within a few minutes she's on the gentle rise where the boy's tree stands, looking down on the place where she sleeps.

The boy is not there, as far as she can tell, and neither is anyone else. *Quickly, now*: she lifts the hem of her skirts in her right hand and hurries down the slope, fishing with her left hand for the digging spoon in the Louie bag.

At the bush, she sees her extra plastic sheet, folded tightly and wadded beneath the bush's lowest branches, right where she left it, and a rectangle of white that turns out to be the take-out bag from the Isaan restaurant that she had left for the boy with the furious eyes. She takes three paces toward a small round stone she had half buried there, however long ago it was, drops to her knees and sticks the spoon into the earth, and the phone buzzes again.

She drops the spoon and is fumbling for the phone, thinking about throwing it as far as she can, when a man says, "You're not taking calls?" and then something that has to be a boot hits the center of her back and she sprawls forward, the spoon flying from her hand.

The Sour Man says, "Burying something?"

She's flat on her stomach with one side of her face on the cold, wet grass.

He says, "Get up."

She finds her way to her hands and knees and then she feels again the flare of pain from her ear that announces that he's clamped it between his fingernails. "Up," he says, tugging her ear sharply enough to make her whimper. "Up, up, up."

Instead, she rolls to the right, feeling the flesh in her ear tearing, and then, with no plan in mind, she crawls away from him as fast as she can. When she gets unsteadily to her feet, he is a couple of meters away, looking at her in a way that seems half-amused and almost affectionate. Small as he is, he terrifies her. He steps toward her, but she backs up, and he shakes his head as though to note that she hasn't learned *anything* yet. Standing where she dropped the spoon, he slides a boot over the earth and bends down to look, and it feels like her heart has stopped. But then he shakes his head and straightens to bring his eyes back to her. "Well," he says, "if you buried anything here, it was a long time ago, so you've still got what I want. Give it to me."

"He didn't give me anything."

"Why were you hiding?"

"I wasn't hiding." There's a warm, feathery touch at the side of her neck, and she knows it's her own blood.

"You didn't call me. You didn't answer my call. You were hiding. Where is it?"

"I don't have any—"

In two long steps, he's on her, and he punches her in the face, and then she's down, flat on her back, the world rippling through tears, and when she sniffs she tastes blood at the back of her throat.

"Not one word," he says, standing over her. "The bag."

She peels the bag off her shoulder and, still lying on her back, holds it up to him. He starts to rifle through it, giving it his attention, and she thinks, *Roll away and then get up*, but he's standing on her skirt, and he feels the tug and says, "Uh-uh."

He pulls things out of the purse and drops them at his feet. When it's empty he turns it upside down to shake it, and suddenly, there's a long, silvery knife in his hand and he slits the bag open—the knife, she thinks, must be very sharp—and he pulls the lining out and then tosses the whole thing aside. He says, "Take off your clothes."

She says, "I'll scream."

"Make one sound, and I'll cut your throat. Where's the money?"

"He didn't give me any."

"You had your phone off for hours. What were you doing, singing him lullabies?"

"He didn't give me—"

"If that's true, you can get dressed again. Up, up. Get out of those rags." He backs away.

To get up, she has to roll to her hands and knees, where she waits, head hanging down, feeling as though she'll pass out if she stands. She wobbles to her feet and holds the pose, waiting to see whether she's going to fall, and then, with his eyes on her, she pulls the outer skirt up and over her head, keenly aware of the stiff little rectangle of folded bills in the waistband of her underpants. She begins to ball up the skirt so she can toss it to him, but he says, "Shake it out. Four or five times. Shake it hard."

She does as she's told.

"Throw it over there, to your right, I don't want it near me. Now the next layer. Where do you *find* these rags?"

It's a blouse. Beneath that is another blouse, and beneath that is her bra. When she's standing there, the bare skin of her belly and back prickling with goose-flesh in the night air, he says, "Pants."

As she unbuttons the pants she finds her mind gliding away from him, gliding away from this moment, and she thinks, *I'll never see Miaow again, I'll never be anyone she would want to*—And then a kind of warmth comes over her, floods through her, actually, and she almost smiles. *So easy.*

"Get them off," he says. He waves the knife at her, just a reminder, a little back-and-forth. She thinks about how sharp it is. It glints, catching some stray beam of light that has infiltrated the trees, and suddenly she's seeing the glint of the sun off the hood of Hyukk-Hyukk's awful car, seeing him smiling at her in the rearview mirror, and she thinks, *That was the last time things could have gone right for me.*

"Hurry *up*," he says.

"I'm doing it as fast as I can," she says, peeling the pants down. She kicks them over to him, trying to keep her eyes on him, waiting for her chance, and almost going over backward. Nothing left now but the bra and the underpants with the money in them. As he bends to pick up the pants the certainty blooms in her; she thinks *Now* and screams something, anything, and he straightens quickly, the knife pointed directly at her, and she takes a fast step and launches herself toward the gleam of the knife. She feels it when it enters her abdomen, but it's more like a punch than a cut, and she thinks, *Sharp edge is down,* and grabs his shoulders and pulls herself up, and then, for the first time, she experiences the knife as a cutting object making a deep, lengthening slice in her body. She has to let go of him because she doesn't seem to have control of her arms anymore, but she knows that the cut is deep enough and long enough, and she closes her eyes as she slides down his slender body, suddenly slick with blood, all the way to the ground, where she folds herself as small as she can, suddenly seeing a bright rectangle of light, a rearview mirror, with a boy smiling at her, and then it's gone and she just waits for it—whatever it is—to take her.

31

Standing on a Stack of Books

THIS TIME HE knows that he's overslept even before he rolls over on the couch because he smells coffee. Weak coffee, but coffee. He turns his head to the left and opens one eye. He has, even with his eyelids down, unerringly located the cup, which is steaming happily on the glass coffee table. Behind it, and out of focus, a small figure grows smaller as it recedes toward the kitchen.

"Thank you, Fon," he croaks.

"Sleep more," she says. "You out all night, give lady money, must be you need sleep."

Her last word is almost drowned out by a tangle of women's voices, electric with energy, from Rose's room. This story will be all over Bangkok by dinnertime.

"Someday, I'll tell you the whole story," he says, sitting up and draping his sheet over him.

Pausing in the doorway to the kitchen, Fon says, "Rose wan' egg. You wan'?"

"No, no thanks." Fon regards an egg yolk as a pouch of deadly poison that should be mashed into submission the moment it hits the pan and then cooked absolutely solid.

Once she's in the kitchen, he downs the coffee in two scalding gulps, turns the sheet into a toga, and stands up. He yawns and stretches, one hand keeping the sheet in place, and he's turned and started for the hall before he realizes what he had glimpsed in his peripheral vision. It's enough to make him reverse course and go back to the coffee table.

Miaow's copy of *Pygmalion*, the one she's been using to run lines with Edward, is pretty much where it's been since the previous evening. But the book's back has been broken and then the book torn into two equal pieces, straight down the crease in the spine. He wraps the toga around himself more securely—he wouldn't put it past Fon to yank it off and then call all the girls in for laughs—and pads across the room to the kitchen, stopping on what he hopes is the practical-joke-proof side of the counter. "Where's Miaow?"

"In room. She get up, she get orange joot, she go back to bed."

"What day is this?"

"You not know?" She cracks an egg and opens it, all one-handed, dead-center in the skillet. All that flash, he thinks, and no talent.

"If I think about it, I'll know," he says. "But I don't want to think about it."

"Friday."

"That's what I thought."

"Then why you bother me?"

"Because I can," he says. "Because I know it irritates you. Is Rose mad at me?"

"*This* question," Fon says, smashing the egg into a viscous, undifferentiated fluid, "you answer without me."

"Right. Well, thanks for the coffee."

"I make for Rose," she says, and he thinks, *Whoops, she really is angry*, but then she turns and gives him the patented Thai smile, the one that seems to start at the toes. "I grind bean this time."

He has to laugh.

"I can tell," he says. "So, she *is* mad at me."

"Who?" Fon says, the image of innocence.

"Skip it." He heads for the bathroom but stops to knock on Miaow's door. He gets the kind of *what?* that only a teen can produce, the *what?* of someone who's been interrupted at the precise moment she's found the solution for all the ills of the world but really needs to write it down.

"I want to talk to you."

"So talk."

He tries the doorknob, but it won't turn. He says, "The door is locked."

"I know. I'm the one who locked it."

"Okay, fine, I'll keep yelling so that everyone in the house can hear me."

She says, "Who cares?"

"Why aren't you at school?"

"I'm taking a personal day," she says. "Isn't that what they say in America, *a personal day?*"

"What happened to your book? The one on the table."

"Well, as you just mentioned," Miaow says, "it's my book."

"Yeah, and I'm doing you the favor of assuming that it broke accidentally, as opposed to you being a big enough, self-absorbed enough, idiot to have done it on purpose." To Fon and Yim and—what was the name?—*Claudia*, it was Claudia—who are peering down the short hallway at him, he says, "Do you *mind?* My daughter and I are having a crisis," and they all pull their heads back, although he'd bet all the money he has left, after the previous evening, that they're pressed against the wall, just an inch out of sight, with their hands cupped to their ears.

To Miaow, he says, "I didn't hear you."

"That's an encouraging sign," Miaow says, "because I didn't say anything."

"You know," he says, crossing his fingers, "there is a key to this door."

A pause. Then she says, "Is not."

"I'm going to get it," he says. "The next sound you hear will be this door opening."

"I don't believe you."

"Fine," he says. "But if I have to get the key, I'll take the lock out for good."

"You wouldn't even know how."

"Hold that thought. When the door opens, you can apologize. No one has apologized to me in days."

He hears a word she never would have used a year earlier, at least, not in his hearing, and then the lock pops and he pushes the door open to see her retreating backward toward the bed, as though she'd half expected him to grab her by the hair. "The book," he says. "First, that's not how we treat books—"

"So that's what you want to talk about. Not what happened last night, but a book."

"That's what I want to talk about."

"It's my book." She sits at the head of the bed, as far away as possible, heavily enough to make the frame creak.

"It's the *world's* fucking book," he says, watching her eyes widen at the profanity, which he rarely uses when he's talking to her. "It belongs to anyone who reads it. It belongs to people who haven't even heard of it yet. We don't treat books that way, not in this family. But that's not the point, is it?"

"You don't—"

"All the *work* you've done. All the progress you've made. You're just going to walk away, tuck your tail between your legs, and cry *weee weee weee* all the way home. Who the hell do you think you are?"

She stands up, her face scarlet with anger. "You know who I am."

"I didn't ask who I thought you were. I asked who *you* thought you were. And now, I guess I know. You're that poor little kid whose mom abandoned her—didn't happen quite the way you think it did, by the way—the kid who had to sell gum on the sidewalk, and beg, and slit purses from time to time. And you think when you go onstage as Eliza, the whole audience is going to be whispering, *She's not acting, she really was a street kid, but a lot dirtier and poorer.* I can hear them now, just *bzzz bzzz bzzz.* Maybe a giggle or two. Well, let me tell you that my heart is just breaking in two. Saddest thing I ever heard. The second thing I want to say to you is that you owe Edward an enormous apology if you think he would tell anybody in the world about what happened last night. The third thing is something an American woman named Eleanor Roosevelt once said: 'We wouldn't worry so much about what others think of us if we knew how seldom they do.' The kids at your school don't actually spend all their time thinking about you because you're not really the center of their universe and they have other things on their minds. You know, their parents, their classes, their boyfriends and girlfriends, their grades, their complexion, their weight, their height, why they're not more popular on WeChat or Instagram or, I don't know, BiteMe, some bullshit like that. You're about number twelve thousand and forty-two on their list of topics to think about."

She's looking at him, but he can't tell whether she's listening or counting silently to fifty.

"When I asked who you thought you were, I was trying to figure out whether you see the same Miaow your mother and I do. Not the kid whose first bath took two hours, so long I had to go down to Mrs. Pongsiri's to pee because you just couldn't stop warming the tub up. So, no, not that Miaow, but one of the other Miaows. Maybe the one who could just barely read her name and a few Thai and English words and who got thrown into a really difficult school, a *no excuses* school, where she caught up with her class level in less than a year and got permission to take a couple of classes *above* her level, and who stepped onto a stage for the first time in her life in Shakespeare, no less, and who was the best thing in the production. I thought maybe you thought you were *that* Miaow, or the one who walked away with *Small Town* as Julie and had your mother and me crying when you came back to say goodbye to the world. Or maybe the Miaow who Edward has fallen in love with, the one who's brave enough to go after the part of Eliza and good enough to get it and kick the hell out of it. And you know what? Whoever you are now, my dear, however far you've risen, you're fucking standing on a stack of books. So you can do what you want, you can drown in self-pity, you can make your mother unhappy, you can make Edward unhappy, you can turn into a coward and walk away from a part you were born to play and you can even decide you've been wrong about wanting to be an actress. When we ask ourselves who we are, I think there are only two answers: whoever I used to be, and who I am now. I don't *know* who you think you are or what direction you're going to take, but you will fix that book the best you can, and then I'll donate it to the library if you haven't got a use for it."

She's been looking down at her lap as he talks, and she doesn't look up at him now, but she nods once.

"I'll fix it," she says to her lap. "I can use it to help Edward. I already know my lines."

"I pretty much assumed that."

"Well," she says, looking at the disorderly heap of blankets on the bed as though it were the most interesting thing in the world, "you know how I am, I mean, that I'm not always fun."

"I do," he says, "and in spite of that, I'm always proud of you." He can hear her breathing, he can hear the whispers from the women eavesdropping around the corner. He can hear his own heartbeat. When he's sure she's said everything she wants to say, he adds, "There's no key to this door. There was, but I lost it right after we moved in. You can lock it and sit in here feeling sorry for yourself or do some work or go back to sleep as long as you want. Let us know if you get hungry."

She's still studying the blankets. As he's about to turn and go, she says, "Was I really that good as Julie?" and then she shakes her head. "No, no, not that. That's not what I want to ask. What was she—what was my mother like?"

"You promise you'll fix the book?"

The doorbell rings.

"I'll do the best I can," Miaow says, and now she's looking straight at him, with an intensity he can almost feel on his skin. "Did she talk about me? What did she say? What do you *mean*, it wasn't the way I thought it was?"

The doorbell rings again, and there are male voices coming from the living room, and then he hears someone hurrying down the hall. It's Fon, as wide-eyed as though she'd just stepped on a snake, and she says, "It's the police."

32

Help Hom

THERE ARE TWO of them, both in uniform. Fon, who is standing directly in front of them, has allowed them to come in only a foot or two, not far enough to close the door. The thin, dark-complected one, who's eyeing the apartment as though he suspects that there are booby traps beneath the carpet, wears the two-chevron insignia of a corporal. The uniform of the other, a well-fed, slow-looking man who greases his hair and combs it straight back in a style that hasn't been popular since Rudolph Valentino, proclaims him to be a sergeant. Both of them seem confused by the women in the room—Yim and Claudia, who are eyeing them without much warmth, Fon, who's blocking their way, and, coming out from the bedroom, the one who calls herself Fanta. Fanta was obviously doing her eyes when the doorbell rang because one of them is lined in black beneath a spidery fringe of false eyelashes, and the other is as naked as a baby's bottom, giving her a permanent wink.

Rafferty has taken a moment in Miaow's room to wrap his sheet a bit more securely, but he knows that what they see is a *farang* who's not even dressed by noon and who is surrounded by what must look like a hired harem. Sergeant Valentino, catching his eye, gives him a conspiratorial *you dog, you* smile and takes a step forward to navigate past Fon, but then his gaze slides to something behind Rafferty and he stops as abruptly as a mime who's walked into a pane of glass. Rafferty doesn't bother to look around to see what it is; it can only be Rose.

"Let them in, Fon," Rose says in Thai. "I'm sure they've got a good reason for being here, although I can't imagine what it could be."

Sergeant Valentino is about to say something as he steps forward, but then his eyes shift again and his face hardens. To Rafferty, he says, in English, in an unexpected tenor voice, "How old is *she?*"

"Well," Rafferty says without bothering to turn. "Until recently, we thought she was fourteen, but it turns out she's fifteen."

The sergeant flutes, "You didn't even ask how *old*—"

Miaow says to Rafferty, "I *am?*"

"That's one of the things we'll talk about," Rafferty says to her.

The baby begins to cry, and Rose turns and vanishes into the bedroom. "You've just met my wife," Rafferty says to the sergeant. "This is our adopted daughter, Miaow. My wife had a baby a couple of weeks ago, and her friends have come to help. If you have children, you know what I'm talking about. And I'm wearing a sheet because it's my house and I can wear whatever the hell I want, and I haven't had time to get dressed yet."

"Boy or girl?" the corporal asks in English.

"Boy. I guess that's supposed to be better."

"Boy *is* better," the corporal says, glancing at the sergeant as though to make sure this is a permissible opinion.

"You don't work," the sergeant says, making it sound like an accusation.

"I work at home. I write books. Tell you what. Fon, can I ask you to make these gentlemen either some tea or some of your excellent coffee while I put some clothes on?"

Fon nods without moving, not bothering to make it polite. Women who work or have worked in Patpong have no affection for the police. She stays where she is just long enough to make her point, then steps aside to let them enter and shuts the door loudly enough to make the corporal start.

"Not quite as strong as what you gave me this morning," Rafferty says. "These gentlemen are armed and we don't want them to get jumpy."

The sergeant says, "We don't need anything. But we do need to talk."

"Give me a minute to pull some pants on, and we'll get right to it."

"He'll go with you," the sergeant says, tilting his head toward the corporal.

Rafferty feels sudden anger wrap its fingers around his throat. "Like hell, he will. I have an apartment full of women, my daughter, and a new baby. You think I'm coming out with a machine gun? What do you want with me?"

"Just to talk. A few minutes, maybe five or ten."

"Well, good, then we can do that right here. The ladies will go in the other room, won't you, ladies? You, too, Miaow. We'll cancel the coffee and tea, stop pretending to be buddies, and have our chat, and if my sheet slips, well, don't let it distract you. Come over to the couch. It's lumpy, but if I can stand it, so can you." He precedes them so he can snatch the bottom sheet off the lumps and toss it next to the wall. Then he sits on the hassock, demurely crossing his legs. In a few seconds the three of them are alone, although neither bedroom door has been closed and Rafferty knows they have an avid audience. He says, "So, what can I do for you?"

The corporal suddenly has a notepad and pen in his hand. The sergeant reaches into his shirt pocket and pulls out a rectangle of paper housed in a small, transparent plastic envelope with a snap to hold it closed. The sergeant says, "What can you tell us about this?"

He knows what it is before he reaches for it, and it feels like the apartment has started to tilt and spin, but he keeps his hand steady, gives it a quick look, breathes in and out and in again, and says, "It's one of my business cards."

"Do you give out many of them?"

"I've only had them six months or so. I've given out, I don't know, forty or fifty." He smiles as though amused by the notion of having to explain. "That's what you *do* with them, you give them out."

"Who do you give them to?" the corporal asks.

"Whoever asks for one. I'm a writer." He swallows, wishing he could take it back because he knows it's a giveaway, and says, "Magazine and newspaper people, book publishers, novelists who want some kind of expertise, occasional foreign investors. I've advised on a couple of movies."

"Have you given any out recently?"

"I give them out all the time, but why *recently?*"

"Look at the card. It's clean, it's not wrinkled—"

"I don't know about you," Rafferty says, the intentional interruption a way of reminding them they're on his ground and, so far, by his sufferance, "but when someone gives me one of these things I slip it into my wallet until I either need it or stumble across it at the end of the year when I'm cleaning all the crap out. If you had let me put my pants on, I could probably show you three or four right now, most of them from months ago, and they'd all look like they were printed this morning." He readjusts the sheet, telling himself he's showing so much leg it borders on rudeness, but then he figures *fuck it* and just dives in. "Why don't we try this the other way around? Why don't you tell me why you're asking me about it? Start with who had it."

The corporal looks at the sergeant with the silent-movie hair, who nods, and Rafferty sees the division of labor. The corporal will talk to him and take notes and the sergeant will watch him. The corporal says, "Have you given any of these to street people?"

Rafferty says, feeling his heart sink, "Street people."

"Homeless. Beggars. That kind of—"

"One. A woman who sometimes begs on Patpong and Silom."

"How old?"

"Hard to say. She could be forty or sixty. She's kind of beat up." He's suddenly overwhelmingly aware that Miaow is certainly listening to all of this in her room. "I give her a little money now and then."

"And your *card*?" the corporal says, eyebrows raised.

"Not long ago I was chatting with her when she spotted a kid picking the pocket of a Japanese tourist, and she yelled 'Thief' loudly enough to be heard in Phnom Penh. The kid ran without getting the wallet and the Japanese guy didn't get his trip ruined. So, yeah, I thought I'd give it to her. Someday when she's hungry, I thought, she might find a way to call me."

The two cops look at him so expressionlessly that they might be waiting for a punch line. He knows it's supposed to make him uncomfortable, so he asks his own question. "How did you come to have it?"

The corporal says, "When did you see her last?"

"Why?"

"Please answer the question."

"Last night."

"Where?"

He chooses the place where the largest number of people probably saw them together. "On Silom, maybe nine o'clock. I passed her on the sidewalk and asked how she was, and she said she was hungry, and I said something like, 'If you could eat anything in the world, what would it be?' She said a banana, so I took her into the Baskin-Robbins that's right there and bought her a banana split. Actually, two. We talked for a while."

The corporal glances at the sergeant, whose attention is entirely on Rafferty. Rafferty leans forward and asks the sergeant, "What's this about? Has something happened to her?"

The sergeant says, "I think we should continue this conversation at the station."

"That's all you're going to tell me?"

"We're asking," the sergeant says. "*You're* telling."

"Well," Rafferty says. He's having difficulty keeping his face blank; whatever happened to her has to be very bad indeed. "Hang on a second." He gets up and goes to the pile of clothes and slips his wallet out of the hip pocket of his jeans. "No gun," he says. "But here, have a look." He fishes through a thin stack of cards and hands one to the sergeant. "I've had it for months, and it still looks new."

It actually is *relatively* new; it's Arthit's card, the one that celebrates his promotion a few months earlier to full colonel, which puts him right outside the door that opens directly into the smoky, greasy Nirvana of the top cops, from whom all authority flows downward and up to whom all graft rises. He hands the card to the corporal, who glances at it, his eyes widening, and hands it to the sergeant so quickly it might be too hot to touch.

"While I get dressed," Rafferty says, "you can call him and tell him you're hauling me to the station. He'd want to be informed."

"You know him?" the sergeant says.

"He's my adopted daughter's—the one you just met?—he's her godfather. I'm *his* adopted daughter's godfather; in fact, I introduced him and his wife to the child they adopted. We're sort of godfathers-in-law. I'd call him myself, but I thought I should let you pay him a courtesy by telling him you're pulling me in; maybe explain the situation to him in your own words, give him the opportunity to be there and ask some questions of his own." He pulls on his trousers and then drops the sheet as he zips up. He bends to pick up his T-shirt, looks at it, and says, "I'll just get another shirt."

"No, no," the sergeant says. "Wait."

"I've been wearing this shirt for *days*," Rafferty says. "I think people should always be interrogated in a clean shirt. A gesture of respect for law and order."

"No one is going to *interrogate* you," the sergeant says. "In fact—" He shifts his weight to pull a little notebook from his hip pocket, opens it, licks a finger, makes a show of leafing through it, and ponderously nods his head. "Yes, I'm right. We've asked you every question on my list."

"Well, then," Rafferty says, "since I'm no longer useful to you, I'll just slip into the bedroom and get a clean shirt."

"Oh, certainly," the sergeant says heartily. "Certainly."

"Right back," Rafferty says. He goes into the hallway, seeing Miaow take a quick step back into her room, her face rigid, and then turns into the bedroom, where he gets a round of soundless applause, hands not actually meeting, from the women. He makes a little bow, pulls a T-shirt from the second drawer in the dresser he and Rose share, and slips his arms in. He's just finished pulling it over his head as he gets back into the living room to find the cops standing at the door to the outside hallway, eager to escape.

"So," he says, "why do you know she had one of my cards in her pocket? What's happened to her?"

"She's dead," the sergeant says. "Foul play. We didn't suspect *you*, of course. We just wondered whether you could tell us something that would help us to—"

"Where did you find her?"

The cops meet each other's eyes for a moment. "In Lumphini," the sergeant says. "Near the lake."

"Right, right." He can't think of anything to say, so he says what's actually on his mind. "Last time I saw her, she was finishing a banana split, and then she, ummm—" To his surprise, the room ripples and he realizes he has tears in his eyes. He blinks them away and says, "She had such a rotten life."

"We're so sorry to have bothered you," the sergeant says, in a tone that's the verbal equivalent of licking Rafferty's bare feet. "Thanks for all your help."

"My pleasure, I guess." He opens the door. "Wait a minute. Killed how?"

The corporal looks at the sergeant, and the sergeant says, "Knife."

Rafferty says, "Jesus. She didn't deserve that. Well, good luck catching whoever did it."

"We will," the sergeant says.

Rafferty closes the door and says, "In a fucking pig's eye." He pulls his phone out of his jeans and hits the speed dial for Arthit. On his way to the couch, he sees Miaow standing just outside the door to her room, staring at him as though she's forgotten who he is. He disconnects and puts the phone away. "Sorry about the language. You, umm, you heard, right?"

Miaow steps forward, glances into the bedroom, undoubtedly seeing a panorama of wide eyes, and quietly shuts the door. Then she comes the rest of the way into the room and takes her usual seat on the hassock. She's studying the floor as though she might have dropped something on it. Just as he's about to repeat the question, she says, "Yes. I heard."

He says, "I'm sorry."

"Why? You didn't do anything to her." Her left foot is jiggling up and down, and she regards it for a moment and then gets up and goes to the couch, where she pulls her knees up against her torso and wraps her arms around them, making herself, at least in

Rafferty's eyes, as small as possible. He stays where he is, unwilling to intrude on her even by moving. A very slow minute or two goes past.

"I sat like this all the time," she says at last. "It's one of the things I remember. I was always sitting on the floor and I had my knees up like this. And my back was against a wall."

He waits, and when she lets her head droop so that she seems to be studying her lap, he says, "Why?"

"So they wouldn't notice me."

"Did they hurt you?"

"Not with their hands." She's rocking, very slightly, back and forth.

"Were you . . . afraid of them?"

She says, "I'm not afraid of anything. Just stupid things, like the play or people not liking me."

"But you didn't want them to . . . notice you." He crosses the room and takes the seat she vacated in the hassock.

A pause, so long he thinks she might get up and go back to her room, but instead she says, "My father . . ." She swallows. "My father didn't like me. He never said anything nice to me. I don't think he ever held me, never so much as picked me up. Even when I was in a corner, I felt like I was in his way. Except for that, I mean except for the way I *felt* about him, I don't remember him much. What I do remember is that he had really big hands and he smelled dirty. Sometimes my mother smelled dirty, too. What it felt like to me, what it smelled like to me, was that they stayed up all night and never cleaned themselves. When it got really bad, I used to think about how nice everyone had smelled at Sonya's."

"Sonya's."

"A place they used to leave me when I was little. I pretended for years that Sonya was my real mother and that she didn't know where I was so she couldn't come and get me. And then, when I was on the street, I smelled even worse than my father had. That bath you were talking about, I was trying to scrub off a whole layer of skin." She puts her head back and closes her eyes and says, "A knife, huh?"

"So it seems."

She sits there hugging her knees, folded as tightly as a paper clip, staring up at the ceiling. She grabs a deep breath, and he thinks she's going to say something, but instead she shrugs her shoulders as high as she can, practically to her earlobes, and keeps them there, then lets them drop. She blows the air out slowly and says, "Knives. It was a knife that Boo used when he came and got me, when he took me away that day."

He says, "Yes?"

"Yes, what? You know the rest."

He starts to reply and stops dead. Should she know this or not? He doesn't know how she actually feels about Hom's death, and he doesn't want to give her a reason to grieve any more than she might already be mourning. On the other hand, the deepest wound is the desertion, being thrown away like that. He says, "She followed you. That day. She hid where you couldn't see her, and she followed you."

Miaow brings her head up so quickly that he sits back. She looks enraged. "Did *she* say that? Liar."

"She described the place. Saw Boo, saw the other kids."

"Liar," Miaow says, "liar, liar, *liar*," and then she's up on her feet and actually running around the corner to the hallway. He hears the door slam.

He sits there, weighing options, and the best one seems to be giving her some time. He's punching the speed dial for Arthit when the door to the big bedroom opens and Rose looks out. He said, "You heard?"

"Yes. I'll talk to her."

As Rose goes down the hall, Arthit picks up and says, "The new father. Getting any sleep yet?"

"Not that you'd notice. Listen, I just had some of your colleagues here."

"Friendly visit?"

"Not exactly. Seems like somebody, a homeless woman, was murdered in Lumphini last night, and she had one of my business cards on her."

"A *homeless* woman? Do you know a lot of—"

"I know, I know. I'll tell you about it sometime. What I want to know is how seriously they'll look into this."

"Off the top of my head, unless she turns out to be related to somebody who matters and who might make a stink, I'd say that going to see you was probably the whole investigation."

"That's what I thought," Rafferty says. "No money, no media interest, no brown envelopes stuffed with cash. Tow her away and forget about it." He turns and walks to the balcony at the far end of the living room. When he turns back, he sees a line of women crossing the hall to Miaow's room.

Arthit says, "Is this important to you? Is there something you're not telling me?"

"No, no. I'm not involved, and it doesn't really concern me, I just gave her some money from time to time, and I thought you should know that I was briefly a—what's the phrase?—a person of interest."

"Then I'd say it's over."

"So, uhhh, the cops said she was found in Lumphini. Do you know—which is a way of asking, can you find out—*where* in Lumphini?"

"Poke," Arthit says. "There's something you're not telling me."

"No, don't be silly. I just liked her, that's all. But, you know, she's not likely to have a funeral, I just thought I'd go pay my respects to her spirit. I promise not to get involved. Listen, I'll tell you about it later, but can you have someone call me, tell me where it happened?"

"I probably can," Arthit says, "although that means I'll need to have someone talk to the cops who talked to you."

Rafferty says, "The sergeant's name tag said Theeravet."

"A prince among men," Arthit said. "Must have been disappointed you didn't slip him a few thousand baht. Someone will get back to you."

"Thanks."

He rings off and looks around the room, thinking how odd it is that, in all their years there, they've never tried to make it more comfortable. He squeezes himself into his work chair and gives himself a moment of silence as he tries to figure out what's next. Rose comes out of Miaow's room, herding the women into the big bedroom. She gives him the big eyes that mean, *Are you just going to sit there?* and then she follows her retinue.

He rubs his face with his hands and swivels in the chair for a minute, which makes it squeak. Then he tugs a few pieces of blank paper out of the printer and centers them on the desk. He thinks better with paper in front of him. The jar full of ballpoints and dried-up felt-tips is at the far corner of the desktop and he pulls it toward him and chooses a pen. He's drawing spirals with it to make sure it doesn't skip when Miaow says, "What are you going to do about it?"

He looks up. He's obviously missed her trip to the bathroom because her face is wet and there's water dripping from the spiky ends of her hair.

"I'm working on it. But if I *were* going to do something about it, would you be interested in helping me?"

The silence stretches out until he puts his hands on the arms of his chair to get up, and then Miaow says, "Do something like what? Helping you how?"

"By finding me some big pieces of cardboard I can write on, and the thickest, brightest felt-tip we have in the house. A color you can practically see in the dark."

She turns her head away until he can see her profile. He can't find her mother in it. "How big?" she says. "Like a shirt cardboard?"

"Jesus, do we have any of those?"

"Yes, as you'd know if you ever wore anything but T-shirts. Haven't you noticed that none of your nice shirts are in the closet anymore?"

"I just thought Rose needed the hanger space and that they were probably being used to line the baby's crib."

"Try the fourth drawer down in that big thing in your room. Rose has been taking them to the laundry, and they come back folded." She does a big sniff, but that seems to be all that remains of her weeping, if she's been weeping.

"Let's tape some together to make a bigger sign."

"A sign," she says. "I'll be right back." She disappears into the big bedroom, and he hears a little breeze of whispering break out.

He realizes that the bright-colored Sharpie is on a shelf at the bottom of a small whiteboard he bought a few years ago in a brief fever of organization. He'd hung it in the kitchen, visualizing it neatly filled out with tidy little shopping and *to do* lists, maybe bits of inspirational prose and witticisms, even the occasional love note, but most of the time he saw a gradually improving caricature of him, recognizable by the beaky Western nose, and then *that* gave way to a series of occasional, rather skillful pornographic line drawings in an eye-popping magenta that depicted people who were sexually entwined in physiologically improbable ways. He didn't know who was responsible for the drawings until Rose came home with the baby, bringing Fon with her. Since then, there has been a new one almost every day. He has taken to erasing the bits that would have been retouched or blurred in a less permissive medium, only to find them redrawn, often with a little extra zing. The pen he takes from beneath the board is the magenta one.

He goes back into the living room to see a lot of shirts he'd forgotten he owned, all lined up on the coffee table as Miaow works the cardboard out. She says without looking up, "How many?"

"I don't know. Six? It needs to be big, so maybe we could overlap six so that the whole thing would be thicker, to make a single rectangle. You know, put about a third of each of them under the one next to it and tape—"

"I'm ahead of you," Miaow says, busily tearing tape. "What do you want to write?"

"Actually," he says, "I want you to write it."

"So it'll be in Thai?" To her, his inability to master, or even befriend, the Thai alphabet has been a reliable source of humor for years. She's taping away, using multiple lengths of tape to secure the joins. "We should put a stick in the back so it can be held one-handed or even jammed into the ground."

"Great idea."

"Well, since I've had a great idea, what's yours? Why are we doing this?" She looks up, and her face brightens. "Oh, that's the pen I was going to suggest."

"I'm taking it to the park. She slept there most nights, I'd guess, for who knows how long. She must have known people there. I'm just doing the cops' job, trying to find out who cared about her and who might have seen something."

She looks down at the cardboard. "Cared about her."

"Well," he says, at a loss. "You know." He doodles on the page and realizes he's written what the sign should say, and he gets up.

She's on the couch, so he takes the hassock and says, "The biggest, clearest Thai you can write. Nothing flouncy, just—"

"You've never seen me do anything flouncy in your life." She holds her hand out for the pen, eyes on the cardboard. "What do you want it to say?"

"I think it should be direct and simple and, I don't know, to the point. I think it should say HELP HOM."

"Help Hom," she says, and he can barely hear her. She begins to write.

33

The View from the Top of the Hill

THE TREES' SHADOWS are long and just beginning to go soft
at the edges by the time he finds his way into the park. For a place
that looks so peaceful, it's amazingly noisy. Just on the other side
of the trees are Bangkok streets that are perpetually jammed, but
now, at rush hour, it's as though some demonic physicist has found
a way to force time and matter into a metaphysical blender and
come up with a new matrix that allows him to double the number
of cars the road was built to hold.

The noise follows him into the shadier area beneath the trees
and begins to diminish only as he nears the little lake. He hasn't
been here often, and he makes a half-hearted resolution to come
back at a happier time.

His heart feels like something he has to breathe around, cold,
heavy, and inert. He is certain that he was—unknowingly and
with all the usual good fucking intentions—responsible for her
death. And the only amends he can think of is crude, blunt-force
revenge. If he's even capable of that.

All he's got with him are the sign, in Miaow's best magenta
Thai calligraphy, and a paper supermarket bag containing a long-
sleeve shirt to put on against the virtual certainty of whining
clouds of mosquitoes or the slightly less likely event of a drop in
temperature, whichever comes first. The bag also contains a thin
circular cushion that normally tops one of the stools at the

kitchen counter. If the shirt is mainly for mosquitoes, the cushion is mainly for ants. He's also got one thousand baht in hundred-baht notes by way of persuasion.

Beneath the cushion is his Glock, just in case the killer should feel compelled to return to the scene of the crime. He doesn't believe that happens anywhere nearly as often as it's said to, but he wants to feel prepared if he's wrong, as he seems to have been over and over during the past couple of days.

"Hey," someone says, and he whirls in a spasm of panicky surprise to see a tall young woman in jeans and a T-shirt, the front of which says, in Day-Glo letters, WAIT UNTIL YOU SEE THE BACK. It takes him a long, socially awkward moment to recognize her as Kwai Clemente—*Officer* Clemente—a top-of-the-line cop who had been methodically discriminated against for being half Filipina and all female until Arthit discovered her and put her to work at a more appropriate rank. He's never seen her out of uniform before. Her most striking feature is her eyes—with their deep brown irises fringed all the way around with gold, beautiful enough to make even men she's arresting look twice—but this time he's distracted by her hair, which is generally stuffed into her uniform cap. Minus the cap, it's much longer than he would have imagined, falling to the tops of her shoulders, and lighter in color than he remembers in the bits he's seen, with a reddish tint calling attention to itself through the black.

"Little jumpy, are you?" she says. "Probably a good thing you're not armed." She laughs, and he joins her, although it doesn't feel very convincing, even to him. She looks at him more closely. "You're not, are you?"

"Of course not. It was just, um, your hair. It's not the way I—"

"Do you like it?" she says, and then she breaks into a deep, full-throated laugh. "Don't bother, that was a joke. The color was a mistake. I was so busy talking to Anand that I bought the wrong bottle, but I think it's okay. He thinks it's okay, too." She pulls a lock down in front and goes cross-eyed looking at it, and adds, "Maybe."

"How *is* Anand?" He doesn't wait for her answer. "Listen," he says, "I'm always glad to see you, but—"

"He's the same as always," she says, "but I stick with him anyway. You were going to ask me what I'm doing here, and I'm going to save you all that work by saying that Arthit figured you wouldn't be able to stay away, and he wanted you to see a couple of the crime scene pictures. I suggested we could email them to you, but Arthit got a little starchy about how they were police property and they couldn't be allowed to get loose in the ether, so my being here, dressed like this, is his compromise with his conscience."

Rafferty says, "What a guy."

"And we also figured, given your sense of direction, you could use all the help you can get. So here, take a look." She holds up her phone and does a couple of swipes, and suddenly he's looking past a tall, dark tree of some kind. He's not big on trees, but this one seems to be growing on a gentle slope that angles down to a clearing with a big bush in it; at a guess, the bush might be shoulder-high on Rafferty. The bush seems to have something large folded beneath it. "This is where she was found," Clemente says, using a bright orange nail to indicate the area of the bush. "Could be where she slept; that thing under the bush is a big plastic sheet that she might have used when it rained. It's a mark of how important this case was to the investigating officers that they left the sheet there; you'll be able to see it for yourself unless someone has taken it. To the right, see that little mound with what looks like a rock on it? It's soft dirt, like it's been dug up recently—maybe to pull up a bush or something—and it's got two deep footprints on top of it and a spatter of dirt behind it. She was stabbed low in the chest and then cut downward, and Arthit thinks the dirt spatter might mean that she jumped from this mound at whoever had the knife and it caught her just below the center of the rib cage, which suggests that he was either lucky or knew what he was doing, and then he yanked it down to open her up. She had skin and hair under her nails, and some blood, too, so the way we see it he was standing a little below her, and when she jumped him she also went after his eyes or something with her nails. Most of the blood is *here*." She taps the screen to indicate a location six or eight steps from the mound and enlarges it. "This is where she was found. The little rise where she was standing is about a meter and a half away, back there to your right. So she jumps, they stagger, him going backward and her plowing forward, he cuts her, she falls." She swipes again, and he's looking at the mound from a new angle that reveals a clutter of clothes off to one side.

"She was up there when he ordered her to undress, which we know because the clothes are scattered to her right, and she was right-handed. We know *that* because she'd written all over her left palm."

"Yes, she did," he says, feeling like there's something pulled tight around his throat.

The glance she gives him is full of curiosity. "Right, Arthit said you met her. How was she?"

"Sad and confused and lonely and cheated. Not much left in the will-to-live tank, I thought."

She's regarding him in a way that suggests she might be guessing his pulse rate. "Arthit didn't say how *you* came to meet her."

"That's because I didn't tell him."

She takes a step back, away from the intrusion and into the world of professionalism. "Are you sure you're neutral enough to get involved in this?"

"I never said I was neutral. What's that?"

"What's what?"

"The thing with the straight edges." He indicates a small white rectangle in the photo, on the ground near the bush.

She enlarges it. "It's a bag. It's a little greasy from having had food in it, but whoever emptied it re-folded it as though it were a napkin for a formal dinner."

"Make it small again. Over here, the little cloth—"

"Those are her underpants," Clemente says, her voice absolutely flat. "All her other clothes are over there, near the mound, but the underpants were found over here, beside her. They're the only thing she was wearing that has blood on it. What that suggests to Arthit is that he was searching her for something—see, over there, that pile of stuff? That came out of a bag she carried."

"Her Louie Vuitton," Rafferty says, belatedly recognizing the brown object from the earlier shot. He wants to turn and spit.

"Yes. The guy turned it over, dumped it upside down where he was standing—where most of the blood is—and slashed the lining. We figure that when he couldn't find what he wanted in the bag, he made her undress. But she wouldn't take off her underpants, either because she was modest or because that's where she'd put whatever he was looking for, and she was wearing them when she jumped him and got stabbed. What was he looking for?"

"Damned if I know."

"Mmm-hmmm." She turns off the phone and takes a diplomatic break, long enough to let her slip it, deliberately and over-carefully, into her purse. "One other thing. One of her ears had been pierced, torn, really, not at the lobe, but at the top. It was like she'd gotten a fishhook through it and then somehow she tore it loose. And there were two of those, one a day or two old and one that was, umm, fresh. None of us has ever seen anything like it."

"I noticed something on her ear, the left one, I think, when I met her. But it wasn't a tear. Looked like a puncture that got infected. She scratched it once or twice, very carefully."

"Well," she says, "this one was new, and it tore the top of her ear open." She takes a deep breath, steps back, and looks him over. "So the sign is supposed to be an invitation for people to talk to you?"

"Can you think of anything better?"

"I didn't mean it as a criticism. I wish you luck. And if you learn anything helpful, you'll let us know, right?"

"Almost certainly," he says.

She nods. "I'll tell Arthit you said yes, absolutely, first thing you'll do. So, right now, look around for a minute. See the lake?"

"Sure. It's that thing with the water in it."

"Okay, bear left so the lake is to your right and stick close to it, eight or ten yards from it at most. In three minutes or so the ground will begin to rise to your left, just a gentle slope, easy for a man your age."

He says, "Hey."

"At the top of the rise is a tree, a pretty big one, the one you saw in the first picture. Go stand next to it, with the lake still to your right, and you'll be looking down from exactly the place where the first picture was taken, and you can walk straight on down to the big bush. Clear?"

"Clear."

"Good. So the baby is a boy, huh?"

"Yeah. And lucky enough to look more like her than me."

"Well, that's good, I suppose, although you're not exactly nightmare material. Anand and I will come by sometime in the next week or two with a teething ring or a savings bond or something. The interest rate is just about what you'd get if you kept the money in your pocket, but it's what people gave my mother, and I'm hopeless with babies." She slips past him and heads back the way Rafferty came. Over her shoulder, she says, "Call us if you get anything good."

SURE ENOUGH, THE view from the top of the hill, once he gets there, is the vantage point from which the first picture had been shot. Beside him is a tall, straight tree with thick foliage and occasional branches starting about five feet up the trunk, making it potentially climbable in a squeeze, at least by someone more sure-footed than he is. Below him is the place where Hom drew her last, probably horrified, breath. He reaches into the shopping bag and puts the Glock on top of the cushion, even though he'll be taking the cushion out once he gets to the bush she had presumably slept beneath. He feels slightly more at ease knowing he won't have to fumble past anything to get to the gun.

Once he's gone down the hill, it's easy to see the disturbance on the little mound from which Hom had seemingly sprung at her killer. She had not been a small woman, so the man with the knife must have been strong not to go over backward. He walks around the mound twice, seeing the throw of dirt where she had launched herself at him. The stone he'd seen in the pictures proves to be a smooth gray oval, maybe eight or nine inches long and five wide at its broadest point, shaped more or less like a potato and half-buried at one side of the mound. It's so out of place that it looks like a marker, and he taps it lightly with his toe, not thinking about it, as he eyes Hom's last home.

Everything that was movable in the photos Clemente had showed him is gone now, except for the plastic sheet and the stone on the mound, and even the sheet has been shoved back until it's mostly out of sight. The things people possess, even if they look like rubbish to others, carry a kind of energy, imparted to them by the people who owned and used them, and the absence of Hom's things makes Rafferty feel that he's in a place where everything important is missing. He's chosen the spot where he'll sit—near the mound because the earth is softer there—and now he pushes the sign into the dirt so it stands on its own, puts down the cushion, and seats himself cross-legged.

This bit of park, with its bush and its mound, had been Hom's space. Even stripped of the things that were there when the last outrage took place—the scatter of clothes, the fake Louis Vuitton tote, the precisely folded white bag—even without these things, this place still reverberates from the shock of multiple crimes, crimes of neglect and exclusion and indifference. It's still a place in which a woman had been left to sink into herself and her regrets, alone. This is where she'd landed after falling so far, from the village to the city to the street, losing her child and everything else that mattered on her way down. And now it's just a clearing in a park that houses a bush with some plastic under it.

In a better world, he thinks, he would have found her, or she would have found him, earlier, when there was still a chance of some kind of rescue and reconciliation, some eccentric but work-able version of an extended family with him and Rose and Miaow, Hom orbiting them like some dotty aunt until she and Miaow reached a kind of equilibrium.

A voice startles him. "How can anyone help her?" a man says in Thai. "It's too late."

Rafferty looks up to see a very thin man in, perhaps, his bat-tered forties, his graying, receding hair chopped, apparently aimlessly, to half a dozen lengths. He wears a random-looking assortment of clothes that seem to have been dragged for miles behind a truck. Rafferty says, "We can find out who did it."

"And how will that help her? Maybe you should have done something when she was alive. I don't think many people will want to talk to you. Whoever killed her, it would be better not to make him angry. She was ready to go, anyway."

"She clawed his face," Rafferty says. "I'll interpret that as a *no* vote."

The man looks down at him for a moment, and then he says, "You're still young. You don't know yet that even people who are sick of life usually fight to keep it. It's the animal in us. When we're cornered, it's all claws and fangs."

"Thanks for the thought. I'll stay here anyway."

"Got a cigarette? Or three or four?"

"No, sorry."

"Only the poor smoke," the man says. "The only people who need cigarettes are the ones who can't afford them."

"Did you know if she was afraid of anyone? Did she talk about—"

"We don't talk about things like that here. We talk about food, we talk about alcohol or dope, about a good dumpster we've found. Things we *need*. If you start to talk about what you're afraid of you'll be alone in no time, and if somebody stays with you it's probably because he wants to take something after everyone else is gone."

"What did you know about her?"

The man looks over at the bush and Rafferty follows suit. "She was here. She wasn't as old as she looked. Some days she had trouble remembering things. She liked chocolate."

Rafferty reaches into his pocket and comes up with a hundred-baht note. "Tell people who knew her that I'd like to talk to them, would you?"

"Sure, but I won't tell them about this," he says, pocketing the bill. "People who never heard of her will be lining up."

"Fine. Thanks. People who knew her, then."

The man turns to go. Over his shoulder, he says, "Good luck."

During the next half hour or so, he sees ten or twelve people, all Thai, some in family groups, who give him a wide berth. One kid, a boy of thirteen or so, nicely dressed and wearing horn-rimmed glasses so big they look like they could conceal a secret identity, detaches himself from his group to say, in English, "Who Hom?"

"Thai woman," Rafferty says.

"Well, duh," the boy says. He squints for a moment, evidently assembling his next remark. "American kid, do they still say *duh*, or no?"

"No. They stopped saying it when I was your age. You need to get some new DVDs."

One of the women in the boy's group—three young teens and two harried-looking adults—calls him.

"Okay," the boy says to Rafferty. "Nice to rap with you."

"Rap on," Rafferty says, pointing a fist in the air.

"You joking me," the boy says. "Bye-bye."

There's a lull during which Rafferty is alone with his sign, the bush, and the mosquitoes. Only one homeless person reads the sign and stops, but she had disliked Hom and has nothing to tell him. He uses the time to think about Miaow, about how this may yet affect her, about the potential for delayed emotional explosions. His daughter keeps everything in, and that makes her especially vulnerable to slow fuses. He sighs and looks around. It's definitely on the edge of getting dark. Giving in to a persistent itch of curiosity, he goes to the bush, kneels down, and pulls out the sheet of plastic.

Someone behind him, whose approach he has not heard, half whispers in Thai, "Nothing there," and Rafferty is so startled that he jumps to his feet, sustaining several scratches from the bush on his arms and cheeks.

It's an emaciated teenager, nothing to him but bones and, judging from his eyes, anger. He has a snarl of long dark hair and a deep dimple in one cheek that's visible even though he's not smiling. It looks like it was put there with a nail. He wears a filthy T-shirt that began its life as blue, a pair of jeans so big on him that the waistband is ruffled beneath his battered belt, and mismatched rubber flip-flops, one of which is held on his foot with twine. He has something white in his hand.

The kid says, "Who are you?"

"Someone who wants to find out what happened."

"Why?" The boy's voice sounds scratchy from lack of use. "And where did you learn to speak Thai? What do you care what happened to her? She was just an old drunk who took dope at night."

After the boy runs out of words, Rafferty says, "Are you finished?"

The kid just watches him.

"What's that?" Rafferty is looking at the white rectangle in the boy's hand.

"Why do you care?" the kid says.

Rafferty takes him in, the sheer boniness of him, the fire in his eyes. He looks like someone whom someone else periodically tried to beat to death without ever quite succeeding, and all that's been left to stalk through the world are skin and bones, held together by fury. Rafferty says, "It's a bag that had food in it, isn't it? There was one down here, too, but it's been taken away. By the cops."

At the word *cops*, the kid spits. Then he says, "So?"

"Okay," Rafferty says. "Why do I speak Thai? I'm married to a Thai woman. Why am I here, why do I care what happened? My wife and I adopted a kid off the street, a little girl, a few years ago, and it turns out that she—Hom, I mean, this woman—was my daughter's real, I mean, *first* mother, the one who gave birth to her."

The kid rocks back on his heels once or twice, as though he might be shifting his weight to turn and run, but instead, he says, "And you just found that out?"

"Yes."

"What's your daughter's name?"

His stare is almost impossible for Rafferty to meet, but he forces himself to do it as he considers the question. He can't find a reason not to answer it. "Miaow."

After a moment, the kid looks down at his pitiful flip-flops. Then, after a long, charged silence, he sighs and sits on his haunches, on the other side of the mound from Rafferty's cushion—just, Rafferty thinks, inches beyond slapping distance.

Rafferty takes his seat again and waits for him to begin. When he doesn't, Rafferty slowly holds out a hand and says, "May I see that?" The kid hands the bag over, so reluctantly it might have been the last of its kind on earth. When he has it, Rafferty turns it over and makes a guess. "You gave her the one that was here when she was killed. It was folded just like this."

The boy swallows, loudly enough for Rafferty to hear it. "She gave it to me, first," he says. "When it had food in it."

"You, ummm . . ." Rather than looking into the boy's eyes, he studies the bag in his hand. "You folded it very carefully."

"I was . . ." His voice trails off. "I was trying to show respect."

"Did she feed you often?"

"I don't know. Maybe five times, maybe six. More than anyone else."

"Did you talk to her much?"

"Never."

"Why not?"

"I don't like to talk."

"But she gave you—"

"When she talked she was mostly loaded on *yaa baa*. She didn't even know she was speaking out loud. Sometimes when she got *really* high I followed her around to make sure nobody hurt her."

"And that's when she mentioned Miaow?"

"Yes. A lot of times."

"Mentioned her in what way? Did she talk about why she had to—" He breaks off, looking for a word. "Why she had to part from her?"

The boy is studying the ground between his feet. "She didn't talk like *that*. She was rattling. She talked to trees, she talked to people who weren't there. Miaow was one of them. It wasn't like she was telling *stories*." The tone is scornful, but he seems calm, even distracted: he's pushing his index finger through the soft dirt of the mound. When he gets to the stone, he taps on it twice with a long, dirty fingernail.

Rafferty says, "But you heard her say Miaow's name."

A silence. Then the boy says, "That's why I sat down."

"Where do you stay?"

The boy regards him so long that Rafferty thinks there won't be an answer, but the gaze feels as though the boy barely sees him; he's focused on something inside. Finally, with the reluctance of someone who is divulging a secret, he says, "You were standing under me. Before. When you were up on the hill."

Rafferty looks past him, looks at the hill. Standing at its high point, almost glimmering with energy, is the tree. For the first time in his life, Rafferty has the impression that his heart has literally skipped a beat and then accelerated to catch up. He starts to speak but swallows instead, and when he's sure he's got his voice under control, he says, "You saw it."

THE WORLD HAS gone dark while he wasn't paying attention. What illumination there is comes from a low reef of clouds, bouncing a fraction of Bangkok's ambient light back down at them, a pale gray, sky-wide, low-wattage lamp that brings solid objects into a kind of dull and shadowy relief. Here and there, through a gap in the foliage, a bright fragment of neon sizzles its way across the night to remind him that the city is still there, but the nearer world, the small world in which the boy is talking, is just silhouettes. If anyone other than the two of them has come near, Rafferty isn't aware of it. What the boy is saying is the only thing that matters. The boy's name is Lamon, which means *gentle*, but Rafferty can't reconcile the name with the hate in the boy's eyes. If the kid dialed it up, Rafferty thinks, he could melt lead just by looking at it.

"She knew I was somewhere near the hill," Lamon says. He is telling the story his way, and Rafferty has no intention of breaking the flow, not even with a question. "She put food near the tree a few times, probably when she couldn't finish it. But she never seemed to look up at the tree. I don't think she knew I spend the first part of every night in it. I think she put the bag there just because the tree is the only *thing* up there. She had to put the bag somewhere, and the tree is the only place that's different from the rest of the hill. So she left it there."

There's a silence that Rafferty steps into, partly to keep Lamon talking, and partly to make sure he understands. "You're there the *first* part of each night?"

The way Lamon is sitting, Rafferty is looking at his profile: the small, delicate nose, the shock of hair. Except for those unnerving stares, he seems to ration out eye contact. "It's hard for me to sleep," he says. "When it's light, I'm on the street. When it gets dark, I need a place to go where no one can see me. I can't sleep when there are people moving around anywhere near me. When it gets dark, I climb into the tree. There's a place to sit up there. I have to wait until I know that anyone who's here is asleep. Then I come down and sleep until the first light begins and people start to wake up."

"Sleep where?"

A pause. "Over there." He lifts his chin to his right, just indicating a general direction.

"But last night, you were still up there."

"It wasn't time for me to move yet. So I was there when she came. I heard her, talking to herself, before I saw her. I have dog's ears. I hear everything."

"When did you see *him?*"

"After she came. She came a different way than usual, from a different direction. Over the hill. She stood under me and looked down, like she was making sure no one was there. Then she went down and got something from under the bush. She had to pull the sheet out to get it. And then she came here, where we are, and got down on her knees. And then he was there, behind her, and before I could shout to warn her, he kicked her, and it all started. It happened pretty fast."

"At some point he had her take her clothes off, so it couldn't have been all that fast. But you didn't do anything?"

The boy closes his eyes. "If you were in that tree right now, where I was," he says, "you'd see a little rise behind the bush, maybe fifteen meters away. He had two guys up there, a big one and a little one, just in case he got into trouble. It was dark, but the big one was wearing a light-colored shirt. Once I saw him, I spotted the little one because he moved."

Rafferty starts to speak, but Lamon holds up a hand. "Even if I hadn't known they were there, I wouldn't have done anything. I thought he was just going to take something, maybe beat her up a little just for fun or to make a point. I've thought about it all night and all day, and I still don't think he wanted to kill her. The way she jumped, it was like she was aiming for the knife. He even tried to back away, but he couldn't move fast enough. I've seen it over and over again in my mind, and it still feels to me like he didn't come to kill her. It was like she used him to kill herself."

Rafferty says, "That doesn't mean he should stay alive."

A shrug. "Big talk."

"I'm not trying to make an impression," Rafferty says. "Besides killing her, the cops say he did something to her ear."

Lamon leans forward and pulls back the thick bush of hair. The top of his left ear ripples with scar tissue. "He likes to do that. With his nails. He grows them long and files them sharp. Usually it's ears. But once I saw him cut a guy's tongue off. With a knife, I mean. The guy had talked to some people. You have no idea how much a tongue bleeds."

Rafferty sits back and then shifts his weight on the cushion. "You *saw* this. So you know who he is." Lamon nods and lightly rubs his fingers over the stone. He seems interested only in its surface, as though something is written there, something Rafferty can't see.

"Why would anyone do something like that?"

"He was making an impression. He was showing us what would happen if we didn't do what he said."

"Who was *us*?"

This time the pause is so long that Rafferty has inhaled to ask his question again by the time Lamon answers him. "Just us. Kids. Thirteen, fourteen years old. He had us doing something we weren't supposed to do. For him, I mean. He was the boss. Six of us. Girls, too. That's all I'm going to say. But he would have been in big trouble if he got caught, so he cut the guy's tongue."

"Can you give me his name?"

"Sure," Lamon says. "But it's a nickname. Yai."

"Would you point him out to me?"

"If I can do it from a distance, if I can do it from somewhere he couldn't see me. For *her*, I mean." He swallows loudly. "Or for her daughter."

"But not for the cops."

"Fuck the cops. If that was me all bloody down here? They'd have turned me upside down to shake the change out of my pockets, then gone to have a drink. If I tell them who the guy with the knife is, you know what they'll do? They'll take what's in his pockets, kick him in the butt, and sell him my name or the name of whoever tipped them."

"Then the name is fine. I can find him from that."

Lamon says, "Now you tell me something. What did he want? What he took was small. My guess was money. But where would she get it?"

RAFFERTY KNOWS THAT the light reflecting off the clouds can't have gotten brighter, but he seems to be seeing more clearly, and he can follow Lamon's hand as he plucks a mosquito out of the air for the eleventh or twelfth time. "So she knocked on your door. How did your daughter feel about that, seeing her like that?"

"I can tell you how she *acted*," Rafferty says, "but I actually have no idea how she felt."

"And Yai sent Hom to you. And she tried to keep the money. Bad idea. Asshole."

"I'm going to do something about him."

"Easy to say." He's running his fingers through the loose dirt on the mound.

"What makes it even worse is that I don't have anywhere near as much money as he tried to get."

"I didn't say he was smart."

Rafferty says, "Where are your parents?"

Lamon leans over and spits into the dirt. Then he says, "Maybe one of the reasons she came to your door was that she still loved her daughter."

"I suppose it's possible. The way she told the story, she didn't want to abandon her."

"But you didn't believe her."

"I don't know what to believe. I'm pretty sure my daughter doesn't believe it."

Lamon says, "Look." He shifts himself around until he's facing Rafferty, and picks up the smooth stone. "This is a marker," he says. "I saw her dig here, with a spoon, over and over. One night when she was still out on the street, I looked to see what it was. When she came back last night, this is where she went, right here. I think it's what she came back for, and I think she'd want you to have it." He scrabbles through the dirt and comes out with a small plastic bag, tightly folded, and hands it to Rafferty.

Rafferty unfolds the bag, takes out the piece of paper inside, which is the size of a playing card, and turns it over. The boy snaps a lighter and Rafferty finds himself looking at the long-lost first act.

The color has faded and one of the corners has broken off, but that doesn't diminish the heartbreak. Three people on a bench in front of something dark and featureless, a backdrop, maybe. A barely recognizable Hom is on the left, young and beautiful, sitting straight-spined with a proprietary air that says that the whole thing was her idea. On the right is a guy Rafferty dislikes at sight, someone, he thinks, he could spot in a high school yearbook as the class jerk. Must be the father, better-looking than was good for him, broad-shouldered, and, apparently, moments from standing up and stalking off.

And *she's* between them: two years old or so, and already well on her way to being Miaow, except that her shoulders are hunched as though she's afraid she might be taking up too much space on the bench, and Rafferty feels an immediate spurt of hatred for the man on the right, who barely seems to know the child is there. Miaow's expression, even at that age, reflects at least two emotions; she's looking at the camera as though she's terrified that it might eat her, and she's also half hoping that it will. Her mother's gaze seems to say, Look. *Isn't my baby beautiful?*

"Yes," he says, and then he surprises himself by swallowing. "Yes, here she is." He looks over at the boy, who's rippling like someone at the bottom of a pool, and he realizes his eyes are wet. He wipes them as the boy studies him curiously. "You're, umm, you're giving this to me?"

A shrug. "It's not mine."

Sniffling loudly, Rafferty reaches into his pockets and pulls out the remaining hundred-baht bills and passes them to Lamon, who folds and pockets them without a glance. Carefully putting the picture back into its plastic envelope and then slipping it into the pocket on his T-shirt, Rafferty says, "Why do you—" He breaks off, and re-frames the question. "You're young, you're smart, you're energetic. Why do you stay here?"

The boy says, "Because it's better than there."

AS THE PARK recedes behind him, he can feel it all churning in his gut, a seething, unstable mixture of rage and pity and regret that seems to roll around, as fluid and as heavy as mercury. When he crosses a street and trips as he steps up onto the curb he realizes that he's exhausted, and he ducks into a restaurant, one of the Western chains that have broken out like blisters all over the city. He wants the energy and the clarity he usually finds in a cup of coffee. He sits alone at a plastic table, still damp and smelling of sponge from its most recent wipe-down, and by the time the cup is empty he's dialing his phone.

"I'm eating dinner," Arthit says.

"At this hour?"

"This is the post-crisis hour, as you, the parent of a teenager, should know."

"This won't take long. I know who killed Hom. I have an eyewitness who described it in details that perfectly match your reconstruction of what happened. Good work, by the way. The witness is the one who put the mysterious white bag there. She sometimes gave them to him, full of food, and he meticulously returned them to her, empty but finely folded."

"I need to talk to him."

"You won't. He won't have anything to do with the police. Incidentally, he's got an ear that was mauled exactly the way Hom's was. That was done with a fingernail, and the guy it belongs to is named Yai. He operates or used to operate some dodge with kids in Patpong or someplace nearby."

"Yai?"

"Yai."

"Underage kids?"

"If the witness was one of them, and I think he was, they were, definitely underage."

"Just so I'm clear on all this, give me the three-minute version."

Rafferty has to take a couple of deep breaths to steady himself, to put some distance between him and the story, before he can boil it down. When he's finished, his armpits are wet and it takes him a moment to bring himself present. "That's it," he says, "as far as I understand it."

"Why all the stuff about making her follow you?" Arthit says. "He knew where you lived. Why didn't he just take her there?"

"Yeah, I've been thinking about that. He told Hom that she'd get a share of the money, but I think he planned from the beginning to kill her and take it all. Murder was a serious enough charge, I think, that he wasn't taking any chances on anyone seeing him with her anywhere near my house. She was, umm, conspicuous. He probably worried that people would remember. Just keeping his ass safe, I think." He sucks in a deep breath and blows it out. "She was always going to be killed."

There's a silence on the line, and Arthit says, "Call you back."

Rafferty's heart is going double-time. He gets another cup of coffee and stares at it until it's room temperature. Then he sips it, makes a face, and gets another one. As he sits down again, the phone rings.

"He's a bad boy," Arthit says. "Pimp, dealer, bully, enforcer, extortionist. With a record like his, if by some happenstance he was arrested by a couple of honest cops who found a huge amount of dope on him, he could be put away until the next Great Flood. Would that make you happy?"

"He's not going to carry that much dope around."

There is a silence on the line.

"Oh," Rafferty says.

Arthit says, "Are you okay?"

"I feel like I've spent the last week as a crash test dummy, but other than that—"

"But I've just given you good news, right?

"Right."

"Then suck it up. Go home and do your *real* job. Be a father. Don't worry about Yai."

Rafferty leaves the new cup of coffee steaming on the table.

34

She Has Two Parents

WHEN HE CLOSES the apartment door behind him, feeling a thousand years old and a thousand pounds heavier, he's startled to see Rose coming out of the kitchen with a cup of something in her hand. He had thought it was much later; his sense of time has abandoned him, but a glance at his watch tells him it's a little after ten.

She stops, her upraised eyebrows asking the question, and he says, "It went fine, I guess. I learned a lot." He turns toward the hall, heading for Miaow's room.

"You know," she says behind him, "you have two children."

"Yes, but only one of them is in trouble right now."

"How would you know?"

He turns back to see her sipping from the cup, and the smell of peppermint, which he loathes, finds its way to him.

"He's got you," Rafferty says. "He's got more aunts than I have fingers. He eats on schedule. What could be wrong?"

"He needs you, too. He's a boy. Even at this age, he needs to have men around him. And you've got to grow up and stop seeing him as competition."

The little envelope with the photograph in it feels warm in his pocket. He says, "Give me ten minutes."

Rose says, "No." She sips again and holds out the cup. "Would you like some?"

"Peppermint tea? I'd rather have a glass sandwich."

Rose says, "We're all out of glass. You know, you have two children and Miaow has two parents."

"What does that—"

"It means that you've barely included me in any of this. It's about a mother and a daughter, you know, and you've left out the only person in this house who's been both."

"You're . . ." He stops, mentally bumping into what she's just said.

"You were going to say that I'm busy with the baby, and yes, I am. But I'm *her* mother, too. Her door is locked, by the way. Edward came over without warning and she sent him home, and then she slammed her door so hard the picture in the hallway fell off the wall. It's still locked, you don't know where the key is, she won't open it, and you're not going to knock it down, so just come into our room with me—it still *is* our room, you know—and say hello to your son, and then tell me what happened. We'll talk about it. Together. Remember *together?*"

Rafferty says, "Beer," and heads for the kitchen. Rose stays where she is, and he says, "You don't actually have to wait for me. I'm not going to dash for the front door, escape into the night. I just . . . I can't actually think of a time when I needed a beer more than I do right now."

"And I can't think of a time when you and I went in to see Frank together. This will be the first."

He stands in the light of the refrigerator and tries to remember why he opened it. "That's hard to believe."

"Only for you. Go ahead, get your beer. My tea is getting cold."

"Okay, okay, getting the beer." He pulls out a small one to show her how seriously he's taking the discussion, even though he knows she won't appreciate, or even notice, it. *The things men do for women,* he thinks, going back into the living room and finding her exactly where he left her. He stops and just looks at her. "You *are* beautiful."

"I know. Worse men than you have told me that. Come on, put your free arm around my shoulder, and I'll put mine around your waist, and we'll go in together. He needs to see things like this so he begins to realize that people can come in pairs. Right now, you're just the only *farang* in the crowd."

"The door isn't wide enough."

"I can solve that," she says, and she does, pivoting them about forty degrees without breaking the embrace as they pass through it, and, joined at the hip, they detour around the bed, drinks in hand, and move in tandem to the crib. "He's asleep," she whispers. "He sleeps there for hours now. Pretty soon, it'll be all night and we can be roommates again." She leans against him and rests her head on his shoulder, and he inhales the scent of her shampoo in what seems like the deepest breath he's drawn in days. It feels like coming home.

"Look at him," she says, her lips to Rafferty's ear. "My little *farang.*"

In spite of a sudden, unexpected glow of pride, Rafferty says, "He doesn't look like me."

"Look at that nose. Not a Thai nose. Not as big as yours, which is good because we'd have to get a bigger apartment . . ."

"Hey," he whispers.

". . . but not as small as a Thai nose. And look." She puts her hand beside the sleeping baby's face. "Not dark."

The baby opens his eyes and looks at both of them as though from a great distance, and then closes them again. His thumb goes into his mouth, and Rose waits, one hand up to caution Rafferty not to speak, and after a count of ten or twelve, she hands him her tea and very gently works the thumb free. Then she licks her own fingertips and whispers, "Our son tastes good."

Rafferty says, "I'll take your word."

"You would make a terrible woman."

He says, "If I'd known you wanted a woman . . ."

"They were standing in line," she says, "if I had wanted one. Give me my tea and come on," she says quietly, "let's catch up."

He sits beside her on the bed and takes a first hit off his beer. Instantly, muscles he hadn't even known were tight relax, and he lets out a sigh.

Rose says, "That's a nice sound. So here's what's happened here. Frank ate everything I gave him for dinner and he hasn't spit any of it up yet."

"That's nice."

"Adjust your scale," she says. "These things are important to me and to Frank. We both need them to be important to you, too. We're not a TV show and you can't change the station when the pace slows down. If you're not interested, tell me now and I'll stop trying. It's too much work to have to deal with *two* babies. If you can't find a way into this . . . this relationship, you and I are going to have problems."

"I don't want us to have problems."

"Then get to know your son. You've been acting like he bites."

"I'm just . . . I don't know how to do this."

She reaches over and takes the beer out of his hand. "You love me, right?"

"Of course."

"Well, he's half me." She takes a long swallow of beer. "So you've got a head start. Love that half of him and after a while, maybe you'll learn to love the half that's you, too. I'm going to need help, Poke. The girls won't be here forever, you know."

"Fon will."

She laughs and hands him the beer. "Yes, Fon will be around

for a while. And he loves her. He's going to love you too, if you'll give him a chance. Can you promise me that you will?"

"Do I have to change him?"

"Once in a while."

"How can something so small poop so much without turning inside out?"

"He's just trying to impress you." And then she's laughing. "And I already *know* you can be a parent, because I've seen how you do it with Miaow."

He says, "Thanks."

"You've been more of a parent to her than I have."

"She needed a father."

"So does he."

"And speaking of Miaow," he says.

She says, "Give me the bottle again." She drinks about a third of it and says, "How bad is it?"

"Well, it's awful in some ways, but in others it's not actually as bad as we always thought it was, either." He tells her the story Hom told him, and when he's done, she sits there, holding the bottle as though she's forgotten it's in her hand.

At last, she says, "That's her side of the story."

Rafferty said, "She carried everything she owned around with her except for one thing, which she buried in the ground where she slept. Buried it for safety. According to someone in the park who knew her, she dug it up and looked at it all the time."

He works the picture, still in its plastic envelope, from his pocket and hands it to her.

She puts her teacup in her lap and looks at the photograph for five or ten seconds and then squeezes her eyes closed and scrubs at her forehead with her fingertips, hard, almost violently, as though she's trying to push something right through the skin. When she looks up, her forehead is bright red and her eyes are wet. "I'd know her anywhere," she says. "Even at that age, she's Miaow. Poor her. Poor both of them."

"So," Rafferty says, "I was going to go in and—" But he stops because Rose has gotten up and is holding out the bottle of beer, now almost empty. "I'll do this," she says. "It's a mother thing."

He takes the beer and watches her detour to the closet, where she slides one of the doors aside and goes up on tiptoe to get something off the top shelf. It's a key, and Rafferty recognizes it.

"You kept losing it," she says. "If I'd told you it was there you'd have lost it again. You—you go talk to Frank or something." And then she's gone, closing the door behind her.

He has no intention of eavesdropping, but having two closed doors between him and them seems excessive, so he waits until he hears Miaow's voice and the sound of her door closing before he very quietly opens the one to the room he's in.

As long as he's up, he tiptoes into the kitchen and gets another beer, then tiptoes back to the bedroom and hovers, suspended, just inside the door, feeling so little contact with the floor he could be a puppet whose strings are too short. He hears Rose's voice, low and soothing, and Miaow's higher and thinner, and then Rose talks for a long time and he can't understand a word and he's ashamed of himself for trying, so he drifts across the room toward the crib.

The kid *is* lighter-skinned than Rose, although Rose isn't very dark. Rafferty can't spot the incipient Western beak yet, but he'll take Rose's word: She's been studying this face nonstop for, what is it, fourteen days now, fifteen? He hears a raised voice in Miaow's room—Miaow's—and then Rose's voice, lower in both pitch and tone, and he's trying to catch a word or two when he sees, out of the corner of his eye, a change in the baby's face.

He looks down into the bluest eyes he's ever seen. They seem to be looking at Rafferty's forehead, and without knowing he's doing it he goes up on tiptoe to intercept the baby's gaze. Now Frank is waving his fists around, and Miaow lets out something that could best be described as a yelp. Listening for all he's worth, Rafferty puts his hand into the crib and touches the back of the baby's hand, and Frank wraps his infinitesimal fingers around Rafferty's index finger, and the world falls away until there's nothing but the blue of the baby's eyes, the warmth of his son's fingers around his, and the sound of his daughter's voice and then his wife's, the two of them talking a mile a minute at the same time, and Rafferty leans down into the crib and says to the baby, "Get used to it, kid. It's music."

35

Coda

WHEN THE PHONE rings early the next morning, he rolls
over blindly to grab it from the glass-topped table beside the
couch, and falls out of his and Rose's bed, hitting the edge of
the night table with his hand and bringing it down on top
of him. The phone slides off and lands on his right cheek, and
he grabs it even before he does a damage assessment and croaks,
"Hello?"

"Wow," a woman says in English. "Guess I woke you up."

"Guess you did." Frank is crying, probably frightened by all the
noise, and Miaow is suddenly in the doorway, her eyes so puffy
they might have been stung by bees, saying, "You guys fighting
already?"

"Who are you fighting with?" says the woman on the phone.
"Oh yes, sorry, this is Jillian Trelawney, lives next door to Mr.
Campeau? There's someone in the apartment."

Rafferty is feeling a bit blurry from lack of sleep, and his head
hurts. "In your apartment?"

"No, silly, in his. Would I call to tell you there's someone in *my*
apartment? I'd be celebrating it privately. But next door, in his, I
can hear them moving around."

Rose is up now, bent over the baby, and Miaow goes over, a bit
gingerly, and stands beside her.

"Oh, Lordy, you've got a baby," Jillian Trelawney says. "Bad on me. But, still . . ."

"I'll come over in a bit," Rafferty says. "Push your bed against the door."

"Oh, no, really?"

"No," he says, "not really," and he hangs up.

He reaches back and pulls the bedsheet on top of him and then wraps himself in it yet again, feeling like he could probably get rich designing a line of sheets with snaps or Velcro or something for men who are never allowed to wake up naturally. Miaow says, with her back to him, "I've been thinking."

"Really," Rafferty says. He's up and working on his hemline.

"That picture," she says, and she grabs a breath, "you know, that picture?"

"I know the picture," he says, and Rose shoots him a glance that, while somewhat fond, quite clearly means *shut up.*

"Well, I was thinking," Miaow says again. "Ummm, it's not hard to see that it's me, right? And that it's—it's *her*, I mean, even though it was so long ago. Right?" She sniffles and swipes furiously at her nose.

"I could see it," Rose says.

"Well, what I was thinking was—I mean, why don't we *use* that to, you know, prove she was my mother and, and that way we could, ummm, we could make sure she gets a funeral, some kind of good funeral, with monks chanting and . . ."

Rose says, "We'll do it. We'll all three go down there, and—"

Rafferty says, "I can probably do it through Arthit."

"Well, then," Miaow says, and she looks down at her feet.

"If anyone had ever told me," Rafferty says, "that my daughter was as smart as she is good-hearted and beautiful, I would probably have said it wasn't possible."

Miaow, who is thermometer-red, says, "You're so *corny.*"

* * *

"*WHAT?*" CAMPEAU GROWLS as he opens the door. Then he's blinking rapidly at Rafferty. "Oh, it's you."

"Getting a lot of Jehovah's Witnesses?"

Campeau sees what Poke is looking at and yanks his hand, which has been holding the door, out of sight. The thick gauze bandage around his wrist is professional and neatly done, but dirty enough to need changing.

"We were worried about you."

"Who's *we?*"

"Your landlady, Toots, the woman next door. Trix." He watches Campeau's eyes widen in something that might be panic, grabs a quick breath, and says, "Me."

"Woman next door—the Australian?"

"She heard a lot of noise the night you left. It frightened her. She knocked on your door a bunch of times the next morning and then called the landlady. Landlady called me."

"Had a fight with myself," Campeau says. "We were evenly matched."

"I know how that is."

"Do you," Campeau says. It's not a question. "Well, listen, I've got to—"

"More or less." He looks past Campeau at the woman who's just come into view behind him, probably from the bathroom. She's slender and white-haired, with symmetrical, delicate features and an unusually full mouth. She's probably in her early seventies, and he's seen her eyes before. "Good morning," he says.

Campeau turns as though he hadn't been expecting anyone to be there. "Oh," he says. Then, to Poke, he says, "This is, this is Malee."

"I thought it might be." To her, he says, "It's very nice to meet you."

"This is Poke," Campeau says. He looks intensely uncomfortable.

"You are friends," Malee says, looking slightly surprised. Her English is almost unaccented.

"Like *this*," Poke says, holding up his index finger and middle finger, pressed together.

"So, uhhh, listen," Campeau says, "we should all go out sometime, me and Malee and you and, and, um, Rose."

"Just the four of us," Rafferty says, wondering how much it's going to cost him to sell Rose on it. "That would be great. Just great. Well, hey, I don't want to butt in. Just needed to make sure you were okay."

"Yup, sure," Campeau says, shifting from foot to foot. "You bet. Right as rain."

"Can't tell you how happy I am about it."

"Oh, for Christ's sake," Campeau says, "get out of here." But he closes the door gently.

He's no sooner hit the sidewalk than his phone rings. It's Fon. She says, "You can buy diaper?"

AFTERWORD

A LONG TIME ago when the world was young—in 2006, in fact—I began a book called *A Nail Through the Heart* with a scene in which the protagonist, an American travel writer, holds his adopted daughter's hand as they follow his wife down a Bangkok sidewalk, shopping for groceries.

I knew that it wasn't the most electrifying opening in thriller history, but I wanted to say on the very first page that this was not a novel about Bangkok in which beautiful young Asian women threw themselves incessantly at uninteresting Caucasian men. My line of thought was something like wife + daughter + groceries = family.

The word *family* did the trick. Since I don't know how to plot in advance, I barely knew who these people were, but the moment I realized they were a family, I thought that it might be interesting to drop a normal—if intercultural and self-assembled—family, who are trying to preserve relationships along traditional lines, into the world capital of instant gratification. It felt to me like the family might serve as a friendly campfire in a world of cold neon.

Most writers, I am convinced, make decisions on the fly because a notion feels right at the moment, and then they are forced to live with that decision for the rest of the book. Or, in this case, nine books. Miaow, who, on that very first page, was little more than a prop to make readers think, "Look, a family man," became, for me, the heart of the series. That's why I think it's fitting to end it with the solution to the longest-running mystery of them all: why, all those years ago, Miaow was tied by a piece of twine to that bus bench and abandoned there. I couldn't leave that unresolved.

The claim Miaow staked on the series' narrative line was a total, and not always welcome, surprise. I had never written a child before and I've never fathered any in real life, and there were times when the challenge of getting her onto the page kept me up at night. But somehow, she always knew what to do, even when I didn't have a clue. *Especially* when I didn't have a clue. I'm going to miss her. Hell, I'll miss all of them. Well, okay, most of them. Even Bob Campeau.

Writing is similar to theater in that characters—both major and minor—are like actors: some stick to the script; some rewrite their parts on the fly; some fight their way downstage center and demand more lines; and some just want to hide in the wings. When a series grows, those wings get crowded as characters from earlier books begin to congregate there, shuffling their feet and clearing their throats from time to time, hoping to be called back into action. Some made it and some didn't. I had good relationships, if that doesn't sound schizophrenic, with most of them, and the ones who refused to rise to the occasion were simply omitted from the following books or, in a pinch, got killed. Fortunately for writers, literary characters don't have unions.

I want to thank all the people who wrote me letters about the books over the life of the series, primarily the Vietnam vets who took the time to say I had come close to the way they felt about what they had been through, and also the families who were navigating the sometimes treacherous waters of intercultural adoption. I even met one of those adopted kids, and that was a kind of high spot in my writing life because she told me I got it mostly right. And thanks to the thousands of fans who wrote once or twice or three times to suggest music for me to write to or to tell me they liked the books but how could I have abandoned this character or that character, or to inform me that this or that fictional establishment wasn't where I said it was (they would have found it *exactly* where I said it was if they'd been on a fictional street). And a specific kind of thanks to the hundred or so who wanted me to understand that I don't know beans about guns.

Very special thanks to the people who turned these daydreams into books at (chronologically) William Morrow/HarperCollins— especially the late, great Marjorie Braman—and then at the wonderful Soho Press, in the hands of the tactfully authoritative Juliet Grames, who has edited all of these for the past eight years and has made every one of them better than it was when she got it. People who haven't yet had a book published often think that their relationship with a publisher will be a familial one, and are usually disappointed when the family turns out to be the House of Atreus. But I felt like these books have had two happy families, the one on the pages and the one at Soho that transformed these noodlings into something people might want to read. One of my favorite movie lines comes from the 1939 comic masterpiece *Midnight*, in which the central character, played by Claudette Colbert, who works in a Paris hat shop, is forced to wait on the unpleasant wife of the man she loves. She brings her hat after hat and then backs up and says, "This one *does* something for you, it . . . it gives you a chin." The people at Soho have given these books a chin.

And thanks to you for getting this far, and a very special, heartfelt thanks to my wife and muse, the one and only Munyin Choy. And three more. First, in this book, my Bangkok friend Norm Smith prevented me from making some very embarrassing mistakes about Lumphini, Patpong, and their environs. Second, Everett Kaser took the first five or six books and created *The Poke*

Rafferty Book, a total reference resource on every character, every location, every theme. And third, thanks to Laren Bright, whose early reading of this manuscript, and many others, trimmed and tuned the writing from start to finish. Sometimes a writer is only as good as his friends.

In closing, goodbye to this little world. It's been a privilege, most of the time, for me to be here.